Ben's breath stirred the tendrils of hair hanging loose from her ponytail.

Kate leaned her back against the solid wall of muscles that was her bodyguard cowboy. The warmth of his arms around her reassured and scared her all at once.

Her hands shook so badly, she thought she might drop the gun.

"Are you afraid?" he whispered.

Yes, yes, she was afraid. Afraid of falling in love with a stranger. Afraid of investing her emotions in someone who would leave as soon as the threat was neutralized. Afraid she would be heartbroken when the dust settled on the Flying K Ranch.

TRIGGERED

BY
ELLE JAMES

First published in Great Britain 2013
by Mills & Boon, an imprint of Harlequin (UK) Limited,
Eton House, 18-24 Paradise Road, Richmond, Surrey TW9 1SR

© Mary Jernigan 2013

ISBN: 978 0 263 90366 9
ebook ISBN: 978 1 472 00731 5

46-0713

Harlequin (UK) policy is to use papers that are natural, renewable and recyclable products and made from wood grown in sustainable forests. The logging and manufacturing processes conform to the legal environmental regulations of the country of origin.

Printed and bound in Spain
by Blackprint CPI, Barcelona

A Golden Heart Award winner for Best Paranormal Romance in 2004, **Elle James** started writing when her sister issued a Y2K challenge to write a romance novel. She has managed a full-time job and raised three wonderful children, and she and her husband even tried their hands at ranching exotic birds (ostriches, emus and rheas) in the Texas Hill Country. Ask her, and she'll tell you what it's like to go toe-to-toe with an angry three-hundred-and-fifty-pound bird! After leaving her successful career in information technology management, Elle is now pursuing her writing full-time. Elle loves to hear from fans. You can contact her at ellejames@earthlink.net or visit her website at www. ellejames.com.

This book is dedicated to cowboys
of all shapes, sizes and sexes.
These brave men and women work hard,
play hard and have a sense of loyalty,
decency and ethics we should all aspire to.

Chapter One

Necessity, burning curiosity and a Hummer limo brought him here, but as Ben Harding sat in the leather armchair surrounded by three other men, he wondered what the heck he'd gotten himself into. He glanced around the room again. The only thing he had in common with the others was that they each wore a cowboy hat, jeans and boots.

Beyond that, he knew nothing about the men gathered in billionaire Hank Derringer's home. The Raging Bull Ranch lay in the heart of the back of beyond, South Texas, where men were tough, the drug runners were tougher and a property owner stood a good chance of getting killed riding across his own spread.

Ben had done his homework. Hank Derringer had become a recluse since he'd lost his family over a year ago in a botched kidnapping attempt. The man had made billions and continued to make more in the oil and gas industry. All facts that were easy enough to find. But why bring these men here? Why now?

Ben would have blown off the invitation to come if he'd had any other choice. His career at the Austin Police Department at an end, he'd been pounding the pavement looking for work and finding that no one, until now, wanted to hire a man who'd been kicked off the force for killing a man with his bare hands.

Did he regret what he'd done?

No.

And he'd do it again, given the same circumstances.

His gut clenched and he fought to push the rage and lingering images to the back of his mind as a tall, slightly older man joined them.

He wore a black Stetson and looked very much like the other men seated around the room. "Gentlemen, I'm Hank Derringer. Thank you all for coming to the Raging Bull Ranch." He sat near the huge stone fireplace, facing them. "I brought you here because you are the best of the best."

"Best of the best what, Hank?" The muscle-bound, blond-haired man across from Ben spoke first. He nodded toward Ben and the other two men. "And who are these guys?"

Hank tipped his head toward the man questioning him. "Patience, Thorn. I'm getting to that. For the rest of you, meet Thorn Drennan, the best sheriff Wild Oak Canyon ever had. A man the people could count on to fight for truth and justice."

Thorn's eyes narrowed. "You're forgetting—I'm no longer the sheriff."

"Precisely." Hank turned to the man with brown hair, brown eyes and a wicked scar across his right cheek. "Chuck Bolton. Your friends call you Big Tex, born and raised on a ranch near Amarillo. You know how to ride, rope and build fences like the best of them. Served two tours in Iraq and one in Afghanistan where you wiped out an entire Taliban stronghold against your commander's orders."

The man sat up straighter, his broad shoulders straining against the seams of his chambray shirt. "Got the boot and a bum leg for that."

"A man with courage and determination to fight the good fight," Hank said.

Big Tex shrugged. "I guess it depends on your definition of 'the good fight.'"

Hank moved on to the next person, a man sitting back from the rest, dark circles beneath his eyes, an intense, haunted expression in his green eyes as he stared out the window. "Special Agent Zachary Adams, one of the FBI's best undercover operatives working to stop the drug cartels along the border. Got caught in a bad situation on the wrong side of the border. Yet you survived."

"For what it was worth." The man's gaze shifted from the window to Hank. "And, just for the record, former FBI. I quit."

Hank nodded. "Right."

Derringer turned to Ben, his smile warm, welcoming. "And then there's Ben Harding, the most highly decorated officer on the Austin police force."

"*The* Ben Harding?" Big Tex snorted. "Weren't you the guy who was fired for strangling Frank Davis to death with your bare hands?"

Ben stiffened. He'd seen what the high-powered CEO had done to that young girl in a run-down warehouse on the seedier side of Austin. He'd watched him run from the scene of the crime with the child's blood on his hands and clothing. Ben hadn't cared who he was or what big company he ran. All he cared about was making the man pay for what he'd done to the girl.

Ben's stomach roiled as he recalled the scene and the memories of another very similar crime involving the deaths of his wife and young daughter.

His fingers balled into fists and he rose halfway out of his seat, ready to take on the world. "Yeah, I killed a man, what's it to you?"

Big Tex shrugged. "Just wondering."

"I read about it. Davis was a sick bastard into hurting little girls. I'd have done the same," the man called Zach said.

"You gave him what he deserved," Thorn agreed. "Why

waste money on a system that would have turned him loose to do it again?"

The starch taken out of his fight, Ben sat back against the soft brown leather of the wingback chair. He was disappointed he wouldn't have a brawl to release all the tension balled up in his gut since he'd arrived. At least now he felt more of a kinship with the others in the room.

Hank's mouth twisted into a wry grin. "You are all highly trained in your fields, and because of your various circumstances find yourselves unemployed."

Ben snorted. "Unemployable."

"Wrong." Hank's lips spread into a smile. "I'm here to offer you a position in a start-up corporation."

"Doing what? Sweeping floors? Who wants a bunch of rejects?" Zach asked.

"I need you." Hank rose from his chair. "Because you aren't rejects, you're just the type of men I'm looking for. Men who will fight for what you believe in, who were born or raised on a ranch, with the ethics and strength of character of a good cowboy. I'm inviting you to become a part of CCI, known only to those on the inside as Covert Cowboys, Inc., a specialized team of citizen soldiers, bodyguards, agents and ranch hands who will do whatever it takes to see justice served."

"Whoa, back up a step there. Covert Cowboys, Inc.?" Big Tex slapped his hat against his thigh. "Sounds kind of corny to me. What's the punch line?"

"No punch line." Hank stood taller, his broad shoulders filling the room, the steel in his eyes indisputable. The man was on the up-and-up. "Let's just say that I'm tired of justice being swept under the rug."

Ben shook his head. "I'm not into vigilante justice, or circumventing the law."

"I'm not asking you to. The purpose of Covert Cowboys, Inc. is to provide covert protection and investigation services where hired guns and the law aren't enough." Hank's gaze swept over each of the men in the room. "I handpicked each of you because you are all highly skilled soldiers, cops and agents who know how to work hard, fire a gun and are familiar with living on the edge of danger. But mostly because of your high moral standards. You know right from wrong and aren't afraid to right the wrongs. My plan is to inject you into situations where your own lives could be on the line to protect, rescue or ferret out the truth."

Ben stood, his body tense, his first reaction to the older man's words to leave and never look back. "I'm not a vigilante, despite what the news says."

"I'm not hiring you to be one," Hank said. "I'm asking you to join CCI as a protector, a man willing to fight for truth."

"Truth, huh?" Zach said. "It's hard to find people who care about truth anymore."

Hank's lips thinned. "My point, exactly."

"Tell me, why should I work for you?" Ben asked.

The older man's shoulders straightened and he looked directly into Ben's eyes. "I care about truth and justice." He walked to the desk in the corner and lifted four folders. The first he held out to Ben. "Are you in?"

What did he have to lose? Ben had nothing to go back to in Austin. No job, no family. Nothing. Against his better judgment, Ben nodded. "I'm in."

Hank handed him the folder. "Your first assignment is on the other side of the county working undercover on the Flying K Ranch. As far as everyone else knows, you're hiring on as a ranch hand. Your job is to help get the ranch operational, but most of all to protect the woman who just inherited it."

"Sounds easy enough."

"Don't count on it. This county is in need of cleanup. I'm hoping you gentlemen will be the men to help in that effort. It's our first challenge for CCI." Hank stared at the other men. "Who else chooses to take on the challenge?"

One by one the men threw their hats in the ring and grabbed a folder.

Ben opened the file and stared down at the image of a beautiful woman with long strawberry-blond hair, green eyes and skin as pale and smooth as porcelain. His gut told him he was stepping into waters way over his head. What did he know about providing protection to a woman? He'd been a street cop, not a bodyguard. Hell, he hadn't been able to protect his own family. A knot of regret twisted in him, but he asked, "When do I start?"

"Tonight. Grab your gear and get on over there, she should have arrived today."

Ben's eyes narrowed. "You were sure I'd take the job?"

"If not you, I'd be out there doing it myself. Don't get me wrong. I won't ask any of you to do anything I wouldn't be willing to do myself."

Ben clapped his hat on his head and headed for the door. It was a job. He didn't have to like it; he just had to do it until he found something else.

"'THE COW DOG saved the little girl and became her very best friend. The end.'" Kate Langsdon closed the book and set it on Lily's nightstand. "Now it's time for little girls to go to sleep." She leaned over and kissed her daughter's forehead, her heart squeezing in her chest with the amount of love she felt for this pint-size person with the long, loose curls of silky, strawberry-blond hair, much like her own.

"Mommy?" Lily yawned and rubbed her emerald-green eyes. "Can I have a cow dog?"

"Sure, sweetie. Just as soon as we can find one as good as Jess the cow dog." Kate switched the light off on the night-stand and straightened her aching back, got up and headed into the bathroom. The past few days had been strenuous and emotionally draining, the amount of work taking the spunk right out of her. She'd driven from Houston to Wild

Oak Canyon, Texas, cleaned a house that had been standing empty for two months, emptied as much as she could of the moving van she'd rented and poked through the belongings of a man she'd never known and never would.

Her father.

Tears welled in Kate's eyes. For years, she'd thought her father dead. All this time, the man had been living in South Texas on a ranch near Big Bend National Park.

Kate dug her hand in her pocket and thumbed the key she'd received a week ago in an envelope from an attorney, including a letter, last will and testament and one corrupt video disk. The day that package arrived everything in Kate's life had changed.

She pulled the key from her pocket and tossed it into her makeup kit, stripped out of her dirty jeans and climbed into the shower. She stood for a long time as the warm spray washed down over her body, releasing the stiffness from her shoulders and tempering the ache in her lower back.

She wished all her worries could wash away with the water. As she stood in her father's house, on the ranch he'd bequeathed to her, she wondered if she'd done the right thing bringing Lily here.

She'd come to start over and to find answers. For one, what did the key fit? The video had been all static and with a brief glimpse of her father, but it cut off before her father could tell her what the key belonged to. Her father's letter left instructions for her to get help from the only man he trusted, Hank Derringer, the owner of the Raging Bull Ranch in Wild Oak Canyon. He'd help her with whatever she needed.

She hadn't called Mr. Derringer at first, taking a day to digest the fact that her father hadn't died when her mother had told her. The news had been so shocking that it took that long for it to sink in. Contacting his trusted friend was the furthest thing from her mind.

Until someone broke into her apartment in Houston while she had been at work and Lily had been at day care.

When she'd come home to find the apartment she and Lily had called home for four years looking as if the place had been tossed in a Texas-size salad bowl, she'd been angry and scared.

How dare someone break into her home? Kate knew she couldn't stay in the apartment, not after it had been violated and especially not knowing the reason. Nothing had been taken, as far as she could tell.

She'd packed up her daughter, boxed their belongings and headed west to Wild Oak Canyon and the Flying K Ranch to find the answers. How permanent this move proved to be was up to what she found, but she'd quit her job and given up her lease before she left. Either way, she couldn't go back and pick up where she'd left off.

Alone in the world except for Lily, Kate had turned to the phone number of the stranger her father had recommended.

Hank Derringer had answered on the first ring. He'd tried to talk her out of coming to Wild Oak Canyon. When she'd insisted, he'd promised to send a cowboy to her, one who could help her get the ranch back up and running and provide the protection she and Lily needed. Her cowboy would be there before they turned in for the night. Or so Hank had promised. Kate wondered what kind of protection she needed on a ranch out in the middle of nowhere.

She'd waited as long as she could to take her shower and still the cowboy hadn't arrived and probably wouldn't until morning.

When the water grew tepid, Kate turned it off and grabbed for the fluffy white towel she'd unearthed from one of the boxes she'd brought with her in the moving van. Bent over, her head upside down to wrap her long hair in the towel, her hands froze. Was that a sound downstairs?

She strained to listen.

Nothing.

Kate shrugged, worried her imagination was getting the better of her. She continued towel drying her hair when something crashed below and a low curse followed.

Her breath caught on a gasp and her pulse raced. She'd turned out the lights on the main floor and locked all the doors before she and Lily had come up for the night. Whoever was down there was moving around in the dark. *Inside* the house.

Kate wrapped the towel around her and ran into the master bedroom she'd planned to share with Lily the first night until she could prepare another room just for her daughter.

Lily lay sound asleep, oblivious to the danger, the only light in the room the glow from the open bathroom door.

With nowhere to run, Kate quietly gathered her daughter, blankets and all, and hurried to the closet where she'd hung all of the clothing she'd brought with her next to those of her father's. Kate thanked her lucky stars that Lily slept soundly. The little girl didn't stir as Kate laid her down in the back corner of the closet, tucking the blankets around her, blocking her from view.

Once she had her daughter hidden, Kate tiptoed back to the nightstand, slid the drawer open and removed the 9 mm Glock she'd brought with her.

A board creaked on the stairs, sending Kate scurrying toward the door where she eased it closed.

Her hands shook as she alternated between holding up her towel and balancing the pistol. She wished she'd had time to dress, wishing more that she'd loaded the weapon. She prayed that the sight of it would scare a trespasser into leaving without hurting her or Lily. On second thought, she turned the gun around and held it by the barrel. Hitting the man would be better than pointing an unloaded pistol.

The doors down the hallway opened one by one. Kate held her breath as the intruder made his way toward the room she and Lily occupied. What she wouldn't give for cell phone reception.

Though, what good would it do when the sheriff wouldn't reach her ranch for fifteen to twenty minutes? She was on her own.

Where was the cowboy? Why hadn't he arrived already? Was the man moving down the hallway her cowboy? If he was, he had a lot of nerve barging in and sneaking around. He deserved the same as any thief and Kate would give it to him.

With Lily in the closet and her own hands shaking, Kate couldn't chance it. She had to divert attention and get the attacker away from the room where her daughter lay sleeping.

Kate prayed the man would give up and go away.

As she watched in horror, the doorknob turned. She wished it had a lock on it she could twist to buy her a little more time. Maybe not having a lock would work out for the better. She raised her arms and waited, her breath caught and held.

A dark figure stepped through the door. The man wore a ski mask. Anyone in a ski mask meant trouble.

As soon as his head cleared the entrance, Kate slammed the butt of the pistol down on his skull so hard the gun bounced out of her hands and skittered across the floor.

The man lurched forward and dropped to his knees.

Kate flung the door wide and leaped past the intruder.

Before she could take two steps, a large hand snagged her ankle.

Her forward momentum brought her down hard, knocking the breath from her lungs. She clawed at the carpet, kicking with all her might with her free foot, landing a couple hard heels in the attacker's face.

His grip loosened and Kate scrambled to her feet, running as fast as she could for the stairs, thankful and terrified when she heard the intruder's footsteps behind her.

She had to get the man as far away from Lily as possible.

If he hurt Kate, maybe he'd leave her for dead and never find the little girl hiding in the closet.

Kate took the stairs two at a time, missing the last one, toppling to the floor and wasting precious seconds.

The man above her came crashing down the steps and leaped over the railing to land beside her.

Kate swallowed her scream, fearing she'd wake Lily. She rolled to the side, her fingers wrapping around the cord of a lamp.

She yanked the lamp toward her, grabbed the base and turned in time to see the man flying at her. He landed on top of her, knocking the wind from her.

With her hand still around the base of the lamp, Kate swung as hard as she could. The ceramic lamp made contact with the ski mask and bounced off, crashing to the wooden floor, shattering into a million fragments.

Out of options, Kate remembered the self-defense training she'd taken when Lily was little. She knew she was the only one there to defend her small daughter. With the desperation of a trapped mother bear, she freed one hand and jabbed her thumb into the man's eye.

He yelled and punched her face.

Pain radiated across her cheekbone, her vision blurred and Kate knew she wasn't going to last much longer. For Lily, she tried to hang in there, forcing the darkness back, struggling beneath the weight of her attacker.

As the intruder reeled back to hit her again, Kate squeezed shut her eyes.

Before the fist connected with her face, all the weight on top of her shifted backward.

Kate's eyes popped open.

The man in the ski mask fought against another man wearing a black T-shirt and a cowboy hat. Fists flew, and bodies banged against the old furniture. The cowboy hat flew across the room, landing in a corner.

Kate sucked in air, filling her lungs and clearing her fuzzy thoughts. She scrambled to her feet, clutching the towel around her, searching for a weapon of any kind. Her hands wrapped around the legs of an end table. She lifted it high and waited for the right moment.

The two men tumbled and flew around the room, knocking over furniture. With the lights out, Kate could barely tell who was who.

Then her rescuer hit the floor on his back and the man in the ski mask pulled a knife from his belt, the metal glinting in a ray of moonlight shining through a gap in the curtained window.

Kate's heart thudded against her rib cage.

The man in the ski mask closed in on Kate's rescuer.

Without thinking past saving the man on the ground, Kate rushed for the one with the blade and slammed the end table down over his head with enough force to break the small table into several pieces.

The attacker dropped to his hands and knees. He swung his arm out, clipping Kate in the back of her legs.

She fell hard, her head hitting the corner of a coffee table. As she landed, she heard shuffling of feet and tried to rise to see what was going on. When she lifted her head, her vision swam.

No. She couldn't give up now.

Pain radiated from the back of her head. She closed her eyes, praying for them to clear and let her get back into the fight. Lily depended on her.

Hands gripped her arms. Kate struggled, but the grasp was strong. Too strong for her to fight off.

"Shh. It's okay. I'm not going to hurt you." The voice was a deep rumble, the tone rich and warm, resonating from deep in his chest, wrapping her in a reassuring blanket.

"Bad guy?" she asked, without opening her eyes.

"He's gone." A hand brushed a wisp of hair out of her

eyes. "Are you okay?" The same hand trailed softly over her cheekbone where the masked man had punched her.

Kate winced, and she opened her eyes to stare into the bluest eyes she'd ever seen. Her breath caught in her throat, and not out of fear. "Who are you?"

"Ben Harding. Hank Derringer thought you could use my help."

Thank God. The cavalry had arrived.

Chapter Two

Ben stared down at the woman, her long wavy strawberry-blond hair lying in damp ringlets against the wood floor. Wrapped only in a fluffy white towel, she looked like a fallen angel, her creamy smooth skin begging to be touched, the towel riding up her shapely thighs.

"You're staring." The woman blinked up at him, her fingers pulling the edges of the towel together over her chest. She tried to sit up, pressed a hand to the back of her head and sank back. "Must have hit harder than I thought."

"I'll call for an ambulance."

She shook her head and winced. "No. I'll be all right, just give me a minute." One arm rose to cover her eyes. The top edge of the towel slipped lower over the swell of her breasts, capturing Ben's attention.

He really needed to focus on the situation, not the female lying almost naked at his feet, which proved hard when the woman had a great figure and very touchable skin. A pang of guilt and sadness knotted his gut. He hadn't felt like touching a woman in more than two years. Not since… "Any idea what the guy was after?"

"None," she answered, the arm dropping to her side. "I'm just glad he's gone and you're here. I'm Kate Langsdon." She held out a hand, a frown denting her pretty brow. "What took you so long?"

"I just got the assignment an hour ago."

"Well, Mr. Harding, I'm glad you came when you did. Any later and…" She shrugged and tried to sit up again. "I have to get up."

"You should stay put and let me call an ambulance."

"No, I have to get upstairs."

"Why the rush?"

"I just need to." She sat up, swayed and started to fall back. "Damn it, I can't be dizzy."

"Pigheaded woman." Ben caught her before her head hit the floor.

"Stubborn man," she whispered.

He scooped her into his arms and lifted her off the floor.

She tensed, her arm automatically circling his shoulder. "You don't have to carry me. I'm perfectly capable of standing on my own two feet."

"Not with a knot on your head and a crazy determination to get upstairs."

"Give me a minute and I'll argue this point." Her uninjured cheek lying against his chest belied her ability to put up much of a resistance. Her free hand struggled to keep the towel in place.

Ben ignored her protest and carried her up the stairs. "Which room?"

She sighed. "Last one on the landing. And really, I can get there on my own."

"No need. From what Hank told me, I'm the hired hand, here to help rebuild a ranch and protect its owner."

"Hank's words?"

"Right." His lips twisted, a frown creasing his forehead. "Let me do my job."

She chuckled, a smile curling her lips, making her face shine even with the nasty bruise turning her cheek purple. "Somehow, I don't think carrying a woman to her bedroom is part of the job description." The smile faded. "But thanks."

For a brief moment the sun had shone in the woman's face, tugging at a place Ben thought buried for good with his wife and daughter. He shook the thought from his head and turned left on the landing.

When they crossed the threshold into the room, the woman twisted in his arms, her gaze darting toward the closet.

The door was open, blankets spilled from inside, some half-dragged out on the floor. "Let me down." She pushed against his arm, her nails digging into his skin.

"I will, but I'm not dropping you."

"Let me down." She shoved harder.

He lowered her feet to the floor, his arm remaining around her waist.

She stood for a moment, swaying, and then lunged for the closet, her eyes wide, her face tense. "Lily?" Her voice was strained, desperate.

"Who's Lily?" he asked.

Kate didn't answer as she dove into the back of the closet, rifling through blankets. When her face appeared at the edge of the closet door, it was pale and pinched. "Lily?" She leaped to her feet and nearly fell on her face.

Ben was there to catch her, his arms crushing her against his chest. "Who's Lily?"

"Mommy?" A tiny voice called out from the bathroom. "Mommy?"

Kate's head came up and she fought her way out of Ben's arms, dropping to her knees in front of a little girl with a mass of golden-red curls very much like her mother's drying wispy locks. She stood silhouetted against the light streaming from the bathroom, like an angel descended from heaven.

"Oh, Lily." Kate hugged the child to her.

Sweet Jesus. Hank hadn't said anything about a little girl. Ben stood like stone, his feet rooted to the floor, unable to move, forgetting how to breathe.

The little girl was about the age of Sarah before she'd been murdered. Though his Sarah was as different from Lily as night and day, they were about the same size and age.

Before Sarah had been killed. She'd been four years old. She would have been six now, if a man Ben had captured and had subsequently been released on a technicality hadn't targeted Ben and his family.

Ben hadn't been home when his wife and daughter had been brutally stabbed to death. Had he been, he'd have killed the murderer with his bare hands, just like he'd killed the man who'd murdered fifteen-year-old Angelica Garza.

Seeing Kate Langsdon on the floor holding the little girl in her arms brought back too many painful memories. Ben's feet moved one at a time as he backed toward the door. With his heart lodged in his throat, he couldn't breathe or think. His gut told him to run as far from Kate and Lily Langsdon as he could get.

Before he reached the door, the curly-haired angel noticed him for the first time. "Mommy, who's that man?"

Kate eased her hold on her daughter and looked up at Ben, the fear of a few moments ago still evident in her pale face. "That's Mr. Harding. He's the man who came to help us on the ranch."

"Are you going to help my mommy?" she asked, her gaze open, direct, piercing the wall wrapped tightly around Ben's heart.

He yearned to run and keep running until the child's trusting eyes were erased from his mind. But he knew he couldn't leave this little girl and her mother when the intruder he'd chased off earlier might return.

"Yes, ma'am. I'm here to help your mommy." He nearly choked on *mommy*. His daughter had called his wife Mommy. His daughter had looked at him with complete trust, as if he could never let her down.

But he had. He hadn't been there when she'd needed him most. He had been all about the job, bringing in the bad guys.

He'd never taken into account that the ones that got off might come back to haunt him. Until it was too late.

Kate's eyes narrowed. "Are you okay?"

No. Ben's gaze went from Lily to Kate. For a tough cop, used to facing down danger on the streets of Austin, he was more terrified of these two women than any criminal he'd ever confronted. "I'm fine." He cleared his throat. "I'll just bed down in the barn."

"No." Kate stood and swayed, her hand on her daughter's shoulder.

Before he could think through his actions, Ben was there, steadying her with a hand under her elbow, the other around her waist.

"Stay here. In the house." She leaned into him for a moment. When she'd steadied, she pulled away and looked up into his face. "Please."

Her green eyes pleaded with him, her hand on his arm burning a path through his defenses. How he wanted to leave, but couldn't. Despite his vow to never care again, he'd proved over and over he just couldn't honor that vow after all. Killing the high-powered child murderer was evidence. Damn Kate and Lily for making him care. "I'll stay on two conditions."

Her shoulders straightened. "Anything."

He scooped up the gun she'd dropped earlier and handed it to her. "First, put this away, take it to a pawnshop or learn to use it."

She took the gun from him, keeping her body between the gun and her daughter's curious eyes. "Check. I'll learn to use it." Her chin tipped upward. "And the second one?"

His gaze swept over her, taking in the smooth lines of her shoulders, the gentle swell of her breasts and the curve of her thighs peeking out from under the terry cloth. If he had any hope of staying neutral in this situation, he had to put distance between himself and Kate. She was too damned attractive.

He forced an uninterested rise of his brows. "If I'm going to get any work done around here, you have to keep your clothes on around me."

Kate gasped, hugging the towel closer, her cheeks flaming red.

"I'll be on the couch downstairs." He stepped out into the hallway and closed the door between them with a firm click.

Kate stared at the barrier between them for a long moment, stunned at the cowboy's abrupt words and departure. "As if I planned to be standing in front of him in nothing but a towel," she mumbled.

"Mommy, why was I in the closet?" Lily's hand slipped into hers and tugged, dragging Kate's mind back to what was important. Her daughter.

She scrambled for an answer that wouldn't scare her small daughter. "I thought it might be fun to pretend to be camped in a cave in the mountains."

Lily tipped her head to the side as if debating whether or not she believed Kate's lie. Then she smiled and pulled Kate toward the closet. "Will you camp in the cave with me, Mommy?"

"Oh, baby, I don't think so. I'm pretty tired and bed sounds more comfortable. You can sleep in the closet, if you want."

Lily stared from the bed to the closet and yawned, her eyelids sagging. "No, I'm tired, too. Maybe tomorrow."

Kate grabbed the blankets from the floor and flung them across the bed as best she could, tucking Lily in on the side away from the door.

As she pulled out a pair of pajamas that would fully cover her body, she thought of Ben Harding's condition. A spark of defiance shot through her and she replaced the pajamas in the drawer, reaching for the filmy light blue baby-doll nightgown she'd bought one hot, impulsive day in Houston.

She slipped the silky garment over her head, letting the towel drop to the floor, and recalled the feeling of being held in Ben's strong arms as he effortlessly carried her up the stairs to her bedroom. Her skin sizzled where his hands had been beneath her thighs and very nearly touching the side of her breast.

Now that she had time to think beyond defending her life, she realized the cowboy Hank had sent was everything a girl could dream of—tall, dark and handsome. Add a brooding, mysterious look in his blue eyes and he was devastatingly appealing.

She hadn't felt like this since…before her husband, Troy, had been killed in Afghanistan, a month before she'd delivered Lily. Four years ago. A wave of guilt washed over her for thinking such thoughts about a man who wasn't her husband. But, then, Troy had been dead a long time, she hadn't. The man downstairs had triggered a strong physical response she thought she'd never feel again.

Kate sucked in a deep breath and let it out, the tips of her nipples tight little points poking at the sheer fabric of the nightgown. She reached for the hem, telling herself that wearing the gown was asking for trouble.

Her hands stopped before they could lift it over her head. Who was she kidding? The man wasn't interested in her any more than she should be interested in him. He was there as the hired help. Hank had promised protection for her and Lily until they could figure out who was responsible for the break-in in Houston and now at the Flying K Ranch.

As she lay down on the sheets, her thoughts drifted to the man sleeping on the couch downstairs. He'd had a strange look in his eyes when he'd seen Lily. His brows had furrowed into a fierce frown, scary in its intensity. It hadn't looked like an angry frown so much as one of great pain and sorrow. What would cause such a look on a man's face?

She didn't know. In fact, Kate didn't know much of anything about her hired gun. Hell, she didn't know anything about Hank Derringer for that matter. This area was rumored to have a big drug cartel influence. Had she asked for help from one of the local mafia?

Kate lay staring at the ceiling, wondering what she'd done by bringing Lily here. Not that she'd been any safer in Houston. Not after her apartment had been ransacked.

A yawn nearly dislocated her jaw, forcing Kate to give up trying to make sense of all that had happened. Tomorrow she'd ask the questions burning in her mind. Who the hell was Ben Harding and what kind of hired hands did Hank Derringer provide? Even more importantly, did he have any hired hands that were a little older and less attractive?

Kate rolled over and punched her pillow before settling down. Her bruised cheek reminded her of the intruder and her near miss with death. She reached out and looped her arm over her daughter, pulling her close. If anything happened to Lily, she'd never forgive herself.

Tomorrow she'd start her search for answers.

Chapter Three

A knock on the door brought Ben off the couch and up on his bare feet in seconds. He must have fallen asleep after tossing and turning on the narrow couch. Every noise had kept him awake until way into the wee hours.

The sun shone through the filmy curtains, lighting his path through the boxes and furniture. From what he could see of the front porch, two men stood there in tan uniforms.

The local law enforcement.

As he pulled the door half-open, footsteps sounded on the stairs behind him.

"Who is it?" Kate descended the flight of stairs in a light blue baby-doll nightgown, pulling a robe over her shoulders that only came down to midthigh. Her creamy legs and the glimpse of her breasts through the thin material of the gown had Ben's jeans tightening.

With the door gaping, he had no choice but to open it the rest of the way.

The two men in tan uniforms stared at him, then their eyes drifted to the woman on the stairs behind him.

A flash of anger burned through his bloodstream and Ben moved to block their view as much as he could. "Can I help you?"

The bigger man stepped forward. "I'm Sheriff Fulmer, this

is Deputy Schillinger. We're here to see Katherine Langsdon."

Ben's eyes narrowed. "For what reason?"

The sheriff's lips pulled up on one side in a sneer. "Now, I guess that's between me and the lady."

"It's okay, Ben." Kate laid a hand on Ben's arm and stepped up beside him. "I wanted to call on them this morning anyway. We had a break-in last night."

"Sorry to hear that. Can you describe the perp?"

She shook her head. "No, he was wearing all black and a black ski mask."

"Not much I can do to help without a detailed description."

She tipped her head to the side. "Then why did you come out?"

"Ms. Langsdon, as the only living relative of the late Kyle Kendrick, you have been served." The sheriff handed her a thick envelope, his face poker-straight.

"What?" She took the packet, her cheeks blanching, making the bruise stand out even more.

"What's this all about?" Ben slipped an arm around Kate as she opened the envelope, every protective instinct on alert in the face of the sheriff and his deputy.

"Back taxes? The will said nothing about back taxes." She looked up at the sheriff.

"Sorry, Ms. Langsdon, I only deliver the bad news, I don't create it. Your father was the one who didn't pay. Since he left the ranch to you, you're responsible now."

Ben didn't like the sheriff's tone or the way the man hit her with the notice so soon after coming to her father's ranch.

"Twenty-seven thousand?" She snorted softly. "I can't afford twenty-seven *hundred*." Kate stared at the paper in her hands. "That would completely wipe me out and then some."

The sheriff shrugged. "You might consider selling this dump. Pretty young woman like you will find it difficult to manage a place this size all alone."

It was all Ben could do to keep from punching the sheriff for his patronizing words. Ben barely knew Kate, but any woman would resent the sheriff's inference that a woman couldn't run a ranch.

"I'm not alone." Kate clutched the envelope to her chest, her chin rising. "I have Ben." She edged nearer to Ben.

His chest swelled, his arm automatically tightening around her middle, pulling her closer to him.

The sheriff's brows rose. "Hired hands don't always stick around."

"He's not the hired hand. He's…" Kate's hand waved, in search of the right word.

Afraid she'd say he was her bodyguard, Ben finished for her, "I'm her fiancé. We will be working the ranch together."

The sheriff's eyes narrowed. "What did you say your last name was?"

Ben's lips twisted. "I didn't. Now, if you'll excuse us." He moved to shut the door.

The sheriff shoved his foot in the way. "Don't cross me, cowboy."

Ben's brows rose and he stared down at the boot in the doorway. "Did you have more business to discuss?"

The sheriff stared at Ben for a long moment, then replied, "No."

"Then have a nice day." Ben glanced down at the boot and back up at the sheriff. Ben's free hand clenched into a fist, ready to take on the arrogant sheriff if the need arose. He'd seen law enforcement officers who let the power of their position go to their heads. This sheriff appeared to be one of them. He made a mental note to watch the man. He could cause trouble for himself and for Kate.

The sheriff finally moved his foot. "I'll be seeing you around Wild Oak Canyon."

Ben shut the door, muttering, "Not if I can help it."

Kate turned away, her gaze on the legal document the

sheriff had given her. "Twenty-seven thousand dollars." She looked up at Ben, her eyes glazed. "That's more than I have in every savings account."

"Surely you have a thirty-day notice on it."

"Thirty days until they seize the property for back taxes owed." She shook her head. "I don't believe this. I should never have come."

"Can't you go back where you came from?" As he made the suggestion, his gut clenched. If Kate left, he wouldn't have to be around her. He could forget the way she made his body hum to life.

Kate shook her head. "No. I quit my job. They've already leased the apartment we lived in. Not that I'd go back. It's no safer in Houston than here."

"What do you mean?"

"I left Houston after my apartment was broken into and ransacked."

"In Houston?"

"Last week. The day after my father's will was read."

Ben didn't like it. Hell, she wasn't any safer in Houston than in Wild Oak Canyon. Ben resigned himself to being her protector until he could convince Hank he had the wrong man for the job. "Was your Houston apartment in a bad neighborhood?"

Kate shook her head. "I hadn't had any problems in the four years I lived there. Whoever did it tore everything apart."

"Any writing on the walls or threats?" Ben asked.

"No. They even ripped the cushions on my sofa. Every drawer was tossed, even the contents of the refrigerator."

"They're looking for something," Ben stated. "The day after your father's reading, you say? Did your father leave you anything besides this ranch?"

Kate's eyes widened. "Yes." Before Ben could question her, she ran up the stairs.

The blood racing through Ben's veins had nothing to do with whatever item she might have received from her father and more to do with the way her bottom swayed side to side and the vision of smooth, creamy skin visible along the curves of her legs. "More clothes. She damn well better wear more clothes," he muttered.

Kate paused at the top of the stairs, glancing down at Ben, her brows dipping. "Did you say something?"

"I'll get my clothes on." He strode back to the couch he'd spent the better part of the night lying awake on, thinking of the sexy legs on a woman he had no business looking at that way.

Hank Derringer was paying him to provide protection from a problem, not to become the problem or one more thing Kate had to be protected from.

He pulled his T-shirt on over his head, calling himself every kind of fool. If he had any cell phone reception at all, he'd be calling Hank and asking for a different assignment. One with a less attractive woman and...no kids.

"Hi."

Speak of the devil.

Ben's head poked through the neck of his T-shirt and he stared down at the pint-size version of Kate. Light reddish-blond curls lay in bright disarray around the child's shoulders.

She held out a brush. "Mommy told me to brush my hair."

Without thinking, Ben took the brush from the girl. He'd brushed Sarah's hair so many times he could have done it with his eyes closed. He knew just how to ease the tangles free without making her cry.

His throat closed as an image of his dark-haired daughter flashed into his memories. God, he missed her.

Lily looked up at him, her green eyes so like her mother's. "Please?" She turned her back to Ben and fluffed her mane of red-gold hair out behind her, waiting expectantly.

Just like Sarah had.

All of the air left Ben's lungs as if he'd been kicked hard in the gut. Yet his hand moved, reaching out to lift a lock of silky red-blond curls. He dropped to his haunches and ran the brush along the strand, picking out the knots with care.

He hadn't felt this emotionally wrung out since Sarah and Julia had died. But the more he brushed Lily's hair, the more his shoulders relaxed and the tightness in his chest loosened.

By the time he finished working the tangles out of the child's hair, he could swallow again. "All done," he said just like he had when he'd brushed Sarah's hair.

"Thank you." Lily turned and hugged him tight, her fresh, baby-shampoo scent filling Ben's senses.

Over the top of Lily's head he spied Kate standing on the bottom step, her eyes round. Was that a tear trickling down her cheek?

Kate ducked her head, a hand swiping at the moisture. Seeing Ben brushing Lily's hair had hit her like a Mack truck. Lily's father had died before she was born. Kate had been a single parent from day one. Seeing someone else, especially a man, brushing her daughter's hair sent a flood of longing through her, for Lily and herself.

Lily didn't know what it was to have a daddy. Just like Kate. Kate swallowed hard on the lump forming in her throat. "Lily, sweetie, go get dressed."

Her daughter's face lit. "Are we going outside to play?"

Kate smiled and patted her daughter's head. "You can play, but I have work to do outside."

"Yay!" Lily darted up the stairs, her bright curls bouncing as she went.

Kate descended from the last step and held out her hand. "My father left this key for me and a video disk."

She dropped the key and the disk into Ben's hand.

"What does the key go to?" Ben turned it over in his fingers.

"I don't know. I've tried to watch the disk, but I couldn't get it to work. The letter from the attorney had a note from my father to contact Hank Derringer for help."

"Maybe Hank can get someone to look at the disk and see if they can pull the information off."

Lily was down the stairs again, wearing shorts, cowboy boots and pulling a shirt over her head.

"Stop, young lady," Kate ordered, afraid her daughter would miss a step and tumble the rest of the way down the stairs. "You can't go out without me, and I'm not dressed."

"Please, Mommy." Lily looked up at Kate with a slight pout on her pretty pink lips.

"I'll take her," Ben offered. "We can discuss the key later." He handed it back to her, setting the disk on an end table.

Kate curled her fingers around the key. "I'll be ready in a minute. I need to finish unloading the rental van and get it back to town."

Ben smiled and raised his hands palms upward. "I'm here to help."

Kate's heart skipped several beats as the man's smile transformed his face from frowning, brooding darkness to sunshine. "You should smile more often," she said without thinking.

Immediately, his face changed back into the brooding cowboy, his forehead creasing. "I find little to smile about these days."

Kate wondered what made him so sullen and sad but didn't want to push the issue, not when he'd thrown up a no-trespassing sign in the way his body stiffened and he turned away. He took Lily's hand in his. "Ready?"

The two left through the front door.

Yes, sir, the cowboy had issues. Hell, didn't everyone?

Kate climbed the stairs, her footsteps slow at first and speeding up as she neared the top. For the first time in months, she wanted to get outside and enjoy the sunshine and fresh air. She refused to believe the hired hand had anything to do with her sudden surge of energy.

A pair of jeans, a snug-fitting ribbed T-shirt and tennis shoes completed her outfit. After she pulled her hair up into a ponytail and settled a baseball cap over her head, she hurried out to join Lily and Ben, her steps light, eager to finish unloading and settle into her new life.

Ben and Lily squatted beside the moving van, pointing at something on the ground.

"That's a scorpion, Lily," Ben was explaining. "Don't try to touch or pick one up, they have a really bad sting."

Lily hunched over, staring at the insect crawling across the ground. She looked up and spied Kate. "Mommy, come see the scorpion."

Kate smiled and squatted beside her. With the three of them all gathered in a circle so close, her stomach knotted. This must be what it would feel like to be a family unit. Mommy, daughter and...daddy. Troy would have been a good father to Lily. He'd been so excited about the arrival of his firstborn, only to be robbed of ever seeing her.

Lily was a beautiful baby and an even prettier little girl with a grown-up sense of responsibility and a child's joy of exploring.

"The day's not getting any longer. I guess we better get this van unloaded so that I can return it to the rental center in town." Kate stood, pulled the padlock key from her pocket and unlocked the back of the van.

For the next twenty minutes, Kate and Ben worked in silence, carrying boxes and furniture into the house. Lily helped a little, then lost interest and wandered around the yard, picking flowers and investigating her new home.

Kate kept a close eye on her. After last night's break-in, she wasn't feeling exactly trusting of her new environment.

Lily had strayed to the corner of the house when Kate

and Ben hauled out the sofa with the repaired cushions she'd brought with her from her apartment.

Getting the sofa through the door took them several tries, tipping it in multiple directions, before they finally shoved the item through. When the sofa cleared the door frame, Kate tripped over a throw rug and landed on her bottom, the edge of the sofa coming down hard on her ankle. "Ouch!"

"Are you all right in there?" Ben called out over the top of the sofa.

"Yes, just not very graceful." Kate stood and put pressure on her ankle and felt pain shooting up her leg. She swallowed a yelp and lifted her end again. There was no time for injuries. The van needed to be back before three o'clock or she'd have to pay for another day's rental.

Once they got the sofa settled into the living room, Kate headed toward the door, trying to hide her limp.

Ben shook his head and pointed to the sofa they'd just placed. "Sit."

"I'm fine, just a little sore. It'll work itself out." When she tried to walk past him, he grabbed her arms and made her stop.

"Let me see." His grip was firm but gentle and his tone the same.

The warmth of his hands on her arms sent shivers of awareness throughout her body. "Really, it's fine," she said, even as she let him maneuver her to sit on the arm of the couch.

Ben squatted, pulled the tennis shoe off her foot and removed her sock. "I had training as a first responder on the Austin police force. Let me be the judge."

Kate held her breath as he lifted her foot and turned it to inspect the ankle, his fingers slipping over her skin.

"See? Just bumped it. It'll be fine in a minute." She cursed inwardly at her breathlessness. A man's hands on her ankle shouldn't send her into a tailspin.

Ben Harding was a trained professional. Touching a woman's ankle meant nothing other than a concern for health and safety. Nothing more.

Then why was she having a hard time breathing, like a teenager on her first date? Kate bent to slip her foot back into her shoe, biting hard on her lip to keep from crying out at the pain. Her head came very close to Ben's. When she turned toward him she could feel the warmth of his breath fan across her cheek.

"You should put a little ice on that," he said, his tone as smooth as warm syrup sliding over her.

Ice was exactly what she needed. To chill her natural reaction to a handsome man paid to help and protect her, not touch, hold or kiss her.

Whoa, there, girl. Kate jumped up and moved away from Ben and his gentle fingers, warm breath and shoulders so broad they could turn a girl's head. "I should get back outside. No telling what Lily is up to."

Ben caught her arm as she passed him. "You felt it, too, didn't you?"

Kate fought the urge to lean into him and sniff the musky scent of male. Four years was a long time to go without a man. "I don't know what you're talking about."

Ben held her arm a moment longer, then let go. "You're right. We should check on Lily."

Kate hurried, no, ran for the open door, her heart racing, her breathing ragged. Just as she crossed the threshold into the open breezy, South Texas sunshine, a frightened scream made her racing heart stop.

"Lily!" Kate burst out onto the porch.

The sound of engines racing up the gravel driveway greeted her. A man wearing a do-rag over his head with a bandanna pulled up over his mouth and nose straddled a huge motorcycle in the middle of the yard, holding a doll by its hair. He laughed, the sound so evil it made Kate's skin crawl.

"That's Lily's doll." Kate flew off the porch and would have scratched the man's eyes out if an arm hadn't circled her waist and yanked her back.

"Go back to the house. Now," Ben said into her ear, his voice tight around the command.

"But Lily—"

"Go." He shoved her back behind him.

Kate hesitated.

The roar of engines rose to a crescendo. An army of bikes swarmed into the yard, stirring up dust where the grass had long since died.

Kate ran for the house. Before she could reach the porch, a motorcycle cut her off. There must have been twenty bikes racing around the yard in a tight circle, trapping Ben and Kate in the center. The dust rose in a cloud, choking visibility to everything beyond.

Beyond panic, long past frightened, Kate screamed into the smoke screen, "Where's my child?"

Chapter Four

Ben had left his Glock on top of the refrigerator inside the house while they'd been working to unload the trailer. Now he wished he had it. Two unarmed people against a biker gang weren't good odds in anyone's experience.

A rider broke the ring, circled the pair and then swerved toward Kate.

Fear for her spiked his adrenaline and he lunged toward the motorcyclist. Grabbing the closest handlebar, Ben twisted it hard toward the man astride. The sharp turn on the forward-moving bike caused the bike to flip over, rider and all.

Ben snagged Kate's hand and pulled her closer to him into the center of the circle.

The man he'd toppled pulled himself out of the dirt, his face bleeding from where he'd crashed into the gravel drive. He glared at Ben and Kate and roared, veins popping out on his forehead.

Kate shrank against Ben. "Oh, God."

They had nowhere to go; the ring of motorcycles tightened. The man with the doll eased toward them, dark eyes glaring through the slit between his do-rag and bandanna. "You need to leave, lady, before it's too late." He ripped the head off the doll and flung it at Kate's feet.

Kate reached for the doll, but Ben held her back. "When

I make my move…run toward the house," he said into her ear. Anger surged and Ben threw himself at the lead man, knocking him out of his seat.

Kate ran.

Ben got one good, hard punch at the man's face before two goons ditched their rides and jerked him off their leader. Caught between two beefy Hispanic men, Ben struggled, twisting and kicking, determined to keep their attention long enough for Kate to escape.

Ben jabbed an elbow into the gut of the guy on his right.

The man loosened his hold.

Ben ducked beneath his arm. No sooner had he shaken free from his captors' hold than he was slammed to the ground from behind, a bull of a man hitting him low and hard.

The wind knocked from his lungs, Ben lay facedown in the dirt, willing his body to move. A foot in the middle of his back kept him from doing anything, especially refilling his starving lungs.

Kate screamed.

A shot of determination rocketed through Ben. He rolled onto his back; at the same time he grabbed the man's leg who'd planted his heavy boot into his back. With a hard twist, he sent the thug flying backward, landing hard on his butt.

Two more men grabbed him, hauled him up and yanked his arms behind him, hard enough that spasms of pain ripped through his shoulders.

The leader lumbered to his feet and stalked toward Ben. He hit him with a hard-knuckled fist, square in the jaw. Ben's head jerked back, hazy gray fog encroaching on his vision. Another punch to his gut would have had him doubling over, if he didn't have two big guys holding him up.

Through the torture, his gaze panned the yard, searching for Kate and Lily.

The bikers had broken the circle and raced around the

yard, running over bushes, ramming into a rose trellis. One drove up onto the porch and ripped the porch swing from its hooks.

Another cut off Kate's attempt to get to the house.

Kate shot a glance over her shoulder and dodged to the left.

The biker sped past her and spun to renew his attack.

Ben planted his feet in the dirt and struggled, twisting and turning in an attempt to go to Kate's rescue, his mind conjuring his wife's last minutes on the earth, fighting to protect their daughter.

Then, he hadn't been there to help Julia. His job now was to protect Kate. If only he'd been more vigilant and not lulled into believing danger wouldn't strike during the daylight hours.

Hell, the fight wasn't over.

The gang leader swung again.

Ben jerked to the side hard enough that the guy on his left tripped. The leader's blow hit his own man in the cheekbone. The man yelled and grabbed his face with both hands, letting go of Ben.

Using the weight of the other man's body, Ben rolled into him and sent him flying over his shoulder.

Kate ran toward the road.

The biker who'd missed her straightened his bike and hit the gas. The back tire spun, then gripped the ground and shot forward.

Ben came at him sideways, plowing into the biker.

The bike and rider rolled over to the side, the rider moving sluggishly in the dirt.

One down, nineteen to go.

Kate ran on, but another bike raced after her.

Ben wouldn't catch up before the biker reached her.

A loud air horn broke through the roar of racing motorcycle engines, followed by a cloud of dust storming toward them on the gravel drive leading to the highway. Another air horn burst and a truck swerved around Kate, aiming straight for the biker in pursuit of the fleeing woman.

A shotgun's nose poked out of the passenger window and blasted a hole in the ground in front of the bike tire. As a result, the biker spun so fast, the back wheel whirled all the way around and out from under the rider.

The gang members Ben had thrown off caught up to him and knocked him to the ground. He came up spitting dirt and ready to tear into them. He swung again and again, pummeling one man in the face. When that one went down, he kicked out and sent the other sprawling on his backside.

Another shot rang out, peppering bird shot at the gang members.

One man yelped and sent his bike skittering out of the shooter's range.

The leader of the gang yelled something and circled his hand in the air, then pointed to the road.

All of the bikers revved their engines and rode out, leaving a lung-choking cloud in their wake.

Their leader left the yard, shouting, *"Dejar o te vas a morir!"*

As the dust cleared, the driver and passenger of the truck dropped to the ground.

Ben laughed, the effort making his split lip and sore rib cage hurt. He leaned against the gnarled trunk of a live oak tree, his knuckles bleeding and every muscle in his body screaming.

The driver was an older Hispanic man with a decided limp. The passenger, the one holding the shotgun, was a woman who could only be described as grandmotherly. Thank the lord for help in all shapes and sizes.

Ben's next thought went to Kate and Lily.

Kate rounded the back of the pickup and ran back into the

yard, tears making muddy tracks down her cheeks. "Lily!" she cried out.

A whimper sounded from the tree branches over Ben's head.

Hidden between the leaves was a little girl with a curly halo of hair, clutching a ball of fur to her chest, tears slipping down her cheeks. "Mommy?"

"Lily?" Kate skidded to a halt beneath the tree. "Oh, baby. I'm so glad you're okay." Kate grabbed a branch and started up the tree.

Ben snagged her arm. "Let me."

"I can do this."

"It would be better if I could hand her down to someone she knows."

Kate backed away and let Ben take the lead.

He ducked beneath the low-hanging branches and climbed upward. "Hey, Lily. How'd you get all the way up here?"

She hiccuped, her bottom lip trembling as she clutched the fuzz ball to the curve of her neck. "I followed Jazzy."

"Is Jazzy one of your toys?" He spoke in calm, soothing tones, careful not to grimace when a shard of pain rippled across his hands or ribs.

Lily shook her head. "No, Jazzy's not a toy."

A soft mewling erupted from the fur ball and little paws reached out to latch onto Lily's shirt.

"Jazzy's a kitten." Lily's eyes rounded as she stared down into Ben's eyes. "Can I keep her?"

Ben chuckled, his body hurting with every breath. He wanted to crush the little girl and the kitten to his chest and hold them there for as long as he could. He couldn't tell if the pain he was feeling stemmed from sore ribs, bruises or heartbreak. "You'll have to ask your mommy."

"Will you ask her for me?"

"You bet." Ben settled on a thick branch and wrapped his

legs around it before he reached out. "Come on. I think your mother wants to fix you lunch or something."

"I'm scared." She glanced around at the ground below her. "Are the bad men gone?"

Rage burned in Ben's throat as hot as acid but he fought to keep it from his face and voice. "Yes, baby. They're gone." This child should not have been exposed to the violence of those men.

She leaned toward him and stopped, her arm around the kitten that clung to her, its blue eyes as big around as Lily's. "You're bleeding."

"It's okay. It doesn't hurt, just a little cut."

"I want my mommy," Lily whimpered.

"I'm going to hand you down to her. Come on. You're so brave to save that kitten. Now let me be brave and save you from falling out of the tree."

Lily smiled. "Silly, I'm not falling out of the tree."

"Your mother thinks you will." He winked. "But I know better. You're good at climbing trees, aren't you?"

She nodded, then let him grab her around the waist and lift her onto the branch he sat on. He hugged her to him, relief washing over him in such a rush that his eyes glazed over and he couldn't see.

"Give her to me, please," Kate cried.

Ben blinked several times before he loosened his hold on the little girl and handed her down into Kate's outstretched arms.

Kate gathered Lily into a hug so tight, Lily grunted. She sat on the ground in the dirt and hugged her some more, tears trickling from the corners of her eyes.

"I'm okay, Mommy." Lily patted Kate's face. "See?" Her empty hand pressed against Kate's face, urging her to look into her eyes. "I saved the kitten." Her smile broadened. "Can I keep her? Her name is Jazzy."

"Sure, honey. You can keep her." Kate dashed the tears

from her cheeks and hugged Lily again. Then she climbed to her feet, lifting Lily to perch on her hip. "Come on, let's clean up."

Ben slid out of the tree and dropped to the ground beside the two, his hand going around Kate's waist. "You two going to be all right?"

"I hope so." Kate's eyes widened. "You're bleeding."

Lily grinned at Ben. "Told you."

Kate cupped Ben's cheek. "Come in the house and let me take care of your cuts before they get infected."

The light touch sent fire through his veins. Ben pushed her hand aside. "I'm fine. I'll just stay out here and see what I can do to clean up the mess they made." Anything rather than being close to Kate. She brought out too many feelings in him, feelings he'd thought long dead, emotions that made a man vulnerable.

The woman holding the shotgun waved her hands at them. "You three go get cleaned up and let us take care of the mess. Eddy and I can set things to rights in no time. Can't we, Eddy?"

The short Hispanic man had wandered off, picking up broken bush branches. *"Sí, señora."*

Ben stepped between the woman and Kate. "Could we at least know the names of our rescuers?" He tried to smile, his lip hurting with the effort. "I'm Ben Harding, Kate's my...fiancée."

"Oh, goodness, yes." The woman shifted the shotgun into her other hand and gripped Ben's hand in a firm, capable grasp. "Margaret Henderson. But most folks 'round here call me Ma or Marge. This here's Eddy."

"Mrs. Henderson, Eddy, glad to meet you." Ben nodded at the gun. "Good shootin'."

"No boys in my family, so my daddy taught all his girls to squirrel hunt." She grinned. "And I make a mean squirrel soup."

"I'll bet you do." Ben let go of her hand. "Thank you for showing up when you did. I think they were about to get the best of us."

"I don't know. You were holdin' yer own pretty well."

Ben didn't want to argue with the woman. He'd gotten his butt whipped and Kate would be in a world of hurt had Margaret and Eddy not come along when they did. Guilt with a hint of heartrending regret tugged at his empty belly. What made Hank think a washed-up cop was the right man for this job? It had taken an old woman with a shotgun to chase off the latest threat. Some bodyguard he'd turned out to be.

Margaret smacked Ben on the back. "Twenty-to-one odds needs a little more encouragement than bare fists. Don't let it get ya down. Question is why they were here in the first place."

Eddy stuck a long blade of grass between his lips and rocked back on his heels. "Their leader shouted *'Dejar o te vas a morir'* as he left." The man had a decided Mexican accent.

Kate shook her head. "I don't know Spanish. What does it mean?"

Eddy's gaze captured Kate's, his lips tightening for a moment before he spoke. "Leave or you will die."

KATE'S HEART SANK into her belly. Holy smokes, what the hell had she done to the bikers to warrant a death threat?

"Well, now, isn't that a nice way to welcome the new neighbors." Marge turned to face Kate, the stiff, tough persona fading with the softening of her eyes. "You must be Kate."

Kate held on to Lily, refusing to let her child out of her sight for even a moment. Her legs still shook and she couldn't keep her hand from trembling when she held it out to Margaret. "Should I know you?"

"Kate Kendrick—" the woman folded Kate's hand in both of hers "—you're the spittin' image of your father."

Kate shook her head. "I go by Kate Langsdon." She gripped the woman's hand with her free one. "Did you know my...Kyle Kendrick?" She still couldn't manage to refer to him as her father. Throughout her life, her mother had told her that her father had died in a car wreck. Growing up without a father hadn't given her any practice saying the word. And for the past four years, Lily had been without a father of her own.

"Know him? I worked for him until the day he was m—" The older woman's eyes widened and she clapped a hand over her mouth. "Sorry." Her glance moved to Lily, and her hand fell to her side. "I worked for Mr. Kendrick until he passed. He was a good man."

Kate bit her lip, wanting to refute Mrs. Henderson's statement. What man would willingly walk away from his daughter and never have contact with her? In Kate's mind, that didn't make a good man.

"Thank you for coming to our rescue." Kate smiled and turned to Ben. "Now, let's get you inside and doctored up."

The kitten Lily had been holding mewed.

An answering meow came from beneath the porch and a brightly colored calico cat stepped out of the shadows.

The kitten clawed at Lily.

"Ouch." Lily held the kitten away from her shirt.

Kate pointed to the cat. "That must be the kitten's mother."

Lily hugged the fur ball to her, her brows pulling together in a mutinous frown. "Jazzy is *my* kitty."

"Honey, you have to let her go to her mama."

"But I want a kitten."

"Jazzy will be your kitten, but you'll have to let her be with her mama until she gets bigger."

"I want her to come in the house and sleep in my bed."

"When she doesn't need her mother anymore. You can come and play with her outside until then."

The kitten dug her claws into Lily, scrambling to get to her mother.

"See, she misses her mother." Kate leaned Lily away from her. "How would you feel if someone wouldn't let you come to your mother?"

Lily stared at the kitten and the calico mother cat, meowing over and over. "I'd feel sad."

"And the kitten is sad because you won't let her go to her mother."

Lily wiggled in Kate's arms, so she set her daughter on the ground.

Plucking the kitten's claws from her shirt, Lily settled the animal on the ground.

As soon as she was loose, the kitten ran for her mother, curling in and around the cat's long, sleek legs.

"See how happy Jazzy is?" Kate knelt beside her daughter.

"Can I play with her after lunch?"

"You sure can." If the bikers weren't back or an intruder wasn't rummaging through the only home they had to go to. Kate's chest tightened. "We'll bring food out for Jazzy and her mother."

Lily slipped her hand into Ben's and one into her mother's. "I'm hungry. Can we eat now?"

Kate almost laughed at how quickly Lily forgot the bad men on motorcycles, all her concentration on eating and getting back outside to play with her kitten. How simple to be a child and forget about all the horrible things adults could do to each other.

Ben glanced over the top of Lily's head. "She'll be all right."

The biker's warning echoed in Kate's mind. "I hope so."

Chapter Five

Kate led the way into the ranch house. As soon as she passed through the door, Lily shook her hand free and ran to the bathroom. Kate and Ben followed, filling the tiny room.

Lily stood on a small plastic step, just the right height to boost her little body up to the sink. She pumped liquid soap onto her hands and turned on the faucet, splashing water over her arms and shirt. "Do kittens like milk?"

"I suppose they do," Kate replied, her voice soft, reassuring and less shaky than it had been in the yard after being terrorized by the biker gang.

Ben's gut clenched. He should have been ready—he could have handled the situation better. He reached out and grabbed her hand. "I'm sorry."

Kate's brows wrinkled. "For what?"

"Letting it go that far."

She dragged her hand out of his, closed the toilet lid and pointed at it. "Sit."

Obediently, he did, amazed at the strength in her tone.

While washing her hands, she chewed on her lip, tears welling in her eyes. She dashed them away, apparently not wanting him to see them. Tough tone and tears didn't add up. Ben's chest squeezed. This woman had been scared out of her mind, but she refused to show it.

Lily climbed into Ben's lap. "You have a boo-boo on your mouth." She poked a finger at the drying blood.

The child felt right, her legs dangling over his knee, her feet swinging in and out. As quickly as she'd come, Lily slid off his lap and left the bathroom.

"Stay in the house, Lily," Kate called out.

"I will. I'm going to my room to play with my dolls."

The sound of footsteps on the stairs echoed through the old house.

Kate snatched a clean hand towel from the shelf over Ben's head, leaning so close, the scent of herbal shampoo wafted over him.

Her breasts brushed against his shoulder and he gasped.

Kate jerked back, towel clutched in her fingers. "Did I hurt you?"

"No," he said through clenched teeth. The pain she'd caused had nothing to do with flesh wounds. She'd stirred his heart to life and that was more painful than a broken bone or knife stabbing. He'd thought his heart was firmly locked away after the deaths of his wife and daughter.

Now he sat at the tender mercy of a woman and her daughter, reminding him with every move, every touch and soft word of all he'd lost.

She dampened the towel in the water and touched the cloth to the corner of his lip, dabbing gently to remove the dried blood.

"Lily's a great kid," he said.

"I know." Kate's gaze focused on his wounds, one hand steadying herself on his shoulder. Warmth filtered through his chambray shirt to his skin. Ben's jeans tightened and his pulse quickened.

"Some bodyguard I am," he said.

When he glanced into her eyes, he caught her staring down at him.

"You were outnumbered. You couldn't fight them all."

"I should have had my gun on me at all times," he countered.

"And they might have used it on you or Lily."

"Or you."

"I'll make an ice pack for that jaw. Any other injuries?"

The longer she stood there close enough to touch, the harder it was not to reach out. "No." He shook his head and stood, wincing, his hand automatically rising to press against his ribs.

Kate's brow furrowed. "Liar. Let me see." She pushed his T-shirt up, tucking it beneath his arms.

A bruise the size of a grapefruit was making its dark purple appearance against his skin and everything beneath the mark ached.

"Damn, Ben, you could have a broken rib." She dipped the towel beneath the faucet again, wrung it out and pressed it to his side, her fingers sliding over the bruise. "Does that hurt?"

Ben grasped her fingers and held them away from his skin. "Yes," he lied. Her touch wasn't what hurt, it was the effect she was having on him. If he didn't get away soon, he'd be hard-pressed to walk away without kissing her.

"Let me take you to the clinic in town. They must have an X-ray machine." She tugged her hand free and pressed the cool towel to his side, all her focus on his injury.

Past his level of endurance, Ben tipped her chin up. "I don't need a doctor. I'm not going anywhere."

When her green-eyed gaze met his, he realized his mistake. Her lips parted, and what she might have said next faded away on a sigh.

Ben bent and brushed his lips across hers. He'd only wanted a taste. But like water to a desert flower, the more he tasted the more he wanted.

His fingers curled around the back of her neck, tugging at her hair, tipping her head back, giving him more access to her lips, her throat and the pulse beating wildly at the base.

She leaned into him. Her fingers pressed against his chest, the tips curling into his skin, not enough to hurt, but enough to ignite a flame he'd thought long burned out.

As fire spread through his veins, his arms tightened around her, his lips going from soft and gentle to crushingly hard, desperate to wipe out the stab of guilt that ravaged him from head to toe.

"I'm sorry, Julia," he said against her lips. "I'm so sorry."

The woman in his arms stiffened, her mouth moving away from his, her hands pressing against his skin.

"Let go of me," she said, her voice ragged, her tone strained.

Ben backed up, his hands dropping to his sides. "I'm sorry. That shouldn't have happened."

"Damn right, it shouldn't have." Kate's hand shook as she swiped the back of her hand over her bruised lips. "I don't know who Julia is, but I'm not her." She turned to walk out of the bathroom.

Ben caught her hand. "You're right. I had no business kissing you." Not when he still had feelings for his dead wife. Feelings that amplified his guilt for having kissed this stranger. "It won't happen again."

Without facing him, she jerked her hand free. "I don't think this arrangement will work after all."

"I understand. I'll talk with Hank about a replacement this afternoon."

"Please." Her shoulders rose and fell as if she sighed deeply, then she left the room.

Ben's fists balled. He wanted to hit something, but his knuckles were already like raw meat. He wasn't sure he could handle any more pain, both physical and emotional.

Too much about Kate and Lily reminded him of Julia and Sarah. The sooner he left the Flying K Ranch the better off they both would be.

Images of the intruder on the first night and the terror of

the motorcycle gang nagged his conscience. Would Kate's next hired gun take better care of her? Would he try to kiss her and forget why he'd come?

KATE RAN UP the stairs and peeked in at Lily. Her daughter sat at her little table with her miniature tea set laid out. A teddy bear and two dolls occupied the other seats.

Satisfied Lily was okay, Kate slipped past and into her own room, closing the door behind her. She leaned against the panel and pressed her fingers to her burning cheeks.

He'd kissed her. Her bodyguard had kissed her.

What had her running scared was that she'd liked it. So much so that she'd kissed him back, practically crawling up his body to get closer.

She covered her softly swollen lips and moaned.

It had been four years since she'd known the touch of another man's kiss, the feel of big, strong hands on her skin.

Her body burned with a need she thought had been buried with her husband. Kate squeezed her eyes shut and tried to picture Troy's face, a sob rising up her throat when the only face she envisioned was Ben's.

Kate opened her eyes, her gaze darting around the bedroom to the framed photograph of her and Troy on their last vacation together. They'd gone to the coast, playing in the sun and sand as if there'd be no tomorrow. Tomorrows for Troy had ended with an improvised explosive device that detonated beside his convoy. He'd been killed instantly. One week before he was due to come home. One month before his daughter's birth. Two days before their third anniversary.

Troy smiled back at her from the photograph, his light gray eyes and sandy-blond hair so different from the dark hair and stormy-blue eyes of the man downstairs.

Kate hugged the frame to her breast, again trying to recall Troy smiling down at her as he'd kissed her goodbye. Even holding Troy's photo, Kate couldn't see him. Her mind fixated on the dark-haired, brooding man who'd come to help her keep Lily safe in their new home.

Kate set the photo on her nightstand and hurried into the bathroom. She didn't have time to worry about why her memories of Troy were fading. She had a daughter to take care of, one who needed her to make lunch.

She stared into the mirror and almost cried of fright. Her face was smudged with dirt, her eyes red-rimmed and puffy from tears of joy at finding Lily safe in a tree.

Kate scrubbed her face with cool water, brushed her hair and secured it in a ponytail at her nape. Clean-faced and refreshed, she took a deep breath and resolved to act as if nothing had happened. No more kisses would be exchanged and life would go on as usual.

When she passed Lily's room, her daughter no longer sat at her table, the tea set abandoned.

Her heartbeat quickening, Kate hurried down the stairs.

A quick perusal of the living room found it empty. Only Mrs. Henderson in the kitchen.

Fear pushed Kate out the front door.

Ben was hanging the porch swing that had been knocked down by the gang.

As soon as he settled the chain on the hooks, Lily climbed up on the swing and patted the seat beside her. "Will you swing with me?"

"I don't know." Ben glanced out at the dry Texas landscape, only his profile visible from where Kate stood. The dark circles beneath his eyes and sad, faraway look tugged at Kate's heartstrings.

"Please?" Lily batted her eyes like a pro.

Ben chuckled and smiled. "When you put it like that... sure." He settled on the swing beside Lily and looped his arm over the child's shoulder, pulling her close.

A lump the size of a grapefruit lodged in Kate's throat and

she backed away, racing for the kitchen and a hand towel to dry quickly forming tears.

Marge stood at the kitchen counter, adding lettuce and tomatoes to thick slices of bread layered with lunch meat. "Ah, there you are. I hope you didn't mind me barging in and jumping right in. I worked here so many years, it feels more like home to me than my own house. I've missed coming out."

Kate's mouth watered. "Where did you get all that food?"

"I was the cook and I handled the grocery shopping for Mr. Kendrick. I figured with you just having moved in, you probably hadn't had time to visit the store to stock up. Eddy's a ranch hand. He wanted to check on the horses and cattle, so I asked him to bring me out after stopping for a few things at the market."

"A few?" Kate opened the pantry doors and checked in the refrigerator and gasped. "This isn't a few."

Mrs. Henderson blushed. "I'm sorry. It's kind of pushy of me, but I've been beside myself staying at home since Mr. K. passed. My husband retired last year and we just bump into each other too much. I *need* to work outside the home."

"I'm not sure I can pay you, and I don't expect you to work for free."

"Now, don't you worry none. Consider this a welcome home gift. And once Eddy gets the cattle rounded up and the fences mended, he'll give you a better idea of what this place can do to support you and your little one."

Tears filled Kate's eyes. "Why?"

"Like I said, Mr. Kendrick was a good man. Many times he'd spot me my mortgage payment when my man was out of work." The older woman sliced a sandwich in two and laid it on a freshly cleaned plate. "Now, you just sit right down there and have yourself a bite. You could stand to gain a pound or two." Marge patted her rounded figure. "Not that you want to put on as many as I have." She laughed and moved around the kitchen like one very familiar with its contents.

Ben entered, carrying Lily on his arm. "Someone is hungry. I wonder who it is."

Lily's hand shot up. "Me!"

He swung her up in the air and caught her.

Kate's heart warmed at her daughter's giggles. Oh, to be young enough to forget so easily. Today could have turned out very badly. Any one of them could have been hurt or killed. Thank God Lily had been climbing a tree, although Kate wasn't all that comfortable with a four-year-old climbing unattended. What if she'd fallen?

If the impact on the ground hadn't hurt her, the biker gang could have.

Ben set Lily on her feet and laid a hand on Kate's shoulder. "She's all right. I won't let anything bad happen to her."

"I know that." Kate's gaze followed Lily around the kitchen, but her mind was on the hand warming her shoulder. "I was just thinking that I should be mad at Lily for climbing a tree, but I can't find it in my heart to be. If she hadn't…" Kate glanced up into Ben's eyes.

A muscle in the side of his jaw twitched. "We'll have to do a better job of keeping an eye on her. She's a very active little girl. Aren't you, darlin'."

Marge trimmed the crust off a sandwich and cut it in triangles, then set it on a plate in front of Lily. "Eat up, half-pint."

"You'll spoil her," Kate protested.

"It's my biggest fault." Marge smoothed Lily's hair back from her forehead. "Never had any of my own. Guess I do go a bit overboard."

"It's hard not to, even when they're yours." Kate smiled at Lily. "She's all I've got."

Marge smiled. "You have Ben, too. When are the two of you lovebirds gonna tie the knot?"

Kate's face burned. She hated lying, but if it helped keep

the rest of the town off her back, she'd do it, and she didn't know Marge well enough yet to set her straight on the fake engagement. "We haven't set a date."

"No hurry, huh? Too many young couples meet each other one day, marry the next and file for a divorce within a year." Marge crossed her arms. "You're smart to wait. Seems Mr. Kendrick and your mama were in that category. Young and crazy stupid in love. Mr. Kendrick never considered whether his new bride would be happy out in the middle of nowhere Texas. She wasn't suited for the rugged life of a ranch owner. Too bad she didn't stay around long enough to find out."

"My mother never talked about my father. She told me he'd died in an automobile accident."

Marge shook her head. "Nearly broke Mr. K.'s heart when your mama left him. He didn't even know you existed until after your mother died and her lawyer notified him, or I'm sure he'd have done more to get to know you sooner."

"My mother's been dead for nearly five years. Why didn't he come find me then?"

Marge shrugged. "I asked him again and again. He just said the timing wasn't right. Might have been because he'd been doing a lot of traveling." The housekeeper leaned close. "He never said, but I think he worked for the government, secret service or something. He'd pack and leave a note that he'd be gone awhile. Never said how long, when he'd be back or where he was going."

"Any idea where he went?" Ben asked.

"I think he had business in Mexico. The man spoke Spanish like a native."

Kate frowned. How sad to learn about her estranged father from a stranger. Especially when he'd lived in Texas all her life and hadn't bothered to get to know his daughter even after he'd learned of her existence.

"Mrs. Henderson?" Ben began.

"Call me Marge. Please."

"Marge." Ben smiled. "What exactly happened to Mr. Kendrick?"

"Now, that's a very good question. You'll get a different answer depending on who you ask."

"What do you mean? Didn't a coroner determine cause of death?"

"The county coroner is a good friend of the sheriff. He'd put whatever the sheriff wanted him to put on the death certificate."

Kate's eyes widened. "I was under the impression Kyle Kendrick died of natural causes."

"The coroner stated he'd died of heart failure."

"And you don't believe him?"

"Oh, I'm sure Mr. Kendrick died of heart failure, but the cause of the heart failure, in my opinion, had nothing natural about it."

Ben pulled up a chair at the table and sat beside Kate. "Why do you say that?"

"The man had bruising around his throat. I'm sure his heart failed when his lungs could no longer get air."

Kate gasped, setting her sandwich on the plate, all hunger forgotten. "Someone choked him?"

"I watch enough crime scene investigation shows to know a man with bruises around his throat didn't run into a door."

"Did you say anything to the sheriff?"

Marge shook her head. "If they couldn't see what was in front of them, either they're just plain stupid or were in on the killin'. Sayin' somethin' to them wouldn't bring back Mr. K., and it might have bought me the same demise."

A chill slithered across Kate's skin. "Who would want to kill him?"

"I can't even imagine." Marge tidied the counter, talking as she went. "Mr. K. was quiet, but well-liked in the community by the few who got to know him. He never had a bad word to say about anybody. He was kinda reclusive, but that could be expected of a confirmed bachelor like himself." She paused and stared out the window. "Could be someone involved in the troubles around here."

Kate frowned. "Troubles?"

"The Flying K is smack-dab in the middle of an area known for drug trafficking from across the border." Mrs. Henderson glanced at Lily. "Maybe Mr. K. got cross-ways with one of them. They found him here in this house. No sign of forced entry, but the place was a shambles. It was like someone he knew killed him, then ransacked the house. As far as I could tell, the only thing missin' was the computer out of Mr. K.'s office. Eddy thinks it was Larry Sites, though why Larry would take the computer…" Mrs. H. shrugged. "The man could barely read, much less find his way around a keyboard."

"Larry Sites?" Kate shook her head, trying to take it all in.

"Larry was a ranch hand here at the Flying K. Worked with Eddy. But no one's seen him since the day we found Mr. K." Marge clucked her tongue. "Poor Mr. K."

A lead weight settled in Kate's belly. "The more I hear the more I'm beginning to think Lily and I need to move back to Houston."

"Oh, honey," Marge said as she laid a hand on Kate's shoulder. "I'd hate to see you go when you just got here."

"Mommy, can I go out now?" Lily asked, her hands and face covered in peanut butter and jelly.

"Sweetie, it'll have to be later. After you wash your hands and face, we're going to town. I have some business to do there."

Mrs. Henderson was there with a clean, wet washcloth before Lily could move a muscle, scrubbing the sticky jelly from her face and hands.

"What do you say to Mrs. Henderson?" Kate prompted.

"You missed a spot." Lily's tongue slid along her lips and she smacked them loudly.

Marge laughed and dabbed at the stickiness.

Lily jumped down from her chair and skipped toward the hallway. "Thank you for making lunch, Mrs. Henderson. It was delicious."

Kate pushed her plate away and stood. "Thank you for the sandwiches, Marge." She rummaged through drawers to find something to wrap hers in.

"Don't you worry about that. I'll put it away for later. You go on. The town rolls up its sidewalks at five o'clock. If you have business there, you need to skedaddle."

"We'll find dinner in town. No need to cook anything here."

"Will do, Kate." Marge gave her a hug. "I'm glad you're here. I've missed Mr. K. and you're the spittin' image of the man, only prettier."

Kate thanked her again and hurried out of the kitchen, her mind running through all Mrs. Henderson had said.

She should have looked this gift horse in the mouth before accepting it and moving out to Wild Oak Canyon in the middle of South Texas. Now that she was here, she had to make the best of it. First things first. She wanted to know more about her father's death and the people with whom he'd done business.

BEN FOLLOWED KATE out of the kitchen. "I have a bad feeling about this."

"You and me both." She stopped at the base of the steps. "I want to freshen up a bit, then I'll be down. I assume, as my bodyguard, you'll be coming with me to town?" This last question she spoke in a whisper.

"That's right."

"In my car or your truck?"

"My truck."

"Good. I'll meet you in five minutes." She ran up the stairs.

Ben almost groaned aloud at the sway of her hips. The woman was far too distracting for him to keep his mind on the task at hand. Julia hadn't been quite as curvy as Kate. Her frame had been slight, so much so that giving birth had been especially difficult. Their obstetrician recommended that she not have any more children due to her narrow frame and complications of high blood pressure and prenatal diabetes during pregnancy.

Ben had been disappointed, wanting a whole brood of children. But he'd hidden his regret well. The sight of baby Sarah, so perfect and pink, had been all he'd needed.

Until a brutal murderer had taken her away from him.

All these thoughts stemmed from the one short glimpse of Kate's swaying fanny.

He shook his head, squared his shoulders and climbed the stairs behind her, heading for the room she'd assigned to him where he changed into a clean shirt and jeans.

Once he'd smoothed his hair into a semblance of order, he stepped into the hallway and ran into Kate.

He knocked into her, throwing her off balance. Ben grabbed her and pulled her into his arms, crushing her against his chest, his heartbeat hammering through his veins. Had he hit her any harder, she would have fallen right over the railing and down to the hardwood flooring.

Once he had her securely in his arms, he couldn't make himself let go. Her curves fit him in all the right places, so soft and tempting.

She looked up, her lips inches from his. "What are you doing?" she whispered.

"Keeping you from falling over the rail." Ben couldn't believe how cracked his voice sounded. "I promise to be more careful in the future."

Her tongue swept across her bottom lip, moistening it. "Please."

"Please what?" Why hadn't he let go of her already?

"Be more careful." She dragged in a deep breath and stepped free of his arms, straightening her shoulders while tugging the hem of her blouse. "I need to get to town. I want to run by the bank before they close."

He nodded, his hands dropping to his sides, the heat still burning within. "I need to touch base with Hank while we're there."

"Good. Then let's get going."

At least one of them had the wherewithal to get past the awkwardness Ben had instigated.

"I'll get Lily." Kate dodged past him like a scalded cat and ducked into Lily's room.

"I'll be in the truck," Ben called out, taking the stairs two at a time. He breezed through the kitchen. "You need a ride back to town, Mrs. Henderson?"

"No. I see Eddy headed this way. I'm sure he'll be wanting to get home and he promised to take me. Don't worry none about locking up. I still have a key." She patted her pocket.

Ben almost frowned, but caught himself. "Are you the only one who has a key besides Ms. Langsdon?"

"As far as I know." Marge's brows furrowed. "Why?"

"Just wondered. I'll make a stop at the hardware store to buy all new locks and keys. Just for safe measure."

She nodded. "Don't want anything bad to happen to those girls."

Ben's jaw tightened. "No, we don't." Whether it was him or one of Hank's other cowboys taking care of her, it wouldn't hurt to change out the locks on the house.

He pulled his truck around the side of the house, got out and grabbed the booster seat from Kate's car, securing it in the backseat of his truck. He tucked his 9 mm pistol into the glove box.

Lily burst through the front door and skipped across the yard, all smiles, her light strawberry-blond curls bouncing around her shoulders. She wore a sundress with a bright yellow-and-white daisy pattern. She was all sunshine and happiness, oblivious to the dangers around her.

That's how a child should be—carefree and happy.

Ben's fingers tightened around the steering wheel, memories threatening to overwhelm him. Scenes in his mind he'd tried so hard to push away.

Kate followed Lily out the door. Her pretty red-blond hair was pulled up in a loose bun at the back of her head. She wore a pastel yellow sundress and sandals, looking like spring and everything right with the world.

God, he had to get Hank to find someone else to take this job. He wasn't cut out for this. It was too soon. Every time he looked at the mother and daughter, a knife twisted in his gut. Sadly, he feared it was already too late to walk away.

Ben couldn't imagine leaving them to whatever peril the wild Texas landscape, and even wilder men who'd already threatened her, had to offer.

He opened the back door, helped Lily up into the booster seat and buckled the belt across her lap.

"I'm impressed," Kate said as she inspected his work. "You did that like you've done it before."

Ben backed away and rounded the truck, wordlessly, his teeth clenched. He'd buckled Sarah in a hundred times, careful with his precious daughter, wanting to keep her safe in case of a traffic accident. Too bad he hadn't kept her safe from her killer.

Kate climbed up into the passenger seat, her brows puckered. "Did I say something wrong?"

"No." Ben sat behind the wheel, fighting for control. Finally, he shifted the truck into Drive.

Her brow remained puckered as she sat back.

Lily fell asleep in the backseat almost as soon as they hit the highway.

Ben's grip tightened on the wheel, his knuckles turning white. His gaze panned the long stretch of road, looking for any hidden hazards, man-made or in the terrain. As knotted up as he was, he'd exhaust himself before nightfall. He inhaled and let the breath out slowly, willing himself to relax.

When they neared the town of Wild Oak Canyon, he had his control back.

Until Kate spoke, her soft tones warming him inside and out. "I believe the bank is on the next corner."

Ben shook his head. "We're stopping at the sheriff's office first."

Chapter Six

Kate climbed down from the passenger seat before Ben could come around and open her door. He insisted on lifting Lily out of her booster seat. Still sleepy, the child stirred and lay across Ben's shoulder. Her eyelids fluttered, then closed.

The sight of Lily sleeping so peacefully on Ben's shoulder was sweet and disturbing. On the one hand the three of them gave the appearance of being a family. On the other, Ben wasn't a fixed variable in Lily's life. When they figured out what was going on and cleared the threat, Ben would be gone. Lily would wonder what she'd done to chase him off. She might even blame herself. Kate reached out. "I'll take her."

Ben turned away, refusing to give up Lily. "Let her sleep."

It only made sense. Kate wasn't too happy, knowing this was temporary. They'd made the mistake of claiming Ben was her fiancé. In a town the size of Wild Oak Canyon, that little tidbit would already have made its rounds.

Kate led the way into the sheriff's office, determined to take charge of this situation, starting with reporting the biker attack.

Deputy Dwayne Schillinger sat in a chair behind a desk, his feet propped on a stack of paper, his hand curled around a burger. "Well, well. To what do we owe the pleasure of your visit so soon?" The man let his boots drop to the floor with a thump and laid his lunch in the wrapper.

"I want to report another attack on my property and a death threat," Kate said.

"What kind of attack might that be?" Dwayne wiped his hands down the sides of his uniform, leaving a streak of yellow mustard. He finally pushed out of his chair and stood.

"A gang of bikers rode through my yard, attacked Ben and damaged property. As they left, they shouted out a death threat."

"Can you describe the men?"

"They wore bandannas around their faces and they rode motorcycles." Kate's fists clenched. "I think they were Hispanic."

"That's not much to go on. Without more detailed physical descriptions, I can't go out and arrest anyone. You have to do a little better than that."

Kate let out a frustrated huff. "Don't you know the people of this county? There can't be that many and surely you know who owns motorcycles and who doesn't."

Ben stepped up beside Kate and added softly, "One of the men had a tattoo of a snake. It wrapped around his wrist and forearm."

"Now *that* I might be able to do something with. Sounds like Guillermo Ramirez. His friends call him Snake."

A shred of relief rippled through Kate. A name for her attacker was better than nothing. "I suggest you arrest him for trespassing and assault."

"As soon as I can find him. Like his nickname, he's pretty slippery and difficult to track."

Kate fisted her hands on her hips. "I have a child living with me. I don't want this to happen again. Are you going to do your job and track down the man? Or do I need to call in the state police?"

Dwayne patted her arm. "Now, don't get your panties in a wad, young lady. We take our work seriously out here. We'll get right on it."

Kate nodded to the stack of papers on his desk. "Aren't you going to take notes, a statement or anything?"

"Don't need to." He tapped a finger to his temple. "I'll remember."

Kate dragged in a deep breath, closed her eyes and counted to three. "Thank you for caring." She turned and marched toward the door.

As she reached for the knob, the deputy called out, "Wouldn't have to be scared for yourself or your daughter if you weren't living on the Flying K."

Kate spun. "And what's that supposed to mean?"

Deputy Dwayne shrugged. "Nothing good's come of living at the Flying K. Look what happened to your father."

Kate walked back toward the man. "Are you telling me my father didn't die of natural causes like the medical examiner claimed?"

Dwayne's squinty eyes rounded. "No, ma'am. Just saying it ain't a healthy place to raise a family."

"You know something I don't?"

The deputy raised his hands. "No, ma'am. Just saying."

"I suggest you find this Snake guy and arrest him. That would go a long way toward making the Flying K a healthier place to live." Kate left the building.

Ben followed, chuckling. "Nice."

"I don't need your patronization. I need answers." Kate stomped to the truck and yanked on the handle. Her nail bent back for her effort and the door remained closed. "Dang it!"

"Mommy?" Lily's eyes fluttered open. "Why were you yelling at that man?"

All the starch went out of Kate. "Oh, sweetie. I was just a little disappointed with him." Inside she bit hard on her tongue. "A little disappointed" was a huge understatement.

Ben clicked his key fob and the locks on the truck popped up. "Bank next?" His mouth twitched on the corners.

If Kate wasn't mistaken, the man was fighting a smile.

A shot of anger flared and died as she tried to picture her tirade with the deputy from Ben's view. Okay, so it must have been amusing to the man to see a woman dressed in a sundress and sandals rip into Deputy Dwayne with all his self-importance, attitude and mustard tracking down his shirt. "Smile and I'll serve your teeth on a platter," she warned, her own lips quirking upward. After the tension of the night and early morning, she could use a good laugh, even at her own expense.

"I wouldn't dare." Ben settled Lily in her booster seat and stepped back, allowing Kate to buckle her daughter in.

Her mood a little lighter, Kate climbed into the passenger seat and leaned back. "Not the bank yet. I want to go to the county tax assessor's office. There has to be a mistake about my father's back taxes."

Ben drove the three blocks from the sheriff's office to the county offices. When he pulled up in front of the building, he left the engine running. "I have a call to make. Will you be all right on your own for a few minutes?"

"Hopefully Lily and I will be safe inside the county offices. When we're done there, we'll go next door to the bank. Take your time." Kate climbed out, lifted Lily from her seat and took her hand, entering the cool interior of the county offices.

"Can I help you?" An older woman with gray hair and a pair of glasses perched on the end of her nose smiled a greeting.

"I hope you can." Kate pulled the letter from her purse and laid it on the counter. "I need information on the Flying K Ranch and any taxes owed on the place."

The woman grimaced. "Ma'am, I'm sorry but the computer is down and has been for two days now. The technician hasn't been able to fix it and we're waiting on someone from state to help." She pushed a form toward Kate. "If you'd like to fill out this form and leave it with me, I'll check the records as soon as I have access."

Kate sighed. "Thanks." While Lily stood patiently beside her, Kate filled out the form, then showed the woman her driver's license and a copy of the deed to the ranch as proof of ownership.

"Do you know when they'll have the system back up?"

"Not a clue. Check back tomorrow. Hopefully it'll be up then."

"Thank you." Kate left, Lily's hand clasped in hers, no less tense than when she'd entered the building a few minutes earlier. No use obsessing over a downed computer; she had only thirty days to come up with the cash, should she need it. No time like the present to see what the bank could do for her. She entered the cool, brightly lit bank lobby, her shoulders back, a smile pasted on her face.

ONCE THE TWO girls were out of the truck, Ben glanced at his cell phone. Two bars. *Here's hoping.* His cell phone had been such a big part of his life in Austin. Out here in South Texas, he was lucky to use it at all.

He hit the speed dial for Hank Derringer and held his breath, not letting it out until the device sent a ringing sound back to him.

"Howdy, Ben," Hank answered.

"We need to talk."

"I take it you've met Kate?"

"I have." He inhaled and let out the breath before jumping in. "I need you to reassign me."

A long pause met his request.

"Did you hear me?" Ben prompted.

"I did. Only I've already assigned the other three members of CCI to cases." Hank cleared his throat and continued, "Is something wrong with Kate?"

"No. It's just that I'm not the right man for this particular job."

"I have full confidence in your abilities. I didn't choose you for this case by acci—"

"You didn't tell me she had a child." Ben cut him off, not wanting to hear Hank's arguments.

"Ah." That one word said it all.

"I'm not cut out to play bodyguard to this woman and her little girl. You need someone who…that… Well, damn. Get someone else."

"This has to do with Julia and Sarah, doesn't it?" Hank asked softly.

It was Ben's turn to leave dead air between the two of them. He swallowed hard on the giant lump clogging his throat before he could croak out his answer. "Yeah."

"Look, Ben, it was exactly the reason I hired you for this job. You have more of a stake in this case, more of an understanding of what's at risk, than anyone else on the team. I picked the right man."

"I can't do it."

"Yes. You can." Hank's voice softened even more. "I heard about the intruder last night and about the biker gang attack this morning. I wish I could send someone else to help you, but I just don't have the resources yet."

Ben snorted. "Good news travels fast, doesn't it?"

"What can I say? It's a small town and I have a few friends."

"In the meantime I'm stuck, is that what you're telling me?"

"You've met Kate and Lily. You've seen a little of what they're up against. At this point, could you really walk away?" Hank left a pregnant pause for Ben to respond. When he didn't, Hank went on, "I stand by my decision. I think you're the right man for the job."

"So it's take this one or resign?"

"You're not the kind of man to resign, if I read your dossier right."

Damn the man. He'd done his homework. He knew Ben more than Ben knew, or would admit to knowing, himself.

"Is that all you have?" Hank asked.

"No, can you use your connections to run a background check on Larry Sites and Guillermo Ramirez?"

"Had a check done on Larry Sites when the man disappeared after Kendrick's death. Newspapers reported that he was suspected of Kendrick's murder, that he's wanted for questioning. Otherwise, he didn't have an arrest record."

"Know anything about Ramirez? The man has a snake tattoo on his arm. He seemed to be the leader of the biker gang attack."

"I'll get an official background check on him, but from what I know, he's a thug for hire. It's rumored he works for whatever cartel will pay him the most. He's walking a thin line doing that. I'm surprised someone hasn't put a bullet in him yet. Part of it has to do with his ability to disappear. We suspect he slides across the border when it's hot on this side."

"Nice." Ben's fingers tightened on the cell phone. Kate was in a lot more trouble than just a biker gang harassing her. "Let me know when you find my replacement. Until then, I'll do the best I can."

"Thanks, Ben. Kate and Lily need you out there." Hank clicked off.

Ben sat for a long moment, staring at the street, heat waves rising from the asphalt, making mirages rise up before his eyes in wavering images of his dead wife and child.

Maybe it was the heat waves, maybe it was the tears. Ben blinked and Julia and Sarah disappeared.

He fought the urge to step on the accelerator and drive. Out of town, away from this job, from Kate and Lily. Hell, out of Texas altogether.

Instead he placed another call while he still had reception.

"Jenkins speaking."

Ben immediately recognized the voice on the other end of the connection as Detective Jenkins of the Austin Police Department. "Jenkins, Ben Harding here. I need some help."

"Ben? Is that you?" Jenkins pitched his voice low, almost to a whisper. "Man, where are you? As far as anyone knows you fell off the face of the earth."

"I'm in South Texas near a little town called Wild Oak Canyon."

Jenkins chuckled. "I guess it's true, then. You did fall off the face of the earth. What can I do for you?"

Ben jumped in. "Who's handling my case?"

"Man, you know I'm not at liberty—"

"Damn it, Jim. Who's handling it?"

Jenkins sighed. "Masters was assigned after you left."

"Anything new?"

"Not much. I think Masters tracked down the man who supplied the girls to Frank Davis. We don't have much, other than hearsay, so we haven't made an arrest yet."

"Girls?" All he knew about was the one Davis had killed.

"Apparently Davis was more deviant than originally suspected."

Ben's hand tightened around the cell phone. He wanted to kill Davis all over again. "Who was the supplier?" he asked through clenched teeth.

"You know I can't give you that kind of information. You're not on the force anymore."

Ben slammed his palm against the steering wheel. "When did you start following all the rules?"

"When you got fired." His tone was flat, final. "Why do you want to know?"

"I killed a man for killing a girl. I want to know it wasn't in vain. From the sound of it there are more women and girls being trafficked."

The silence on the other end indicated he'd gotten his friend's attention.

"Who supplied the girls to Davis? If they are victims of a human trafficking ring, it has to stop."

"I don't like going against department rules."

"Lives could depend on this." Ben's hand tightened on the receiver as he waited for his friend's response.

"Look, we know that. Masters is working the case."

"So let me help. What's it going to hurt?"

"You, me…I don't know, but I don't like playing both sides of the law."

"I'm no rogue and I doubt I could get into much trouble way down south where I am, but if there's any way I can help, I will."

After a long pause, Jenkins said, "His name is Rolando Gonzalez. He's here in Austin, but we suspect he has connections to the Mexican Mafia. As a matter of fact, he's got family in South Texas. Let me pull the file and get back with you. If you could do some looking around while you're down there, we might get more on him and who he's working for. Just don't do anything stupid."

Like killing him before they could get information out of him? Ben knew he'd gone beyond his limit on Davis. Seeing that girl lying on that cot, beaten, bleeding and past help… Ben stared out the window, his heart racing as if he was there all over again.

A movement on his right jerked him back to the present.

Kate and Lily exited the county tax assessor's office, waved at him and walked next door to the bank. If Hank got him off this case with Kate, he would have time to check out the lead Jenkins was talking about.

"I don't get reception out on the ranch where I'm working, so leave a message on my cell. If it's urgent, contact Hank Derringer." Ben left Hank's number with Jenkins. "I'll be waiting for that information."

"Will do. And Harding…stay safe. If this is as big as I think it is, you don't want to get caught in the cross fire of the Mexican Mafia."

Hell, he couldn't afford to get in the middle of the Mafia, not when he had Kate and Lily to protect. He'd wait to make any inquiries until Hank found a replacement.

"I NEED TO take out an equity loan on my father's—my ranch and open a three-thousand-dollar line of credit until I can withdraw money from a CD I set up for Lily's college." Kate leaned forward, her anger building with each time Art Manning tapped his pen to the loan application form in front of him.

"I'm sorry, Ms. Kendrick."

"Langsdon."

"Ms. Langsdon. I'll have to perform a complete credit check on you and have our corporate underwriters approve this before I can give you an answer. In the meantime I suggest you open an account here. We can't loan money to anyone who is not a current client of our bank."

"I see." Kate stood. In the meantime, she was running low on cash and she needed money to pay Eddy and Ms. Henderson's salaries, not to mention putting food on the table and all the deposits she'd needed to get the electricity and gas switched over to her name.

"While your underwriters are thinking about it, I'll be thinking about whether or not to open an account." She gathered Lily's hand in hers.

"Ms. Kendrick."

"Langsdon."

"Without a job and a current income, I doubt the underwriters will take your application seriously."

"The land isn't enough collateral to secure a mortgage?"

"Not given the history of that particular parcel and its location."

"You mean I won't be able to get a loan?"

He shook his head. "I doubt it."

Kate breathed in and let it out before speaking again. "Thank you for your time, Mr. Manning."

She headed for the door, ready to be out in the heat, away from the stuffy air-conditioned atmosphere of the bank building.

"You look like your father." The voice belonged to a businessman dressed in a tailored suit leaning against the stand containing blank deposit slips.

Kate's steps faltered and she glanced at the man, her eyes narrowing. "Seems to be the consensus. If you'll excuse me…" Impatient and tired after a sleepless night and the fright of the morning, Kate had no intention of stopping to chat and she veered to the side.

The stranger stepped out, blocking her path to the exit. He stuck out his hand. "I'm Robert Sanders. Your father and I were friends."

To avoid being outright rude, Kate clasped the man's hand and shook it briefly. "Nice to meet you, Mr. Sanders. I'm Kate."

"Kate Langsdon." He held on to her hand longer than Kate wanted, then let go. "You have his eyes."

"I thought the hair was the dead giveaway."

"Your father's hair was much darker." Sanders raised a hand to touch one of Kate's curls.

She backed away.

The man's hand fell to his side. "But the green eyes are unmistakably his. I believe your mother had blue eyes, did she not?"

His comment took the wind out of Kate's sails. "You knew my mother?" So far, no one in town had mentioned her mother. Most people she'd run across in Wild Oak Canyon mentioned Kyle Kendrick, but not her mother, as though she'd never been there.

"No, but your father had a picture of his ex-wife on his desk. You don't look much like her at all."

That made Kate smile and her gut twist at the same time. "My mother always said I was a constant reminder of my father."

"Your mother must have been a very special woman. Your father never married after she left."

A spike of anger flared in Kate's gut. She'd loved her mother until the day she'd died. But if she had one regret in her relationship, it was that her mother had chosen to lie to her about her father, claiming he was dead, instead of alive and available if she'd wanted to meet him.

Kate suddenly felt stifled in the bank. "If you'll pardon me." She wanted out. Knowing Ben was waiting made her all the more anxious to leave, ready to get back to safe territory.

That thought gave her pause.

Damn.

After only one day, she'd come to rely on the strength and presence of Ben. If things didn't get better soon, she ran the risk of becoming too dependent on him.

Since her husband's death, Kate had been hesitant to date, unwilling to drag her daughter through relationships that wouldn't last. Not many men wanted to date a woman with a ready-made family.

Not that she wanted to date Ben. But the close proximity of a bodyguard could lead to the same outcome. Lily could become attached.

As she stepped around Mr. Sanders, the man handed her his business card. "I feel somewhat responsible for the well-being of my friend's daughter." When she didn't take his card, he lifted her hand, laid the card in it and curled her fingers around the paper. "Please, if there is anything I can do, don't hesitate to call."

Kate clutched the card. "Thank you." When she turned to leave, his hand caught her elbow.

"If you don't mind, I'd like to visit the ranch and make sure you're doing okay out there all alone."

"That won't be necessary."

"I insist."

"I'm not alone. I have my...fiancé staying with me. I'm quite all right."

Sanders's eyes narrowed fractionally, then his brows rose. "So, wedding bells are in the near future for you, are they?" He grasped her hands again. "Congratulations, my dear. I'm so happy for you."

Kate pulled free of Mr. Sanders's grip. "Thank you." She snatched Lily's little hand and turned away, hating the lies she was telling this town, but feeling more comfortable with the fact that Ben's presence would keep her safe. At least it might make others think before they set foot on her property. The more the people of the county thought a man lived there full-time, the better off she was. A lone woman on a ranch could be considered a target. Especially a ranch in cartel territory.

Houston was looking better every minute. But Kate had come too far to turn back now. She wanted to find out why her father had died. If he hadn't died of natural causes, Kate wanted to know who had killed him and why.

BEN HAD HIS hand on the gearshift ready to pull away from Wild Oak Canyon, to start a new life...elsewhere. As he flexed his arm to move the gear, Kate pushed through the glass doors, leading Lily by the hand, a troubled expression on her face.

Instead of driving away, Ben found himself climbing down and opening the rear passenger door before Kate reached the vehicle. The slump in her shoulders and the dullness in her eyes plucked at his heartstrings more than he cared to admit. "I take it that meeting didn't go well."

"County computers are down until further notice, so I struck out there."

Ben lifted Lily into her seat and buckled her belt. "We can come back tomorrow."

"Then the bank..." Kate stepped on the running board and slid into the passenger seat. "I only asked for a home equity loan to help me catch up in case I owed back taxes, and a line of credit loan to last me long enough so that I can sort through my father's will and cash in some certificates of deposit I have set aside for Lily's college fund." She snorted. "You'd think I'd gone in there asking for a fortune."

Ben didn't trust himself to comment. His insides churned. He didn't want to admit to Kate how close he'd been to leaving her and Lily in Wild Oak Canyon. What kind of coward left a woman and her child to fend for themselves?

Once they were all in the truck and belted, Ben rounded the truck and climbed into the driver's seat.

Kate sighed. "I guess the only good thing out of those two stops is this." She held up a business card. "This Robert Sanders claimed he was a friend of my father's and gave me his card in case I needed anything."

Ben reached for the card. "Let me see that."

Kate handed it over. "Looks legit."

Robert Sanders of Sanders Homes. Real Estate Broker and Construction.

Ben turned the card over, then handed it back to Kate. "Let me have Hank check him out before you get too chummy."

Kate nodded and slid the card into her purse.

Ben would keep an eye out for Sanders. If he really was a friend of Kyle Kendrick, he shouldn't be a threat to Kate. But then Kyle's place hadn't been broken into. He'd known his attacker.

Ben shifted into gear and pulled out onto the road.

"I need to stop at the hardware and feed stores for the things Eddy wanted me to get." Kate pulled a sheet of notepaper from her purse. "He handed it to me on the way out of the house." She glanced over her shoulder at Lily. "Then we can go to the diner and have supper. Would you like that, Lily?"

Lily's eyes widened, a smile lighting her face. "Do they have milk shakes?"

Kate let her daughter's happiness wash over her and she smiled back. "I don't know, but we'll find out."

"Can I have a chocolate milk shake?" Lily's feet bounced on the seat back.

Ben laughed. "We'll see when we get there."

In less than an hour, they had what they needed loaded into the back of the truck.

"Guess it's a good thing *you* drove today. I haven't had the chance to go through my father's barn and see if he had a truck. This ranching thing is all new to me."

"I can help you there."

"I thought you were a bodyguard. Were you a cowboy in your former life?"

"I grew up on a ranch." He'd loved living on a ranch, riding horses and raising cattle. But his family didn't own the ranch. Once his father's health declined to the point he could no longer handle the hard work, they'd moved to Austin where both his parents died in a multicar pileup on the interstate the week after Ben graduated from college.

"So is it true, once a cowboy, always a cowboy?" Kate's question pulled Ben back to the present.

He wasn't looking at her, but he could feel Kate's direct stare, and it made him uncomfortable. Why did she have to ask so many dad-burned questions?

He didn't respond with anything more than a shrug.

Her lips twisted. "Nice to know. You must be a man of many talents. Anything else you'd like to share with me?"

"No." Ben pulled into the parking lot of Cara Jo's Diner. The timing couldn't have been better. He shouldn't have shared anything about his existence before Kate. None of that existed anymore. Not his parents, not his wife and child and not his work as an Austin police officer.

His slate was clean. What he did with his life now was the only thing he could do.

Start over.

A pretty young woman wielding a broom swept the sidewalk in front of the diner and smiled brightly when Ben stepped from the truck. She stopped to reach into a big cardboard box. When she straightened, there was a round-bellied puppy in her arms. "Howdy. I don't suppose ya'll want a puppy."

Kate had just set Lily on her feet and reached back into the truck to retrieve her purse, a hand holding on to the child's.

Lily wiggled free of Kate's grip, squealed and ran for the box. When she tried to step up on the curb, her sandal caught and she tripped, her little body slamming into the sidewalk.

Before Kate could reach her, Lily raised her arms for Ben to pick her up, tears streaming from her eyes.

Ben gathered her in his arms and cradled her. When he glanced up, his gut clenched at the paleness of Kate's face. He tried to pry the little girl's arms from around his neck, but she wouldn't let go. "Don't you want your mama?"

Lily buried her face in his shirt. "No, I want you."

Chapter Seven

Lily's knees and hands were scraped and bleeding. Her big emerald-green eyes filled with tears. "Am I gonna die?"

Ben smiled down at Lily. "No, baby, you'll be just fine."

Kate's heart skipped a few beats. A pang of jealousy tugged at her. But more than that, her chest tightened at how quickly Lily had assimilated Ben into her life. When he left, he'd leave a hole in her daughter's world that Lily wouldn't understand. She wouldn't be fine.

"Let's get her inside." The woman with the broom set the puppy down in the box and leaned her broom against the wall. "I have a first aid kit in the kitchen."

As Ben stepped into the diner, Lily practically crawled over his shoulder. "I want to see the puppies," she cried.

Kate followed Ben. "After we clean up your boo-boos, sweetheart, you can see the puppies."

"Can I hold one?" She sniffled and rubbed her arm over her nose.

Kate handed Lily a tissue from her purse. "If the nice lady says you can."

The broom lady chuckled. "My name's Cara Jo Smithson. And yes, you can hold one."

Lily grinned, her tears disappearing.

"So you're *the* Cara Jo?" Ben asked. "You're not what I expected as the owner."

Cara Jo laughed and batted her eyes. "I hope you mean that in a good way." The diner owner glanced over her shoulder at Ben, her footsteps slowing.

Kate had a sudden urge to scratch Cara Jo's eyes out for flirting with Ben. Then she had to remind herself the engagement was just a big fib. She had no hold on Ben and no right to be jealous if he flirted with the stunning Cara Jo. "The first aid kit?" Kate prompted.

"Oh, yes. This way." The woman marched to the back of the dining room and through a swinging door. Cara Jo held the door for Ben, Lily and Kate. "The washroom is at the rear of the kitchen. The first aid kit is in there under the sink."

Kate assumed the lead, stepping past shiny stainless-steel preparation tables and a huge gas stove.

"Let's get you fixed up." Cara Jo eased past Kate and Ben and entered the employee washroom, where she reached beneath a counter for a large, red plastic container with a big Red Cross sticker plastered to the top.

Ben set Lily on the countertop.

Kate moved to stand beside Ben, her hip so close it rubbed against his. A shot of awareness winged through her and she almost pulled away.

Cara Jo pulled bandages, sterile gauze and an accordion of alcohol prep pads from the kit, handing them to Kate.

While Kate dressed Lily's wounds, Ben distracted the child. He smoothed the red-gold curls out of Lily's face. "How many puppies do you have in that box, Cara Jo?"

Kate smiled, glad Ben's words captured Lily's attention, drawing it away from what Kate was doing.

"There are five, but one is already spoken for."

"What breed are they?"

Cara Jo laughed. "Purebred mutts, as far as I can tell." She opened an alcohol pad and handed it to Kate. "The vet seems to think they're a mix between Australian shepherd and border collie. All I know is that they're fuzzy and cute as can be. I'm having a hard time letting them go. But one dog in the family is enough when I'm working so much here at the diner."

Kate wiped the alcohol pad across Lily's skinned knees. Lily grimaced and reached for the knee. "Ouch."

Ben caught her hand before she could touch the cleaned wound. "You're doing so well, Lily. I didn't know you were such a big girl. So far, not a single tear."

"Big girls don't cry, do they, Mommy?" Lily darted a look at Kate.

Kate could feel the next sentence coming before her daughter even said it.

"Big girls can take care of puppies, can't they?" Lily's eyes rounded, her head tipping up and down.

Kate's brows furrowed. "I don't know. Puppies are a lot of work. Someone has to feed them every day and take them outside a lot until they learn to go out on their own."

"I can do that." Lily's eyes widened, her bottom lip pouting outward, just a little. "Can I have a puppy, Mommy? Please."

"You just found a kitten. Isn't a kitten enough?" Kate couldn't resist her daughter's sad puppy look. And now that they lived on a ranch, not in an apartment in Houston, she had no excuse. A puppy was a definite possibility. Still, it meant committing fully to living in Wild Oak Canyon. A puppy in a Houston apartment wouldn't work for Kate or the puppy.

"Let Mommy think about it, Lily," Ben said.

"Ben's right." Kate could have kissed Ben, the thought strangely appealing, more so than she wanted to admit. "I need to think about it."

Lily slumped.

"Hey, why the sad face?" Ben chucked a finger beneath her chin. "She didn't say no."

Teardrops shimmered on Lily's eyelashes. "She didn't say yes."

Kate shook her head, smiling. "I want to think about it."

"They'll be ready to wean from their mother any day now," Cara Jo added. "I hope they all have a home soon."

"Based on the one you were holding up before Lily fell, I'm sure they'll be snatched up," Ben said.

A bell jingled from the dining area. "If you two can handle this, I've got a customer. By the way, my special this evening is meat loaf and mashed potatoes, if you plan on staying for dinner."

"We can handle it from here," Ben reassured her. "And yes, we're staying for dinner."

Alone with Ben and Lily in the washroom, Kate's body tingled at the man's nearness. Heck, his broad shoulders practically filled the small space and his strong, capable hands dwarfed hers as he held her daughter.

Fingers fumbling, Kate applied a bandage to the sore knee, then bent and kissed the covered injury. "There, all better."

"Not quite." Ben pulled the rubber band from Lily's ponytail that had been hanging drunkenly to one side. Strands of silky golden-red curls fell loose about her shoulders. "Can't let this brave young lady walk out of here with a lopsided pony." Carefully, he bunched the hair into his hand, smoothing all the lumps, and secured it again in the band.

Kate's breath caught and held throughout the process. Clearly, the man had done this before. She didn't know anything about Ben. For all she knew, he could be married with a little girl of his own. A family he'd soon go home to.

Her stomach flip-flopped, a sense of impending loss leaving an empty space inside. How could this be? The man was nothing more than a hired gun, a bodyguard to protect her. He'd only been around for a day.

Kate had never believed in love at first sight. Not that

what she was feeling was anything like love. Respect, maybe. The man was strong, self-assured and handy to have around in a fight...or fixing a little girl's hair. That pretty much summed up her knowledge of Ben Harding. That, and he'd been a first responder for the Austin Police Department in his past life. What had made him leave to go work for Hank Derringer as a bodyguard for hire? The little bits of information she'd gleaned from the quiet man only made Kate want to learn more.

"Come on." Ben swung Lily up in his arms. "If it's all right with your mother, we'll go see those puppies now."

"I was thinking dinner would be a good idea."

The disappointment on Lily's face made Kate reconsider. "Okay, but only for a few minutes. I'll order our food while you two play with the puppies." She raised questioning brows at Ben. "Anything you'd like in particular?"

For a long moment, he stared down at her, with Lily perched on his arm. His blue eyes smoldered, his gaze lowering to somewhere south of Kate's nose.

Her pulse quickened, her mouth going dry. Kate ran her tongue across suddenly parched lips. "Food...what kind of food would you like?"

His mouth twitched. "Cara Jo's mention of meat loaf and mashed potatoes sounded great. I haven't had meat loaf in a long time."

"Meat loaf it is." Kate couldn't get out of the washroom fast enough. Heat suffused her entire body at the thought of Ben's full lips, that blue-eyed gaze bearing down on her, reminding her she was more than just a mother. She was a young woman with needs and physical desires she'd thought long gone with the death of her husband.

In an attempt to get her ragged breathing under control, Kate sat at one of the empty booths and waited for Ben and Lily to step outside before she dared follow them with her gaze.

"You're one lucky lady." Cara Jo stood at her elbow, a pad and paper in her hand.

"How so?" Kate wasn't feeling so lucky. At the moment, she felt trapped by her own raging hormones and latent desires.

Cara Jo spread her hands, palms up. "Why, your husband, of course."

"Fiancé," Kate corrected.

Cara Jo glanced out the big window at Ben squatting beside the box, handing Lily a puppy. "That man's hot, and he's really good with your daughter."

Kate's gaze followed Cara Jo's. "Yes, he is." Too good with her daughter and too handsome for Kate's own good.

"Let me know if you ever decide to give him up."

"Why?"

"He's just the kind of guy I'm looking for."

Kate's teeth ground together and she fought to keep from saying something stupid like *he's mine, keep your greedy hands off him.* Once again, she had to remind herself that she had no claim on Ben and that he wasn't even her fiancé. "You'll be the first to know," she said through tight lips.

Cara Jo laughed. "Lighten up. I'm not going to steal your man. He's in love with you, not me."

If only.

Kate's eyes widened and she almost jumped up from the table and ran. What the hell was she thinking? Ben wasn't her man. They'd only known each other for a day. He didn't—couldn't—love her and she'd better get such crazy thoughts from her head before she did something even more stupid, like falling for the big guy.

"Are you ordering for yourself or your family?"

"All of us." Kate had let the family comment slip right by so easily without trying to correct Cara Jo. At this point, she couldn't retract the lie without backtracking with the sheriff's office and anyone else who'd spread the rumor.

"So you're the folks who've moved onto the Flying K Ranch? I'm glad."

Kate's gaze shot to Cara Jo's. "You are? Why?"

Cara Jo shrugged with the hint of a smile. "Gets kinda lonesome out here in the middle of nowhere. There's not nearly enough women our age to talk to." Cara Jo's smile widened. "A girl could always use a friend."

Kate's eyes misted. "Thanks. I was feeling a bit overwhelmed by the acres of land between me and my nearest neighbor."

Cara Jo's sunny face darkened. "I hear you had some trouble out your way."

"Someone broke into the house the first night I was there."

"And what's this I heard about a motorcycle gang tearing through your yard?" Cara Jo shook her head. "What's with people? It's as though they're trying to scare you off or something."

"I'm getting that feeling, too. I just don't know why." Kate tipped her head to the side. "Did you know my father?"

"A little. He stopped by the diner for supper occasionally." Cara Jo gazed into Kate's eyes. "You have his eyes. I remember them being a pretty shade of green."

"So people say. I wouldn't know." Kate glanced toward Ben and Lily. "I never met the man."

"Really?" Cara Jo's pretty brow furrowed. "I think he traveled a lot. He never said much when he came in, but he was always polite and tipped well. He had a great smile, but apparently he didn't talk to anyone else about his life or what he was up to on the Flying K. He was a recluse."

"I wonder why he didn't get to know his neighbors."

Cara Jo leaned closer. "Some say he was involved in the Mexican Mafia. I'm usually a good judge of character. I didn't see it in him."

"I wish I'd had the chance to get to know him." Her comment was no more than a whisper.

Cara Jo's frown deepened. "Yeah and if wishes were horses…"

"…beggars would ride," Kate finished.

The diner owner bent toward Kate and hugged her with her free arm. When she straightened, she swiped at moisture in her eyes and laughed. "Hey, what say we do lunch sometime?"

Warmth washed over Kate. Nobody in Houston had volunteered to be her friend. Rarely had she gone out to lunch with anyone other than Lily.

She'd been casual acquaintances with her coworkers at the hobby store where she'd been employed. Scraping out an existence for her and Lily on what little she made and the money from her husband's life insurance became an exhausting job. Spare time was spent with her daughter, going to the parks and zoo.

"I'd love to do lunch." Kate smiled up at Cara Jo. "Maybe you'd like to get out of town and come visit the ranch? I can make a mean grilled cheese sandwich." Kate glanced around the diner. "I'm not a grand cook."

Cara Jo snorted. "And you think I am? I have the usual. If I change things up, I get complaints. People can be such creatures of habit."

"Cara Jo," a gray-haired older man called out from a booth on the other side of the entrance.

"I'll be right with you." Cara Jo grinned. "Don't be surprised if I show up on your doorstep real soon. In the meantime, what's your poison?"

Kate gave her new friend their order and sat back, admiring the tall, curvy young blonde's happy efficiency at handling her customers.

A squeal from outside drew Kate's attention.

Lily squatted on the wooden planks of the front porch, reaching out to a rambunctious black-and-white pup that nipped at her fingers. She jerked her hand away from the dog's sharp teeth and giggled.

Ben sat back on his haunches, smiling at the child. Every once in a while, his smile dimmed and his gaze grew somber.

Kate sat forward, studying the man.

The bodyguard had dark wavy hair hanging down to his collar. His square chin and lean, muscular body spoke of strength and discipline. But those smoky-blue, brooding eyes held too many shadows. Someone or something had hurt this man.

Kate closed her eyes and told herself she didn't want to know who and what had caused him so much pain. She couldn't keep them closed long. Lily squealed again and Ben's rich laughter made her want to go outside and join them.

"You should go see the puppies. They're too cute to miss." Cara Jo was at her side again. The diner owner set three glasses of ice water on the table and utensils wrapped in bright red cloth napkins. "Your food won't be ready for a few minutes. Go on before I do. That man is too yummy to be left alone long."

"No, I'll just wait here." Kate was already too aware of the man and the magnetism that pulled at her.

Lily giggled again, making Kate's heart leap.

"Have it your way, but those puppies will steal your heart." Cara Jo walked away to tend to another customer.

Lily squealed again, and Ben's laughter followed. Unable to resist, Kate rose from the booth seat and pushed through the front door out onto the porch. "Okay, you two are having entirely too much fun. Let's see what you've got."

Ben grinned up at her, the shadows gone from his eyes. "I think Pickles is her favorite."

"And which one is Pickles?" Kate dropped down on her knees and peered into the large cardboard box.

Five fluff balls growled in their puppy voices while tear-

ing at a stuffed toy that had seen better days. Each puppy
had its own unique coloring. Three were the mottled gray,
white, black and red of the Australian shepherd. Two were
black-and-white like a border collie.

In the corner closest to where Lily stood, one of the black-
and-white pups leaped against the side of the box.

"Look, Mommy, Pickles has pretty blue eyes." She dangled her hand in the box and Pickles snapped at it, his high-
pitched bark playful.

Lily laughed and hid her hand behind her back, looking up at Kate with shining eyes. "Can we take him home?
Please, Mommy."

Kate lifted the puppy from the box and held him in the air.
The gyrating ball of fur wiggled its way out of her hand. Kate
caught Pickles before he hit the ground, her heart lodged in
her chest. "You are a mess, little fellow."

"No, he's not. He's happy you picked him." Lily pointed
at Pickles's long black tail tipped with white. "See, he's wag-
ging his tail."

Kate held the puppy up to her face. The little fellow licked
the air, trying to get her nose, making her laugh at his per-
sistent attempts.

Raised by her mother in a small condo in the city, she'd
never been allowed to have a pet. No one was home to take
care of it for hours and her mother thought it was unfair to
animals to be left alone for so long. That and they could
barely afford to put food on their table, much less buy food
for a dog.

Kate hugged the puppy to her chest. Closing her eyes, she
inhaled the unique scent of puppy fur and puppy breath. The
defenseless pup reminded her of a time when she held Lily
in her arms, alone in the maternity ward. She'd clung to her
baby, after the miracle of her birth, realizing Lily was the
only person she had left to love in her world.

Tears welled in her eyes and she blinked to keep them from falling. When she looked up, her gaze met Ben's.

All the pain of her own loneliness shone back to her like a mirror in his eyes.

Ben stood, his jaw tightening until a muscle jerked on one side of his face. "I'll wait in the truck."

Her heart squeezing in her chest, Kate asked, "What about supper?"

"I'm not hungry," he called out without looking back.

Chapter Eight

Ben walked away. He would have run if he thought it would help. But no matter how far he ran, he couldn't escape the image of Kate staring at him through tear-soaked eyes.

As he dropped down off the porch, the sound of Lily's voice reached out to him, slamming another bullet into his heart. Sarah had been that enthusiastic, filled with a beautiful love of life. His daughter had been the joy of his existence.

For a few short minutes, he'd let Lily into his heart, laughing for the first time in two years. Letting her happiness revive his dead heart. Guilt swamped him, dragging him into that bottomless pit he'd crawled into after he'd discovered his wife and daughter murdered in their home.

How could he let another little girl fill that void?

And Kate's tears had touched him like nothing else since Sarah's death. He shouldn't be having these feelings. He'd lost his chance at love. He'd squandered it by not being there to protect them. Instead he'd been chasing his career as a cop, fighting to keep criminals off the street.

Ben jumped into his truck and slammed his door, then he hit the steering wheel with his palm so hard, pain reverberated through his hand and up into his arm. He welcomed it, using it to refocus on why he was there.

He had to regain his self-control or risk the lives of the

people he was there to protect. No matter what, he couldn't let Kate and Lily suffer the same fate as his family.

"YOUR DINNER IS ready." Cara Jo appeared in the doorway. Her smile turned into a frown. "Where'd Ben go?"

"He's waiting in the truck. I'm sorry. We're a little tired from all the excitement last night and this morning. Could we get the meal to go?"

"Absolutely. Give me a minute and I'll bring it out."

Kate returned the puppy to the box and then fished in her purse for her wallet, extracting enough cash to pay Cara Jo for the food and a tip. "I don't need any change."

"Honey, consider it my gift to the new girl in town."

"I insist. This is your livelihood." Kate placed the money in Cara Jo's hand and closed her fingers around it. "Please."

Perhaps the other woman saw the moisture in Kate's eyes, because she didn't press the issue. "Okay. Give me a minute."

A couple minutes later, she returned with a bag filled with take-out boxes. The heady scent of hot food wafted beneath Kate's nose and her belly growled. "Thank you. And please, come out whenever you'd like."

Lily stared down into the box, her lip trembling. "Can we take him home?" She looked up at Kate, pressing her hands together like she was praying.

"Not today, sweetie. Pickles has to stay with his mommy for a few more days."

"Then can we bring him home?"

"If he's not one of the puppies Ms. Cara Jo has promised to someone else."

Lily's gaze shifted to Cara Jo. "Can I have that one?" She pointed to Pickles, who'd resumed jumping against the side of the box, barking at Lily.

Cara Jo smiled. "You're in luck. He's still available."

Lily squealed and jumped up and down.

Anxious to leave and find out what had made Ben depart

so abruptly, Kate reached out and hugged Cara Jo. "Thanks for everything. I look forward to seeing you soon."

Cara Jo patted her back. "Let me know if I need to bring my shotgun out with me. You stay safe."

Kate slid her purse strap up over her shoulder. One hand held on to the bag of food while the other grabbed Lily's little fingers. "Come on, it's time to go home."

Ben stood beside the truck, his head bent, his hat tipped low, shading his eyes.

As soon as she stepped off the porch, he opened the back door and swung Lily up into her booster seat, buckling her in place. Wordlessly, he took the bag from Kate and settled it on the back floorboard, out of range of Lily's swinging legs.

Kate climbed into the front passenger seat and closed the door, unsure how to broach the subject of his sudden retreat.

When Ben slid in behind the wheel, he didn't look at her; instead he backed away from the diner and headed out of town on the highway leading to the Flying K Ranch.

"Just so you know, I asked Hank to find a replacement for me." His soft-spoken words took a moment to register.

When they did, Kate's head jerked toward him, her heart hitting the bottom of her stomach. "Why?"

"I'm not the right man for this job."

After the craziness of the day, the invasion of her home by a faceless man and the biker gang threats, Ben's announcement scared her the most. Tremors rippled through her body. A chill that had nothing to do with the truck's airconditioning wrapped around her and she shook uncontrollably. Keeping her voice as even as possible, she remarked in a tone she hoped sounded unconcerned, "You've done pretty darned good so far."

"Nevertheless, when he's got someone else lined up, I'll be leaving."

What could she say to that? Her logical left brain said to

leave it, nothing she could say would convince him to stay if he really wanted to go.

Her emotional right brain urged her to beg him to stay. He'd saved her more than once and she trusted him to do it again.

Instead, she whispered into the darkness, "Why did you walk away from Lily, me and the puppies?"

At first she didn't think he'd heard her and she let it go. Maybe she didn't want to know after all. What if he answered that he didn't like children or that he didn't like her? Nothing made sense. The way he'd been so happy and laughing with Lily led Kate to believe he liked children.

"I couldn't handle it." Ben's words broke through the frigid darkness.

Her heart already strained from his announcement that he'd be leaving; Kate wanted to know more than he was giving her. First she glanced over her shoulder at Lily.

Her baby's head dipped toward her chest, her eyes closed, chest rising and falling in deep, even breaths. Blessedly asleep, unaware of Ben's announcement that he'd be leaving.

Anger cleared Kate's head and forced her to sit up straighter. "Just what is it that you couldn't handle? Is it the constant threats out at the ranch?"

He didn't answer, ratcheting up Kate's annoyance with him for his vagueness and her desire to get to the bottom of the issues.

"Is it me? Am I too demanding?"

He shot a glance at her. "No, it's not you."

"Does Lily have you running scared? I can see that. Most four-year-old children terrify me. Especially ones who idolize me and dog my every step."

Ben's lips curled on the corners in a hint of a smile that never reached his eyes. The light from the dash didn't reflect in their dark depths. "No, Lily is a beautiful little girl."

Kate sucked in a deep breath and let it out between

clenched teeth. "If it's not the situation and it's not me or Lily, what the hell had you running?"

Another long pause lasted a couple miles.

Kate turned away from Ben and stared out at the darkness. Only she couldn't see past the glass reflecting her image and Ben's behind her.

The man stared straight ahead, his eyes smoky dark, the shadows beneath them deep and disturbing.

"I lost people I loved." His voice was agonizingly deep, and the words spoken so softly Kate thought she'd imagined it.

She turned toward him, studying his face. Had he spoken or had she imagined the words?

His hands gripped the steering wheel so tightly his knuckles had turned white. That and a tick in his jaw were the only indications of something going on more than him driving the truck.

"Who did you lose?" Kate asked, daring to believe she'd heard correctly.

"My wife and daughter. Sarah was Lily's age when she and Julia were murdered."

All the air left Kate's lungs and a weight settled on her chest that crushed the will from her. Julia. The name he'd called her when he'd kissed her. "Oh, God. I didn't know." She reached out and touched a hand to his arm.

Being with Lily had to be killing him.

Kate's worst nightmares had been those where she'd lost Lily, but every time she'd awakened to realize it had only been a bad dream.

Ben had lived it.

Her stomach roiled, the pain of loss almost as palpable as if she'd lost Lily. She swallowed hard on the giant lump choking her throat. "I'm sorry." Kate's voice caught on a sob. She looked back at Lily, counting her blessings, knowing that every minute she had with her little girl was precious.

Ben didn't have that anymore. His Sarah was gone.

Her bodyguard, the man who'd protected her and Lily, drove on as if he hadn't spoken at all. His face inscrutable, his lips pulled into a tight line.

As they turned off the highway onto the road that led to the Flying K Ranch, movement caught Kate's attention out of the corner of her eye. Before she could react, something hit the passenger-side door with the force of a freight train, flinging Kate sideways. If not for the seat belt, she'd have slammed into Ben and possibly gone through his window.

Lily screamed from the backseat as the truck lurched sideways and skidded across the road toward the ditch.

Ben fought to keep the vehicle on the pavement, but the driver's-side tires bit into the shoulder before he could right the vehicle.

Kate barely had time to straighten before the truck was hit again. All she could see before she was tossed against the restraining belt was a dark grille and the glass of headlights that hadn't been turned on.

Ben cursed, grinding his foot to the accelerator, trying to get away from their attacker. The impact pushed them off the road and down into the ditch so fast the truck teetered on two wheels.

Her breath caught in her throat as the truck wavered, then dropped to all four tires, the jolt flinging her against the door.

Lily cried out.

"Hold on, baby," Kate called out.

Switching the truck into four-wheel drive, Ben gunned the gas pedal. The tires slipped on the gravel, then the knobby treads dug into the dirt and the truck shot back out onto the road.

The dark, steel-gray haze of dusk surrounded them.

Kate twisted in her seat, peering into the semi-darkness of a cloudy starless evening. Behind them, taillights gleamed, two specks of red racing back toward Wild Oak Canyon.

Lily cried softly in the backseat.

The danger past for a moment, Kate unbuckled her belt and crawled over the front seat into the back.

Ben flipped the overhead light on. "Is she all right?" He drove slowly toward the ranch, his gaze darting to the rearview mirror.

Kate cupped her daughter's face.

Other than silent tears trailing down her cheeks, Lily appeared to be okay. "We're okay, aren't we, baby?"

"Want me to take you two back to town?" Ben offered. "We could report in to the sheriff's office and let him know what happened."

"No. I don't want to risk being out of the vehicle if that guy returns. I just want to go home." She sat in the middle of the backseat beside Lily, holding her child's hand. Soon the tears stopped and Lily fell back to sleep.

Kate trembled in the darkness, afraid of staying where someone obviously didn't want her. She was pissed off that she was being forced out by thugs.

When they arrived at the ranch, Kate unbuckled Lily.

Ben opened the door from the outside and draped Lily's sleeping body over his shoulder.

Kate dropped to the ground, her body stiff from being hurled around the interior of the cab. Her shoulders were sore and her right breast was tender from the force of her body hitting the shoulder strap of her seat belt.

While Ben carried Lily into the house and up the stairs to her bedroom, Kate went from room to room, switching on the lights. When she reached the kitchen, her hand paused on the light switch.

A noise in the pantry captured her attention.

A moment before, she'd been so tired she could barely stand. In an instant, she was on alert. She flipped the light switch on and grabbed for the broom she'd propped beside the door early that morning.

She waited for the next sound that would indicate where the intruder stood.

Her teeth clamped down hard on her lip to keep her from screaming.

A loud click sounded from the pantry and the lights blinked out.

"Kate?" Ben called out from the staircase behind her.

Kate flipped the light switch and nothing happened.

Then something moved in the direction of the walk-in pantry. A door thumped open and footsteps scuffled across the tile.

"Stop or I'll shoot." Kate held the broom up like a shotgun. Her eyes had yet to adjust to the darkness. All she could make out was a shadowy form.

"Then shoot," a voice called out. He lunged for the back door and ran out before Kate could do anything.

And what could she have done? The broom wasn't a gun. At best she could have thrown it at him. At least he hadn't attacked her.

"Kate!" Ben's voice echoed in the living room. "Where are you?"

"In the kitchen. I'm okay."

"What happened?" Footsteps sounded on the wood floor in the hallway and Ben skidded to a halt behind her, his hands reaching out to gather her into his arms. Ben crushed her to his chest. "You scared the hell out of me. Why didn't you answer me the first time?"

"We had an intruder in here. I didn't want him to know where I was."

"Are you all right?"

"I'm fine." *Now that you're here.* She leaned back against him, wrapping his arms securely around her middle.

He turned her in his embrace and tipped her chin up.

Already her eyes were adjusting to the limited lighting. A

soft blue glow poured in through a nearby window as clouds skittered across the sky, freeing the moonlight.

Kate stared up into Ben's dark eyes. "Why is this happening?"

"I don't know." He smoothed a hand over her cheek and it found its way to the back of her neck. He tugged her hair, tipping her head backward, making her lips more accessible to his...kiss.

Ben's mouth closed over hers, sending wave after wave of sensations rippling through Kate's body.

Her hands climbed up his chest, twining around his neck. She applied pressure, wanting more, needing him to deepen their connection, to warm her body with his. To chase away the shadows of fear making her tremble.

His tongue twined with hers, thrusting deep, sliding long and slow, in and out.

When his hands slipped downward, over her shoulder blades and to the small of her back, she didn't protest, couldn't tell him to stop. Not when all she wanted was for him to shove her up against a wall, wrap her legs around his waist and drive deep inside her.

How long had it been since she'd made love to a man? Since before Troy had left for war. Almost five years. More than any woman should have to grieve.

BEN'S MEMBER STRAINED against the stiff denim of his jeans, pushing against the button fly, waging a war for freedom. His hand tangled in Kate's thick, lush curls, cupping the back of her head as he bent her over his arm and took what he wanted in the form of a kiss. But it wasn't enough.

The lingering shock waves of adrenaline pulsed through his system, urging him to take action. With no enemy to attack and no imminent danger, his relief could only be derived from making mad, passionate love to this woman whose body warmed his hands and awakened desires long buried.

Kate melted against him; her hands smoothed down the back of his neck and then squeezed between their chests. Her fingers searched for the buttons on his shirt, opening one after the other until she slipped through the opening and touched his skin.

Cool, slim fingers set off a string of explosions inside Ben, sparking nerve endings to life.

Before long, she had all his buttons undone and was tugging his shirt out of his waistband.

Ben found the hem of her dress and pulled it up over her head, tossing the garment to the floor. A black lace bra was all that stood between him and her perfectly rounded breasts.

When her hands locked on the top button of his jeans, his heart skipped several beats and he sucked in a raw, ragged breath.

He closed his hands over hers. "No."

She froze and glanced up, her green eyes shadowed. Then her chin dipped and she backed away. "You're right. I shouldn't have done that. I'm sorry."

Ben's hands fell to his sides, regret burning in his gut. He couldn't let himself be distracted, not with Kate's and Lily's lives at stake. He reached around the wall, feeling for the light switch, and flipped it.

Nothing.

"Know where the breaker box is?" he asked.

"I saw it in the pantry earlier today. The intruder must have known where to look because that's where he was hiding."

"This has got to end." Ben felt his way through the kitchen to the pantry he recalled from unloading Kate's furniture and supplies. There was a sound of rustling fabric, a drawer opened and closed behind him and a beam of light clicked on.

"This might help." Kate, now redressed, followed him into the closet-size room and shone the light on the breaker box. Her presence in the tight confines of the tiny space lined with canned vegetables and boxes of cereal only made matters worse.

He was so tense, he fumbled with the handle to the breaker box before he could get it open and find the tripped switch.

Once the switch had been returned to the on position, light poured through the open pantry door.

Kate backed out, turning off the flashlight. "Just so you know, there are several flashlights in the drawer at the end of the counter here." She slid the electric torch into the drawer and closed it, her hands shaking.

Her gaze slipped up to his, her eyes wide and haunted. "I won't attack you again. I promise."

Ben leaned in the door frame of the pantry. "You didn't attack me. If anything, I was all over you. I've never wanted to kiss someone as much as I wanted to kiss you."

Her brow furrowed. "Then why...?"

"It's wrong. I won't be here long and I don't want to lead you on in any way."

She nodded. "Good, because I'm not in the market for a man. I only need a bodyguard. I don't know what came over me. Must have been the adrenaline rush. Don't worry. I'll leave you alone."

When she turned to leave, Ben shot forward and captured her arm. "Don't get me wrong." He lifted her chin and stared down into her flashing green eyes. "I wanted to kiss you. And I still do." He bent until his lips barely touched hers.

Kate's gaze caressed his mouth, then her eyes rounded and she backed away, spun and ran up the stairs.

It took every ounce of Ben's self-control not to follow her.

Chapter Nine

After lying awake in her bed with her eyes wide open and her mind spinning until the early hours of the morning, Kate finally fell into an exhausted sleep.

Not until Lily skipped into her room the next morning did she open her eyes and squint at the sun shining through her window.

"Oh, baby. I should be up by now to fix your breakfast."

"Mrs. Henderson fixed it for me."

Kate sat up, the T-shirt she'd slept in bunched around her. "She did?"

"Uh-huh. Can I go outside and play?"

Before her daughter finished her sentence, Kate was shaking her head. "Not until I'm up and dressed. You're not to go outside without me or Mr. Harding. Do you understand?"

Lily sighed and crawled up on the bed. "Could you hurry? I saw a lizard on the front porch."

Kate ruffled Lily's strawberry-blond curls. "No rest for the weary, is it? Okay, okay. I'm getting up. Why don't you go down and help Mrs. Henderson in the kitchen?"

"Okay." Lily rolled to the edge of the bed and dropped onto the floor.

The patter of her feet warmed Kate's heart and made her want to get out of bed and join the day.

The fear of the night before faded with the steady heat of the midmorning sun.

She quickly brushed her hair, secured it in a low pony-tail at the base of her head and washed her face. A glance at her wan complexion in the mirror triggered her to dig in the drawer full of cosmetics for powder, blush and a little mascara. No sense looking like death.

Not when there was a handsome man close by. One who'd admitted to wanting to kiss her.

Excitement filtered through her body as she thrust her feet into jeans and pulled them up over her hips. A soft rose T-shirt and pointed-toed pink leather cowboy boots completed her outfit. She hurried from the room and down the stairs to the kitchen, peeking into the living room and ranch office on the way. If she were honest with herself, she'd admit she was looking for Ben.

"He's outside in the yard with Lily," Marge said as she appeared at the kitchen door.

Kate started. Having another person in the house took some getting used to. "I was looking for Lily."

"She's out there with Mr. Harding. They are too cute to-gether. He's hangin' a tire swing for her. Eddy's out round-ing up strays. We got here two hours ago."

Kate peered out the window over the kitchen sink at the man hanging from a tree branch. He expertly tied a rope to the branch, then swung out of the tree to land on his feet be-side the four-year-old.

Lily grinned up at him, clapped her hands and giggled. "Do it again, Mr. Ben. Do it again," she cried, loud enough Kate could hear her muffled words through the window.

"He scrubbed an old tire he found out back with a brush and dish soap and he found a length of rope in the shed." Mrs. Henderson dried a pan as she gazed out the window, a smile lifting the corners of her mouth.

The image of the man and child made Kate's heart ache.

Lily really needed a father figure. She needed a man in her life to teach her to be adventurous, to show her how to make things and climb trees.

Kate chuckled. Not that the child hadn't learned something about tree-climbing on her own. Kate's smile faded. And thank goodness she had. No telling what the biker gang would have done had they found her outside alone.

A chill shook Kate's body.

"Got a plate of scrambled eggs warming in the oven. Sit yourself down while I pop bread in the toaster."

Kate sank into a chair at the big kitchen table. "You don't have to go to the trouble."

"Now, don't argue with me. I like doin' for others. Makes me feel useful. Oh, by the way, your telephone is working now."

Kate hopped out of her seat. "Good, I want to call the sheriff."

"Oh, honey, I heard about your intruder last night. Ben— Mr. Harding already put a call into the sheriff's office reporting the incident. He said they were sending a deputy out today to look around."

Dropping down to the seat, Kate shook her head. The man was always a step ahead of her.

Marge continued talking as she scooped eggs onto a plate and set it in front of Kate. "I checked around to see if anything had been taken. I could swear I had several cans of soup and tuna I'd planned on using for lunch today. And the loaf of bread I'd laid out was gone." She shook her head. "Looked to me like someone who was hungry slipped in and took what they needed."

"Why wouldn't that person just knock on the door and ask for food? Why steal it?"

"Could have been undocumented immigrants." Marge's brows dipped. "Sometimes a steer will go missing. No telling what's been taken since Mr. Kendrick passed. Eddy said the cattle are all over the ranch. It'll take him days to account for what's left of the herd."

"I suppose I could learn to help him. Do you think Lily would be all right out riding along with us?" Kate had ridden horses a couple times, but she was by no means an expert. Lily had never had the opportunity.

"I could keep her here with me. I'm sure we could find plenty for her to play with around the house."

"I don't want to be a bother."

"No bother. I love little ones." Mrs. Henderson set a glass of orange juice beside Kate's plate. "Eat now. Better to make your decisions on a full stomach."

Kate ate the scrambled eggs and toast, enjoying being waited on for the first time since her mother died. She carried her plate to the sink and ran it through the warm soapy water Mrs. Henderson had used to clean the dishes. No dishwasher in this house.

"Look, he's got the tire up." Mrs. Henderson pointed out the window.

Lily lay on her belly through the hole of the old tire, swinging and laughing out loud.

Her happiness made Kate's heart lighter. She deserved to have a yard to play in and a real home, not an apartment in a busy city.

What would it take to find the ones responsible for trying to run them off the property? Kate wanted a place to call home, for herself as much as she wanted it for Lily. This ranch was the only thing her father had ever given to her, and she'd be damned if she let anyone take it away.

Determination and a sense of purpose flowed through her veins, giving her the inspiration she needed to fight for what she wanted for her and her baby. "Mrs. Henderson, do you know the number for Cara Jo's Diner?"

"Sure do."

Kate called her new friend Cara Jo. Then she brushed

her teeth, stopped in her bedroom for her pistol and a box of ammunition. She shoved the box into her pocket. She held the pistol behind her back, then headed outside to fulfill her promise to herself.

Ben lifted Lily out of the tire and set her on the ground.

Her hair was falling out of her ponytail and she wore a thin coating of dust and a smile. "That was fun. Can we do it again?"

"After a while, sweetie." Kate dropped a kiss on her tousled hair. "Right now, I want you to go inside and help Mrs. Henderson bake cookies."

Lily squealed and ran for the house.

Kate inhaled and let out her breath in a slow, steadying release. "I want to take you up on that offer."

Ben's gaze dropped to her lips. "What offer?"

Heat spread throughout Kate's body at the thought of Ben's kiss. She shoved the image aside and squared her shoulders. "I want you to teach me to shoot my gun." She pulled the weapon from behind her back and held it out.

Ben touched a finger to the tip of the barrel and pointed it away from him. "You start by never pointing a gun at someone unless you want to shoot them."

"It's not loaded." She dug the box of ammo from her jeans pocket and held it out in her other hand.

"Trust me. Make it habit not to point a gun at anyone, loaded or unloaded, unless you intend to shoot him."

"Okay."

Ben took the weapon from her hands and inspected it. "Do you own cleaning supplies for this?"

"Yes."

"Good, it looks good for now, but after we shoot, it'll have to be thoroughly cleaned." He tipped it back and forth and weighted it in his grip. "It's a nice 9 mm Glock. Where did you get it?"

"It was my husband's." She'd almost made him get rid of

it when she'd discovered she was pregnant. After his death, she couldn't bring herself to sell it. Now she was glad she hadn't. "Is it a good brand of gun?" she asked.

"One of the best." Ben clicked a button and the magazine dropped out of the handle. He caught it with his other hand. "Let me see the rounds."

Kate plunked the ammo box in his open palm, careful not to touch him, afraid to set off another bout of uncontrollable lust. That would be a disaster, considering he didn't want anything to do with her. Hadn't he said he was leaving as soon as Derringer arranged a replacement?

Ben loaded the bullets into the magazine. "Make sure your bullets are pointing toward the barrel of the weapon." He showed her how to slip the magazine into the handle and how to release it. Then he handed the gun to her. "You do it."

She didn't care how basic the lessons were, she wanted to learn and get it right the first time. When Ben left, Kate's and Lily's lives depended on Kate's ability to protect them.

Kate held the weapon, searching for the magazine release button. When she found it, she released the magazine and it fell to the ground.

"You'll want to keep your weapon as clean as possible." Ben chuckled, the sound warming Kate's insides.

As Kate bent to retrieve the magazine, a vehicle rumbled down the gravel drive, stirring up a cloud of dust.

"Must be the sheriff's deputy." Ben took the Glock from her and reassembled it, stuffing it into the back of his waistband.

The SUV pulled to a stop. The cloud of dust drifted to the ground and Deputy Schillinger climbed out. "I hear you had another intruder."

"We did," Kate responded. "He was here when we got home after dark yesterday."

Schillinger had a lump of tobacco stuffed between his

teeth and his lower lip. He spit a dark stream of nasty juice on the ground at Kate's feet. "Did you see who it was?"

Kate stepped backward, her breakfast roiling in her gut. "No, he didn't happen to announce himself or show his face. He did get away with some pantry staples and bread."

"Probably illegals."

When Schillinger looked like he would spit again, Kate frowned. "Do you mind?"

The man paused, then let loose anyway, wiping a dark drop from his chin. "Not at all."

Kate stared at the mess on the ground and back at the deputy, then crossed her arms. "And let me guess...you can't do anything without a full description." Kate let out a tight breath. "I don't know why we bother to call you. I'll turn this over to the Customs and Border Protection guys. Maybe they will do something. Thank you for your time."

Another vehicle approached. It slid in beside the deputy's SUV and Cara Jo's long, lithe form stepped out. "Hi, Kate. Got a surprise for Lily." Cara Jo pushed her shoulder-length blond hair back behind her ears, opened the back door and reached in, extracting a black-and-white puppy from the backseat.

Lily burst from the house, racing toward Cara Jo. "It's Pickles! It's Pickles!" She skidded to a stop in the gravel and reached up.

Cara Jo laughed and handed her the puppy. "You have to be very careful with puppies. They're smaller than us and can be hurt easily."

"I'll be very careful. I promise." Lily clutched the squirming puppy against her chest and ran to Kate's side. "Look, Mommy, Pickles is here."

"That's great, honey. Can you take him in the kitchen and get Mrs. Henderson to help find feeding bowls? You can get one of the boxes we used to pack and use it for his bed."

Lily ran toward the house, the puppy flopping in her arms.

Cara Jo joined the group of adults. "What's happening?" She glanced at the deputy. "What are you doing here, Dwayne?"

Kate could have laughed at the way the deputy's lips thinned at being called by his first name. "I was called in on business." His chest puffed out a bit more and he looked down his nose at Kate's new friend.

Cara Jo's brows rose and she turned to Kate. "Business?"

"Unfortunately, the sheriff's department is better at serving papers than they are at finding intruders." Kate gave the lawman a pointed look. "If you're not going to dust for prints or at least write down a statement, I see no further need of your services."

Dwayne's eyes narrowed. "This isn't the place for a woman. You really should consider selling before the bank takes the ranch."

"The bank's not taking anything." She didn't know how, but she'd find a way to come up with some money.

"Then you might want to leave before anything bad happens to you or your little girl."

Ben slipped an arm around Kate's waist. "She's not going anywhere she doesn't want to."

"Besides, it's ridiculous to even consider leaving," Cara Jo said with a snort. "Give up a ranch because the sheriff's department is too scared or lazy to do anything about the growing crime rate in the county?" She hooked Kate's arm and stared at the deputy. "Why are you on the force if you can't do your job?"

Dwayne's face bloomed a ruddy red, his eyes narrowing at Cara Jo. He shifted his attention to Kate. "Think about it, Ms. Langsdon."

Ben's arm dropped from around Kate's waist and he stepped toward the deputy, his fists clenched.

Kate grabbed his hand and slipped it back around her. "He's not worth it."

Schillinger turned and marched to his SUV, climbed behind the wheel and spun out in the gravel on his way out of the drive.

"That man always has a sour look on his face," Cara Jo remarked.

Kate laughed. "I thought it was just me."

"No, it's definitely him." Ben brushed a lock of Kate's hair back behind her ear.

"Thanks for being here for me." Even if Derringer had sent him, Ben had gone above and beyond on more than one occasion. Kate couldn't imagine having to deal with everything that had happened on her own.

"I need to make a call. You going to be all right for a few minutes?" He gazed into her eyes.

Her heart flipped at the worry reflected in his eyes. "I'm fine. Cara Jo's here."

"Go on. We need time for girl talk." Cara Jo waved Ben toward the house.

Once he left them, Cara Jo faced Kate. "Now, what's this about the county foreclosing on your ranch?"

Kate shook her head. "You don't want to know."

"I wouldn't have asked if I didn't care." Cara Jo touched a hand to Kate's arm.

Cara Jo had it right, Kate had needed someone she could talk with and Ben wasn't necessarily the right person. He was the hired help. He couldn't dig her out of her financial hole. Nor did she want him to. She dragged in a deep breath and let it out. "The sheriff and Deputy Schillinger served me with papers that the county is going to seize the property for almost thirty thousand in back taxes."

"Holy moley." Cara Jo flattened a hand to her chest. "That's a lot of cash."

"Yeah." Saying the amount out loud made it sink in all the more, threatening to overwhelm Kate. "I just need time to figure things out. Hire a lawyer or something. But the local bank probably won't loan me any money to keep things going in the meantime."

"I've got a loan on my diner through that bank. But then I grew up here. They know me."

Kate sighed. "I'm an unknown and not a very safe bet." She glanced around at the barn and outbuildings. "And I'm sure the rumors about the attacks aren't giving the bank faith in my abilities to run a ranch and protect my interests."

"You can't help that someone is attacking you." Cara Jo nodded toward where Ben had been. "And you have your fiancé living here. Ben looks fully capable of handling any difficulty."

"Having Ben here didn't help me one bit in the eyes of the bank loan officer." Kate snorted. "I don't even have enough to pay Eddy and Marge until I can get my hands on my daughter's college fund."

"How much do you need?" Cara Jo propped her hands on her hips. "I can't afford thirty thousand, but I can spot you some money until you can get to yours."

Kate's chest swelled, her eyes filling. "No, I can't take advantage of you like that. You barely know me. I'll figure things out. Heck, I've only been here a couple days. Things are bound to get better."

"Sometimes things get worse before they get better. But then, don't let me be the downer here." Cara Jo hugged Kate. "The offer's open if you need it."

"Thanks." Kate gave her a watery smile. "I'll wait and see what the county assessor says when the computers come up again. No use borrowing trouble. I have enough as it is."

FROM THE HALLWAY where the phone was located, Ben could keep an eye on Kate and Cara Jo outside. He dialed Derringer.

"Hank, Ben here."

"Got the phone line hooked up at the Flying K, did you?" Hank asked.

"It's working."

"Good. Had some news on that DVD you sent to me. My contacts in the state crime lab may just be able to recover what was on it. They told me they should have it by this evening. Whatcha got?"

Ben watched as Kate and Cara Jo hugged. What were they talking about? "Can you do some digging on Deputy Dwayne Schillinger and a Mr. Robert Sanders?"

"Why?"

"Schillinger's been out here twice to investigate break-ins, and done nothing but warn Kate to leave."

"Hmm. That doesn't sound right."

"That's what I'm thinking."

"I'll get my contacts on the deputy. I take it you had another break-in last night?"

Ben's hand tightened on the receiver. "We did."

"Anyone hurt?" Hank asked.

"No, he left without attacking."

"As for Robert Sanders, he's pretty well-known in the area, what with his ties to real estate and construction. But I'll have my folks do a little digging to see if he's got any dirt hiding under his rug."

The pounding of horse hooves made Ben glance toward the south. "Hank, I gotta go. Let me know if anything comes up."

"Will do. And, Ben, be careful out there. Ranches can be like islands. You're out in the middle of nowhere with no one to depend on but yourselves."

"I know that. And the local authorities aren't helping at all."

Ben hung up and burst through the door as a horse and its rider galloped across the dry grasses toward the house.

"That's Eddy." Mrs. Henderson stood on the porch, wiping her hands on a dry dish towel. "He's in an all-fired hurry."

Kate was halfway to the fence, with Cara Jo following, when Ben leaped off the porch.

Eddy's mount galloped across the dry Texas paddock of sparse grass and scraggly vegetation. By the time he reached the gate, Kate was holding it open for him.

Ben ground to a halt beside her. "What's wrong?" Ben asked.

Eddy slipped from the saddle, his boots hitting the ground, stirring up a puff of dust. "Found several steer carcasses along the southern boundary."

Chapter Ten

"I didn't know if you wanted to come out and inspect, or if you wanted me to notify the sheriff's department and let them handle it." Eddy waited for Kate's response.

Kate glanced at Ben. "I don't think the sheriff will be much help. Let's get out there and see what we've got." Kate headed for the barn. "Oh, wait.... Lily." Kate performed an about-face and headed back to the house.

Just inside the kitchen door, Lily held Pickles to her cheek as she stood beside Cara Jo.

"Kate, go on, do what you have to do." Cara Jo waved Kate toward the barn. "Don't worry about Miss Lily. She and I are going to start training Pickles. Aren't we, dear?"

Lily nodded. "Mrs. Henderson's making treats for Pickles."

Kate bit down on her lip. "Are you sure?"

Cara Jo smiled. "Absolutely."

"Don't you have to be at the diner?"

"Not today. I give myself a day off every once in a while. I can do that." She smiled. "I'm the owner."

"Thanks." Kate spun and hurried to the barn where Eddy and Ben stood.

Her first time in the barn, Kate stared around at the tack hanging from hooks on the walls. "Is there a four-wheeler or a horse I can ride?"

Eddy shook his head. "No four-wheelers, but I've got a couple horses in the stalls in the barn."

Ben captured her arms and turned her to face him. "You're not going. You need to stay and look after Lily."

"You saw what Marge is capable of." Kate nodded toward Eddy. "She wields a powerful shotgun, doesn't she?"

Eddy slapped his hat against his thigh. "Scares me, if that's whatcha mean." He slipped a rifle into the holster on his saddle.

Kate felt a little better knowing they'd be heading out with a little more firepower than her Glock, which was tucked neatly into Ben's waistband, along with the one he wore on a shoulder holster over his blue chambray shirt. She made up her mind. "Lily will be fine with Mrs. H. and Cara Jo will be there as well to entertain her and keep an eye out for trouble."

Ben crossed his arms. "Sounds like you thought this through."

"I did."

"I still don't think it's a good idea."

Her brows rose. "Why not? This is my ranch, and it's my responsibility to see to the safety of the people and animals on it." She stepped toward one of the occupied stalls. "I'm going."

Ben followed, his boots stirring the dust around her. "Have you ever ridden a horse?"

"Plenty," she lied. Well, it wasn't a lie if "plenty" meant five times in her entire life.

"Right." Ben's one-word response told Kate he didn't believe her for a minute.

Eddy led a horse from the middle stall. "This is Lucky. She's a little older and as calm a horse as we have on the Flying K."

"As compared to what?" Kate asked as she stared up at the horse, thinking the mare was bigger than any of the horses she'd ever ridden.

"She's been out roaming the pastures since Mr. K....left." Eddy breathed deeply, his jaw tightening. "She won't be hard to ride."

Kate refused to be intimidated by the animal's size. "You'll have to show me where everything is."

Eddy led the way to the racks of saddles stored in the tack room. He nodded toward a brightly colored blanket. "If you'll toss that over Lucky's back, I'll handle the saddle."

Rather than push the point and take the saddle herself, Kate led the way back out to the horse and eased the blanket across Lucky's back.

The animal eased sideways, whickering softly.

Kate stepped away and let Eddy settle the saddle on the horse's back. She studied Eddy's moves, committing them to memory for the next time when she'd insist on doing it herself.

"When you cinch the girth on Lucky, do it a couple of times. She likes to blow her belly out. If you don't do it more than once, she'll fool you and when you get going, the saddle will slide to the side, dumping the rider."

Kate nodded. "I'll remember."

Once Eddy had the saddle securely fastened, he handed the bridle to Kate. "You can do this."

Kate nodded, trying to remember, from the five times she'd ridden at a farm outside Houston, how to slip the bridle between the horse's teeth and over its head.

Eddy walked away, calling over his shoulder, "She'll bite down to keep you from getting it between her teeth. Stick your thumb in the corner of her mouth to get her to open."

While Eddy adjusted the girth on his horse, Kate worked at sliding the bridle between Lucky's teeth. After several failed attempts, the horse stomped her feet and swished her tail, slapping Kate at like a pesky fly.

"You're going to wear this bridle," Kate said between gritted teeth.

In her peripheral vision, Kate could see Ben walking toward her. She'd be damned if she couldn't accomplish this one little task. With her teeth clenched as tightly as Lucky's, and the bridle held in one hand, Kate shoved her thumb in the corner of the animal's mouth and tugged.

Lucky smacked her lips and her teeth opened wide enough for Kate to slide the bridle between her teeth and loop the strap over her ears. "There. That wasn't so bad, was it?"

The mare opened and closed her mouth as if adjusting to the metal bit.

Kate tightened the strap beneath Lucky's chin and the one around her head. When Lucky was ready, Kate walked her to the barn door and glanced at the stirrup, wondering how in hell she was going to get her foot up that high. She glanced around the barnyard, spying a wooden step close to a hitching post. She tugged the reins, urging the horse to follow.

Lucky straightened her legs, refusing to move.

Ben had saddled a gray Arabian gelding and stood in the barnyard watching Kate struggle with the mare. "Need a hand?"

"No, I have this," she insisted.

"Lucky doesn't like the step." Eddy led his gelding out and swung up into the saddle.

Ben closed the distance between Kate and himself.

An uncontrollable surge of excitement swept over her, setting Kate's nerve endings alight.

"Let me help," he whispered. "It by no means implies you need it." Ben stooped, cupping his hands.

Kate leaned close. "I don't like relying on you." She stepped into his palms.

"Why?" He rose, lifting her high enough to toss her leg over the saddle.

"Because you won't always be there. I'll have to take care of myself and Lily." She held on to the saddle horn with one hand.

Ben nudged her calf.

His fingers touching her, even through the thick denim of her jeans, had her blood racing through her veins. She held her leg well out of his way while he adjusted the stirrup on the right and rounded the horse to adjust the left. When he had it positioned correctly, he guided her foot into the stirrup. Then he handed Kate the reins and stepped back.

Lucky danced to the side, setting loose a swarm of butterflies in Kate's belly. Now was the time to admit she hadn't ridden a horse in over ten years. But she clamped down hard on her bottom lip and held on for dear life.

Ben swung up in his saddle, turning the gelding all in one smooth motion, like he'd done this a thousand times before.

Since he'd grown up on a ranch, he probably had.

Her back ramrod-straight, Kate nudged Lucky with her heels and followed Eddy to the gate.

Ben covered the rear.

Eddy leaned down and pulled the lever, opening the gate.

Lucky bolted through and set off at a gallop.

Her heart in her throat, Kate pulled back on the reins, wishing she hadn't been so quick to say she'd ride out. No matter how hard she tugged on the leather straps, her efforts only slowed the mare marginally.

Ben and Eddy caught up to her before she'd gone far.

The ranch foreman passed her and led the way to the southwest corner of the ranch.

Ben and his gelding kept pace beside her.

"This is the first time you've been out to see what you now own?"

She nodded. The thought of all that she could see around her belonging to her seemed a bit overwhelming. "What do I do with all this?"

"That's why you hire people like Eddy to take care of the horses, cattle and whatever else you decide to raise."

"I've never been one to sit back and watch others do all

the work. It bothers me to have Mrs. Henderson cooking meals and cleaning up after me. I've never had anyone wait on me. Not even my own mother." Kate stared at Eddy's back, wondering what it meant to be a working rancher and if she had what it took to do it.

"Ranching is hard work."

Kate sat up straight, though her tailbone was beginning to hurt. "I'm not afraid of hard work."

"It's twenty-four hours a day, three hundred and sixty-five days a year."

She smiled. "So is parenting."

"Lily needs a mother to take care of her."

"And I need to make this place operate at a rate that can support us. Otherwise, I'll have to find a job to support *it*. And out here in South Texas, I doubt there are jobs that pay enough to support a woman and her child, much less her ranch."

Ben touched the brim of his hat. "You have a point. Owning a ranch is a big responsibility. Are you sure you want to bite off that much?"

Kate frowned at him. "Now you're sounding like Deputy Schillinger. I'm not a quitter."

"What about the danger?"

"I'm not a quitter," she repeated, staring ahead at Eddy.

"What about Lily?"

Kate bit down on her bottom lip. That was the rub. Had it just been Kate, she'd have jumped in with both feet ready to rip into anyone stupid enough to try to run her off her land. Now she had a child to protect. And she had to give Lily a home.

Funny how, after only two days, she'd started thinking of the Flying K as home. Her home. Though she still didn't know much about the man who'd lived here, the man who'd been a big factor in bringing her into this world, she felt a tenuous connection to him and wished not once but a hundred times that she'd had the opportunity to know the man. "Lily needs a place to call home."

"Isn't home where the heart is? Wouldn't she be happy anywhere as long as she's with you?"

Anger bubbled up in her chest. "Are you trying to talk me into leaving?"

"No, I'm trying to figure out why you want to stay when all you've gotten out of it so far is threats and attacks."

As quickly as it rose, the anger ebbed away. "I've also made a new friend." She smiled. "And I met you." She glanced at him, her brows rising.

Ben's gaze remained forward as if he avoided hers. "That's not much of a bonus."

"I think so." She gave him a moment of silence before asking, "I understand we're a painful reminder of your family. But is it that bad that you still want to leave us?"

"Damn it, yes." His response startled the horse beneath him.

The gelding sidestepped, bumping into Kate's.

Ben's leg brushed against Kate's calf. He jerked the reins to the left and the horse danced away. But the brief contact had been enough to leave Kate's breath ragged, her hands shaking.

For a few long moments, Kate rode in silence, her heart hammering against her ribs. Ben wasn't afraid of evil men with guns. He feared her and Lily. It all made sense.

He'd lost his wife and daughter. Seeing Kate and Lily had to be tearing him apart. Kate's heart tightened as if someone had hold of it, squeezing mightily. She'd lost a husband she'd loved with all her heart. Kate couldn't imagine losing her spouse and her daughter all at once. She doubted she'd be strong enough to go on living.

Ben was afraid to care again.

Eddy shouted and kicked his horse in the flanks. Black

buzzards rose from the ground ahead, their huge wingspan filling the air, stirring dust into a cloud.

Relieved to have something else to concentrate on, Kate eased her horse forward, bringing the mare to a halt beside Eddy.

The stench of decaying flesh almost knocked her out of the saddle. Kate gasped and sucked in another lungful of the putrid air. She pulled her shirt up over her nose and breathed through the fabric.

Spread across the ground was the carcass of a black Angus steer, mostly picked over by the scavenger birds who'd located this meal.

Eddy and Ben dropped out of their saddles and squatted beside the dead animal.

"Whoever killed it used a knife." Ben pointed to the smooth edges of cut skin on what once had been the steer's throat.

Kate gagged and swallowed hard to keep from vomiting. She sucked in a deep breath through her shirt and let go of it. Then she grabbed the saddle horn, slipped her feet from the stirrup and slid down the horse's side, landing with a thump on her butt.

Ben was beside her, grasping her beneath her arms. "You all right?"

"I'm fine, except for my damaged pride." She stood and brushed the dirt from her hands and backside. "Who would have done this?"

"Considering they cut away the biggest chunks of meat, I'd say someone who was looking for a meal. *Madre de Dios.*" Eddy rattled off a couple sentences in Spanish before he shook his head and stood.

Ben was circling the dead animal. "There are footprints all around." After a moment he looked off into the brush to the south. "They lead toward the canyon."

"Shouldn't we follow them?"

Ben shook his head. "Only if you want to die."

A shiver rocked Kate's frame. "You think the people who killed this cow would shoot at us?"

"No, but they might slit your throat to keep you from disclosing their location."

"Oh." Kate wrapped her arms around her middle, the warmth of the day turning cool. "What now?"

Eddy looked out over the land. "We need to herd all the strays closer to the ranch house and barn where we can keep a closer watch on them."

"Doesn't that limit the amount of grazing?" Kate cast a glance at the dry land, where vegetation was sparse.

"Do you have a better suggestion?" Ben asked.

Kate stared across at Ben and Eddy. "We could call in the Customs and Border Protection and have them run interference until they get the drug trafficking under control."

"We'll report it," Ben said. "But getting the illegal activity under control won't happen overnight." He gathered his reins and led the gelding away from the dead steer. "In the meantime, we need to do like Eddy said. Otherwise you'll continue to lose cattle."

Eddy glanced at the sun tipping toward the horizon. "We can start tomorrow. It's getting late and we shouldn't be out here after dark."

Kate walked her mare a few steps away from the carnage and reached high for the saddle horn, dragging herself up enough to get her foot in the stirrup. At last she was able to sling her leg over the saddle. Proud she'd gotten up by herself, she almost cried when she noticed the reins hanging from the bit down to the ground.

A soft chuckle sounded beside her.

Ben walked across the dry ground, bent to retrieve the reins and handed them up to her without a word. That quirky smile almost made her want to kick him. At the same time it made her insides heat with want. She pushed aside her desire and focused on the next step.

The three of them rode back the way they'd come, with Eddy taking the lead again.

Halfway back to the barn, Ben shouted to Eddy, "Go on ahead. Kate and I are going to do a little target practice."

Eddy chuckled. "Can you wait until I get out of range? I prefer to remain in one piece."

"You bet." Ben reined in beside Kate and dropped to the ground. He grasped her around the waist and lifted her out of the saddle.

When she opened her mouth to protest, he covered her lips with a finger. "I know you can get down all by yourself. Just humor me. It'll be faster and you won't need to spend any more time with me than you have to."

She rested her hands on his shoulders as he let her slowly slide down the front of his body until her feet touched down. Kate clamped hard on her tongue, afraid she'd say what she really thought. That his hands on her waist had been deliciously sexy, the broad fingers spanning her middle, his muscles flexing and the ease with which he'd lifted her had left her breathless. But not nearly as air-deprived as the feel of his body against hers as she'd slid down him to her feet.

She'd do best to keep her mouth shut and get this lesson over with. The more time she spent alone with Ben, the more she couldn't imagine him leaving. Dangerous ground to be sure.

BEN REGRETTED LIFTING her from the saddle as soon as his hands closed around her. He compounded the regret by letting her body brush against his. Now all he wanted was to do it again, only this time for her to wrap her legs around his waist, her breasts pressing against his chest.

He pulled the Glock from his back waistband and checked the safety.

Kate stood with her back to him. She'd pulled the rubber band from her hair, letting it fall free around her shoulders. After she'd finger-combed it several times she gathered the long tresses in a bunch.

Ben shoved the pistol into his pocket and pushed Kate's hands aside, plucking the band from her fingers. In two quick motions he had the ponytail secured. His hands dropped to her arms, turning her to face him.

She blinked up at him, her lips parted, full and kissable. "You do that like a natural."

"Comes from having a daughter, much like Lily." His hands fell to his sides and he turned away.

He strode several feet away from Kate, needing the distance to keep from pawing her like a teenager. His member strained against the tight confines of his denim jeans. God, he wanted the woman. Instead, he scanned the terrain, searching for a target.

"Kate," he called out.

She came to him, her hands twisting together, her brows just as knotted. "We can do this another day," she said.

"No, you need to know how to use that gun if you plan to keep it."

"Okay." Kate nodded. "Show me."

He handed her the Glock and wrapped her fingers around the grip, lacing one finger over the trigger.

Her body shook against him.

"Think of it as an extension of your arms." He helped her cup her trigger hand with the palm of her empty hand and raised her arms.

"Look down the barrel and line up the sight with the target."

"What am I aiming for?" she asked, holding the gun steady.

"See the prickly pear cactus there with the three lobes facing us?"

"Yes."

"Aim at the top center lobe. Once you have the sights lined up, press the trigger slowly."

Her pulse hammered through her veins. "Will it kick?"

"Not much."

"How much is not much?" she asked.

"Just shoot it and you'll find out."

She aimed the barrel toward the cactus, breathed in, then out, then closed her eyes and pulled the trigger.

The pop wasn't as loud as she'd expected and the kick wasn't bad at all. She focused on the cactus, noticing all three lobes remained intact. "Did I miss?"

"Yes, and you scared the crap out of me." He pushed his cowboy hat back on his head and circled behind her, his arms coming up on either side. "Let's do it again. Only this time, keep your eyes open."

Ben spooned her body with his, bringing his arms up on either side of hers. His hands closed around her fingers and he inhaled her unique scent of honeysuckle and citrus.

His groin tightened and he knew he was in trouble.

Chapter Eleven

Ben's breath stirred the tendrils of hair hanging loose from her ponytail. Kate leaned her back against the solid wall of muscles that was her bodyguard cowboy. The warmth of his arms around her reassured and scared her all at once.

What would it be like to lie in his arms naked?

Her hands shook so badly, she thought she might drop the gun.

"Are you afraid?" he whispered.

Yes, yes, she was afraid. Afraid of falling in love with a stranger. Afraid of investing her emotions in someone who would leave as soon as the threat was neutralized. Afraid she and Lily would be heartbroken when the dust settled on the Flying K Ranch. "N-no," she lied, "I'm not afraid."

"Good. This time keep your eyes open and caress the trigger like a lover."

Holy shotgun blasts! Was he kidding her? All his words did was make her even more aware of the ridge of his fly pressing into her buttocks. She wanted to caress something, and it wasn't the trigger of her 9 mm Glock.

Perspiration beaded on her forehead. "Is it getting hotter?"

"You bet." His hand curved around her again. "Ready?"

Oh, hell, yes, but not for what he was thinking.

Focus, woman. Hell, how could she when she had the hottest cowboy in Texas wrapped around her?

Think of Lily. Images of her daughter brought Kate back to the real reason for her shooting lessons. Living alone on a ranch, she had to have the ability to protect herself and her daughter.

Her hand tightened around the grip and she forced air into and out of her lungs, focusing her concentration down the short barrel, lining up the sights with the target. Then, like Ben said, she stroked the trigger, keeping her eyes wide open.

The weapon kicked backward and Kate almost dropped it.

The acrid scent of burned gunpowder filled her nostrils and she blinked to clear her vision.

"I'll be damned." Ben leaned to her side and stared at her, his brows furrowed. "Are you sure you haven't done this before?"

"No." Dear God, his face was close enough to kiss. So much for maintaining focus on the lesson. "Why?" Her voice cracked and her body trembled.

"Take a look." He faced what was left of the cactus. The top, middle lobe had a hole blasted through it.

Kate squinted, afraid she was seeing things. Sure enough, there was a smooth round hole, dead center. A thrill of excitement rippled through her. "I did that?"

"You did." He chuckled. "I think you've taken me for a ride. How many times have you handled this gun?"

Kate shook her head, floored by her accuracy. "Other than using it to hit the intruder over the head the other night, never."

"I believe you have a promising career ahead of you as a sharpshooter or sniper."

"It was luck." Kate laughed shakily.

He nodded toward the cactus. "Do it again, only this time, aim for the right lobe." His hands fell to his sides and he backed away.

Standing alone, she didn't feel as confident or steady. But

she also wasn't distracted by body contact. She looked down the barrel and lined up the right lobe in her sights.

"Remember…caress the trigger." Ben's words slid over her like melted chocolate in the dry Texas heat. Her hand tightened around the grip and the trigger and the weapon discharged.

Kate yelped. "Dang. I wasn't ready." She glanced at the cactus. "Did I hit anything?"

Ben chuckled. "The dirt in front of the plant."

Widening her stance, Kate glared at Ben. "I'm going to get this."

He nodded. "I have no doubt."

"Shh." This time her hands didn't quiver, her body didn't budge and the bullet nicked the lower corner of the lobe she'd aimed at. Her gaze shot to Ben. "Does that count?"

"If it had been a man, you most likely would have hit him where it would hurt him." Ben grinned. "That's good."

Kate couldn't look away. When Ben smiled, his entire face lit up and his blue eyes shone bright and clear. She tipped her head to the side. "I like it when you smile."

Immediately, his mouth straightened and he glanced away. "Adjust how you line up the sight based on where it hit last time, and keep practicing." Ben strode to where they'd tied the horses.

Kate took her time and fired again. The bullet bit into the top corner of the cactus lobe. Her concentration alternated between the target and Ben. He'd gone from happy to glum in seconds and it was driving her nuts.

"You know, it wouldn't kill you to smile more often." She cast a glance over her shoulder at the silent man.

He flipped the stirrup over the saddle on his horse and he tightened the girth before he muttered, "Have to have something to smile about."

"I heard that." Kate lined up the sights and squeezed off another round. The bullet pierced the center of the right lobe.

Kate smiled and looked back at Ben, careful to point the nose of the pistol away from him. "How about waking up every day?"

"What about it?"

"Aren't you happy when you wake up every day?" Kate continued. "How can you be unhappy when the sun is shining?"

"The sunshine makes it incredibly hot out here in South Texas."

Kate fired off the remaining rounds in her ten-round magazine. Some of the shots went where they were supposed to, others hit the dirt in front of and behind the cactus plant, never touching it. When the last bullet was spent, she hit the magazine release button and caught the magazine before it hit the ground. The sun dipped low on the horizon, lengthening Kate's shadow.

She crossed to where Ben stood holding his horse's reins and stared up into his eyes.

The shadows were back and his jaw was tight, a muscle twitching in his left cheek.

Before she could overthink her reaction to his somber look, Kate smoothed her hand over the twitching muscle. "You must have loved her a lot."

Ben grabbed her wrist so fast, Kate cried out. "I loved Julia and I loved Sarah," he said, taking her gun in his other hand and tucking it back into his waistband. "But nothing I do now will bring them back. Nothing. They're gone."

His fingers hurt where he crushed her wrist, but Kate couldn't pull it free, nor could she back away from the intensity of his gaze.

"Julia and Sarah died, Ben." She pressed a hand to his chest. "But they never left you."

Silence settled like dust between them.

For a long moment, nothing stirred, neither one of them moved.

Then Ben yanked her hard against his chest, his lips crashing down over hers, his mouth claiming hers in a savage kiss. He let go of her wrist, one hand cupping the back of her head, the other clutching her bottom, grinding her pelvis against the hard ridge beneath his fly.

When he let her come up for air, his lips moved over hers, sliding along her chin. "I loved my wife."

"Yes, you did. But you didn't die with her."

"I know, damn it." He grabbed her arms and shook her. "I should have."

"No, Ben. You're still here for a reason."

His head whipped up. "What for? To punish me for failing to protect them?" He shoved her away from him. "I wasn't there for them."

"You didn't kill them."

"I could have stopped him."

"You couldn't be everywhere. He'd have found a way."

Ben stalked away, breathing hard, his face a ruddy red.

Kate's heart squeezed so hard in her chest, she thought she might have a heart attack. The anguish in Ben's face, the agony in his tone, ripped her apart.

"We need to go. It's getting dark."

When Ben passed her to get to his horse, Kate touched his arm.

He shook off her hand. "Don't." His glare scorched her.

Kate flinched, drawing back her hand as if he'd burned it. "I'm sorry. I shouldn't have brought it up."

He snorted and swung up into the saddle without offering her a leg up.

Kate managed to mount on her own, struggling to keep Ben's anger and withdrawal from bringing her all the way down. The man had some issues.

Hell, so did she. Only she'd had four years to work through them. Two years and a wake-up call in the form of Kate and Lily hadn't been enough time to lessen Ben's loss. He was still mourning his wife and child and nothing Kate could do or say would mend that kind of broken heart.

As Kate turned her mare north toward the house, a light blinked from the south. A shot of adrenaline raced through her system and she tugged hard on Lucky's reins, wheeling her around to face south again.

"Did you see that?" Kate glanced over her shoulder at Ben.

Lucky jerked her head and whinnied, trying to get Kate to turn back toward the barn.

Ben was already a few yards north when he reined in and twisted in his saddle. "See what?"

"A light." Kate pointed. "Out there."

Ben urged his horse around and came to a halt beside Kate. "Where?"

As dusk settled in around Kate, her eyes adjusted to the darkness. A flash of light blinked on, then off, a tiny pinprick on the horizon. "There." She gathered her reins. "Should we go check it out?"

Ben studied the light. "No."

"But—" The light grew more steady, pointed directly at them.

"No, looks like they're headed this way and we don't have time to outrun them." He spun his horse and dug in his heels. "Come on."

Kate stared at the light a fraction of a second longer. It was getting bigger. Which meant Ben was right, the vehicle causing the light was headed their way. Whether it was friend or foe, Kate had no intention of sticking around to find out.

She swung Lucky around and took off after Ben and his gelding, letting Lucky have her head.

Ben raced across the ground, dodging cactus, sage and saw palmetto. When he came to a dry ravine, he reined in so fast, Kate's horse struggled to stop in time. Tire tracks led down the banks and back up the other side.

Ben was off his horse and reaching for her reins before Kate had time to think. "Why did we stop?"

"We won't make it back to the safety of the ranch before they catch up. We have to find a place to hide." He reached up, grabbed her around the waist and pulled her off the horse. "Hurry."

Ben took the reins of both the horses and ran down the banks, following the meandering creek bed.

Kate hurried after him, slipping and sliding on the loose gravel and rocks. "Do you think whoever is out there is dangerous?"

"You want to stick around and find out?" he said over his shoulder.

Kate closed her mouth, conserving her energy to keep up with Ben's headlong race down the wash.

When he came to a point where the creek bed curved north at a huge boulder, he tugged the horses behind the outcropping and tied their reins to a scrubby root. They were a good two hundred yards from the tracks. "Stay here."

Kate skidded to a halt, breathing hard. "Why? Where are you going?"

"Back to see who's trespassing." He turned and started back the way they'd come.

Kate laid a hand on his arm. "Not without me, you're not."

"It'll be dangerous."

"It's my land. I need to see what's going on." She let her hand slip down to his.

"It's safer staying clear." The darkness was settling in around them and the stars popped out of the sky one at a time.

Kate couldn't read the expression in Ben's eyes, but she wouldn't let him go without her. She dropped his hand and crossed her arms. "If you don't take me with you, I'll follow you anyway."

Ben sucked in a deep breath and let it out. "You're a stubborn woman."

"I've been known to be. Are you going to stand around arguing or are we going to go and find a good place to hide closer to the road?"

"I don't like it."

She snorted. "So noted."

"Then stay behind me and keep quiet."

"Yes, sir." Kate popped a salute that was all but lost on him as he turned and jogged back down the creek bed, hunkering low so that he wouldn't be seen over the banks.

Kate followed, copying his technique, her heart pounding, her breathing erratic. What was she getting herself into?

All she knew was that she didn't want to be left behind while Ben risked his life to see what was going down on her ranch.

Light glinted above them, casting a beam over the top of their heads.

Ben came to a sudden stop and flung his arm out, catching her before she barreled past him. "We hide here."

He ducked behind a boulder no bigger than a sheep and dragged her down beside him. Ben pulled the Glock from the back of his jeans and handed it to Kate. "Don't use this unless I tell you to." He removed his 9 mm from his shoulder holster and held it in front of his face.

Kate's hand trembled. Sure she'd been practicing shooting, but the thought of pulling the trigger on a person...

Her shoulders stiffened, her resolve strengthening as she thought of Lily. She'd do whatever it took to protect the ones she loved.

The rumble of an engine grew louder and the light brighter. Then it angled down the creek bank and came to a grinding halt, dust flying all around, forming a hazy glow in front of the truck. The driver turned the vehicle off and silence engulfed the scene.

As the dust settled, Kate peered at the back of the pickup.

Four men perched on the sides, wielding what looked like automatic weapons, the type used by the military.

Kate gasped, then clamped a hand over her mouth and stared wide-eyed as one man hopped out, his feet crunching as he landed in the gravel. He stretched, his gun arm rising high into the night sky. He said something in Spanish and the driver responded.

Another man, brandishing a similar weapon, dropped down and shone a flashlight in a wide beam around the pickup, turning it slowly toward the position where Kate and Ben lay.

Ben whispered, "Close your eyes."

Kate squeezed them shut and ducked her head low behind the boulder.

The crunch of gravel grew louder. Kate fought her instinct to look up and see how close the men had come, but she was afraid that if she looked, the flashlight would glint off her eyes and give away their position.

"Brille la luz aquí!" a voice shouted closer than Kate had imagined.

Ben pressed his lips to her ear. "Don't move," he whispered.

He didn't have to worry. She froze, holding her breath, waiting for the men to move away.

Light shone on either side of the boulder.

Then a loud bang blasted through the night and kicked up dust around where Kate hovered. She bit hard on her tongue to keep from crying out.

Footsteps crunched closer and then a heavily accented voice called out. *"Serpiente para cenar!"*

Men laughed and the light bobbed skyward.

The footsteps moved away.

Kate let go of the breath she'd been holding and dared to peer around the side of the boulder.

One man had his gun slung over his shoulder and he held

a long fat snake out to the side, speaking in rapid Spanish. The driver and the other gunmen laughed.

The crackle of a radio broke through their merriment and the driver responded to the call. When he finished, he waved a hand out the window. *"Vayamos!"*

The snake man dropped the reptile and leaped over the side of the pickup. The other men leaped in beside him. The truck pulled up the other side of the wash as another set of lights crested the bank behind them and dipped down into the creek.

In that one instant the light from the second vehicle illuminated the truck in front of it. Kate could see into the first truck's bed.

Huddled low and holding on to one another were several women and young girls.

One cried out.

One of the gunmen slapped the girl. *"Silencio!"*

Kate lurched forward, her heart lodged in her throat.

Ben captured her arm and dragged her back to the ground. "Don't move." He pushed her back to the ground and started to get up himself.

This time she caught his arm and held on to Ben. "There's too many of them."

"Alto!" The gunman with the flashlight shone the beam over the creek bed for a long moment, the light hovering over the top of the small boulder.

Kate ground her teeth and fought her instinct to leap out and scratch the man's eyes out who'd slapped the girl. But even she knew it would be crazy. They outnumbered Kate and Ben and outgunned their two pistols. Taking a stand would be suicide.

After a moment, the gunman waved the driver on and the truck topped the incline and pulled away. The second truck lumbered down into the ravine and up the other side, revealing the back filled with four more gunmen and from the dark forms hunkered low in the bed, another load of people.

Ben lay still for a long time, even after the second truck exited the creek and moved off across the desert.

"Why didn't we stop them?"

"My duty is to protect you. We were outnumbered. The best we can do is get back to the ranch and report this to the Customs and Border Protection."

"But those women and the girls..." Kate stood and brushed the dust off her jeans.

"Coyotes would just as soon kill them, ditch them and save their own butts." Ben headed back down the creek bed toward where they'd stashed the horses.

Kate was left to follow, wishing with all her heart she could have done more to protect the frightened people in the back of the trucks.

Ben untied the horses, bent to give her a boost up and swung up into his saddle without speaking another word.

They hurried across the dried grasses, dodging cacti and stumpy palmetto palms illuminated by the sparkling blanket of stars in the sky.

"Do you think they could be the people responsible for killing the steer?" Kate called out over the thrumming of horses' hooves.

"Probably."

"We should have stopped them."

Ben shot a glance her way. The moon had begun to rise, reflecting light off Ben's eyes. "The only way we'd go back out there at night is with a full contingent of soldiers and the Customs and Border Protection agents leading the way. Even then, *you're* not going out there."

A chill gave her gooseflesh as she recalled the guns every one of the men carried.

Ben urged his horse into a gallop, cutting off any further conversation.

Kate dug her heels into her horse's flanks, her gaze panning the horizon, searching for the lights of the two vehicles. Her breathing returned to normal only after the glowing windows of the ranch house came into view.

They rode up to the gate at full gallop.

Eddy stood ready, swinging the gate open for them. "You two are in a hurry. Run into trouble?"

"Two trucks full of gunmen and people." Ben dropped down off his gelding. "We had to lay low until they passed."

"You did right getting back here." Eddy nodded toward his horse. "I was getting worried and was about to come out searching for you."

Kate led her horse into the barn. Before Ben or Eddy could offer to help, she'd flipped her stirrup up over the saddle and loosened the girth. Not so hard. She could get used to riding the range and checking on cattle.

When it came time to haul the saddle off the horse, Kate tugged, expecting it to be difficult. But she pulled too hard and the saddle slid right off, the weight sending her flying back.

Ben's arms circled her waist, steadying her.

Kate leaned into him for a moment, appreciating the solid muscles and the earthy scent of a man who'd been working with horses. She could get used to having him around.

Kate pushed away. "We need to get up to the house and call the CBP." She ducked around Ben and hurried to deposit the saddle in the tack room before she did something stupid...again.

Brush in hand, Eddy stood beside Kate's mare. "I'll take care of the horses. You two head on up to the house."

"Thanks." Ben hooked Kate's arm and led her out of the barn and up to the house.

She was kind of glad to have him so close. After hiding from gunmen, the night's shadows caused her a lot more heebie-jeebies than ever before. Before she'd seen the two truckloads of coyotes and women, Kate had been more than ready to call this place home and make a stand for the land her father left for her and Lily. But now...

Kate and Ben only made it halfway across the yard when Lily burst through the screen door and raced down the steps. "Mommy!"

Ben let Kate's arm drop. "I'll make the call."

"Thanks." Kate gathered Lily up in a bear hug and swung her around. "How's my sweetie pie?" She held the child longer than normal and inhaled the scent of baby shampoo. An image of the women and girls in the backs of those trucks had been indelibly etched in her memory. She couldn't imagine being so desperate she'd subject Lily to the danger of stealing across the border in the middle of the night with men who'd just as soon take the money and leave them for dead.

"We made cookies. I found a horny toad, but it got away. Pickles piddled in the hall twice and he's asleep now." Lily glanced over Kate's shoulder at the barn. "Can I ride a horse?"

"Not now, baby."

"When?"

"Another day." A day when Kate felt more comfortable about the horse she'd be riding, and after they found the gunmen traversing her land and jailed them where they couldn't traffic humans or drugs ever again. Maybe then she could be more certain about making the Flying K their home forever.

"Come see our cookies." Lily wiggled out of Kate's arms and ran for the house.

Kate followed Ben and Lily into the house.

Once inside, Ben headed for the hallway.

Kate entered the kitchen where Lily showed her the cookies she'd made with Mrs. Henderson and Cara Jo.

Cara Jo was stacking cooled cookies in the cookie jar. "I'm so glad you two made it back when you did. I was about to call the sheriff."

"I'll tell you about it after Lily is in bed." Kate glanced around. "Where's Mrs. Henderson?"

"Her husband picked her up an hour ago."

"Thanks for staying with Lily. I owe you."

"I enjoyed it as much as I think she did."

"Now, let me see if these cookies are edible." Kate grabbed a cookie from the pile and bit into it, her empty stomach rumbling. "Oh, yes. They are wonderful. Snicker-doodles?" she asked.

Lily laughed. "How did you know?"

"My mother used to make these." Tears welled in her eyes at the memory of her mother and the weekends they'd spent making cookies and hanging out when she was little like Lily. At times like this, she missed her so much it hurt.

Kate glanced at the clock. "Holy smokes, it's way past your bedtime, young lady."

"I already had my bath. Miss Cara Jo let me stay up until you got home so that I could show you the cookies."

Cara Jo winced. "I hope you don't mind. She was so excited."

Kate shook her head. "Not at all. But now it's time for bed."

Lily danced ahead of Kate. "Can Miss Cara Jo read a book to me?"

"I'm sure she would like to get home sometime tonight and it's a long way back to town."

Lily grabbed one of Kate's hands and one of Cara Jo's and looked up at them both with her wide green eyes. "Please?"

Cara Jo laughed. "I'd love to and it'll give you a chance to wash up and have dinner."

"You're sure?"

"Absolutely." She swung Lily's arm. "Lily and I are best buds, aren't we? Why don't you grab Pickles and let's get her settled in her box upstairs."

Lily chased Pickles down the hallway and up the stairs.

Kate hugged her new friend. "Thanks, Cara Jo."

"Really, Kate. I love Lily, she's a great kid." Cara Jo climbed the stairs behind Lily, leaving Kate at the bottom.

Ben slipped up beside her. "I made the call. They're sending out a chopper to see if they can locate the trucks."

Kate faced him, her heartbeat speeding up at his proximity. Why did this man she'd only known a very short time have that kind of pull on her? "Any chance they'll find them?"

"The trucks have a big head start in the amount of time it took us to ride back to the ranch." He shrugged. "They could be just about anywhere by now."

Kate rested her hand on the banister and stared up the stairs, her heart heavy. "Do you think they're helping illegal immigrants or trafficking women?" Kate gazed into Ben's eyes.

His brows dipped low and a muscle jerked in his jaw. "As far as I could see, there were only women and girls in those trucks."

"Dear lord." Kate sagged and her stomach roiled. "We should have stopped them."

"No. We were outnumbered and not as heavily armed." Ben gripped her arms and turned her toward him. "Let the Border Patrol deal with it. They have the resources and the weapons necessary to handle the coyotes. Had we intervened, we would only have made matters worse."

"Still…"

"Have faith in the CBP."

"Do you?"

Ben's lips tightened. "At this point, I have to. I have to focus on you. I can't risk your life chasing after bad guys." He turned and would have walked away, but Kate put a hand on his arm.

"Ben, what happened out there?"

"What do you mean?"

"Between us." She stopped, her gaze dropping to where her hand touched his arm. "Before the coyotes... The kiss."

He stiffened, drawing up to his full height. "What happened out there...shouldn't have. I won't let it happen again."

Kate braced her palms on his chest. The solid muscles beneath his shirt made her long to run her fingers across his naked skin. "I shouldn't have encouraged it. But..."

"It won't happen again. I'm here to protect you and Lily. Nothing more." He backed away, his tone brooking no more argument, his face set in stone.

Kate tucked her hands in her pockets to keep them from shaking. She wanted to say more, to tell him she'd felt his response, he wasn't immune to her. Instead, she turned and walked up the stairs.

IT TOOK ALL of Ben's self-control to keep from going up the stairs after Kate. He wanted her so badly it hurt and the turmoil it was causing inside him was more than he could stand.

Kate was as different from Julia as night from day. She'd already proved she wasn't afraid of anything. When the gunmen had shot so close to them, Kate hadn't fallen apart like a lot of women would have. She'd held steady and stayed low.

He wondered what Julia would have done. What she had done when she and his daughter had been...

Ben's breath lodged in his throat when he realized he couldn't even remember Julia's face. He closed his eyes, but all he could see was light auburn hair, glinting like copper in the sun.

Ben stepped out onto the porch.

Eddy was coming up from the barn. "I have the horses settled in for the night and gave them an extra section of hay."

"Thanks."

Eddy climbed the steps and stood beside Ben, staring out into the night as he rocked back on his boot heels. "Well, I'll be heading home unless you think I need to stay."

"No. Go on home. I'll take it from here."

"Think she'll stay?"

Ben didn't have to ask who Eddy was talking about. "Kate's a pretty determined woman."

Eddy nodded. "If she's anything like her father, she won't give up easily."

No, she wouldn't, but in this case, maybe she should. The situation was too dangerous.

"I'll be goin'. *Buenas noches.*" Eddy climbed into his pickup and drove away, leaving behind him a deep silence.

Darkness closed in around Ben as he crossed to the barn, checked inside, made a pass around the outside and the perimeter of the other outbuildings.

When he was satisfied there were no intruders, he climbed the steps to the house and went straight to his room. He grabbed fresh jeans and a clean shirt and ducked into the bathroom down the hall.

When he emerged, he peeked in at Lily, who lay sound asleep, her puppy in a box beside her bed, also asleep.

Sounds from the kitchen drew him down the stairs when he should have gone straight to bed.

Kate stood with her back to him at the kitchen counter, wearing a worn T-shirt and frayed denim shorts, and she was barefoot. Her hair hung in limp, wet strands, dampening the back of her shirt. "You can wash your hands in the sink, here. Your plate will be ready in a moment."

Knowing it was a mistake, yet unable to help himself, he crossed to the sink and stood beside her. He squirted dish soap onto his fingers and cleaned his already clean hands. He couldn't resist any excuse to be closer to her.

As he dried his hands, she smiled at him.

"Sit. Cara Jo left after reading two books to Lily. Mrs. Henderson left the best roast beef and potatoes you've ever tasted warming in the oven. I'll have a plate full for you in two shakes."

Kate stood within reach and, if he was right, she wasn't wearing a bra. Dear God, he wanted her.

Ben swallowed hard and backed up several steps. "I'm not hungry." For food.

When she turned with a heaping plate in one hand and a glass of iced tea in the other, she frowned. "No argument. You need to eat." She set the plate and glass on the table and pointed at the chair. "Sit."

Too tired to argue, or maybe just too tired to fight it, he sat in the designated chair. Two candles stood in the middle of the table with a box of matches beside them. Ben struck the tip of a match against the matchbox and applied the flame to the wick.

"Sorry, forgot the silverware." Kate dived for a drawer, pulling out a knife, fork and spoon. She hit the light switch on the wall, plunging the room into an intimate hazy glow.

She returned to his side and leaned over him to place the utensils beside his plate.

He couldn't take anymore. He grabbed her around the waist and sat her in his lap. "Do you have any idea what you're doing to me?"

Her eyes widened, her mouth opened in an O, and her cheeks turned a pretty pink. She sucked in a breath and let it out, her blush deepening. "Based on where I'm sitting, I could hazard a pretty good guess."

"Damn it, Kate, I promised it wouldn't happen again."

She sighed. "Some promises were meant to be broken." Her gaze dropped to his lips.

Her words, the way she said them, and that shift of her attention was his undoing. "What am I supposed to do with you? You set me on fire."

Her lips turned upward and she smiled. "Burn, baby, burn."

Laughter rumbled up inside him. He fought the happiness, fought to control a surge of hope. In the end, he lost and grasped her cheeks between his hands, kissing her like she was the buoy that would bring him back to the surface of the sea of sorrow he'd been wallowing in since Sarah's and Julia's deaths.

Her fingers plied loose the buttons on the front of his shirt, one by one. She didn't break the kiss until the last button was freed.

Ben's hands slipped beneath her shirt and up her back. As he'd suspected, she wasn't wearing a bra. Heat rushed to his loins, his member straining against his fly.

Kate shoved the shirt over his shoulders and down his arms.

Ben's fingers slid along her sides and upward to cup her breasts. When his fingers found the taut nipples, he paused. "Lily?"

"Will sleep until morning." She kissed his chin, her lips sliding downward to caress his neck, her breasts pressing into his palms.

Even the child conspired against Ben. With nothing but his memories standing in his way, Ben lost the fight. He shrugged the shirt off his arms and lifted the hem of Kate's T-shirt up and over her head, flinging it across the table. Then he lifted her, spreading her legs wide to straddle his hips. In the soft candlelight he gazed down at her, drinking her in like a man dying of thirst.

"Don't stop now." She raised his hand to her breast. "I'm not good at starting over. I married my high school sweetheart. I don't know how to flirt. I never had any practice."

"You're doing a hell of a job." He rolled her rosy nipples between his thumbs and forefingers.

Her back arched, her hair slipping down to her waist, curling as it dried.

"You should eat." She gasped as he took one nipple between his teeth and nipped.

"I am."

"Food, silly." Her fingers wrapped around his head and held him where he was, her thighs tightening against his sides.

"The only thing I'm hungry for is you." He stood, bringing her up with him, wrapping her thighs around his middle.

Her arms circled his neck as she spread kisses along the column of his throat.

Ben carried her up the stairs to her bedroom, kicking the door open softly so as not to disturb Lily and Pickles.

He set her on her feet and stripped her shorts down her long legs.

Kate stood for a moment, bathed in moonlight peeking through the window. Her tongue swept across her lips, her gaze traveling over him and downward. "You're a bit overdressed." Her fingers closed around the metal rivet of his jeans. She pushed it through the hole and slid the zipper downward, slowly, her fingers brushing against his erection.

Past rational thought, he swung Kate up into his arms and, one-handed, flung back the comforter.

About to lay her against the sheets, he paused.

A movement out of the corner of his eye and a dry rattling sound shot adrenaline through him and he jumped back.

"What? Oh, my God!" Kate clung to him, her arms clamped around his neck, her gaze on the bed. "Is that what I think that is?"

Coiled against the cool white sheets was the biggest rattlesnake Ben had ever encountered. And it was angry.

Chapter Twelve

Kate stifled a scream as she clung to Ben, holding her arms and legs as far away from the snake as she could. She'd have crawled over Ben's body and run if he hadn't been gripping her so tightly. "Do something," she cried.

Ben chuckled, struggling to maintain his hold on her squirming body. "I have to put you down before I can take care of the snake." He strode to the door. "Turn on the light."

Kate flipped the light switch.

The snake on the bed rattled again, perhaps angry at having his sleep disturbed.

Kate shot a glance all around them, searching for friends of the snake in her bed. The floor appeared clear of any other slithering creatures. "Put me down."

Ben dropped her feet to the floor and steadied her. "Are you okay?"

She crossed her arms over her breasts. "No. There's a snake in my bed. A poisonous one at that."

"You can wait in the hall if you like."

"No." She didn't want to leave Ben's side. If anyone could handle a tough situation, it was Ben. "What are you going to do?"

"Get rid of the snake," he said, his tone matter-of-fact.

"How?"

He didn't answer. Instead he approached the end of the

bed, careful to stay out of striking range of the big rattler. He pulled the top sheet and comforter completely off the bed and shook them.

Nothing fell out.

Kate lunged for the sheet and shook it again, before wrapping it around her body.

Ben eased the elastic corners of the fitted sheet off the end of the bed. Circling wide, he repeated the process on the other end of the bed, then he gathered the ends and pulled them together quickly before the snake could slither out and onto the floor.

Carrying the fitted sheet like a bag, he held it away from his body and descended the stairs.

Kate followed, checking the floor before she took every step. She stopped at the top of the stairs, shivering in the air-conditioning.

Ben continued down, stepping out the front door onto the porch. "I'll be back. Don't touch anything until I can check your room over."

Kate held her breath until Ben returned, letting it out as he appeared again in the doorway.

"The snake?"

He closed the door and glanced up at her. "Dead."

Kate heaved a sigh. "Thank God." Then her heart thumped against her ribs. "Lily." She dashed into her daughter's room, slapping the light switch on the wall.

Ben burst through the doorway behind Kate.

Kate gathered Lily up in her arms and held her while Ben checked her bedding and room thoroughly.

"Mommy?"

"Shh, baby. Go back to sleep."

Pickles whined in his box.

"Can Pickles sleep with me?" she asked, her voice groggy, a fist rubbing over her eyes.

"No, baby. Pickles has his own bed."

"I want Pickles to sleep—" A huge yawn interrupted Lily's protest. She snuggled down in Kate's arms and fell back to sleep.

The puppy turned around in his box three times and dropped down, his head draped over his paws.

Ben straightened the bedding and waited for Kate to lay the child down. Afterward, he tucked the sheets around Lily and pressed a kiss to her forehead.

Kate swallowed hard on a knot in her throat.

Ben had kissed Lily, the gesture so natural and right it took Kate's breath away.

When he straightened, his gaze met hers. He nodded toward the door.

Kate stepped out into the hallway, tugging the sheet up securely over her breasts, embarrassed about her behavior. She'd more or less encouraged Ben to make love to her. Hell, she'd practically thrown herself at him. Her cheeks burning, she pulled the door halfway closed and turned toward her bedroom.

Two steps in that direction and she stopped, a huge tremor shaking her so hard her teeth rattled.

Ben's hands settled on her bare shoulders. "What's wrong?"

"I can't go back in there."

"I'll check it out."

"Thanks, but it won't make a difference. I won't be sleeping in there tonight."

"I've disposed of the snake."

"Yeah, but you can't take the image out of my head."

"You can sleep in my room."

"No. You need your sleep more than I do."

"We both need sleep." He cupped her elbow with his warm, strong palm and led her past Lily's room to his.

Once inside the doorway, Kate stopped and stared at the

four-poster bed, images of a naked Ben flashing through her mind. "No. I can't do it."

"I'll sleep on the couch downstairs."

"I can sleep on the couch."

"And if something happened to you downstairs, I might not hear anything."

Kate trembled. "I just won't sleep then."

"Don't be ridiculous. Take the bed." He urged her forward, stripped the comforter back and checked the sheets. "See? No snake."

A shiver racked her body yet again. "I can't get that rattler out of my mind. I almost crawled into bed with a snake." She shivered again.

He shoved a hand through his hair. "If it helps, I'll stay with you until you go to sleep."

She glanced at him, her brows pulling downward. "What we were about to do…"

"Don't worry. I'll only stay until you go to sleep. Nothing else."

"I don't know."

"For crissakes." Ben scooped her up in his arms and tossed her on the bed. "Go to sleep before I forget myself again." He turned his back on her and paced the floor.

Kate adjusted the sheet around her body and moved to the farthest side of the bed. "And I'm supposed to sleep while you pace?" She shook her head.

He stopped and shoved a hand through his hair. The button on his fly remained undone, the zipper halfway down.

Despite her best promise to herself, Kate's gaze zeroed in on the dark hairs peeking through. The shivers of dread for the snake changed to the shivers of the kind of excitement she'd felt before the snake had come on scene.

Her gaze rose to capture Ben's, staring down at her.

He groaned. "I can't do this."

"Then don't." Kate fluffed the comforter, checking beneath it one more time before she settled in, her eyes wide. She turned her back to Ben and feigned sleep. After a moment or two, a sensation of something crawling across her leg made her sit up in the bed and drag her legs up to her chin. She shook the blanket again. Nothing fell out or slithered across the bed.

Kate peered over the top of her sheet-covered knees. "Why are you still standing there? The couch is downstairs. I don't need you." Her voice trailed off. The hell she didn't need him. It was destined to be a long, scary night.

His hand rose to the light switch. "Want me to turn out the light?"

Her hand went up immediately. "No!"

Ben sighed, crossed the room and sat on the edge of the bed.

"What are you doing?"

"Going out of my mind. What does it look like?" He swung his legs, jeans and all up onto the bed. "Come here." Ben gathered her in his arms, pulling her body up against his. "Go to sleep."

"I can't."

"Yes, you can. Close your eyes and picture Lily playing with her puppy."

Snuggled against Ben, one hand resting on his bare chest, Kate tried. Instead of her daughter, all she could imagine was trailing that hand across his taut muscles, finding and pinching the hard little brown nipples.

She closed her eyes, inhaling the fresh, clean scent of soap and man. Her hand slipped over a rib, then another, inching south to the waistband of his jeans.

Ben captured her hand. "This can only lead to one thing."

"You think?"

In a flash, he shoved her onto her back, pinning her wrists above her head. "I loved my wife, Kate. I don't need another woman in my life."

"Then why are you lying on top of me." Her gaze met his unflinchingly. She arched her back, her pelvis rubbing against the hard ridge beneath his jeans. "And why are you so aroused?"

He closed his eyes, his breath coming in short, ragged pants. Then his mouth descended on hers. His hands found the edge of the sheet over her breasts and yanked it downward, peeling it from her body, until she lay naked and trembling. Not out of fear, but in anticipation of what would come next.

She raised a hand to his zipper, sliding it lower until his erection sprang free, hard and straight.

"I didn't want this to happen," he said through gritted teeth.

"So noted." Kate's hand circled him, sliding along his length, dipping inside the denim to cup him, massaging his member. "What are you going to do about it?"

He leaped from the bed and stood with his back to her, breathing hard.

She rose behind him, her hands caressing a path, curving around his shoulders, down his sides to his narrow hips. Kate circled around to his front, beyond caring what he thought of her brazen behavior, beyond patient...ready to take him inside her.

She wanted him to fill the void she'd been living with for so long.

Kate pushed his jeans over his hips and down his legs, her hands caressing his buttocks, his thighs and the sharply defined calves.

He stepped free of the denim and threaded his hands in her hair, dragging her to her feet.

She let him, her body sliding up his, skin-to-delicious-skin. Every nerve ending burned, fire radiating from her core outward.

He cupped the back of her thighs and lifted her, wrapping her legs around his waist. "Stop me now."

"I can't." She wove her fingers into his hair, dragging his head downward until their lips met. "I need you."

His member nudged her opening, the tip sliding in. "Wait."

"Really?" Her thighs tightened around him, lifting her up.

"I have protection in the nightstand...by the bed." He groaned and lifted her off him, laying her across the bed, her legs draped over the side.

Kate reached into the drawer and removed a strip of foil-packaged condoms. She tore the packet open with her teeth and rolled the condom over him, her hand cupping him at the base.

Ben stepped between her legs, grabbed her wrists and pinned them over her head, his erection poised at her entrance. "You make me hotter than the Texas sun."

"That makes two of us, then." She wrapped her legs around his waist and tightened, driving him in.

He slid all the way inside, the smooth, slick sensations so erotic, he threw his head back and drew in a deep, steadying breath.

Then he pulled back out and slammed in again, settling into a fast, smooth rhythm.

As the friction increased, heat built and tingling sensations rippled through Kate's body. Her back arched off the bed, her thighs clenching with each thrust until she pitched over the edge, crying out his name.

His fingers dug into her hips as he plunged in one last time. Ben held steady, his face tense, his muscles bunched and his member throbbing against her channel.

As they tumbled back to the earth, Kate's legs disengaged from around his waist and dropped over the side of the bed.

Ben eased her up on the mattress and lay beside her, spooning her body with his.

"Stay with me?" she begged.

His hand rested on her naked hip. "As long as there are no regrets in the morning."

She sighed. "No regrets." Kate snuggled in his arms, feeling more safe and secure than she had since her husband left for war. If only she could count on this to last.

Sadly, she knew she couldn't.

A single tear slid down her cheek and dropped onto the sheet. How could a man come to mean so much to her in such a short time? Was she desperate for male companionship? Or was it *this* man that made her feel this way?

It didn't matter. When his replacement came, Ben would leave. She'd be on her own again.

But for now, he kept the boogeyman and the snakes away while warming her backside.

Kate closed her eyes and fell asleep.

BEN LAY FOR a long time, his arms around Kate's naked body, holding her like they belonged together. Making love to a woman had that effect on him. That had to be the explanation for his sudden desire to stay with her, to become a part of her and Lily's lives.

But that wouldn't be fair to either one of them. He'd had a wife and daughter. He'd loved them both so much it still hurt to think about them. How could he begin to love someone else as much? He couldn't. It wasn't possible. Was it?

Kate stirred against him, her bottom brushing sensitive areas, stirring desire so strong he couldn't suppress it.

He'd asked Hank to find his replacement. What if he did? Could Ben walk away and leave Kate in the hands of someone else? Could he trust that other agent to take care of Kate and Lily, to protect them from whoever was after them?

His arms tightened around Kate, his chest squeezing tight. He couldn't desert them. Not now. Not when they needed him most.

The sound of a puppy's cries pulled Ben from his thoughts. Pickles had to be missing his mother.

Ben slipped out of the bed and stood, gazing down at Kate as she lay deep in sleep, caressed by the moonlight streaming through the window. Her long hair looking more auburn in this light as it splayed across the pillow, her lips parted as if she fell asleep whispering.

Ben brushed a strand of hair from her cheek and bent to press his lips to hers.

"Sweet dreams."

He slipped into his jeans and zipped them, then padded barefoot to the next room.

Lily lay splayed across her bed, her foot dangling over the side.

Pickles looked up at Ben, his soulful blue eyes begging Ben to rescue him from his grief and loneliness.

Ben scooped up the puppy and the box and headed down the stairs to the couch. He understood how Pickles felt. Torn from the ones he loved, but surrounded by the possibility of a new family.

In the night, everything seemed more overwhelming than during the light of day.

As he lay on the couch, his feet hanging over the arms, Ben cuddled the puppy against him and turned over the day's events in his mind.

Two things stood out, touching him with a cold hand of dread.

A gang of coyotes was using the Flying K as a place to traffic human cargo.

Secondly, that snake hadn't gotten into Kate's bed on its own. Someone had put it there.

Chapter Thirteen

Kate yawned, stretched and glanced around her room, disoriented at first. Her tender breasts rubbed against the sheet and she remembered where she was—in Ben's bed—and that she was naked.

"Mommy?" Lily called out.

Kate scrambled to her feet, wondering where Ben had gone. She had just wrapped the sheet around her body when Lily ran by the open door.

"Mommy?"

Her frightened cry spurred Kate forward. "Lily, I'm here."

Lily stopped at the top of the stairs and looked back. "Where's Pickles? He's not in his box."

Kate smiled and shrugged, relieved her daughter hadn't asked why she was in a different room and wrapped in a sheet. "I don't know. Let me get dressed and I'll help you find him."

"Lily?" Ben's deep voice echoed up the stairs.

Kate moved to peer over the banister railing at the man.

He stood barefoot, wearing nothing but his jeans. The sight of his naked chest sent Kate's pulse skittering into crazy palpitations. An image of herself lying naked with him spread warmth throughout her body, and extra fire to one place in particular.

He shot a heated glance at her before he held the puppy up for Lily to see. "I have Pickles down here."

"Pickles." Lily ran down the stairs, her hand trailing along the railing, wild, light red hair flying out around her shoulders.

A sharp tug in the region of her heart made Kate press a hand to her chest. How like a family they were. She had to remind herself that it was nothing but an illusion. A fantasy bubble destined to pop when life returned to normal.

Ben handed Lily the puppy. "I've already taken him outside. He should play all right inside for a few minutes. Stay in the house, please."

"I will." Lily set the puppy on the floor and ran into the living room, squealing as Pickles chased after her, barking in his shrill puppy voice.

Which left Ben staring up at Kate. He stepped up one of the stair risers. "How are you this morning?"

Kate gathered the sheet around her body, a flush of warmth burning up her neck into her cheeks. "I'm fine."

He climbed two more steps, his gaze pinning hers. "Any regrets?"

Her eyes widened, her heart pounding so hard, she could hear it banging against her eardrums. "No regrets." She swallowed hard and forced herself to ask, "And you?"

When Ben cleared the top step and stood with her on the landing, Kate stepped away until her back bumped against the wall.

"None." Ben advanced slowly. When he stopped, barefoot and toe to toe with her, he reached out and touched the rise of her breasts above the sheet. "Seems you were wearing this last night."

A smile fluttered across her lips, shyness weighing on her words. "I think I need a new outfit."

"I kind of like this one." His fingers tugged on the end, untucking the edges.

Kate inhaled, her breasts rising as Ben unfolded the sheet, exposing her body to his piercing gaze.

"Oh, yes. I like this outfit." He bent, capturing a nipple between his teeth, nipping lightly.

Kate's hands feathered through his hair, pressing against the back of his neck. She closed her eyes, letting the rampant waves of desire swarm over her.

"Mommy?" Lily's voice brought her back to earth with a jolt.

Kate jerked the sheet closed, stepped around Ben and leaned over the railing. "What is it, Lily?"

"Pickles had an accident."

A chuckle rose up her throat. "I'll be down in a moment to help you clean it up." When she turned toward her bedroom, Ben blocked her path. She blinked up at him. "You heard Lily, the puppy had an acci—"

Ben lifted her chin with a crooked finger and kissed her hard, his tongue darting out to capture hers in a brief caress.

As quickly as he'd possessed her, he let her go. "I'll take care of the puppy." Then he left her on the landing and padded down the steps, entering the living room in search of Lily.

Kate stood still for several seconds, unable to get her bearings. Hell, she'd been unable to form coherent thoughts since Ben had come into her life. If she wasn't careful, she'd fall in love with a man who still loved his dead wife. And where would that leave her?

Kate eased into her bedroom, on the lookout for anything that slithered or rattled. The room remained silent as she dressed for the day in jeans, a white button-down shirt and cowboy boots. She pulled out the key her father's attorney had given her at the reading of the will and decided it was time to look for whatever it belonged to.

Perhaps when she found the lock, it would unveil the reason why someone wanted her off the property and away from Wild Oak Canyon.

As Kate gathered her ponytail in place, corralling her wild curls with a rubber band, the telephone at the bottom of the stairs rang. She decided to forgo makeup. It wasn't as if she was trying to impress anyone. Certainly not Ben. He wasn't sticking around. What had happened last night wasn't the stuff relationships were made of. Ben was a bodyguard. Kate was the job. When she no longer needed his protection, he'd be gone.

If she was smart, she'd discontinue this sex-only connection with the bodyguard. It wasn't fair to her, to Lily or to him.

With a deep breath, she hurried down the stairs and lifted the phone on the fourth ring. "Hello."

"Kate, it's Cara Jo."

"Hi." Kate's heart warmed at the sound of her new friend's voice.

"Just wanted to let you know the local church in Wild Oak Canyon has a Mother's Day Out program. Lily might enjoy playing with children her own age a couple times a week."

"Wow, that would be great. What days?"

"Tuesdays and Thursdays from nine until three o'clock." Cara Jo called out to someone on her end of the phone.

"Are you at the diner?" Kate asked.

"I am. It being Thursday, I thought I'd let you know early enough to get Lily in today, if you had a mind to." She chuckled softly. "Purely selfish reasons, I assure you. If you come to town, you could join me for lunch and do a little shopping without having to drag poor Lily around."

"That sounds good. I could run by the sheriff's office again and report the dead cattle, for all the good it would do."

Cara Jo snorted. "At least you'd have a record of it."

"Right." Kate glanced at Lily playing on the floor in the

living room with Pickles. The little puppy had as much energy as the four-year-old.

Nothing like jumping into the community. And Lily was used to playing with the children she'd met at the day care in Houston. Kate made the decision. "I'll check it out today. If all goes well, I'll meet you for lunch."

"Make it around eleven-thirty. Twelve to one-thirty is our busy time and it gets hard to find a seat."

"Will do." Kate hung up, ran back up the stairs and grabbed play clothes, shoes, barrettes and a hairbrush from Lily's room.

When she returned to the first floor, the living room was empty.

Sounds of voices and laughter came from the kitchen.

When Kate entered, she was struck by how natural the scene appeared.

Lily sat in a chair on a stack of books, digging into a bowl of cereal. Ben sat beside her with a plate of eggs, bacon and toast. Mrs. Henderson busied herself at the stove, talking to both of them with her back to the room.

Kate smiled. "Good morning."

"Oh, Kate, dear. Sit. I have breakfast for you." Mrs. Henderson lifted a fry pan full of fluffy, yellow scrambled eggs and faced her. "Did you sleep well?"

Kate's face heated. "Yes. I did." *Minus the snake and the musical beds and making love to Ben.* She had slept well once she'd fallen asleep in Ben's arms. She refused to meet his gaze, but out of the corner of her eye she could see the way his lips twitched.

If he smiled now, she'd throw something at him.

Instead he shoved a forkful of eggs into his mouth and chewed.

"Lily, how would you like to make some new friends today?" Kate asked, hoping to pull attention off her red cheeks and focus it on her baby girl.

Lily set her spoon beside her bowl and lifted her cup of milk. "Yes, please."

Kate continued for Ben's benefit, "There's a Mother's Day Out program at the local church. Cara Jo from the diner suggested it, thinking Lily might like to meet some of the local children. I think it's a good idea."

Ben nodded. "Eddy had a few things he'd like picked up in town. We can take the truck."

"I'll take my car, you can follow. I think I'll be safe in town and I might want to do a little shopping while there."

Ben frowned. "Are you sure you don't want me to drive?"

"I don't think it's necessary." Kate remained firm. If Ben was leaving, she needed to get around on her own and not be afraid. "Nothing's going to happen in a town full of people."

Ben's brows didn't rise. "I'm not thrilled with the idea of taking two vehicles. Seems a waste of fuel and time. But as long as you wait for me to follow you back to the ranch, I suppose it's okay."

Kate almost smiled. For some strange reason, she liked pushing his buttons. But she understood his reasons. It was his job to protect her and Lily. "I'll let you know when I'm ready to head home."

Fifteen minutes later, she'd finished her breakfast, brushed her teeth and Lily's, and gathered her keys and purse.

Ben waited outside beside his truck, his brows dented in what appeared to be a permanent frown. He'd already switched the booster seat into the backseat of her car.

Lily ran to his arms. "Pickles cried when I put him in the box."

"Mrs. Henderson will let him out to play once we leave. He'll be fine until you get home." Ben tucked her into the safety seat and buckled the belt over her lap, then pressed a kiss to her forehead.

Kate stood back, once again amazed at how comfortable

the two were together. Already, she predicted it would be hard on Lily when Ben left.

Kate climbed into the car and pulled out onto the highway bound for the little town and the church where Lily would spend the day doing what kids did—play.

The drive was uneventful and Kate relished the time alone with Lily. It gave her the opportunity to think through what had happened the night before. She never would have thought she'd be so quickly attracted to a man, and never had she dreamed she'd jump into bed with a stranger after knowing him such a short time. Having married her high school sweetheart, Kate hadn't dated as an adult. One thing was for sure, she wasn't setting a good example for Lily. Still she didn't regret the magic she'd experienced with Ben the night before.

Kate parked in front of the church.

Ben parked on the passenger side of Kate's car. He got to Lily before Kate and lifted the child out onto the ground, tucking her hand in his.

Kate took Lily's other hand and they walked into the church together.

At the administrative office, Kate filled out paperwork and let them make a copy of Lily's shot records. When it came to filling out the emergency data card, she paused. She wrote down her home phone number and her cell phone number, but the cell number was only reliable sometimes. "If you can't get me on my cell phone, call Cara Jo's diner and ask for me or leave a message with Cara Jo. I'll check in there."

"Leave my cell number, too, as backup." Ben recited his number and Kate wrote it on the form.

Kate and Ben walked with the administrator to the classroom Lily would be in. Six children ranging in age from three to five gathered around tables, wearing cute little aprons. They were elbow-deep in finger painting.

Lily was so excited, she didn't even say goodbye.

Kate left the building, happy that her daughter would have a fun-filled day with children her age.

"Now what?" Ben asked.

"I want to stop by the county assessor, do a little shopping and then meet Cara Jo for lunch." She shot a glance his way, but didn't linger on his handsome face, afraid she'd ask him to stay with her. "What about you?"

"While you're in town, I can take care of reporting the dead cattle to the sheriff's office. At least get it on record. I need to run out to Hank's and check on the status of that DVD. Then I'll drop by the hardware store for the items Eddy needed for the ranch."

Kate glanced at her watch. "Meet back here at three?"

"Three." He caught Kate's arm as she turned away. "Don't go anywhere else without notifying me first, will you?"

"I won't." Her arm tingled where he touched her. Damn. The man had her tied in knots and wanting so much more. Things she shouldn't be thinking in broad daylight came to mind more than she cared to admit. With her thoughts on her bodyguard, she wasn't focusing on what was important. The nutcase causing her grief and the human trafficking happening on her own land.

"Three o'clock." She scooted away from his grip on her arm and climbed into her car. After shifting into Reverse, she left the parking lot, cranking the air conditioner up to chill her suddenly flaming cheeks.

She stopped by the county tax assessor's office to discover no change in the computer situation. They expected someone out that afternoon to work on it.

After she left the county offices, Kate spent thirty minutes in the General Store, exploring the aisles, getting familiar with what Wild Oak Canyon had to offer. It wasn't a huge department store, but they sold jeans, chambray shirts and cowboy hats. That and a few odds and ends in fencing supplies and plain pantry staples, fresh bread and milk. After she'd gone up and down each aisle, it was time to meet with Cara Jo at the diner across the street from the General Store.

When Kate pushed through the diner's door, Cara Jo dashed by her, carrying three heaping plates of food.

"Sorry, one of my waitresses called in sick. I have to work the lunch crowd." She set the plates on a table in the corner where three men dressed in jeans and chambray shirts sat with their forks and knives ready to dig in.

On her way back past Kate, Cara Jo gave her an apologetic frown. "Sorry. Can we do a rain check on our lunch?"

"That's fine. I ate breakfast not long ago."

"Oh, please sit, have lunch. It's on me." Cara Jo whooshed by and grabbed another two plates from the window into the kitchen.

Kate glanced around at the busy establishment. She didn't want to sit by herself, and she didn't feel like sitting with strangers.

Robert Sanders occupied a booth near the far corner, sitting across the table from the sheriff, their heads bent close, intense expressions on their faces.

Kate didn't see herself getting into a conversation with the two men. And they appeared to be discussing business. She caught Cara Jo on her next pass. "I'm going to head out to the ranch. I have some things to do out there. I'll be back in town around three to get Lily. I'll stop by then for a cup of coffee, if you have time."

"Oh, sure. Three will be our slow time. I'll see you then." Cara Jo was off again, snatching up a carafe of steaming coffee and a pitcher of ice water.

Kate left the diner and stood outside on the sidewalk. She dug her cell phone out of her purse and dialed Ben's number. The call went straight to his voice mail. She left a message, or at least hoped she did. With spotty reception, she wasn't sure she stayed connected throughout her call.

With nothing else to do, not feeling like shopping and

with nobody to talk to, Kate decided to do what she'd told Cara Jo she was going to do and head back out to the ranch.

Lily would be happily playing with her new friends and Ben was busy doing errands and updating the sheriff's deputies and Hank Derringer.

A little lonely and a bit anxious, Kate couldn't stand around and wait for someone to show up or free up to babysit her. She still had a lot of unpacking to do. Mrs. Henderson would be there and now that Kate knew how to handle the Glock, she would be just fine.

Kate jammed her hand into her jeans pocket, searching for her car keys and found the mystery key her father had left her. She could spend time searching the house and surrounding outbuildings for the lock the key belonged to. Kate climbed into her car and headed out of town to the ranch. The wind had picked up, buffeting her little car around. With few trees or hills to block the wind, it blew through, hard and fast and filled with fine grains of sand that pinged against the windshield.

In broad daylight, Kate didn't expect to be accosted. But then she hadn't expected a biker gang to show up in her front yard the first morning after she'd arrived. Just to play it safe, Kate kept alternating watching the pavement ahead and behind in the rearview mirrors. Anytime she passed a road connecting to the highway, she studied it carefully, looking for suspicious vehicles, lurking, waiting for her to pass by, alone and vulnerable.

She'd be glad when she got back to the ranch with Mrs. Henderson and Eddy.

Kate gripped the steering wheel so tightly, her knuckles turned white as she struggled to quell her rising fears and to maintain control of the little car being tossed around by strong southerly winds.

By the time she drove through the gate and up to the ranch house, Kate's fingers were cramping. And all for what? Nothing happened on the highway and no biker gang greeted her at the house.

As Kate climbed out of the car, her hair escaped its neat ponytail and whipped around her face and neck.

A rumbling-on-gravel sound made her turn and face the driveway she'd driven in on. Another vehicle turned off the county road onto the gravel drive far enough away that she couldn't make it out, but close enough to send a flash of fear through her.

Her brows furrowed, Kate hurried toward the house, scraping her mind for the location of the pistol and shells.

"Oh, good. You're here." Mrs. Henderson met her at the screen door, her purse hooked over her shoulder. "Mr. Henderson forgot to tell me he had an appointment at the clinic today and the Customs and Border Protection folks called a while ago to say they were on the way out to check on your reports of lights and dead cattle. I'd stick around and answer their questions, but now that you're here…"

"How long did the CBP say they'd be before they got here?" Kate asked.

"There they are now." Mrs. Henderson pointed down the drive.

The vehicle Kate had seen came into view. A big, white Hummer H2, with knobby tires and a green stripe, spit up a wide cloud of dust on the gravel drive.

"When they called about an hour ago, I thought it would be no problem. Eddy said he'd meet them at the barn when they came in. I had just pulled a pie out of the oven when David called to say he was picking me up." The older woman glanced over Kate's shoulder. "That should be Dave now. I wasn't sure what to do with the puppy when I left so it's a good thing you showed up when you did." She gave Kate a half smile. "Sorry. My husband can be forgetful. That's why I go to his appointments with him."

"Don't worry. I'll be fine without you."

Her eyes narrowed and she looked past Kate. "Where's Mr. Harding?"

"He'll be along in a bit," Kate fudged. No use detaining Marge when her husband had already driven out to pick her up.

"I can't leave you alone. Mr. Henderson will just have to go on without me." Marge let the purse slide down her arm and turned in the doorway.

"No, really. I'll be fine. Eddy's around here. The Border Protection is here. And if that's not enough, Ben gave me lessons on how to fire my pistol. It turns out I'm a pretty good shot. You go on with Mr. Henderson. He needs you more than I do."

The older woman's brows dipped. "Are you sure?" She glanced around the immediate vicinity of the ranch house as if expecting someone to be lurking in the shadows. "I don't feel right leaving you like this."

Kate rested her hand on Mrs. Henderson's arm. "You don't have to baby me. I can handle myself and Ben will be along shortly."

"Okay. But do be careful." She squeezed Kate's hand and descended the stairs. "I'll be back to fix dinner around five."

"Don't make the trip out again. I can cook, you know." Another near lie. She wasn't that good, but Mrs. Henderson didn't have to know that.

Marge patted her purse. "Well, then, I'll see you in the morning."

"Thanks, Mrs. H." Kate sighed as Mr. Henderson got out of the driver's seat and rounded the front of the car to open the door for his wife. He waved at Kate and climbed back into the car and turned it around, headed back to the highway and town.

Kate admired the way the old couple relied on each other for things. They loved each other, which was evident in the way the old man took care of Marge and she him.

When Troy had been alive, Kate had never quite pictured them growing old together. Now she supposed that she'd never had enough time on her hands to dwell on such things, what with her pregnancy occurring so close to when they'd gotten married and then Troy leaving before even Kate knew she was with child.

Kate stood in the yard as the officers stepped out of their SUV and strode across the ground to her.

One of the officers held out his hand. "I'm Officer Mendoza with U.S. Customs and Border Protection. Are you Ms. Langsdon?"

"Yes, that's me."

"We're here to review recent reports of suspicious activity in the area."

"I take it the helicopters didn't find the two trucks last night?"

"No, ma'am." The spokesman of the two pulled a notepad out of his pocket. "Could you or your husband show me where you saw the dead cattle?"

Kate let the husband comment pass by without comment. "Your best bet will be to have my foreman show you where you can find the dead cattle and the ravine where we saw the two trucks."

Eddy chose that moment to cross the barnyard, slapping his cowboy hat against his leg, dust rising and whipping away with the wind.

Kate brought the CBP officers up to date on what had happened on the ranch, from the attack in the house, the home intrusions, biker gangs and dead cattle to the truckloads of people.

Mendoza shook his head. "I suggest you get a good guard dog and a bodyguard."

"Got the bodyguard. Working on the guard dog." Her lips curved as an image of Ben came to mind and at the thought of Pickles being a guard dog.

Mendoza glanced over her shoulder and around the yard. "A bodyguard isn't much good if he's not around to guard you."

"He's on his way back from town," Kate lied, realizing she'd been stupid to leave Wild Oak Canyon without him. Without Marge as backup she only had Eddy to protect her should someone cause trouble.

When Kate had told them all she knew, she paused, waiting for their response.

Officer Mendoza closed his notepad and slid it into his shirt pocket. "Could you show me where you found the carcasses?"

Kate turned to Eddy.

"Sí." Eddy eyed the men. "I have extra horses in the barn."

The officer smiled. "Thanks, but we'll stick with the SUV. It gets in most places the horses can go."

Eddy didn't respond, his gaze roving over the huge tires and fancy paint job of the CBP vehicle. Then he shrugged. "You'll have to follow me and my horse." He turned and walked away.

Mendoza grinned. "He always so talkative?"

Kate smiled. "He has to warm up to you."

"How long have you owned the Flying K?"

It was Kate's turn to smile. "A grand total of a week."

Eddy had mounted his horse and stood waiting by the gate to the pasture.

"Guess we better get going." Mendoza nodded at Kate. "Thank you for your time."

"Hope you find the trucks. I'm worried about the passengers as hot as it gets out here." Kate watched as the Hummer cleared the gate and Eddy closed it behind them.

Once the group disappeared across the pasture, Kate dug the key from her pocket and performed a systematic search of the inside of the house, fitting the little key into every lock on the off chance it was the right one. She checked behind furniture, paintings and beneath rugs for any hidden doors.

The attic had been particularly creepy, with spiderwebs and a thick layer of dust. The hot Texas sun had heated the top of the house so much Kate had broken into a sweat as soon as she'd pulled down the attic access door and climbed to the top. After checking out two old trunks and an antique desk, she retreated to the air-conditioned second floor.

She let the attic door close on its springs. So far she'd struck out on finding the lock inside the house. She headed out the front door, letting the screen slap closed behind her.

Living in Houston had conditioned Kate to the constant noise of urban life. Here, the silence was only interrupted by the wail of wind against the windows. When she stepped out on the porch, the strong westerly breeze hit her with a heated blast, slapping her hair around her head. As far as Kate knew, she was the only person within miles of the ranch house. That gave her a kind of lonely, distant feeling. A quick glance at her watch told her she didn't have much time to check out the rest of the buildings if she wanted to be back in town on time to pick up Lily at the church and have a cup of coffee with Cara Jo.

She descended the steps, blinking the sand and grit out of her eyes. Choosing the shed closest to the house as a place to start looking, Kate kicked up dust as she trod across the dry Texas soil and flung open the door to the small building. The interior was packed with an ancient riding lawn mower, an antique car probably dating back to the 1940s, a variety of spare parts and equipment, a large rollaway toolbox and fishing poles.

After the bright sunshine, the interior was dark and deeply shadowed. She flipped the light switch beside the door and nothing happened. She'd need a flashlight if she planned to explore in the outbuildings. How long had it been since anyone had been inside this one? At least long enough to accumulate a thick layer of dust. Which, in this part of Texas, could be as little as a day. At the least, she could check out the toolboxes. They appeared to have tiny locks on some of the drawers.

The shed had no windows and only the one large door. Kate opened it wide and leaned a cement block against it to keep the wind from slamming it shut.

Then she stepped through, blocking the sun for a moment. She hugged the shadows, allowing for as much light as possible.

First, she tried the toolboxes. The key didn't fit the two locks, so she moved on. Kate squeezed between the front of the antique car and the wall of the building to get behind it. A scorpion skittered over a concrete block and down the side into a shadow.

Kate hated scorpions, having been stung more than once living in Houston. A shiver slithered across her warm skin. She'd have to warn Lily about the dangers of picking up rocks and things.

On the other side of the antique auto hung a rack of fishing poles. Below the rack, on the dirt floor was a tackle box with a keyhole on the front.

Ready to try anything, Kate stuck the key in the hole and turned it.

The lock clicked open.

A rush of excitement filled her and she dropped to her knees to better see what might be inside. The lighting behind the car was minimal, dust particles gleaming in the air. Kate held her breath as she laid her hands on the box, her pulse hammering through her veins.

Careful to look for scorpions or black widow spiders, she eased the lid back. From all she could see with the shadows and limited light, it was what it looked like. A fishing tackle box. The top compartment was loaded with dusty lures and faded rubber worms.

Kate let go of the breath she'd been holding. "Why would he leave me a key to a fishing tackle box?"

She sat back on her haunches and lifted the top compartment, exposing the bottom of the container.

Once again her breath hitched in her throat. Beneath a filet knife and a pair of pliers lay a mix of lures and lead weights. Buried among them was a slim silver thumb drive.

Was this it? Was this the item the key was hiding? Kate moved the knife and pliers aside and fished the thumb drive out of the box.

She shoved the data storage device into her pocket and stood.

The heavy shed door slammed shut, cutting off the light, throwing Kate into complete darkness. She reached out a hand to steady herself against the antique car and waited for the wind to blow the door open again so that she could see to find her way out.

The door didn't open.

Kate felt her way back around the old car to the front, her shirt catching on a nail protruding from the wall, ripping through the fabric and tearing into her skin. She screamed and nearly tripped over the forgotten concrete block the scorpion had scurried beneath.

Heart racing, afraid she'd brush against something deadly, sharp or creepy, she moved around the wall until her fingers brushed against a hinge. Finally, she'd reached the door.

Wind whistled through the cracks, a dark, lonely sound.

Kate leaned against the door and pushed. It didn't budge. She tried again, this time putting her full weight into it. The door remained closed. She stepped back, tucked her shoulder and slammed into the door. She bounced back.

As the truth dawned on her, her heart sank to her stomach. The door had been locked from the outside.

Chapter Fourteen

Ben sat across the desk from Hank. "That's what's been happening."

"Too much for young Kate to handle alone." Hank nodded. "I'm glad you've been there to protect her." He leaned forward. "I received word from one of my connections in Customs and Border Protection. They found a dead woman on a ranch adjacent to the Flying K two weeks ago. From what they said, she was an illegal immigrant. How she got there, they would only guess. She died of exposure and dehydration."

"Damn." Ben shook his head. "A dead woman, dead cattle, intruders. You think they're trafficking humans across the Flying K and don't want Kate to interfere?"

"Sounds like it. A deadly situation if Kate gets in the middle. The immigrants aren't who she needs to be worried about. It's the coyotes who bring them across. They don't care who they have to kill to get paid."

"Hank, we only saw young women in the backs of those trucks."

Hank glanced up at Ben. "If they're trafficking young women, we have an even bigger problem. Someone stateside is harboring them and possibly selling them to underground sex dens."

Ben clasped his hands together to keep them from shaking. "Like the one we busted in Austin. I caught one of their suppliers, Marcus Mendez. The bastard got off on a technicality, then he came after my family. Think these are connected?"

"Could be." Hank leaned back in his chair. "I spoke with the regional director of the CBP. They didn't find the trucks you and Kate saw last night."

"Damn it." Ben stood and paced in front of Hank's desk. "I should have stopped them there."

"You had Kate to protect and you were outnumbered." Hank rounded his desk and laid a hand on Ben's shoulder. "You did the only thing you could. Now that you know they're running a human trafficking trade across the Flying K, you have to keep Kate from stumbling into them."

"I'll try but she was real upset by what we saw." Kate had a mind of her own and might try something dumb to help those girls. Ben blew out a long breath and dragged a hand through his hair. "I should be with her now."

"Where is she?" Hank asked.

"I left her at the diner. She should be okay there for a little while." Only now he wasn't so sure. Trouble had been following Kate since she'd arrived in this part of Texas. "Before I go, anything on the video?"

"As a matter of fact, we did make a little headway." He clicked the keyboard on his computer and then nodded toward the flat-screen television mounted on the wall behind Ben. "Look at this."

Static filled the screen, then a wavering image of Kyle Kendrick blinked into view.

"Hello, Kate. If you've received this video, something has happened to me and I'm either dead or missing and presumed dead. I couldn't leave without letting you know that of all the regrets in my life, you and your mother are my most heartfelt."

After a short pause, he continued.

"I can't say that I lived a good life. I didn't go to church, I wasn't a pillar of the community and I avoided jail on more occasions than I'd care to remember."

Ben sat back, his heart squeezing in his chest as he imagined Kate watching this video and her reaction to seeing the man on the screen for her first time.

"Then I met your mother and everything changed. I wanted to be a better man. I wanted to make her proud of me, and I thought I could. But I was in too deep. The people I worked with had me. Imagine being married to the mob. In this case, the Mexican Mafia cartels."

Ben whistled, noting the haggard expression, the dark circles around the man's eyes. Eyes that looked so much like a haunted version of Kate's. "What a life."

"I married your mother, thinking I could shake their influence. I thought I could just quit, stop running drugs and start fresh." The man in the video shook his head. "I was wrong and it almost got your mother killed." He ran a hand through his hair and tipped his head back, squeezing shut his eyes. "I had to let her go. To send her away. I didn't know she was pregnant with you. If they'd known how much I cared for her and anything about my unborn child, they'd have used it against me. I couldn't contact you, couldn't talk to your mother. I had to shut the door to that part of my life completely or risk your lives. It was the hardest thing I've done in my entire life."

Kyle Kendrick stared into the camera, his eyes narrowing. "When the DEA cornered me in Vegas, I knew it was over. They would have sent me to jail, which, in retrospect, might have been easier. Instead, they gave me a chance to redeem myself. If I would become their informant, they wouldn't lock me up." Kyle snorted. "I should have let them send me to jail." Kyle shook his head slowly.

"Once I started ratting out the leaders of the cartels, I

knew my days were numbered. But I hung in there, trying
to find out who the stateside head honcho was."

Ben shot a glance at Hank.

"I've come so close I might be in trouble. I'm sending
this video in case something happens to me. I wanted you
to know how much I loved you and your mother."

After another short pause, Kyle continued.

"In the envelope with this video is a key. It unlocks a
tackle box you'll find in the shed with the old Cadillac. In
the bottom of the tackle box is a flash drive. It contains all
the notes I used to nail the members of the cartel and the
work I've compiled leading up to the discovery of the stateside crime boss. At the time of this video, I know there are
things happening in the area. I leave this information with
you in the event of my untimely but fully expected death.
The data is encrypted, so you'll need to hand it over to someone who can break the code. What you do with it is up to
you. Toss it, ignore it or hand it off to the DEA, I don't care.
Just don't get involved. I would hate to think my work once
again puts you in danger."

Ben narrowed his eyes and focused on the screen.

"As I was saying, several factions are active. Drug running and human trafficking. The coyotes who run the people across the border referred to the stateside connection as
Diablo Patrón, the devil boss. I think I know who's responsible, but haven't accumulated enough evidence to nail him.
If what I think is true…" He looked at his hands clasped in
between his knees. "Let's just say, I want to verify before
I call in the Feds. The stakes are high. Whatever happens
to me, know that I deserved what I got. Whatever you do,
don't get tangled up in this mess. And watch out for the following men…"

As Ben leaned forward, the picture on the screen tilted.

Kyle Kendrick lurched forward to catch the camera, but

missed, and the machine fell to the floor with a loud crash. Then static and gray squiggles filled the video screen.

"Who?" Ben leaped to his feet. "Who was she supposed to look out for?"

Hank stood, as well. "That's the kicker. Nothing else was recorded. Or Kendrick thought he'd finished recording his message and didn't. He must have been in a hurry to get the disk in the mail."

"Holy hell." Ben paced to the end of the French doors and back across Hank's spacious wood-paneled office. He stopped and faced the older man. "She needs to leave now. Go back to Houston, get the hell out of Texas. If the cartel finds out about the flash drive, she's dead."

"Scared the hell out of me, too." Hank walked around the desk and laid a hand on Ben's shoulder. "And there's one other thing I wanted you to know."

Ben looked into Hank's eyes. What else could go wrong?

"I hired another cowboy with the skills necessary to take over for you with the Langsdon woman. You don't have to go back there. He's here on the ranch. I can send him immediately."

Ben pressed a hand to his gut as if he'd been punched. "No."

"Are you sure? He has a stack of medals and credentials almost as impressive as yours."

"No." Ben straightened. God, what was he doing? He had an out. He didn't have to go back to the Flying K and be around Kate, whose body and soul reminded him of all he had to live for. He wouldn't have to face Lily, the child who'd worked her way into his heart in such a short time and left him open to her unconditional love and the heartbreak of leaving her behind when the job was done.

"I'll see this one through," Ben said. He headed for the door before he could change his mind, or before Hank could pull rank on him and change it for him.

"What about the video?"

Ben stopped. "Do you have it in a format I can show Kate?"

"Do you have a computer?"

"Yes."

Hank dropped into his desk chair, plugged a flash drive into the side of his monitor and clicked his keyboard. A moment later he yanked the flash drive from the monitor and handed it to Ben. "Be careful out there. Don't hesitate to call me in or to notify the DEA if things get out of hand."

"Don't worry. I'll be in touch." Ben left, climbing into his truck with a sense of impending doom.

Kate had come to the Flying K with the hope of starting over, of providing a good home for Lily. She'd ended up in a hotbed of danger.

Ben couldn't get back to her fast enough. Thank goodness she'd stayed in town.

The drive back to Wild Oak Canyon passed in a flash, considering Ben broke every speed limit the whole way. Thank goodness the county sheriff couldn't hope to patrol all the roads leading into the community with so few on staff.

Once in town, he pulled into the diner, his gaze searching for and not finding Kate's car. His heart skipped several beats, but he refused to let himself get worked up. He unbuckled his seat belt, dropped down to the pavement and looked around.

Cara Jo stepped out of the diner, her brows furrowed. "Oh, thank goodness you're here."

Ben's adrenaline spiked. "Why? Where's Kate?"

"She left right before lunch to head back to the ranch. She promised to be back in time to pick up Lily, but the woman in charge of the Mother's Day Out program called and said Kate hadn't come and Lily was the last one there. I tried to call you, but you didn't answer. I tried Kate's home phone and there was no answer. I was just about to get Lily myself, but I was afraid I wouldn't be on the list of people allowed to collect her."

Ben was already back in the truck and pulling out of the parking lot by the time Cara Jo finished talking. He whipped out onto the street, drove the few blocks and skidded to a stop in front of the church.

The woman he'd met earlier stepped out the front door of the church, holding Lily's hand. She turned and locked the church.

"Mr. Ben!" Lily jerked her hand free of the woman's and ran toward him, her arms outstretched.

Ben gathered her to him and lifted her off her feet.

"Thank goodness you're here. Lily was upset and worried you had lost your way." The woman looked around Ben. "Is Ms. Langsdon with you?"

"No, she had something come up and asked me to pick up Lily," Ben lied. He held Lily close, his heart aching for the child who'd thought she was forgotten.

Lily leaned back, tear tracks dried on her cheeks. "Can we go home now? Pickles missed me."

Ben nodded. "Yes, we can." He thanked the woman and tucked Lily into the backseat of his truck, buckling the seat belt over her lap. He didn't have the booster seat, but the buckle would have to do until he got back to the ranch and found Kate.

She'd promised not to go back until he could go with her. And why wasn't Mrs. Henderson answering the phone at the ranch?

Questions swirled in his mind throughout the drive out to the Flying K. When he came within sight of the house, he spied Kate's car sitting in the drive.

Nothing moved. No one came out to greet them.

Ben shifted into Park and climbed down. He lifted Lily out of the backseat and carried her to the house. The front door was unlocked. When he pushed it open, he called out, "Kate?"

As soon as he set Lily on her feet, she ran for the kitchen where Pickles's shrill barks created such a loud ruckus, Ben could barely hear himself think.

The house was a disaster. Drawers had been pulled out of the kitchen cabinets, pots and pans lay strewn across the floor.

"Pickles!" Lily cried out. "Where's Pickles?"

A high-pitched whine sounded from behind an overturned chair.

Ben found the puppy's box wedged between a cabinet and the chair and lifted it out, puppy and all.

Lily leaned over the box and let the puppy lick her fingers. "Oh, Pickles, did you miss me?"

Ben checked the pantry and locked the back door, then lifted Lily in his arms. "Sorry, sweetheart, we'll come back for Pickles in a minute."

He didn't want to leave the little girl alone until he was certain whoever had turned the house upside down was no longer there. He carried Lily from room to room.

The child clung to him, probably sensing all was not right. "Mr. Ben, why is the house a mess?"

Ben tried to think of something that would make sense to a child and not frighten her. "Someone must have been playing with things and didn't put them away."

"Where's my mommy?" Lily trembled in his arms and he held on tighter, anger burning below the surface. No child should be afraid to come home.

A quick look around the house, both upstairs and down, confirmed his suspicion. Kate wasn't there and not a single room had been left untouched. Even Lily's room had boxes overturned, clothes flung across the floor and pillows torn open.

By the time he got back to the kitchen, Lily was sobbing quietly. "I want my mommy."

"Tell you what. I bet I know someone who could do with some hugs."

He entered the kitchen and set Lily on the floor.

Pickles barked in his shrill little voice.

Lily ran to the box and lifted the puppy into her arms. "Oh, Pickles." She hugged his neck and held him tight until the puppy squirmed loose and tore out across the floor.

Lily laughed and ran after him into the living room.

Ben followed. Of all the rooms, this one seemed the safest for now. "Stay in the living room, sweetheart. I'll be right back."

He hated leaving the four-year-old alone in the ransacked house, but he didn't know what to expect outside. He jogged to the barn first.

The stalls were empty. He checked the number of saddles in the tack room. All were there and Eddy's truck wasn't in the barnyard. Had Kate gone with Eddy?

Ben couldn't think of a logical reason why she'd leave with Eddy.

Pulse pounding, Ben emerged from the barn and yelled, "Kate! Kate!" He made a complete circle around the barn and scanned the pastures nearby. A few horses trotted over, hoping for a treat. But Ben saw no sign of Kate.

Unwilling to leave Lily alone any longer, he ran toward the house, heart heavy and desperate to find the spitfire redhead. "Kate!"

Moving fast to get back to the house, Ben almost missed the noise coming from the shed.

He ground to a stop and held his breath so that he could hear even the slightest sound.

There it was again. A muffled cry.

"Kate?" He jogged to the shed, careful to limit the crunch of his boots on the gravel.

"Ben! I'm in here," a voice called out, followed by pounding on the wooden door.

Kate.

Ben grabbed the door and yanked. It didn't budge. A latch had been slid home after the door had closed. The wind could have closed the door, but then someone on the outside had to push the bolt through the hasp.

He slid the latch to the side and jerked the door open.

Heat hit him at the same time as Kate's body plowed into his chest.

Her face was red and she wasn't perspiring.

"Holy hell, Kate, how long have you been there?"

"I don't know. It was dark. I must have drifted off. But it seems like forever." She leaned heavily against him and smiled up at him through pale lips. "I could use a drink of water."

He scooped her into his arms. Her skin felt hot and dry. It had to be over a hundred and twenty inside the shed. If she'd been in there for several hours, the saunalike atmosphere could have killed her.

Ben carried Kate toward the house.

"Lily?" Kate's big green eyes gazed up at him.

"She's inside playing with Pickles." Ben's mouth was set in a grim line. "Why did you leave town?"

Kate nestled closer to him, shrugging. "I don't know. I didn't really feel like shopping. I wanted to find out what the key belonged to." She wiggled against him, jammed her hand into her pocket and drew out a small silver flash drive. "I found this."

Ben's eyes widened. "Ah, you found your father's data."

Kate's brows furrowed. "How do you know about it?"

"Hank's team has been busy. I have something for you to watch as soon as we get you hydrated and cooled off."

"I'm fine. Show me."

He shook his head. "Not until I know you're okay."

When they entered the house, Lily ran past, followed by a nipping, barking Pickles. "Hi, Mommy. Someone made a mess and didn't clean up." She stopped in the middle of the floor so fast, Pickles plowed into her. "Why is Mr. Ben carrying you?"

Kate smiled at her daughter, then glanced up at Ben, her brows raised. "Why *are* you carrying me?"

Ben smiled at Lily. "Because I'm big and strong."

Lily giggled and raced off, Pickles nipping at her heels.

Kate moved against him. "You can put me down."

"I will." He glanced at the stairs, then the couch and decided he wouldn't convince her to get in a cool shower. Not when he had news about her father and with Lily playing on the ground floor. Ben laid her on the couch. "Stay."

Kate laughed shakily. "I'm not a dog." Then she looked around the room. "Holy cow."

"Yeah, and it doesn't get better."

Her shoulders sagged. "Will this ever end?"

Her sad expression was almost his undoing. "Sit tight. I'll be back with a tall glass of ice water and a cool rag. But only if you stay."

"I may not be a dog, but I can be bribed." Kate settled back against a tattered throw pillow, her skin cooling in the air-conditioned room.

By the time Ben returned, Kate was shivering, her teeth chattering together so hard she thought they might crack. "I don't know what's wrong with me." Pain stabbed through her calf. She jerked up to a sitting position, grabbed her leg and doubled over. "Ow!"

"What's wrong?" Ben set the ice water on the table.

"Cramp." She tried to rise and fell back against the couch, too dizzy to stand. "I need…to…stretch." She pressed one hand to the cramped muscle, the other to the bridge of her nose.

"Just lay back." Ben pressed her firmly against the cushion, stretched her legs out straight, slid her shoes off her feet and pushed her toes up.

"Ow! Ow! Ow!" Kate reached for his hand, but couldn't quite get there before she fell back against the pillow. Soon, the cramp eased and she lay still, her breathing shallow, the pain gone. "How'd you do that?"

"Works on a charley horse. Figured it would help you with the cramp." He lifted the glass. "Now, let's get some fluids inside you and you'll feel better." He helped her to a sitting position and slid in behind her to hold her up while she drank.

She wanted to drain the glass, but Ben wouldn't let her.

"A little at time. Otherwise you'll just barf it up."

She snorted. "That would be attractive."

"In between sips, you can tell me what happened."

"Before you say anything, I'm sorry." She sipped from the glass, gathering more words as the fuzziness cleared from her head. "I shouldn't have come home by myself."

"Then why did you?"

"I can't rely on you to always be here for me and Lily. I have to be able to handle things on my own."

"When we find out who's behind all the threats. Not a moment sooner."

"I know, I know." Because he was there and she couldn't lie back against the pillows, she let herself lean into the hardness of his muscular chest. "I should have waited for you. And I will from now on." As soon as the words left her mouth, she knew they were a lie. Ben wouldn't be there for her *from now on*. "Or at least until we figure out who's doing this," she added.

"My most immediate concern is getting you hydrated." He pulled her closer and urged her to take another sip.

"Don't worry. I think I could drink a bathtub full of water."

"What happened?"

"I was looking for a lock the key would fit into and had

just found the tackle box in the shed and the flash drive inside it when the door slammed shut. I'd propped the door with a concrete block. Guess it wasn't enough for the gusts of wind."

Ben's arm tightened around her. "It was more than the wind. Someone closed the door on purpose and locked it from the outside."

Kate glanced up, the glass of water forgotten, another tremor shaking her. "Someone locked me in there on purpose? There weren't any windows to let any air in."

Ben's body stiffened beneath hers. "You could have died if we hadn't found you soon enough."

Kate placed the cool glass against her lips, her thoughts on Lily as she plowed through the living room, the puppy chasing after her. "I can't afford to die, Ben. I'm all Lily has," she whispered.

Ben took the glass from her and set it on the table within her reach, then he laid her back on the couch.

She wanted him to hold her longer until the chill of what had almost happened dissipated.

He stood, looking down at her with a frown pulling his brows together. "You're going back to Houston."

Kate tried to push to a sitting position. "Says who?"

"It's not safe here."

"I have nothing left for me in Houston."

"You have Lily."

She started to say something, but bit down on her lip instead. He had a good point. "I can't go back to Houston. It's not any safer. Remember? Someone ransacked my apartment there. I'll bet it has something to do with what's on that flash drive I found."

"You can't tell anyone about it. No one."

"Okay."

"And at least consider leaving here until the dust settles."

She wanted to tell him to quit telling her what to do, but before she could he pressed a finger to her lips.

"I'm not trying to be a jerk. I'm worried about you and Lily. When I came back here and couldn't find you…"

She grasped his hand and held on to it. "I'm glad you did. Mrs. Henderson wasn't due back until tomorrow morning and Eddy could be out until dark working with the cattle. That reminds me."

Ben stared down at her. "Reminds you about what?"

"The CBP was out here investigating the cattle carcasses and asking questions."

Ben's mouth tightened. "Hank says they found a woman's body on the ranch adjacent to the Flying K two weeks ago. She appeared to have been an undocumented alien."

Kate's stomach dropped. "Dead?"

He nodded.

"Wow. I really am in the middle of this, aren't I?" She sat up and waited for the dizziness to clear. "You said you got information off the DVD my father left?"

"We did." He pulled the flash drive from his pocket. "Where's your laptop?"

"It's in a satchel in my bedroom." She sat up and leaned forward, but before she could rise, Ben pressed a hand to her shoulder.

"I'll get it." Ben collected the laptop from her bedroom and returned to the living room where he booted up the system and plugged in the flash drive. "Have you had lunch?"

"No. Marge said she left a pie on the counter and to help yourself." She didn't glance his way, her eyes trained on the screen. When it came up with her father's image she drew in a sharp breath, her heart squeezing so tightly she was afraid it would stop. "That's him? That's my father?"

Chapter Fifteen

Ben entered the kitchen, the sound of the video barely reaching him. He figured he'd chosen the coward's way out by ducking into the kitchen while Kate reviewed her father's first and last words to her. Ben tried to block the words from his mind and Kate's reaction by keeping busy.

As he glanced around, he noted that the back door swung wide open on its hinges, the hot Texas wind blowing into the house. The countertop was empty, no pie there, only a few crumbs. Perhaps Kate had been mistaken. The pantry door also hung open. When Ben peered inside, he noted cans lying sideways on the shelves and strewn across the floor. Someone had been in a hurry to get in and get out of the kitchen. Another unauthorized entry. Since the front door most likely hadn't been locked when Kate left the house to look into the shed and barn, it wasn't a forced entry, but an entry nonetheless. The other break-ins had been just that. The doors had been locked. Whoever had come in hadn't broken a window. He'd used a key or jimmied the lock.

Could it have been the same person responsible for locking Kate in the shed? Ben had stopped by the hardware store and picked up all new doorknobs and keys for the house. He'd gotten enough copies to give Mrs. H. one and one for himself and Kate.

Maybe changing the locks in the house would keep Kate and Lily safer.

God, he hoped so.

Ben quickly made a sandwich out of bread, leftover slices of the ham Mrs. H. had cooked for breakfast and a dab of mustard. Ben didn't know if Kate liked mustard, but he added it anyway. There was a lot he didn't know about Kate.

If he was smart, he'd keep it that way. He couldn't afford to get attached.

His stomach roiled every time he thought of Kate locked in the hotbox of a shed. If he hadn't come when he had...

He wrapped the sandwich in a paper towel, grabbed a bag of chips and hurried back into the living room, bracing himself for the storm of emotions Kate might be experiencing and another chance to hold her in his arms.

Lily had crawled up on the couch with her mother and lay with her head in Kate's lap. The four-year-old's silky, light golden-red hair curled around her face, one hand tucked beneath her cheek. She was fast asleep, petal-pink lips parted.

Kate stared down at her daughter, smoothing her hand across her hair. Every so often, she'd brush a tear from her eye before it fell onto Lily.

Ben froze on the threshold of the room, holding the sandwich and bag of chips, his chest hurting so badly he held his breath to keep the pain from spreading.

Kate blinked and she looked up at him, her green eyes darker than the deepest forest. "My father was a drug runner."

"Yes, but he wised up and went to work for the good guys."

She looked up at him, tears welling in her eyes. "He didn't abandon us."

"No. He didn't. He sent you away to keep you safe."

A single fat tear slipped down her cheek.

Another blow to Ben's insides, tearing away at the wall

he'd constructed against ever falling in love with a woman or a child again.

"I wish..." Kate started, glanced down at her hand and then up at him. "I wish you'd give me that sandwich."

Ben almost laughed. She had been about to say something else, but settled for focusing on something she could control. A sandwich. A lousy ham-and-mustard sandwich.

Kate held out her hand.

Ben shook himself out of the trance and handed it to her. When their fingers touched, Kate flinched, her eyes widening. With her other hand, she twined hers around his, dragging him closer.

He leaned over her, his gaze capturing her green one.

When he was within kissing range, she stopped. "Thank you for being here for us." Then she kissed him, her hand circling behind his neck.

Barely aware of where they were, the child in Kate's lap and the near-death experience, Ben kissed her back, his lips caressing, his tongue sweeping across hers.

Lily stirred and sighed.

Ben broke it off, his lips thinning. "You don't have to kiss me to thank me. I'm just doing my job."

"Well, you're doing a darned good job, then." She tipped her chin up. "And I *wanted* to kiss you, not as payment for saving my life, although I do appreciate that you did. Thank you for helping me learn more about my father. I wish I'd had a chance to know him."

"Based on the video, he wished the same." Ben swallowed the hard knot forming in his throat. "Want me to carry her up the stairs?"

"Please." Kate brushed Lily's hair back from her forehead and pressed a kiss to her temple, then leaned back so that Ben could take Lily from her lap.

Ben lifted the child and headed up the stairs, still reeling from the kiss, more bothered by it than by having made love to her the night before.

The woman trusted him to keep her safe. What scared him most was that he didn't know who to keep her safe from.

Kate followed. "I'm going for a shower, unless you want to go first?"

"You go. I need to make a couple phone calls." He tucked Lily into bed and headed down the stairs, anxious to talk with Jenkins and Hank. When he heard the water come on in the shower, he lifted the phone from the receiver and punched the numbers for his buddy back in the Austin Police Department. A quick glance at the clock indicated the hour was late, but not too late to call Jenkins. He owed him.

"Hello."

Ben recognized the gravelly voice on the other end of the connection. "Harding here. What did you find?"

"Ben? Didn't you get my message?" The gravel left Jenkins's voice.

"No. Reception stinks out here. Give me what you have."

"Masters searched through Rolando Gonzalez's phone records. He's got a cousin he calls pretty often in your area. A José Mendez. I have an address they pulled up based on the phone number. Here."

Ben jotted the address on a notepad and ripped off the page, stuffing it in his pocket. "Any other reason Mendez could be considered a person of interest?"

"He happens to own a commercial driver's license. He drives the big trucks."

"Something big enough to transport people and drugs?"

"Yeah. Since he's in your neighborhood, I suggest you check him out. See what other connections he has."

"Will do." He'd notify Hank and let him track it down.

"Look, Jenkins, I need you to dig into anyone and everyone these guys may have had contact with."

"Hey, information flow goes both ways, you know. What do you know that I don't?"

"They are smuggling women and girls up from Mexico through here. We encountered a couple pickup truckloads last night."

"You called the Customs and Border Protection?"

"Yeah, by the time they got the choppers up, the trucks had disappeared. We need to find them before they are sold or killed."

"I'll get right on it." Jenkins paused. "Oh, and one other thing. That Robert Sanders you had me look up?"

"Yeah, what about him?"

"He was a friend of Frank Davis. Spent time up here in Austin going to social functions. The society pages have photos of them drinking together."

Ben's heart squeezed tight. "Thanks. I'll check into Sanders."

"And Harding," Jenkins began, then paused. "Be careful. The Mexican Mafia can be brutal on both sides of the border."

Ben hung up and glanced at the top of the stairs.

The door to Kate's room opened and she stepped out, wrapped in a soft pink robe, her hair up in a towel turban. Her brows dipped. "Who was on the phone?"

"I made a call to a friend of mine who has connections with the Austin Police Department."

"Why Austin?"

"I might be grasping at straws. But I hope to find something useful that will help me keep you safe and help those women."

"You'll tell me what you find, won't you?"

"You bet," Ben lied. "Want me to check your room?"

Kate stood at the doorway to her bedroom. "No. I can do it myself."

"I don't mind and I'd feel better knowing it's safe." Ben

climbed the stairs, brushed her aside and entered, check-ing beneath the bed, pulling back the covers and sheets and opening the closet. "All clear. No snakes."

She gave him a shaky smile and touched his arm as he passed her. "Thanks."

Ben had to get away before he was tempted to kiss her again. He really wanted to and that would solve nothing and complicate everything even more.

As he descended to the first floor, a shadow passed by the front window.

If he hadn't been looking that way at that exact moment, Ben would have missed it. He focused on the window next to it and the shadow appeared again.

Ben's pulse leaped. He turned out the light in the hallway, lifted his Glock from where he'd left it on top of a bookshelf and slipped out the back door, rounding the house from the opposite direction.

As he eased his way around the side, he ducked low, care-ful to tread lightly and stop to listen every few steps.

When he rounded the corner near the kitchen side of the house, he paused behind a rosebush and waited, his ears cocked toward the front of the house.

A twig snapped close by.

Ben held the Glock in front of him and peered around the bush.

A dark figure hovered in the shadows by the kitchen door. He wasn't very tall, but he was barrel-chested and stocky.

Ben inched forward to a better position. If the man tried to make a run for it, Ben could head him off.

When a shadowy hand reached for the doorknob, Ben stood, pointed the gun at the man's back and said, "Don't move if you want to live. I have a gun trained on you."

The man froze.

For a moment Ben thought he'd listened, then in a burst of movement, the shadow spun and ran.

Even as he shouted, "Stop, or I'll shoot," Ben gave chase, pounding the ground behind the darkly clothed man. He could have just fired off a round and probably hit the assailant, but Ben didn't want to kill the man. He wanted answers and this guy might have some.

The intruder headed for the barn, running hell-for-leather, but he was no match for Ben, who'd been running all his life and kept in good shape.

Before the stranger disappeared around the corner, Ben threw himself at the man's legs, catching enough of a pant leg to bring the man down.

They crashed into the hard-packed dirt.

Ben leaped to his feet, pushed a foot into the middle of the man's back and pointed the gun at his head. "Don't even think about moving." With his spare hand, Ben grabbed the man's arm and pulled it up behind his back. "Get up."

The guy stood. "Let me go, please. I didn't steal anything but food. I'll pay it back, I promise."

Ben pushed the man's arm up to the middle of his back. "To the house."

"I can't. If they see me, they'll kill me."

"Who will?"

"I can't say. I know too much." The man twisted. "If they know I'm here...if I'm caught...I'm as good as dead. Please, let me go."

Ben struggled to maintain his hold on the desperate man. "Slow down. No one's going to hurt you unless you try to get away from me." Ben lifted the arm higher and shoved the man toward the back door to the house. "In the house. Now."

"Ben?" The kitchen porch light blinked on and Kate stepped out, her bathrobe wrapped tightly around her body. "Ben?"

"I'm here." He eased the man forward.

Kate's mouth dropped open for a second, then she closed it and ran forward. "What can I do to help?"

"Take the gun and hold it on him."

Kate took the weapon from Ben and held it with both hands, pointing the barrel at the stranger's head. "Who is he?" she asked.

"I haven't gotten that far." Ben pushed the man forward. "Answer the lady."

"Larry," he said, his head down. "Larry Sites."

"The man who disappeared the day my father died?" She stopped, her eyes widening in the light from the porch. "Were you there when he died?"

"Yes, ma'am," the man answered softly.

Kate jumped in front of him, her mouth set in a tight line. "Was it really natural causes? Or did you kill him?"

Sites stood still, his gaze never wavering from Kate's. "He was murdered. But I didn't do it."

Kate gasped, her hands shaking, the gun tipping wildly. "Who did?"

"Can we take this into the house?" His head swiveled from right to left, his eyes wide, scared. "I'm a sitting duck out here."

"Kate, honey, get inside." Ben glanced around the barn-yard.

"You can let go of my arm. I'm not going to run. I'm tired of hiding." Sites sighed. "I might as well be dead."

Kate stepped up onto the porch and opened the kitchen door. "If you didn't do it, who killed my father?"

"I didn't have any beef with Kyle Kendrick. I just happened to be around when he was killed."

"Why didn't you tell anyone who did it?" Ben pushed him closer to the house.

"No one would have believed me, not when it was—" A loud pop sounded and Larry's body jerked so hard he pulled free of Ben's hold.

"Kate, get down!" Ben dropped to the ground.

Kate threw herself into the house.

After a long minute, Ben whispered loud enough to be heard in the house, "Kate? Are you okay?"

"I'm fine. What happened?"

Ben inched forward to where Larry Sites lay on the ground. His hand encountered warm sticky liquid and his chest tightened. "Someone shot Sites."

"Is he…"

Ben found the man's throat and felt for a pulse. Nothing. "He's dead." Ben crawled over the body and made a run for the door.

Kate stepped aside as he entered and slammed the door behind him. "What just happened?"

"Sites is dead. Someone shot him."

Kate pressed a hand to her chest. "I'll call the sheriff."

She hurried to where the phone sat on the table in the hallway. When she lifted the receiver, her hand shook so much she dropped it.

Ben caught the handset. "Let me." He held the device to his ear only to discover there was no dial tone. "It's not working."

Kate's brows furrowed. "It was working a few minutes ago."

"Either the phone system is down or someone cut your line."

She wrapped her arms around herself. "I don't like this. I should check on Lily."

"Do that, and get her ready to leave."

"Where are we going?" She gathered the edges of her robe closer, her body trembling.

Ben pulled her into his arms and pressed a kiss to her forehead. "I don't know, but we're not staying here. Now go. Stay away from the windows and don't turn on any lights. We don't know if the shooter is still out there." He turned and would have walked away, but Kate's hand on his arm stopped him.

"Where are you going?" she asked.

"To check outside and see what I can find."

Her fingers tightened on his arm. "Don't go."

"I'll be okay. Lock the door behind me and hold on to this." He reached up to the top of the shelf where he'd left her loaded Glock and handed it to her, checking that the safety was on. "You know how to use it. Point, click the safety off and shoot. Just make sure it's not me. I'll call out when I want back in. Otherwise leave all the doors locked. If you have to…leave them locked until morning when Mrs. H. arrives." He kissed her lips this time. He couldn't resist. She looked so vulnerable in her pale pink robe. "Relax. I'll be all right."

Her hand trembled as she cupped his jaw. "What if you don't come back?"

"I will." He kissed her again, this time his tongue pushing past her teeth to slide along hers. It was a lot harder this time to break away, but he did. He needed to know if the shooter was still out there. If he was and he planned to target Ben and Kate, they were pretty much trapped inside the house.

Kate followed him to the back door. When Ben slipped out, she closed the door behind him and locked it, her heartbeat pounding against her rib cage. "Please be okay," she whispered. Then she turned and hurried up the stairs to get ready for whatever happened next.

Fumbling around in the dark, her pulse racing, Kate dressed and grabbed a bag out of her closet. She shoved in a change of clothes for herself, her brush and toothbrush.

In Lily's room, she gathered an outfit, shoes and Lily's favorite doll, shoving them all into the bag and zipping it closed.

Pickles stood, stretched, then leaned up against the side of the box and whined.

Afraid he'd wake Lily, Kate lifted him from the box and cuddled him beneath her chin, inhaling the warm sweet scent of puppy and drawing comfort from the creature. "It's going to be okay. Ben will be back and we'll all be fine."

The minutes stretched by. Kate set the puppy in the box, looped the bag over her shoulder and carried it down the stairs, placing it by the front door. She returned to Lily's room and carried the box with Pickles down the steps. On her last trip, she carried Lily down and laid her on the love seat out of view of the windows. Her little girl barely stirred throughout the process.

Sounds of an engine drew Kate to the living room window. She peeked around the edges, careful not to provide too much of a silhouette should a shooter decide to fire at her.

Ben's truck pulled up right in front of the porch and stopped, the lights glaring out into the side yard. Ben dropped out of the driver's seat and rounded the front of the truck, leaping up onto the porch.

Kate was there, unlocking the door even as he knocked.

He burst through and closed the door behind him.

"Did you see anything?"

"Nothing. I found fresh motorcycle tracks, but whoever rode in on it was gone. Ready?"

Kate nodded. "What about Sites?"

"There's nothing we can do for him but report the murder. We have to get you somewhere safe first. Then we can notify the police."

Ben lifted Lily from the love seat and cradled her in his arms.

Kate slung the bag and her purse over her shoulder and hefted the box with the puppy.

Ben's brows dipped. "You have all that?"

She smiled. "I'm a mother."

"Okay, straight out. I'm right behind you."

Kate sucked in a deep breath and let it out. It did nothing to calm her nerves, but she stepped out onto the porch and down to the pickup, sliding the box onto one side of the backseat floorboard. She tossed the overnight bag onto the other side and climbed into the passenger seat, sitting low.

Ben came out half a minute later, carrying Lily. He settled her into her booster seat, tightened her straps and fumbled with the box containing the puppy. Finally, Ben climbed into the driver's side and shifted into Drive.

Before he'd gone ten feet down the driveway, headlights flashed on directly in front of them and the red and blue of a law enforcement vehicle whirled like circus lights.

Ben had to stop or risk running into the vehicle.

"It's the sheriff." Kate reached for her door handle. "We can tell him about Sites and the shooter."

Ben grabbed her arm. "Stay put and don't say anything."

"Why?"

"Trust me."

"Please step out of the vehicle," Sheriff Fulmer called out, service weapon drawn. He approached the driver's side of the truck while Deputy Schillinger came up on Kate's side.

"Sheriff, what's this about?"

"We had a report of gunshots fired. Please step out of the vehicle and keep your hands where I can see them."

Ben got out slowly, his hands held high. "Your report was correct. Someone shot Larry Sites. His body is lying on the ground outside the kitchen door."

To Ben, his gaze narrowed. "Cool your heels, cowboy."

The sheriff nodded toward Ben, his gun trained on Ben's chest. "Up against the truck and spread your legs."

Kate could barely breathe as she slid down out of the truck. "You're worrying about the wrong man. Whoever shot Sites might still be out there."

Schillinger jerked his gun toward Ben. "Look out, sheriff, he's got a gun."

Kate stepped in front of the deputy's weapon. "He's licensed to carry one."

"But he's not licensed to kill." The sheriff nodded to the deputy. "Check it out."

Sheriff Fulmer removed the Glock from Ben's waistband and tucked it into his belt. While the deputy rounded the house to the kitchen, the sheriff patted Ben down, running his hands up Ben's legs and into his pockets, emptying them of their contents. He opened Ben's wallet and checked the driver's license. "Says he's Ben Harding from Austin." Fulmer tossed the wallet onto the hood of the truck and continued his search. When he delved into Ben's front pocket, he pulled out a small silver flash drive and held it up to the light. His hand closed around the tiny device and he slid it into his pocket.

Kate leaned forward. "Hey, that's not yours."

"And you're wrong." The sheriff continued to search Ben's other pocket. "It's evidence."

"It's mine," Kate said. "You have no right to take it."

"It's on a man who might have committed a murder."

"He didn't!"

"Leave it, Kate," Ben warned her. "We'll get it back when we clear up this mess."

Two minutes later, Deputy Schillinger returned. "It's Sites, all right, and he's dead as a doornail. Gunshot wound."

Kate bit down on her lip, wanting to say more, to stop what was happening to Ben and get back the data storage device her father had placed in her possession.

Sheriff Fulmer grabbed Ben's wrist and pulled it behind him, then the other and zip-tied them together at the base of his spine.

"Am I being arrested?" Ben stood tall. "I know my rights."

"You're being arrested on suspicion of a homicide. You have the right to remain silent and I suggest you do and get into the car." Fulmer shoved Ben toward the sheriff's vehicle.

"Sites tried to break in and when I stopped him, someone shot him."

Kate stepped forward. "Ben didn't kill Sites. Someone else did."

Schillinger waved his gun in her face. "Don't get in the way or you'll be going with him. In which case, we'd have to place your little girl in the care of child welfare services."

As the sheriff pushed Ben into the car, Ben called over his shoulder, "Kate, get Lily to somewhere safe."

Kate's shoulders sagged, her eyes filling with tears. The only person she'd felt safe with was being hauled off in a police car. "Where?"

"Ma'am." Deputy Schillinger stepped between Kate and Ben. "I suggest you climb into the truck and drive into town in front of us. You can't stay here, since this is now officially a crime scene."

"But Ben didn't do it," Kate insisted.

The sheriff stopped in front of her. "Are you admitting to the crimes?"

"No, of course not." Kate's head spun, her vision clouding. What the hell was going on? Had the entire world turned upside down?

"Kate," Ben called out. "Go to town. Get help, call a lawyer, just don't argue with them."

"For a murderer, he gives good advice." Schillinger gripped her elbow, dragged her around the truck and shoved her up into the driver's seat. "Drive."

With no other choice and Lily to consider, Kate did what she was told and drove into town, the rotating lights from the sheriff's vehicle filling her rearview mirror.

She held on to her sanity, her resolve strengthening as she reached the city limits. First stop for her was Cara Jo's Diner where she hoped Cara Jo was home above the restaurant and had a phone she could use. She had to get in touch with Hank.

Chapter Sixteen

Ben leaned over the backseat, his gaze on the taillights of his truck as Kate turned left into the diner parking lot. Good, she was going to her only friend in town, Cara Jo, where she could use a phone and contact Hank with the number he'd given her earlier. Hank would help clear up this mess and send reinforcements to protect her and Lily.

Ben could kick himself for not getting Kate to safety faster. He swiveled in his seat as the sheriff's SUV passed the diner and continued on to the sheriff's office. "If you'll look at the gun, you'll note that it hasn't been discharged."

Sheriff Fulmer ignored him, pulling to the side of the road a block away from the diner. "Schillinger, you're to stay here and keep an eye on Ms. Langsdon."

"Why?" Schillinger asked. "I thought we had our killer."

Fulmer glared at him and said in a deadly tone, "Get out."

Schillinger muttered beneath his breath as he climbed out of the SUV.

The sheriff shot down the road, sliding into the parking lot at the sheriff's station. He got out and left Ben in the backseat as he unlocked the door to the office. Apparently the offices were only open during the day.

Ben waited for the sheriff to come back and lead him into a jail cell.

Fulmer didn't even glance back at the SUV as he entered the office and closed the door behind him.

After a few minutes, Ben frowned, working the zip tie around his wrists, trying to free his hands. Unfortunately, the sheriff had cinched it good and most likely the back doors of the SUV were locked from the driver's control panel. Even if he got the zip tie off his wrists, he'd have to break the window or cage separating the passenger from the driver. Why would the sheriff leave a murder suspect sitting in the back of a vehicle?

A moment later the sheriff stormed out of the office, flinging the door so hard it cracked against the wall. "Where is it?" he yelled, his face red, his eyes round, angry and maniacal. Fulmer yanked open the back door of the SUV, grabbed Ben by the front of his shirt, hauled him out and slammed him against the vehicle. "Where the hell is it?"

"I don't know what you're talking about."

"The database. The information Kendrick left to his daughter. Where is it? And don't tell me you don't know. You spoke to Derringer on the telephone and said you had a flash drive." He shook Ben and flung him against the SUV again.

Without his hands to balance, Ben tripped and fell to the ground.

Fulmer kicked him in the side. "Tell me!"

Pain shot through his side where the sheriff's boot crashed into his ribs. When the sheriff pulled his leg back to deliver another kick, Ben rolled to the side to avoid it. "Why? What's on it that you'd accuse me of a murder I didn't commit?"

"I need that damned data. My wife's life depends on it." Fulmer reached down and dragged Ben to his feet. "Please, tell me. Tell me where it is."

Ben shook his head. "I don't have it."

"Sheriff," a voice called out. "Sheriff!" Deputy Schillinger ran toward them, sweating, red-faced and breathing erratically.

"I thought I told you to watch the girl."

"She went into the diner...with the kid." Schillinger dragged in a deep breath. "Then she left the diner." The deputy doubled over, wheezing. "I couldn't...follow her... without a vehicle."

"Damn! Which way did she go?"

"West on Main."

The sheriff held Ben by the collar of his shirt. "If she has it, I'll get it. If she doesn't, you'll get it for me before you get your precious fiancée back." He slung Ben away from the SUV. "Don't let him out of your sight."

Fulmer climbed into his vehicle and spun the vehicle around, burning a trail of rubber against the pavement.

His heart racing, Ben's gaze followed the sheriff. "What did he mean, his wife's life depends on that data?" Ben asked the deputy.

"I shouldn't be saying this, but the best I can tell, the drug cartel kidnapped her when she went down to visit her family in Monterrey, Mexico." Deputy Schillinger hooked his hand through Ben's elbow and started toward the sheriff's office.

Ben dug his heels into the pavement. "Why didn't he call for help?"

"They threatened to kill her if he told anyone." The deputy tugged on his arm. "Come on. I've got a cell with your name on it." He led him toward the building.

Ben went along with him, every escape scenario he could imagine racing through his head.

When Schillinger dropped his hold on Ben's elbow and reached for the doorknob, Ben stepped back. "I'm sorry, but I can't go with you." Ben ducked his head and rammed into the deputy's back, sending him flying headfirst into the metal door.

He hit with a sickening thud and crumpled to the ground.

With no time to spare, Ben ran back toward the diner, his wrists still bound together.

When he reached the restaurant, he raced around back and kicked the door until Cara Jo peeked out the window, then threw open the door and came out on the landing above him. "Ben? Oh, thank God." Wearing a robe and flip-flops, she rushed down the stairs.

Ben's heart squeezed in his chest and his rib ached where the sheriff had kicked him. "Where's Kate?"

"She brought Lily and the puppy inside, then went back out for her overnight bag. Next thing I know she's driving off without telling me where she went."

Cara Jo pressed her hands to her cheeks. "From what I could see, there was a man in the passenger seat."

"Who was it?"

"I don't know. All I saw was his silhouette as the truck sped out of the parking lot. I called 911 and the dispatcher said she'd get word to the sheriff."

Ben gripped Cara Jo's hand. "Where's Lily?"

"She and Pickles are sleeping in my bed upstairs."

"I need a phone."

"Come up and use mine."

Ben pushed ahead of Cara Jo and raced up the stairs. The living quarters above the diner were small but decorated tastefully. "Where?"

"By the kitchen counter." Cara Jo pointed to the telephone. "You're not going to be able to do much with your hands tied behind your back." The diner owner pulled a butcher knife out of a drawer and sliced through the zip tie.

Ben rubbed his raw wrists for a second to get the feeling back into his fingertips, then dialed Hank.

The man answered on the first ring. "Derringer speaking."

"It's Ben. I need help, ASAP. Someone has Kate and I don't know who it is or where they're going."

"Slow down and tell me what happened."

Ben gave his boss the abbreviated version of what he'd

learned that day. "Someone wants that data file and they're willing to kill to get it."

"Does Kate have it?"

"No."

"They'll use her as leverage to get you to give it to them."

"I figured that." Ben leaned his head against the wall. "The sheriff was with me when someone else took Kate. Larry Sites is dead and I have no idea where to start looking for Kate."

"Ben, hold on." Sounds of keyboard clicks echoed across the phone, then Hank was back. "I had a tracking device placed on your truck. If she's in it, we can find her. I have my IT guy pulling it up as we speak."

"Thank God." Ben sagged against the counter. "Hey, this might be small, but my guy in Austin said Robert Sanders was photographed at a fund-raising event in Austin with Frank Davis."

"The man you killed?"

Ben winced. "Yeah. Did you find anything else about Sanders? He approached Kate the other day, claiming to be a friend of her father's, which doesn't make sense since most people around here claim Kate's father kept to himself. He didn't have friends, just acquaintances."

"From what I'd known of Kyle Kendrick, he didn't talk much to anyone and was always on the road, traveling from here to Mexico and back."

"You think Sanders could be the U.S. link between Mexico and the human trafficking?"

"Could be. Be careful. If he is, he has a lot to lose and he'd gladly take down anyone who gets in the way of his enterprise." Keyboard clicks sounded on Hank's side. "My IT guy says the truck's headed out County Road 949. From what we can see on the satellite map, there's not much out there but a diesel mechanic shop and some storage buildings."

Ben's hand froze on the receiver. "Would the address of the mechanic's shop be 1421 Highway 949 West?"

"Looks like it. Why?"

"My Austin contact said the man who supplied Frank the woman he killed had a cousin who lives at that address."

"Ben, I'm calling in the Border Protection and Texas Rangers. Don't try to go in there without backup. You could be stirring up a rattlesnake's den."

"Hank, they have Kate. She was my responsibility."

"Ben!" Hank shouted.

Ben hung up and sprinted for the door.

Cara Jo stood there dangling a set of keys. "You can't get there without a vehicle. Take my Mustang and bring Kate back safe."

"Lily?"

"I'll take good care of her."

"Do you have a gun?"

"I do and I know how to use it." She lifted a 9 mm Beretta from a shelf in an antique cabinet. "Girl can't be too careful when she lives alone."

"Don't let anyone in. Not anyone until I get back here with Kate. As a matter of fact, hit Redial and get Hank to send someone out to stand guard."

"Will do." She shoved him out the door. "Now go. I want my new friend back. Alive. Oh, and there's another one of these—" she waved her gun "—under the driver's seat and it's loaded."

Ben ran to the bottom of the stairs and leaped into a vintage 1967 Mustang. Seconds later he'd skidded out on Main Street and turned onto County Road 949 headed west, having flashbacks of when he'd gotten home too late to save Julia and Sarah. History could not repeat itself. He wouldn't let it.

His hands tightened around the steering wheel and he

jammed the accelerator to the floor. The car was old, but it packed a lot of power. He hoped it was enough to get him there in time.

"YOU NEVER WERE my father's friend, were you?" Kate stared straight ahead, her hands clutching the steering wheel, thankful she'd unloaded Lily and the puppy first before she'd come back down to the truck for her overnight bag. At least they were safe from this latest threat. She risked a quick glance at the man beside her.

Robert Sanders sat in the passenger seat with a pistol pointed at her side. "We were business partners. He helped me find the drugs in Mexico and I sold them."

Kate's heart sank into her gut. The fact the man was admitting all this to her was a sure sign he planned to kill her when all was said and done.

Tears threatened, but Kate wouldn't let them fall. She didn't plan on dying today. Lily needed a parent to raise her. She'd already lost one. Kate would be damned if she lost another.

"I'll ask you again. Where is the flash drive your father left you?"

"I told you. The sheriff took it from Ben when he arrested him for murder."

"Then you'd better hope the sheriff doesn't decrypt the data before your fiancé gets it back."

"I suppose the information on that thumb drive implicates you in the human and drug trafficking going on around here."

"Amongst others who'd rather not be named."

"What are you going to do with me?"

Before they got too far out of town, Sanders punched buttons on his cell phone one-handed and hit Send. "I have Kendrick's daughter and I know you have the thumb drive. If you don't want your wife to die, you'll meet me at the shop, immediately." Sanders paused. "Ten minutes. Be there or I make the call."

Kate shot a glance at Sanders. "I'm not Ben's wife."

"I wasn't talking to Ben." He slipped his cell phone into his shirt pocket and steadied the gun on Kate. "Faster."

Kate eased her foot onto the accelerator. Sanders had called her on her ploy to slow down enough for someone to catch up. The farther away from town, the less likely Ben would find her.

Although how he'd get free from jail, she didn't have a clue. She hadn't even had a chance to call Hank and let him know what was going on. When Cara Jo discovered her missing, she'd call the police. A lot of good that would do.

After what felt like a very long time, Sanders leaned forward. "Turn left at the next driveway."

Kate slowed as the headlights from Ben's pickup reflected off several large metal buildings and an old barn.

"Stop."

Kate slammed her foot on the brakes.

Sanders shot forward, hitting his head on the dash. "Damn you, woman. You should have left when Snake warned you."

"My father left me that ranch. I wasn't going anywhere." Kate shifted into Park.

"You're going to wish you had." Sanders grabbed her by the hair and dragged her out of the truck through the passenger side, tossing her to the ground. "Get up. And don't try anything. I'd just as soon kill you as look at you. You Kendricks have been nothing but a thorn in my side."

He kicked her in the ribs.

Pain radiated through her rib cage as Kate staggered to her feet, reluctant to stay down where the man could kick her again.

A man with a bandanna and a tattoo on his arm stepped out of the shadows. *"Buenas noches, Patrón."*

"Did Sites spill the truth before you shot him?"

"No, amigo."

"I asked you to take care of him weeks ago."

"He was a slippery one."

"Where are the other men?"

"Moving the first shipment. They will be gone all night."

Sanders pushed Kate toward the man. "Put her with the others."

"Con las putas?"

"Sí. Do as I said."

The man with the snake tattoo grabbed Kate's arm and hustled her toward the derelict barn.

Before they'd gone two yards, headlights swung into the driveway.

Guillermo stopped and stared back toward the road.

Kate tried to wiggle out of his grip, but his fingers tightened on her arm.

Sanders held his pistol out and waved it. "Get out of the car, Sheriff."

The sheriff remained inside.

Sanders shot out a headlight and held up his cell phone. "I'm dialing now. Your wife is as good as dead."

Fulmer climbed out of the SUV with his hands raised. "Don't. Delia is all I have. Don't hurt her."

"If you didn't want me to hurt her, why were you snooping around the Flying K?" Sanders asked.

"I'd heard Kendrick had a flash drive full of the names of the people he'd been working with on both sides of the border."

"Heard? As in, bugged the phone?"

The sheriff shrugged. "I figured Kendrick's daughter might have learned something from her father."

"Her father is dead and we'd been all over the house and found nothing. Even in his computer."

"It didn't hurt to be aware, so I bugged the phone." The sheriff took a step closer. "When I heard Harding talking about a flash drive, I knew you wouldn't want it to get into the wrong hands."

"Wrong like yours?" Sanders held out his hand. "Give it to me."

The sheriff pulled out his pockets. "I don't have it."

"Kate here tells me you picked it off her fiancé."

"I confiscated a flash drive but it wasn't the right one. It didn't contain the data, only a video message from Kendrick to his daughter telling her of the drive and where to find it."

"You lie!" Sanders shot at Fulmer's feet.

Kate flinched.

The tattooed man seemed as reluctant as Kate to leave the little scene unfolding.

"I wouldn't risk my wife's life over a data device. I want her back. Alive."

Sanders shook his head. "You're a stupid fool. Your wife doesn't *want* to come back."

Fulmer's face blanched. "What do you mean?"

"She left you and returned to her family."

"She went back for vacation. Someone kidnapped her. Her parents were beside themselves when they told me."

"They told you what she wanted them to tell you. She's been working for me on the other side of the border making good money sending me the goods."

"No." Sheriff Fulmer backed away a step. "She wouldn't do that to me. Delia loves me."

"She loves money more." Sanders's lips twitched. "And the beauty of it is, you've been working for me to keep her safe. Ironic, don't you think?"

"You bastard!" Sheriff Fulmer lunged at Sanders.

A shot rang out as Fulmer reached Sanders.

The two men staggered, the sheriff falling to the ground, a hand clutched to his chest.

Kate dived for the man, but came up short when her captor jerked her backward.

Blood dribbled from the side of the sheriff's mouth and he stared up at the night sky. "I loved her...."

Kate choked back a sob. The man had to have loved his wife very much to have risked his career and his life to save her.

Her thoughts turned to Ben. If something were to happen to her, he'd blame himself for failing to reach her in time. She refused to be the next victim on his watch. Ben deserved a chance to love again. He was a good man and he'd be a good husband and father again, if only he could believe in himself.

"Guillermo!" Sanders jerked his head toward the barn. "Get her inside and burn the building."

As the tattooed man dragged her away, Kate prayed she'd live long enough to tell Ben...

Tell him what?

That she loved him? After knowing him such a short time? Could it be love? Her father said he'd fallen in love with her mother the moment he met her. Could it have been the same for her?

Love or not, she wanted the chance to get to know Ben better, to see if what she felt for him was love. She'd never thought she'd love another after losing Troy. But Ben...he could be her second chance. Her heart was big enough to love again.

Guillermo unlocked a padlock securing a heavy chain to the door of the barn and pulled the chain through the handles. Before he could shove her in, she backed up sharply and jerked out of his grip, then plowed into his side, sending him sailing through the open doorway. Several female, frightened cries erupted from within.

"Mierda!" the big man shouted.

Before Guillermo could regain his balance, Kate ran for the shadows.

A shot rang out, spitting dust up beside her, but she made

it to where the moonlight cast a deep shadow next to the big old barn.

"Get her!" Sanders shouted.

Footsteps pounded on the gravel behind her.

Her pulse banging against her eardrums, Kate ran as fast as she could, tripping over objects hidden in the dark. When she cleared the back of the building, a wide-open field loomed in front of her, illuminated by the moon.

If she stepped away from the barn, she'd be found. If she stayed where she was, she'd be caught.

The whirring of a helicopter sounded in the distance and a long beam of light moved toward the barn and building complex.

It had to be the cavalry. Kate dropped to her knees and choked back a sob. Ben must have escaped.

An arm circled her neck and yanked her up.

Kate cried out, struggling to get her feet beneath her.

Headlights blasted into the compound and sirens blared in the distance.

Guillermo hauled Kate out into the open and shoved her toward his boss. He flipped a switchblade out, the smooth metal glinting in the beams of the car's headlights.

Sanders grabbed her hair and jammed the gun into her cheek. "Move and I kill her."

"Don't hurt her." Ben's voice washed over Kate like a cool balm in a blazing desert. He climbed out of an older model Mustang, carrying a gun aimed at Sanders. "I have what you're looking for."

He was there. Ben had come, against all odds.

"You give me Kate. I'll give you the device." Ben reached into his pocket with his left hand.

"Why don't I just shoot you and get the device myself?"

"You could do that, but then you might not have time to find it and destroy it before that helicopter arrives, and what would your friends on both sides of the border do to someone who let that kind of information get out?" Ben tipped his head toward the sky. "You only have a few seconds."

"Put your gun down," Sanders demanded.

Ben didn't budge.

"Do it—" Sanders shoved Kate in front of him "—or I put a bullet through her pretty head."

BEN SUCKED IN a breath and let it out slowly, praying for the right move, the right decision, the one that ended with Kate going home to Lily and raising her daughter in peace.

"Don't, Ben." Kate's voice shook. "He's going to kill me anyway. And you, too."

"Shut up." Sanders jerked her hair back hard.

Kate whimpered but didn't cry. "No," she said. "You shut up." In a flurry of movement, Kate slammed her elbow into Sanders's gut and dived for the dirt.

A shot rang at the same time Ben fired, clipping Sanders in the shoulder.

Sanders staggered backward into Guillermo, knocking the other man to the ground. When Sanders rolled over and staggered to his feet, clutching at his belly, Ben was there, his gun drawn, ready to kill the man.

Overhead, the helicopter moved into position, a spotlight filling the yard with blinding light.

Ben held his gun steady. He bent to touch Kate's shoulder. Her face was down in the dirt, but he felt for a pulse. After a second or two a strong, rhythmic thump beat against his fingers and he let the air he'd been holding out of his lungs.

Cars with rotating blue and red lights and sirens screaming whipped into the yard.

Kate stirred, then sat up with a jerk. "Ben!"

"I'm here."

"Oh, thank God." She threw herself into his arms and hugged him so tight she almost knocked him over. "I thought he'd kill you."

As the Texas Department of Public Safety swooped in with guns drawn, Ben lowered his weapon and gathered Kate in his arms, his hands weaving through her hair. He inhaled the scent of her shampoo, a huge weight lifting from his shoulders. "I wasn't too late."

She laughed and captured his face between her palms. "No, you weren't. And you saved more than me." She grabbed his hand and dragged him toward the barn.

The lawmen stepped in front of her, blocking her way.

Hank Derringer appeared beside the lawmen. "It's okay, they're the good guys." He swept past the men in uniform and stuck out his hand to Kate. "I apologize for not coming sooner. I'm Hank Derringer. And you're Kate. You have your father's eyes."

"I know." Kate smiled. "Your timing was good. And thanks for assigning this cowboy. I wouldn't be here shaking your hand without him."

"I knew he was the right man for the job." The older man winked at Ben. "Convincing him was the hard part."

"I'm convinced and glad you put me up to it." Ben touched a finger to Kate's cheek.

"You're not done yet." Kate took his hand and resumed her march toward the barn. "There are people in that barn."

As the words left her mouth, women and young girls peeked around the edge of the open doorway with dirt-streaked faces.

"We found them." Kate smiled up at Ben. "You're a hero. You saved these people."

"No, you did. I just came as backup." He hugged her to him and swung her off the ground. When he set her on her feet, he took her hand in his. "Let's go home."

Kate's smile faded. "I'd love to, but now that the bad guys are caught, you don't have to stay."

"The hell I don't." He slipped an arm around her and

walked toward the Mustang. "I know a little girl who'd miss me, even if her mother won't."

She batted his arm with a light pat. "You're growing on me, cowboy. Given time…who knows…a woman could fall in love with a man like you."

He stopped and turned to face her, cupping her cheeks in his palms. "That's what I'm counting on." Then he kissed her.

Epilogue

Kate sat with Ben on the porch swing, Lily between them, holding a very wiggly Pickles. The sun was setting on the horizon after a hard day's work on the ranch.

"Eddy and I got all the cattle rounded up and accounted for," Ben said, his hand twirling through a strand of Kate's hair.

Kate relaxed for the first time in a long time, content with her life and the direction it was going. "Think we'll have any more trouble with traffickers on the Flying K?"

"With the information Hank pulled off the flash drive, the Border Protection officers rounded up the gang of coyotes on this side of the border and the Mexican authorities claim they did the same on their side. I reckon they won't be hauling people across your spread anymore. You'll be happy to know that the women and girls found in the barn have been returned to their homes."

Pickles leaped from Lily's lap and scrambled across the porch.

Lily squealed and shot after him.

Ben scooted closer, pulling Kate into his arms.

Kate snuggled against him, pulling one foot up beneath her. "Did my father list the name of the kingpin on the U.S. side of the border?"

Ben shook his head. "No. But he left notes that he'd been working on. Hank will follow up on those. He's keeping the information close to his chest because your father mentioned a leak in our government."

Kate sighed. "At least they cleaned up around here, for now."

"You and Lily should be okay here on the Flying K."

Kate sat up straight and gave Ben a crooked smile. "That reminds me. I had some good news today."

"Did you stop by county records?"

"Yes, I did. The taxes were all paid up. The sheriff was just trying to scare me off the land so that Sanders's trafficking operation would go undiscovered and unimpeded. That's good news, but not *the* news."

Ben turned to her, his eyes narrowing. "What is it, then?"

"My father's attorney called. Seems the package I received in Houston wasn't all that my father left me. The attorney's been busy collecting all my father's bank information and sent me a detailed listing of the money my father had put away."

"Drug money?" Ben asked.

"That was my first thought. I wouldn't want any of that, not when people die every day in that business." Kate leaned into Ben, resting her head on his shoulder. "He received a salary from the FBI for his work with them and he set it all aside. Not to mention the FBI also carried a life insurance policy on him and I was named the beneficiary."

"Enough to get the ranch up and running?"

"More than enough." Kate tipped her toe on the porch, setting the swing in motion. "If I manage it well, Lily and I won't have to worry about money ever again."

Ben hugged her to him. "I know you were worried. I'm glad it's working out for you. You and Lily deserve to be happy."

She backed away enough to stare up into his eyes. "The point is…I can afford to hire ranch hands. You can continue working for Hank if you like."

Ben frowned. "Trying to get rid of me?"

"No, but I know deep down you're a cop and fighting for justice is what you do best. If working for Hank is what you want, then Lily and I will be here for you when you're not out on assignment."

Ben shook his head. "You're amazing. I think you know me better than I know myself."

She shrugged. "You're a good man, Ben Harding."

He leaned back and drew her against him. "And to think I didn't want this job in the first place."

Kate smiled up at him. "So what's keeping you?" She pressed a kiss to his lips.

"That, for one." Ben captured her face in his hands and deepened the kiss. "I never thought I could love another woman as much as my first wife." He paused, looking down at her. "I was right."

Her heart squeezing tightly, Kate's smile drifted downward. "What do you mean? You don't like us?"

"On the contrary. I love you more than I could imagine ever loving any woman." He brushed a kiss to the tip of her nose. "You're brave."

"Not where snakes are concerned," she argued.

"You're resourceful." He kissed her right cheek.

"A girl has to be, to get by these days." Kate's blood thickened, spreading warmth slowly across her body.

"And you make a great mother to Lily." He kissed her left cheek.

Kate laughed, her chest swelling with emotion. "What's not to love about Lily?" She clasped his cheeks between her palms. "Get to the point, cowboy."

"I think I'm going to love you for a very long time...if you'll let me."

"I'm counting on it, cowboy." Kate sealed her promise with a kiss.

* * * * *

Even through the thin shirt he could feel the heat of her skin, and his fingers tightened.

His temperature spiked as his gaze lingered on her. He justified the need rumbling through him by thinking about the adrenaline aftermath. Never mind that he'd never had the desire to kiss anyone else but her after a work takedown. Seeing those big eyes and soul-stealing face, he felt his common sense go on the fritz.

It had always been this way between them. Hot and pulsing, both desperate to get the other into bed. They could communicate between the sheets. Real life was the problem.

FEARLESS

BY
HELENKAY DIMON

® and ™ are trademarks owned and used by the trademark owner and/or its licensee. Trademarks marked with ® are registered with the United Kingdom Patent Office and/or the Office for Harmonisation in the Internal Market and in other countries.

First published in Great Britain 2011
by Mills & Boon, an imprint of Harlequin (UK) Limited,
Eton House, 18-24 Paradise Road, Richmond, Surrey TW9 1SR

© HelenKay Dimon 2010

MILLS & BOON

First published in Great Britain 2013
by Mills & Boon, an imprint of Harlequin (UK) Limited,
Eton House, 18-24 Paradise Road, Richmond, Surrey TW9 1SR

© HelenKay Dimon 2013

ISBN: 978 0 263 90366 9
ebook ISBN: 978 1 472 00732 2

46-0713

Harlequin (UK) policy is to use papers that are natural, renewable and recyclable products and made from wood grown in sustainable forests. The logging and manufacturing processes conform to the legal environmental regulations of the country of origin.

Printed and bound in Spain
by Blackprint CPI, Barcelona

Award-winning author **HelenKay Dimon** spent twelve years in the most unromantic career ever—divorce lawyer. After dedicating all that effort to helping people terminate relationships, she is thrilled to deal in happy endings and write romance novels for a living. Now her days are filled with gardening, writing, reading and spending time with her family in and around San Diego. HelenKay loves hearing from readers, so stop by her website, www.helenkaydimon.com, and say hello.

This one is dedicated to all the readers
who requested another miniseries.
I hope you enjoy the Corcoran Team!

Chapter One

Lara Bart picked up her ice water and used her palm to wipe away the puddle left behind on the coffee table. Drops slid down the side of the glass, making her hand slip. She fought the urge to dump the contents down her shirt or at least close the dull brown curtains outlining the window to the right of her chair. The sun pounded on her, filling the twelve-foot-square room with bright light and an almost unbearable heat.

It was summer in Washington, D.C. Between the soaring temperatures and bone-melting humidity she'd already lost the battle with frizz. She could feel her hair morphing from wavy to wide as she sat in the non–air-conditioned, seemingly airtight Capitol Hill brownstone belonging to Lieutenant Commander Steve Wasserman. She had to interview the man as part of a security-clearance check for Martin Coughlin, a retired navy lieutenant looking to obtain a new position with the Naval Criminal Investigative Service.

Steve and Martin had been roommates at the Naval Academy years ago, which was why she sat in the rolling heat with the backs of her thighs stuck to the leather chair and the sweat soaking through her silk blouse and seeping into her navy blazer. She had to talk with people from Martin's past and those familiar with his current life.

And because her luck was at an all-time low, this assignment qualified as a rush. Her boss at Hampton Enterprises, the private firm contracted with the Department of Defense to conduct clearance interviews, said to make this one a priority. Apparently, someone at NCIS wanted Martin hired on there and fast. That meant long hours of searching through records and asking questions, followed by a ton of paperwork.

Not that anyone cared how inconvenient a work rush was for her on top of her regular clearance caseload. That much was evident from the fact Steve had disappeared into his kitchen ten minutes ago and hadn't said a word or bothered to come out since. A wall blocked her view, but she didn't even hear him clanging around in there as expected. He'd got a message on his cell and excused himself, and she'd been stuck in the makeshift sauna alone ever since.

So much for the idea of beating the Thursday afternoon rush-hour traffic back to her condo in Alexandria, Virginia. She'd likely sit on the 14th Street Bridge forever. Good thing she'd grabbed that granola bar before she headed out earlier today.

A loud scrape that sounded like someone dragging a chair across tile broke through her internal grumbling. She waited for another sound, for anything, but the narrow brownstone remained quiet except for the loud tick of the antique clock above the fireplace as the minutes slowly passed. Because she hated having her time wasted, she stood up, ignoring the ripping sound of her skin against the chair and the sharp sting. Despite her host's lack of social skills, this time she put her glass down on a magazine. No need to take her frustration out on his furniture.

Her shoes fell silent on the beige carpet. In two steps she was at the kitchen doorway. Her gaze went to the open back door and the small patio beyond. It took her a second longer to notice the brown shoes and khakis sticking out from behind the butcher-block island.

Guy on the floor. Her mind rushed to fill in the blanks. At fortysomething and in good shape, Steve seemed young for a heart attack. That probably meant he'd somehow fallen without making a sound.

And here she had been sitting in the other room complaining. Tiny pricks of guilt stabbed her as she switched to rescue mode. She grabbed the cell in her blazer pocket as she turned the corner and slipped farther into the kitchen, intending to perform CPR as she called for help. Her fingers fumbled on the buttons so she stopped her rush and looked down, trying to concentrate on dialing something as simple as 9-1-1.

"Who are you?"

The male voice had her head jerking up again. Her gaze bounced to her far right. There in the corner near the sink and tucked behind the oversize refrigerator stood a man. He had brown hair and a furious glare, but the real problem was the knife in his hand.

Her gaze bounced back to Steve's still form. For the first time she noticed the circle of dark red pooling beneath his body and spreading across the once off-white tiles.

"I didn't..." She cupped the phone in her palm and slipped it back in her jacket as she tried to maneuver back out of the room. "I'll just go."

Before she could turn and run, the man pounced. Just as the scream left her lungs, he grabbed from behind and around her middle, choking off all sound. The move trapped her arms to her sides and squeezed the air out of her lungs. She coughed as her gaze darted around the room for some way out of this strange nightmare.

She opened her mouth again and his beefy palm settled over her mouth. "Oh, no, princess. Not one word."

She strained and shoved her shoulders against his hold. Her neck ached from stretching and the activity exhausted her, but he didn't even move. His hand muffled her screams and her lungs burned from the effort. When she finally collapsed against him, she stiffened and moved away from him again just as fast.

Fear threatened to swamp her. She heard a roaring in her ears and her heart thumped so hard she was surprised she couldn't see it through her shirt.

"You picked the wrong day to visit your boyfriend." The attacker's hot breath blew across her cheek as he spoke.

His sick laugh rumbled through her senses and dark spots swam in front of her eyes. To keep from passing out, because that had to be the worst idea ever in this type of situation, she forced her breathing to slow. One more beat at the current speed and she'd be doubled over hyperventilating.

As she struggled to regain control of her body, words raced through her mind, blurred and garbled. She closed her eyes for a second, trying to concentrate and bring them into focus.

Stay calm. Remember what I taught you.

Like that, anxiety stopped pinging around inside of her. Her ex wasn't in the room but she could hear his voice inside her head. He was an expert at self-defense and at breaking a woman's heart. Only the former mattered right now. A brief mental review of the skills he'd taught her stopped the room from spinning.

In a span of seconds her brain rebooted. She let her body go completely limp as she gathered her energy reserves for a big play.

The attacker tossed her around as he walked into the family room. When he finally stopped, he lifted his hand from her mouth but kept it hovering there, ready to slap against her lips again. "Are you going to be a good girl, princess?"

She nodded. Relief crashed through her a heartbeat later when the tight constriction around her chest eased. The man still held her, could crush her windpipe or any other body part if he wanted, but she could breathe without panting again. Oxygen flooded her brain as she waited for her chance.

"Thank you," she whispered, trying to sound grateful and submissive and whatever else this guy needed to feel confident in his power over her.

He spun her around. Only a foot of space separated them as his fingers dug into her upper arms. "What are you doing here?"

"Work."

He leaned in. "What kind?"

Now. She lifted her knee, putting all of her strength behind it, every ounce of will and the adrenaline flowing through her, and nailed him right between the legs. His mouth moved but nothing except a tiny squeak came out. His hands slid down her arms, all pressure from his fingertips gone, as he fell to the floor in a whoosh.

He groaned and swore as he rolled around. After rocking a few times, he tucked into the fetal position and stayed there. Then his breath came back full force. The furious whispering started, filled with swearing and what he planned to do to her before he snapped her neck.

She blocked the words, refused to be paralyzed by them. She had to move and wouldn't get a better opportunity. She shifted around his prone body, ignoring the thrashing and threats. She'd almost stepped to freedom when his big hand clamped around her ankle.

With his body still bent over, his furious gaze stayed on her. He twisted and pulled until she hopped on one foot. She let him drag her closer as she fought for balance. It was either give in to his strength or topple over him and she knew if that happened, she was a dead woman. He'd made that clear.

"Where do you think you're going?" He almost spit as he talked.

The fury in his tone whiplashed around her. Her mind

went blank except for one thing—escape. With one hand pressed against the side of the couch, she reached out, trying to grab for the lamp sitting on the table behind it. As he pulled hand over hand, bringing her closer, she stretched out to full length, ignoring his nails as they dug into her skin.

Keeping her focus on the target, she waved her hand and her fingertips brushed against the shade. The base wobbled and thudded against the wood. Her breath caught as she waited for it to bobble then fall out of reach, but luck was on her side this one time.

With one last lunge she slapped her palm around the long stem and held on. Yanking as hard as she could, she ripped the cord from the wall and dragged the lamp over the back of the sofa toward her chest.

A ripping sound cut through the room as the top of the lamp broke through the shade. She ignored the pain shooting up her leg and the heavy weight in her hand. Pivoting, she turned and held her unexpected weapon directly over her attacker's head. And let go.

His eyes popped wide and he yelled as he moved his head on the carpet. At the last second, he let go of her and folded his arms over his face to ward off the inevitable blow.

Suddenly free, her body went flying from the momentum. She stumbled as balance completely abandoned her. Next thing she hit the floor on her knees and heard a crack. Biting through her lip to beat back the sudden thumping in her knee and scrambling on all fours, she shuffled across the carpet.

The slide against the rug burned her skin and something sharp on the floor dug into her palm. She gave a quick tug to her purse strap where it sat next to her abandoned chair a few feet away, and the contents spilled all over the floor. She grabbed for her keys and left everything else behind.

With a push, she got to her feet. One knee buckled as a sharp sting stole her breath. She ignored it all, keeping her focus on the front door. Freedom sat a few steps away, and she had to get there before her attacker showed off a new weapon. She saw the knife but he could be hiding anything anywhere.

She looked over her shoulder one last time as her hand closed over the doorknob. Her attacker had almost reached a sitting position as he felt around him for something.

Now or never.

Throwing the door open, she tripped across the threshold and down the three steps to the walkway. Every cell inside her told her to look back and see how close he was. She pushed it all away.

After a chirp, the car's locks clicked. Her hands shook as she opened the door and threw her body across the seat. From the corner of her eye she saw a shadow. The attacker stood in the doorway with his hands braced against the sides of the jamb.

When he started down the stairs her heartbeat kicked up until the hammering filled the car. The keys jangled in her hand as she tried to shove them in the ignition. Once, twice, three times she missed, clicking against the steering column. Finally one fit into the slot and she turned it hard enough to twist the metal.

Just as the attacker reached the side of the car, she slammed her elbow against the lock and jammed the gas pedal to the floor. He smacked his hand against the driver's-side window and she put all her weight on that pedal. The tires squealed and her nine-year-old car fishtailed out of the parking space and onto the one-way street, barely missing the motorcycle parked across the street.

With fingers locked around the wheel, she wrestled to keep the front end from smashing into a car right in front of her. This area of town consisted of narrow streets packed with brownstone residents who juggled on-street parking regulations on a daily basis. Her only goal at the moment was to keep from pinging through there like a pinball. And to keep moving.

She ran the stop sign and flew down the street at a speed guaranteed to get her a ticket, and right then she'd kill to see a police car. A few people standing on the sidewalks yelled at her and one shook his fist. Their neighborhood-watch outrage was the least of her worries right now.

Taking the corner too fast, she ripped around to the left at the next intersection and didn't stop while her heartbeat still clanged in her ears. Up ahead she saw a red light and traffic flow in both directions. With her eyes closed or open, no way could she pass through there and live. She needed an alternate route, but she didn't know this part of town well enough to know the best ways in and out.

Easing over, she hooked a right and flew down another residential street. When she finally eased up on the gas, the shaking in her hands had moved to her entire body. Every cell and muscle trembled. She hadn't realized she was mumbling and gulping in breaths until the fog clouding her brain cleared a little.

She let the car slow to a stop as she pulled into a space reserved for buses. Checking the rearview mirror for the hundredth time, she scanned the street, looking for anyone who might be following. Cars passed and people walked by—a few even stared at the lady drawing in deep breaths as she sat frozen in place. But all that mattered was she didn't see the attacker.

Once the air flowed inside her at a normal rate again, she fumbled around in her jacket pocket and grabbed her cell. This time she skipped a frantic emergency call to the police. She needed the one man she'd vowed never to call again—

Davis Weeks, her ex-fiancé and the same man who specialized in crazy combat skills and secretive missions.

He would know what to do. He always did.

Chapter Two

Davis Weeks rubbed his eyes as he walked out of his bathroom, fresh from a shower. Thanks to the sticky Maryland summer heat, he didn't bother changing out of the towel wrapped around his waist. He was tempted to let it fall to the hardwood floor and stand naked in front of the fan. But because he could see the narrow street one floor down from this position, he decided to keep something on. No need to scare the crap out of poor Mrs. Winston next door. The woman had to be over eighty, though from the way she winked at him all the time he wondered if she'd enjoy the show.

Sweat dripped down his back just from the ten-foot march from the bathroom to the bedroom window. Man, it was hot. That would teach him to buy a run-down town house in Annapolis then not be home long enough to fix it up or figure out some sort of air-conditioning solution.

Between the massive summer thunderstorms and the tropical storm that had blown up the coast earlier in the week, the small strip of land behind his house, listed as a backyard on the real-estate sales contract, had morphed into a muddy mess. He'd just burned off some of the extra energy rumbling around inside him by laying gravel over the driveway off the alley.

Why he'd picked a humid afternoon for the task had more

to do with being limited to desk-job duties at work than any-thing else. He wasn't the sit-around type.

Now his muscles ached and his lower back begged for mercy. Three months shy of his thirty-fifth birthday and his bones creaked. He chalked the new pains up to too many years of chasing, shooting and diving for cover. He used to recover from jobs within a day or two. This time he neared day ten and his ribs still ached from where he'd got hit by that car. At least he'd got the bad guy.

He started to stretch his arms over his head and winced from the pull. Glancing around for a clean T-shirt, his gaze fell on the unmade bed. The blinking green light on his phone caught his attention next. With his job at the Corco-ran Team he was on call all the time, and that habit gave him some comfort, but he had forgotten to bring the cell with him when he went outside earlier. He'd been unavailable for two hours, which was a record.

He swore under his breath as he reached over. A few but-tons later and a voice he hadn't heard in months buzzed in his ear. Eleven months and twelve days, but who was counting?

"Davis, it's me. I'm in huge trouble. I...need you. Please be home."

Lara Bart, his former fiancée and the sole reason he went off the grid on a job that ended with busted ribs and a bruised jaw. The passing of days didn't matter. He knew that voice, could hear it every time he closed his eyes.

He also knew something was very wrong. The slight tremor. The stammer. None of that was normal for her. Husky voice, yes. Scared? Never.

The swearing this time included a few extra words and a lot of grumbling. Jamming his finger on the button, he called her back and nearly threw the phone when it went di-rectly to voice mail.

He'd just pivoted and started stalking to his closet when

the doorbell rang. He took off down the stairs with his bare feet thumping against each step.

As he hit the foyer, the rapid-fire knocking started. Breaking from protocol and his usual common sense, he entered the code on the alarm as he opened the door. Lara shoved her way inside and pressed up against him. Her arms wrapped around him as her cheek landed against his bare chest.

"You're home." She was out of breath and trembling as she mumbled the words against his skin.

The touch had his brain cells misfiring. It took a second for all the pieces to register. Her hair was lighter, with touches of blond through the rich brown waves, but still so soft. And his need for her still kicked hard enough to knock him over.

Ignoring the feel of her in his arms, he set her away from him and scanned her body, trying to remain as detached as possible as he checked for obvious injuries. "Are you hurt?"

She shook her head. "Well, except for my knee."

Looking down, he noticed the ripped hem of her skirt and red knee. That, along with the untucked and torn silk blouse, signaled trouble.

"What happened to you?" He almost dropped to the floor and checked her leg, but her next comment stopped him.

"I was attacked."

"What?"

She conducted security-clearance interviews, but there was nothing inherently dangerous about her job. He knew because he'd checked out her company and its independent contractor ties with the Department of Defense when she'd taken the position. Not that she knew that.

And it didn't matter that they'd broken up. He watched over her and always would.

"I should have called the police, but all I could think about was getting to you." Her hands were a blur of constant motion. Her gaze bounced all over the room, and she pushed her shoulder-length hair out of her eyes.

"Okay." Good, even. Being her first thought certainly didn't suck, but he needed her to calm down. "Take a deep breath."

Her chest rose and fell as she took his advice, but her hands kept shaking. "There was blood everywhere."

Dread ripped through him. Didn't sound as though this, whatever "this" was, had happened at the office. It took all his considerable control to focus the energy pinging around inside of him.

He wanted the information fast and clean, but she wasn't a field agent with the sort of delivery skills for that. Then there was the problem where her words kept jumbling together.

He cupped a hand over her cheek and lifted her head until her almond-colored eyes met his. Even terrified and twisted up, she was still the most beautiful woman he'd ever seen. Tall and trim with high cheekbones and a face that you could slap on a magazine cover without makeup.

But none of that mattered now. He needed information. Without it, he couldn't step in and fix whatever this was.

Skipping over the "blood" comment because he'd probably be hearing that one in his sleep, he went for the broader picture. "Can you tell me what happened?"

"My jacket is in the car." She looked around as panic moved into her eyes and turned her movements into uncontrolled jerks. "My briefcase." She turned to head back outside.

The last thing he wanted was her out in public until he ferreted this out. "Wait…"

A shadow moved in the open doorway behind her and the facts clicked together in Davis's head. The adrenaline started pumping through him a second later.

Jeans and a jacket, much too warm for the weather. And

the gun with the convenient silencer screwed on the end. No question what that was for.

Davis assessed and acted. With a hand on Lara's arm, he tugged her around him. She practically flew as he shoved her against the wall and into the small corner at the bottom of the stairs wedged next to the coat closet. Her back hit with a thud, but he couldn't worry about that now. His concentration centered on the guy with the massive body and bald head aiming right for him.

As the attacker stepped inside, a flood of tension filled the air. Davis kicked out, trying to catch the door and knock it into the guy's head. Maybe make him drop the gun. The attacker was quicker. He caught the edge and slammed it shut behind him.

Davis reached for his weapon and touched only the cotton of his towel. No gun, not even any pants. The closest weapon was hidden across the room by the fireplace. That left few options.

He dived for the attacker's stomach. The guy groaned as he crashed into the door and Davis smashed his hand against the knob.

Heavy breaths echoed through the room as each threw punches and aimed kicks. Davis's landed awkward because of his position and the need to keep the barrel of that gun aimed at the empty center of the room.

He slammed the guy once then twice into the hardwood, but he didn't drop the weapon. Barely looked winded.

The guy's knee came up, catching Davis in the jaw. His head snapped back and pain shot down from the base of his neck. Impressive training but Davis's was better. He rammed his elbow into the side of the guy's head and heard a sharp crack.

With the attacker off balance and reeling, Davis connected with a punch to the stomach, then one to the jaw. The guy went down hard on his knees, yelling. The gun flew across the room before spinning under the coffee table.

Davis scrambled, but the other guy wasn't going down easy. He dropped and crawled on his elbows and knees. Blood dripped on the floor from his split lip.

Knowing it was going to hurt like hell, Davis did a jumping dive, landing on the attacker and sending a knee plowing into his back. The guy howled in pain as his head tipped back and he bared his teeth.

Davis didn't wait. He threw his upper body out, ignoring the tearing he felt along his injured ribs, and reached out his hand. The pain smacked him hard enough to close his eyes, but he forced them open again. He couldn't stop. Hesitating meant death for Lara and that was not going to happen on Davis's watch.

Just as he collected his strength and shimmied closer to the weapon, the attacker grabbed his leg. Twisting and sucker punches to the back of the knee came before Davis could brace for the attack. A shocking agony spiraled through him and his breaths came in rushed pants, but he refused to give up.

His fingers brushed against the metal. A few more inches and he'd have it. To get leverage, he balanced a hand against the floor and lifted his sore body up. Out of his peripheral vision, he saw Lara move. She sneaked up behind the men as they fought, carrying the heavy glass lamp that usually sat on the small table right near the double window at the front of the house. The same one she had bought right after they'd put an offer on the town house and he now used to hold his discarded keys each day.

Sensing something, or maybe reading the not-so-secret approach in Davis's eyes, the guy whipped around. He kicked out as he lunged for Lara. In panic, she jumped to the side and threw the lamp. It missed the attacker by a few inches but it gave Davis the diversion he needed. Stretching those last few inches, he grabbed the gun and wrenched around again.

He concentrated, blocking out everything—Lara and the pain shaking through him—to hit that target and nothing else. "Hey!"

The guy pivoted and his eyes went wide. With a roar of fury, he made a final leap for the gun.

Davis didn't hesitate. A crack split through the wrestling sounds of the room. Lara's surprised inhalation followed the guy slumping over on his side, pinning one of Davis's legs underneath.

Blood pooled, seeping into the small carpet. The room, ringing with activity a second ago, fell deadly quiet.

Davis kicked the guy off him then climbed to his knees. He pressed his free hand to the guy's neck, checking for a pulse. Next came a quick search of the attacker's pockets for some sort of identification. Davis peeked up at Lara, standing a few feet away with her hands over her mouth.

"Is he dead?" she whispered through her fingers.

The thump of a pulse grew faint then slipped away as Davis checked. "Yeah."

Her gaze searched the room, over the newspapers stacked on the edge of the couch and the four coffee mugs lined up across the coffee table. "Call an ambulance."

"Too late." With an arm wrapped around his ribs, Davis stumbled to his feet.

Out of the line of sight of the window, he crept around the family room and pulled her out of range at the same time. With his back to the door's edge, he scanned the outside for another gunman. Last thing Davis needed was another attacker blindsiding them.

When he turned back around he saw Lara watching his every move. Time to get her attention off what may be a second burst of gunfire. "Is this the guy who attacked you?"

"I don't know." She didn't even look at the downed attacker.

Davis reached out to her but it was as if she didn't even see the gesture. Her body closed in on itself as she put her hands on her shoulders, swinging her body from side to side and nibbling on her bottom lip. All while she carefully avoided looking at him or the guy on the floor.

The ache inside Davis was no longer about the death match. It was for her. For the sadness he saw pulling at her face and the tiny tremors that moved through her from the second she'd walked in the door and into his arms.

He was all too familiar with death on the job. She interviewed and wrote reports. She was normal. This was a nightmare, complete with splashes of blood and a body. "I know this is hard."

Her gaze went to the attacker then bounced back up again. "No."

"What?"

"It's not him. This is a different guy."

Now, that was a load of bad news. Davis exhaled as he tried to juggle all the questions in his mind. Rapid firing them at her would only shut her down. They had enough history for him to know she didn't react well to the interrogation thing, even if it was well-meaning. "Have you ever seen him before?"

"Definitely not."

Because she still avoided looking at the man in question, Davis tried again. "Are you sure?"

Her hands dropped to her sides as her cheeks flushed. "How can you stay so calm?"

The look was not a mystery. Just like always, anger slowly replaced the other emotions clashing inside her. Lashing out was her natural reaction.

If they had ten extra minutes to do this dance, he'd probably welcome anything that took her away from being scared, but right now he needed her to focus so he could get her out of there.

"Practice." He glanced through the house and out the back door right before he did another visual sweep of the front. Next he turned to the clock above his fireplace and calculated the lead time they'd need if this guy had a partner.

"That's your response?" Her voice dripped with sarcasm.

Good. He could handle that reaction. "I was being honest."

She snorted as she stepped around the downed attacker and came closer to Davis. "Right."

Yeah, she'd definitely shifted to the anger phase. He'd seen it coming. He welcomed it but he also knew he'd have to sit down soon.

He had taken a huge body blow and all that scrambling had knocked something loose inside him. His breathing hovered at the wheezing point. Fearing the damaged rib had slipped from aching to broken, he walked, partly doubled over, to the edge of the couch.

The color left her cheeks as quickly as it had come. "Davis?"

"I need a second." He had to think. Somehow his work life had once again intruded on her safety. She didn't even know about the guy who'd threatened her a few months ago and ended up in the morgue. That guy learned the hard way not to come after the woman of a former Defense Intelligence Agency agent turned private-security expert.

Before Davis could blink, she was at his side. Her hand went to his hair and her eyes filled with concern. "Oh, my... your stomach is black-and-blue. We need to get you to a hospital."

He hissed a sharp breath through his teeth when she tried to wedge her shoulder under his armpit and get him to his feet. "Whoa, honey."

"I'll call 9-1-1."

He caught her around the waist before she could race through the room looking for a phone. Even through the thin shirt, he could feel the heat of her skin and his fingers tightened.

His temperature spiked as his gaze lingered over her breasts. He justified the need rumbling through him by thinking about the adrenaline aftermath. Never mind that he'd never had the desire to kiss anyone else but her after a work takedown. Seeing those big eyes and soul-stealing face, he felt his common sense go on the fritz.

It had always been this way between them. Hot and pulsing, both desperate to get the other into bed. They could communicate between the sheets. Real life was the problem.

"The ribs are from my last job." And Davis doubted they'd heal anytime soon.

"You got jostled."

He slipped his hand over hers, trapping it against his stomach. The dull ache caused by the touch was totally worth it. "Jostled?"

This time it looked as if she wanted to roll her eyes. She refrained but likely not by much. "Davis, don't do that thing where you grab on to words I say and then repeat them back to me in order to ignore or stall a tough discussion."

Most important to Davis, she didn't pull away. Not even when he slid his fingers through hers. "You know me too well."

"Exactly."

"Then you know what I'm going to say next." He pulled her in a little closer and her eyes sparkled with that compelling shade of light brown. "I need to call my team and we need to get out of here."

Her shoulders stiffened. "Police."

"Not until my people—"

"You have 'people' now?"

"—check for identification and scan records to see what hole out of my past the guy crawled up and out of." She glanced down at their joined hands and he thought he saw a smile tug at the corner of her mouth, though what she could possibly find amusing about the situation was beyond him.

"You've never referred to the team at the DIA that way before."

"I'm not working there now."

The smile vanished as fast it had come. "What?"

He understood the tension that suddenly appeared around her mouth and eyes. His job had been a huge wedge between them. Truth was his current position was much more dangerous than the old one, and she'd made it clear the old one had scared her to death. "I'll explain that later, but the 'people' I plan to call first is Pax. He's my brother and, like you, he could be a target, too."

"You think the attack is about you?"

"What else could it be?" With the Corcoran Team, a private group contracted out to government agencies and private companies to assist in high-priority but under-the-radar kidnap rescue missions, the bad guys were very bad.

Davis and his team worked off the grid, taking on the missions others couldn't do within legal parameters. That slapped a bull's-eye on their backs, and it looked as if someone had come looking for payback.

The only question was why they'd included Lara in the plan. Knowing who the attacker was and whom he worked for might answer that question. Until then, Davis was not letting her out of his sight, no matter how much she argued. And he was pretty sure she'd fight the protection.

"You're forgetting the guy who killed the lieutenant commander didn't even know I was in the house," she said, acting as if the out-of-context comment explained everything.

But the news crashed through Davis's mental walls. He'd just come up with a plan, and then she threw this new information at him. Kind of an important piece, too. "Go back. Someone was killed?"

"I mentioned that."

"Uh, no. That's a fact I'd remember."

"I'm not going to argue about who knew what when." Her hand left his stomach and she started pacing. When she got close to the body, she came scurrying right back to Davis's side. "For a second I forgot there was a dead guy on the floor. What does that say about me?"

The conversation threatened to veer off course again, so he brought it back. "You were talking about the murder of a naval officer?"

"Let's just say that's the second time today I fought a guy off with a lamp."

The information nearly stopped Davis's heart. The idea of her injured and scared tore through him with the force of a hurricane, leaving behind a hollow emptiness in his gut. He could go a lifetime without seeing the look he had seen on her face a few minutes ago. But this went beyond fear. She'd been forced to defend herself, and that unleashed a fury inside him that had his head thumping.

He needed details. "Lara—"

"We'll come back to that when we discuss your new job." She put a hand under his chin and let her thumb brush over his lips, which stopped what he was going to say. "And, yes, I will follow you out of here. You're the expert."

Not sure of her game, he closed one eye and looked her over. "That's good to hear. A little surprising, but the right answer."

"I learned some things once you left…" That thumb made one more pass before her hand dropped. "And don't gloat. It's not attractive."

Words backed up in his throat. He had no idea what to say. In his head, the answer was clear—get her out of there now. The rest of his body had a different idea. "I'll call Pax and the rest of the team to deal with this guy and start investigating."

"Only you would use the word *deal,* like a dead man is a broken mug or something. He's a person, and being this close to him is creeping me out. Like, my insides are shaking so hard I might throw up."

That possibility didn't scare Davis, but he trod carefully with his answer because they'd had this argument before and he'd lost—big. "He tried to kill you. Once he crossed that line, I didn't care who or what he was."

When she continued to stare at him, he steered the conversation back where he needed it. "I need the phone."

She slipped away from him only long enough to grab it off the far table—then she was back at his side. "Here."

His hand slid around her waist to rest on the sexy dip of her lower back. "It's going to be fine."

"You should do one more thing before the cavalry comes."

He doubted anything mattered all that much except getting somewhere out of sight. "We'll be long gone by the time they arrive. That's the point."

"Well, before we go, you might want to put on some clothes." Her gaze traveled to his lap. "You're naked."

The words registered in his brain and he jumped up. A visual sweep down his body confirmed her comment...and the amusement in her voice. "What the...? When did the towel come off?"

"Very early in the battle."

"I didn't even notice."

"Impressive, by the way. I had no idea you knew how to bare-body fight." This time the back of her hand pressed against her mouth to stop what looked like a smile.

He had no problem with her looking all she wanted, so he played along. "I've told you before that my talents are endless."

Her gaze took another bounce down and up, then she smiled. "I can see that."

Chapter Three

Less than ten minutes later, they slipped through the kitchen and out the back door. Lara watched as Davis caught the screen before it could slam shut. Always thinking and rarely unprepared. That was how she thought about him, and her mind wandered there often.

They hurried across the porch, the boards creaking under her sensible pumps. His sneakers didn't make a noise. It was as if he placed each step with precision, including his run down the four steps to the muddy square of a backyard.

Her gaze focused on his butt. Not a bad focal point and certainly less scary than looking up into the eyes of another attacker. Two were enough for one day. Davis also made the staring easy. He had put on jeans and a T-shirt and carried a bag Lara wanted to believe was loaded down with clothes and essentials like shampoo but probably only contained weapons. He did love his big-boy toys, but at least he had clothes on now.

Through the haze of panic enveloping her and the sick ball of dread bouncing around in her belly, she smiled. It was not as if seeing Davis naked had ever been a hardship. He stood six foot one with long, lean muscles. If there was an ounce of fat on him, she defied anyone to find it. If anything, he was even more toned, more fit, than when she'd left all those months ago.

Looking at him now and holding his hand while they crept on boards balanced over the big puddles, she watched the muscles on his back tense and flex under his shirt. Nothing new there. The broad shoulders and military-short sandy-blond hair hadn't changed. Neither had the rough edge to his face, complete with a broken nose from years ago that had never healed quite right and a full, kissable mouth.

Put it all together and you got a man who was self-assured and strong, compelling and intriguing without being pretty. He walked by and women turned. He took a woman to bed and she didn't want to leave again for days. Lara knew that last one from experience.

"You okay?" His question, delivered in a monotone voice, almost blended into the sounds of traffic blocks away.

"Except for the whole thing where people are trying to kill me? Yes."

His fingers tightened around hers. "That's the spirit."

They walked to the six-foot fence running between his house and the next-door neighbor's then followed it to the very back end. Unless he planned to chew his way through it, she didn't see this as a viable way out. "Uh, what are we doing?"

"Escaping." He trailed his hand over the wood planks.

"Did you develop the power to walk through walls?"

He shot her a sexy smile. "If only."

Refusing to get sidetracked by the shine in his green eyes, she glanced around the yard. Nothing was out of the ordinary. You'd never know a dead man lay only a few feet away.

The strangeness of life going on, the sun shining and a lawn mower running nearby, struck her. When a person died, the world should stop, if only for a second. But nothing changed.

"Here we go." There was a click and a panel of boards slipped open.

"A hidden door? Of course. Everyone has one." She rolled her eyes, but his back was to her so he missed it. That was a shame because it really fit here.

Davis had a contingency for everything. Well, everything but her, which was part of the reason she'd handed back the ring and still cried over the loss.

"It's my get-out-of-Dodge-fast plan." After ducking his head inside and taking a look around, he held the door open and motioned for her to pass through. "After you."

It was not as if she had a choice. Her life had careened out of control hours ago. Now she just held on and hoped not to throw up. Her knee throbbed and the drum-crashing thumps in her head promised a killer headache any second now.

They stepped inside a fenced-off square consisting of a small shed and what she guessed was a car under that slip-cover. When they reached the shed, Davis flipped open a black box and typed in a code. The gate at the back end of the enclosed space opened. It spilled out into the alleyway that ran behind his house, the same house he'd moved into a week after their engagement had ended.

They were supposed to have bought it together, even put in the offer together, but when the relationship fell apart he went through on his own. Funny how the original sales listing forgot to mention a secret car compartment at the back of the neighbor's property.

"Any chance you're going to tell me what's happening here? I feel like I walked into a movie a third of the way through."

A door Lara hadn't even seen on the house side of the enclosure opened and a tiny older woman walked out. "Is it time, Davis?"

Lara couldn't help but stare. The lady wore a long royal-blue robe buttoned up to her throat, dwarfing her under-five-foot frame. Her shocking white hair was long enough to tuck into her collar but thin enough for Lara to see the woman's pale scalp underneath. Slippers and cheeks rubbed pink with bright blush rounded out the look.

Whoever she was, she knew Davis and wasn't surprised to see him. She walked right up and put her hand on his forearm. Her eyes twinkled as she looked at him.

"Hi, Mrs. Winston." He lifted her hand and kissed the back. "I need the car."

"Go ahead." She patted his arm then turned to Lara. "Well, who is this pretty young thing?"

"This is Lara, my..." He shot Lara a warning glance. "Fiancée."

"Well, it's about time, young man. Come here, dear." Mrs. Winston gave him a squeeze and shuffled over to Lara.

It was her turn. Mrs. Winston hugged her, though her arms barely reached to Lara's back.

"Uh, hello." The older woman was so small and thin that Lara worried about crushing her by accident, so she kept the hold loose.

When the older woman pulled back, she took both of Lara's hands in her curved ones and her smile faded fast. "Did that boy fail to give you a ring?"

Lara glanced at Davis. He stood behind Mrs. Winston with an unreadable expression. Clearly this woman viewed Davis in a grandson sort of way. Lara wasn't about to unload about all their past problems. It didn't hurt anything to let this woman think what she no doubt wanted to hear.

"Don't worry. He gave me a beautiful ring." And technically that wasn't a lie. He had. A perfect solitaire with baguettes on a platinum band.

It had broken her heart, actually shredded it in two, to hand it back. Not because she loved jewelry—that sort of thing never mattered to her—but because of what it symbolized. The commitment she so desperately wanted from Davis.

Mrs. Winston reached out and absently patted Davis's shoulder. "He's a nice boy."

He handed her a cell phone. "You remember what I told you, Mrs. W?"

"Stay inside, don't talk to anyone including anyone in a uniform, put the alarm on, pretend I don't know you and wait for you or Pax to come back." She peeked around Davis's muscled arm. "I guess I can add Lara to the list of people I can trust."

He kissed her on the cheek. "Nicely done, Mrs. W."

"My mind is just fine, you know."

"All of you is." He winked at her. "Now, back inside."

Mrs. Winston padded away without asking for an explanation. The snide part of Lara figured that was why Davis liked the woman so much. She didn't ask questions.

He closed the door, sealing them inside the odd parking space. When he turned back and walked to the front of the car, he whistled. The peppy tune continued as he ripped the slipcover off to uncover a pretty boring blue car.

Not Davis's usual style. He didn't go for flashy, but he usually chose trucks of some sort. This thing barely had a backseat.

With the driver's-side door open, he reached under the dashboard and pulled out a set of keys. He smiled as he jingled them in front of her. "Ready?"

The man looked far too satisfied with this little scene. "What, no helicopter?"

"Not on such short notice."

"Are you kidding me?"

He frowned. "Do you want to drive?"

"I'd prefer an explanation. You involved your neighbor in something dangerous. Since when do you do things like that?" That piece didn't make any sense. If anything, Davis was overly careful.

He used to talk about contingency plans and had even run through a safety drill with her one time. The second time he'd tried she'd threatened to dump a pot of hot coffee over his head. Not that she would have, but coffee was sacred to Davis so he'd fallen for it.

He insisted civilians were the main problem in most difficult situations. Something about them taking away his options and messing up the fluidity of the operations. People without skills were fine as long as they listened. Mrs. Winston obviously listened. Looked as if she harbored a schoolgirl crush, too, but Lara wondered about her ability to follow directions.

"She thinks she's my top secret assistant, but really she's a nice old lady who never gets even a phone call from her deadbeat kids in Delaware. Her husband died more than a decade ago and she's alone. I mow the back lawn, talk to her and, yes, play along with her active imagination, including installing a security system that rivals most high-tech office buildings."

She listened but the questions remained. "I still don't get it."

Nothing in his explanation sounded like the Davis she knew. With his messed-up background he hadn't learned much in the way of family coping skills. His bond with Pax was unbreakable, but coddling elderly women seemed outside of Davis's skill set.

He smiled. "From the time I moved in she tried to wander into the house. More than once she set off my alarm by accident. Almost got shot another time when she snuck in the back while I was out front. It was a problem until she decided I was a spy."

The word clunked in Lara's brain. "Spy?"

"International James Bond type."

They used to laugh about televisions shows and how they portrayed law-enforcement officials, especially those who worked undercover like he did. Expensive drinks and cars were so out of the realm of reality for Davis that he often swore his way through a program.

"You hate that term."

He shrugged. "I tolerate the whole spy thing for Mrs. W because it makes her happy."

The idea of Davis playing into that sort of nonsense to make an old lady happy made Lara's stomach do a little dance. "That's kind of adorable."

"It was necessary. But, yeah, Pax also thought it was hysterical."

The game came together in her head. "So, naturally, you told her Pax was a spy, too."

Davis flashed her that sexy smile that had sent more than one woman into an eye-fluttering swoon. "I wasn't about to go down alone. Point is, she loves it, and the wandering-around thing stopped. Now she watches the house for me and is much more careful because she's *helping* me."

"And she lets you keep a car here." Lara ran her hand over the roof, marveling at how clean it looked for being held outside of a garage.

"I actually bought the spot. Money was tight for her and it worked well with the spy story. Also gave me a place to store the car that I prefer to keep for emergencies."

The little dance turned into a full-fledged stomach jig. He presented this tough-guy tarnished image but underneath he was about helping people. Maybe it came from being abandoned by his mother that he never let anyone else get stuck out there all alone. Whatever the origin, it was one of those things that had made her fall in love with him in the first place.

"You rescued her," Lara said.

"Uh, no. I came up with a way to neutralize her." He walked around to the passenger's-side door and opened it. "Get in."

It was just like him to duck a compliment. He saw admitting to the existence of his bone-decent good side as some sort of weakness. She'd never been able to make him see that the size of his heart was much more impressive than the size of those biceps.

Rather than fight, because, really, there was nothing for her to win on this one, she slid into the seat. She waited until he'd climbed in before asking the obvious question. "Where are we going?"

"Pax's boat." Davis slid the key in and turned. The engine roared to life.

"Is being surrounded by water really the safest choice?" Then there was the problem that she got queasy if the boat rocked too much.

She'd never been on this one, but they'd gone boating with friends before. She'd tried that focus-on-a-spot-in-the-distance thing and ended up losing her lunch over the side of the boat. Not the best impression on his then–work friends.

"It's not registered to Pax. Only a few people know about it and all of them have brutally high security clearances. Whoever is behind this shouldn't have a clue."

She waited until he'd pulled out of the spot and relocked the gate to talk about the point nagging at her. "I notice you didn't ask if I had a boyfriend before you added me to your spy story."

The car grew deadly quiet as she traced a pattern on the inside of the window. When the silence stretched, she glanced over. The rigid jaw and tick in his cheeks told her what she needed to know. This was not his favorite topic. Understandable, but she thought she knew his response, so she was prepared to wait all day. And she let him know that when she glanced over and lifted her eyebrows but didn't say a word.

He exhaled in that women-are-so-annoying way men often did when they were cornered. "Do you?"

He didn't even try to make it sound like an honest inquiry. "Oh, please. I know you know exactly what's going on in my life. Or at least you think you do."

A smile broke over his mouth. "Yeah, I'm single, too."

CLIVE EBERSOLE BROUGHT his car to a slow crawl and stopped behind the designated warehouse on the southwest waterfront in Washington, D.C. He didn't have to look at his watch to know he'd lost some time on this job. Took him longer to clean up Steve Wasserman's row house than expected. Clive had wiped the place down, except, of course, for the evidence he needed the police to find.

Remembering the scene brought Lara Bart to the front of his mind for about the hundredth time in the past two hours. He hadn't counted on her. That one proved to be a fighter and a significant complication.

Good thing she'd left her work case file when she'd run off. The documents inside helped him track her identity and find her apartment. She hadn't run back there, so he couldn't tie up that end, but the trip hadn't been a total waste. Not after he borrowed a few items.

And it had only taken him a few minutes to find exactly what he needed to take back and plant in Wasserman's bedroom. A few pieces of underwear and her address book, along with her laptop and a brush. With all of those pieces, one would hang her.

The move was off script but to his mind brilliant. And perfect in the execution. Not even the best lawyer would be able to dodge the reality of her property and DNA being all over the crime scene, as well as all over the house. She was supposed to have been there for a simple interview, but Clive had created something much bigger. A false past that tied her directly to the dead man.

It would only take a few fake emails to establish the rest of the secret life and a lover's spat. One well-placed hair from the brush and she'd be spending the rest of her days in prison. That would teach her to take him on, to think that she could actually win.

Idiot woman. She may have escaped, but she'd left enough behind for him to implicate her in the naval officer's murder.

His orders hadn't mentioned her. She'd been an unwelcome surprise, but he'd improvised. Wiped his fingerprints and any evidence of his presence away. Instead of framing the murder as burglary-gone-bad as planned, he had a new answer—her.

The question was whether his employer would see it this way. When he'd confirmed the Wasserman termination at check-in everything was fine. Delivering the news about Lara Bart's interference had caused a hiccup. Clive had been directed to appear at this destination at this time. That was rarely a good sign.

He heard the crunch of tires and glanced in his rearview mirror. A black sedan now idled behind him. He didn't wait for the phone to ring on this command performance. Taking the offensive always worked for him, and the two guns tucked within easy reach would even the balance of power.

Exiting the car, he scanned the area for witnesses. He'd been tripped up by one already today and refused to have it happen a second time.

The passenger's-side window rolled down and a thin file appeared in the space. No words, just a tap of a folder.

Pompous and dripping with an overactive ego, his employer continued to act as if he could separate the things he did from who he was. A typical smarmy blowhard dressed in a too-expensive suit. From the sunglasses to the shiny watch to the annoying way he held his head an inch too high, the man's overblown sense of self begged for Clive to put him down.

His usual business philosophy faltered with this guy. Usually, as long as he was paid Clive ignored the overdose of attitude. The second an employer failed to transfer the payment on time and in the right amount, Clive would cut him down— literally. It had happened only twice, but his reputation remained intact. Both of those disloyal men were dead and Clive promised the same to anyone who tried to screw him.

He leaned down but didn't grab the papers. "What's this?"

His employer continued to stare out the front window. Didn't even bother to turn down the news on the radio or give eye contact. "Your one chance to fix your mess."

Clive decided he could do without the overwrought drama, but that was what this guy did best. "I already did."

"You left a witness. Worse, you opened the door to more trouble than you can imagine."

Clive kept his one hand behind his back, next to his weapon, and grabbed the file with the other. "Meaning?"

The employer finally faced Clive, but the dark glasses hid any reaction. "Your backup failed to tie up loose ends, so I am reluctantly trusting you to do it."

The words made the nerve in the back of Clive's neck twitch. "What backup?"

"I always have insurance."

"So do I. That's why Ms. Bart will now take the fall for the murder. Problem solved."

"She is the least of your worries now." His employer turned the radio volume up and looked forward again as if to ignore Clive's very existence on the Earth. "The man referenced in that file is your main concern. Neutralize him immediately."

The car took off before Clive could move away. Only luck and quick reflexes prevented him from becoming a victim of a hit-and-run or losing a foot.

But he would remember. When this was over, his employer might need a lesson. One at the end of a knife, and Clive did so enjoy his knife work.

There would be time for that later. Now he needed to focus. He flipped open the file and read the name at the top and the job history.

Davis Weeks.

Looked as though Ms. Bart had a built-in protector. That was fine with Clive. This Weeks guy would bleed out like any other man...slowly and with as much pain as possible.

Then Clive would pay his employer a much-needed late-night visit.

Chapter Four

Davis sat across from Lara on the back deck of his brother's twenty-six-foot cruiser. The gentle rock of the boat and slosh of water against the side had a hypnotizing effect. So did watching the guy four slips down stack enough supplies on the dock for a four-month voyage. Never mind that his boat was small enough to get tossed around in the ocean. Davis hoped the guy had the smarts to limit his trip to close-in on the Chesapeake Bay and have the coast guard on standby just in case.

But Davis had enough to worry about without adding another person to his Watch List. With his elbows balanced on his knees, Davis looked down at the rough white floor under his sneakers and listened to Lara's description of what had happened at the Capitol Hill town house.

A knife wound. A dead naval officer. An attacker with a gun. Lara wrestling free and going on the run.

It was a lot to take in.

With each word, the adrenaline increased in speed as it raced through him. The need to find the guy and rip him apart nearly swamped Davis. He jammed his teeth together to keep from letting his rage out.

She wound down when she hit the part about leaving the city and heading for Annapolis. With an arm stretched over the top of the back bench, she stared at the locked gate separating the public area from the boat slips. Her mind clearly wandered to other concerns.

He knew where. "No one is coming in here who shouldn't be here."

"What?" She blinked as she looked at him.

He nodded in the direction of the mounted camera on the dock. "My team is watching the area through closed circuit."

"When did that happen?"

The woman could stand to have a bit more faith in his skills. "The second after I called Pax."

She shifted sideways and put her legs up on the padded seat. Thanks to a quick stop at the discount store, she'd changed clothes. Gone was the ripped and professional outfit. He preferred her this way. Relaxed and at ease. With her itinerary today, she'd earned a few minutes of peace.

She now wore jeans and one of those tops barely held on her shoulders with thin straps. It slipped past her waist but not by much. Another twist and he'd get a peek of her sexy bare skin and flat stomach. Not that he needed a reminder. He remembered every inch of her with his eyes open or closed.

She tipped her head back, and the fading sun streamed through her hair. Her husky voice echoed around them as she closed her eyes. "Are you in charge of this team?"

Damn, she was beautiful.

"No." The word caught in his throat, but he pushed it out.

Also fought the urge to make her tell the entire story again. She'd run through it three times, the last one while grumbling and frowning at him through all but the end. She didn't understand the importance of those tiny details that became clearer with each telling. He did.

"When did you take the job with Hampton and start doing security-clearance checks?" He knew her official start date, but the reasons for the change were a mystery.

"When I decided being an office manager at an intellectual-property law firm was not the most exciting career ever."

He'd left her in a safe job with benefits and no danger, other than falling into a boredom coma or getting her shirt caught in the copier. Now she walked in and out of situations with people she didn't know. Yes, she asked questions and collected data for a living, which should be relatively safe, but going into a stranger's house was a whole different level of danger. One he didn't accept for her.

"Isn't protocol to meet interviewees in public places?" he asked.

"Have you been reading my employee manual?"

"I'm serious." And about a half step away from being furious with her for taking huge chances.

"Usually, but this was a rush job and my boss asked me to fit the Wasserman interview in."

The sequence seemed clear to Davis. She broke protocol this one time and the world came crashing down around her. Either her being there was pure coincidence, or someone had set her up. If the latter was true, then the second attack of the day made less and less sense.

So did her sudden change of position on job-related risk. She'd hated that he took them, but now she was plunking that perfect butt right into the middle of some sort of war.

The realization made his hands shake with the need to yell. The growl roared up from his stomach, but he tamped it back down. "So, you switched jobs because you wanted something dangerous."

"I didn't say that."

"I'm thinking it was implied." She was making this conversation more convoluted than necessary, and they both knew it. The fact she didn't give him eye contact gave her away. "And you used to say I was the one with the communication issue."

She made a choking sound as she lifted her head and swung around to face him again. "Speaking of that, what's with all the team stuff? Last I checked, you were flying around the world conducting investigations about military intel."

The brunt of his anger smoothed away. Okay, this part promised to be difficult. He shot the other boater a look just to see if he was listening in. Davis looked in time to see the guy trip over his cooler. That was about as smooth as Davis felt at the moment.

Rather than dance around it, he said it straight. "I quit that job and went with a private firm."

"Oh, really. The same job I begged you to leave." The flat line of her mouth and dead eyes suggested she'd reached the end of her patience.

He couldn't really blame her. They'd gone around and around on this topic when they'd been together. She hated his work and the life-threatening situations it threw him in. That last DIA-related assignment broke them apart. He'd sat there in San Diego, listening on the phone while she begged him to come home. He'd almost crushed the cell under his hand in frustration because he couldn't get to her.

The crying and pleading had been new. Anger he could handle, but hearing the desperate tremble in her voice shredded him. Even thinking about it now started a hollow rumbling in his gut.

She hadn't cared that his old boss was trapped in a nightmare because his fiancée had gone missing or that his boss's twin brother nearly had got killed in an explosion. She asked him to turn his back on everything he knew to be right, and he couldn't do it.

After the tense discussion, Davis and Pax had agreed they needed to finish the job. Just a few more days. Davis had justified it in his head until he blocked out the sound of her voice. The operation ended but Davis had come back to Lara and her packed bags and the engagement ring on the kitchen counter.

He couldn't deal with any of that now. "I see the irony."

"It's more than that, Davis. We broke up over your habit of picking your job over me." In the past, she'd deliver a line like that in a moment of pure female fury. Now she said it with all the emotion of reading a grocery list.

"We broke up over a lot of things." Her lack of support and refusal to accept who he really was being some of the points he remembered.

She opened her mouth twice but nothing came out. Without warning the tension left her shoulders. "I am going to let that go because you saved my life today."

Not sure he'd actually won that round but unwilling to get her riled, he nodded. "Much appreciated."

"I'm guessing you don't sit at a desk at this new job."

There always had been so much about his job he couldn't explain. This was part of that. "I'm sitting now."

"You always were the best at dodging a question." She lifted her hair off her neck. If she was hoping for a breeze, none came.

The air stood still. The heat was actually wet, choking as it burned down your throat. Having her sit there, sun-kissed and hotter than he remembered, made his temperature spike into the danger zone. This heat had nothing to do with anger or the temperature outside. This was pure, unfiltered need. All the fighting and months apart hadn't crushed that.

"Ask me anything, but first answer one question." He rubbed his hands together, debating if this was the right time. "Why me?"

"What?"

"You could have called the police or a friend. You were

thirty miles away and you'd had a huge scare and you got in a car and drove to me."

Amusement lit her brown eyes and a smile inched over her lips. "You're the only spy I know."

He really did hate that word and she knew it. "I'm serious."

"You weren't the best fiancé but you were great at your job. I knew I needed the best." She glanced at the radio on the deck next to his foot. "Anything on the news yet?"

"No." The answer was automatic. It wasn't as if the radio was even turned up loud enough to hear it. At this level it sounded more like static or a low mumble, but he knew how this game was played. "Wasserman was in the military. NCIS probably dropped a net over this while the experts come in to collect evidence."

A different emotion moved over her face. One that looked suspiciously like doubt. "Explain to me again why we aren't reporting the murder."

"I don't want questions from anyone, including NCIS, the FBI or the police, until we know what happened in that kitchen and why."

"I don't get it."

Of course she didn't, because he was purposely not explaining it. That plan might have worked on another woman, one not as smart or intuitive. One who let things slide and accepted things just because someone said them with authority. Nothing about that description fit Lara.

She picked and checked and he'd loved that about her from the beginning. A whiny, clingy type didn't suit him. He wanted vibrant…then he'd had it and lost her anyway.

The least he could do was let her see how this would go. "How many people knew you would be at Wasserman's house today?"

She shrugged. "A few. Why?"

"Did you touch anything?"

"I don't—"

"A table. The door. A glass." He ticked the possibilities off on her fingers.

"All of them. What is your…?" She blew out a long breath. "You think I'll be blamed for this?"

"Possibly." Definitely. The police would look at the forensics, and Davis feared those results would only point in one direction. Hers.

"But not coming forward will only make me look more guilty."

"That depends on why Wasserman was killed." A question Davis wanted answered as soon as possible.

"What are you saying?"

A bell dinged in the distance as birds squawked. "Someone took him out before he could talk with you. Who knows what information he had or why someone would want it silenced."

"Yes, so—"

"He asked specifically to speak with the investigator." Davis switched seats. Instead of sitting across from her, he slid in next to her with his arm running along the back of the bench seat. "Coughlin, the guy you're investigating, didn't put Wasserman on the list. He got there because he came forward. He had something to say and specifically asked to say it that day."

"How do you know this?"

His hand brushed against her back, right near her shoulders. When she didn't pull away or wince, he kept it there. "I know people."

"I'm serious."

His fingers touched her soft hair. The gentle waves wrapped around his thumb. "Do I look like I'm kidding?"

"I don't believe this." She bent forward with her arms

wrapped around her waist. When she started rocking, he moved in closer.

"Hey, come here." That arm slid around her and pulled her in tight against his side. Seeing her confused made bile rush up the back of his throat. "It's going to be fine."

She stared at his wide eyes, and a strain pulled across her cheeks and mouth. "How can you say that?"

"As you pointed out, I'm very good at what I do." His fingers threaded through her hair as his mouth hovered just inches from hers.

"What is it you plan to do?"

Kiss her, deep and hard, and not stop while either of them could still move. He wasn't one to mix business and pleasure, but control deserted him when she was around.

Even after she'd left, he kept the memories of her alive. He wanted to be pissed and still seesawed back and forth, but he couldn't hold on to the rage. The hurt and disappointment, well, those lingered.

But she was talking about work and he forced his mind to focus on that. She needed protection, not pawing. "We'll figure out why Wasserman is dead and why, coincidentally, people tried to take both of us out on the same day."

"I'm confused. Do you think this is about my work or yours?"

He was still deciding. "Until I know, you are pinned to my side."

"I'm not sure that's a good idea." She said the words even as her hand traveled over his chest and down to his stomach.

"Then you should have called your imaginary boyfriend." He kissed the very tip of her nose, thinking the soft touch would satisfy him.

He was dead wrong.

"I had a hard enough time handling the flesh-and-blood

type." Their heads bent so close together that her whispered words blew across his lips.

"From my memory you handled that quite well."

He gave in. One small press of his lips against hers. Quick and gentle, with barely any heat.

"Your ribs."

"I'll let you know if you're too close. So far, we're good." She grabbed a fistful of his shirt. "Davis—"

"Trust me."

The second kiss blew the first away. This one sent energy arcing between them. His mouth over hers, pressing, touring, tasting. His hand in her hair and her cuddled against his chest.

He could feel her fingers slide over his shoulder and trail down his back. Any closer and she would be on his lap. He no sooner thought it then his arm slipped under her legs and tugged them up and over his thighs.

The kiss exploded and devoured. Any idea that they were done flushed out to the bay. When her head fell back and he started to push her down on the bench, he knew his control had snapped and it would take an army to put it back together again.

He'd just decided to tease the edge of that thin shirt and tunnel up when the nerve ticked at the back of his neck. At first he felt more than saw movement on the walkway down to the dock. Then he heard the clang of the gate and thumps of footsteps. If the person wanted to sneak up, they'd failed. No way was this a professional killer. Well, not the enemy kind.

Davis lifted his head and, after a quick look over the side, stared down into Lara's cloudy eyes. "Company."

The boat shifted in the water and the footsteps fell louder. The chuckle came next. "Probably not the best timing on my part, but hello."

Davis looked away from the woman who meant everything and over to the brother he'd called for help. Pax stood on the ladder with a bag of what looked like food in one hand and a folder in the other.

After a quick mental assessment Davis decided all of that, whatever it was, could wait. "Get lost."

"Pax!" Lara jumped off the seat and straight into Pax's arms. He dropped his packages just in time and her smile beamed. "It's good to see you."

Lara had the power to lighten even Pax's darkest moods. They had a sister-brother relationship. They joked and she made fun of the way he hid his dates from her. And put either of them near a tub of raw cookie dough and it would be gone before you could get a spoon and jump in.

The stab of guilt over losing her extended to Pax. Davis had lost the love of his life. Pax had lost someone he cared about, and that list was not very long.

"You, too, though the circumstances need some work." Pax looked at Davis over the top of Lara's head and mouthed the word *sorry*. "You guys okay post guns and knives?"

"I was better five minutes ago," Davis mumbled.

Pax kept an arm around Lara. "And look at you beating up the bad guys. I hear the lamp is your weapon of choice."

"Kind of hard to hide in my pants, but yes."

Accepting the fact the kiss was over and not going to be revived anytime soon, Davis motioned for Pax to sit. "What did you find out?"

Pax guided Lara back to the bench next to Davis before grabbing his dropped belongings and dropping in the seat across from them. "NCIS is on the scene at Wasserman's house. Agents are looking for Lara."

The blip of happiness disappeared. She looked back and forth between the men. "What?"

"And the dead guy on your floor is, or I guess I should

say *was,* a gun for hire. Former military with a dishonorable discharge. Apparently, your boy liked to shoot a bit too much." Pax handed the file to Davis. "So, it looks like we have some work to do."

Lara slumped back in the seat. "I almost hate to ask what all of this means."

The notes were few, but Davis read enough to be concerned. He flipped the pages but put the file down when he realized Lara's total attention was focused on him.

Prettying it up wouldn't help, so he shot right to the truth. "Pax is saying you're likely to be the number one suspect in the murder of Wasserman."

She shifted until her feet hit the floor, then she pulled them up, then they went back down again. Something seemed to be pinging around inside her and making her squirm. "But why would I kill him? I don't have a motive."

Davis switched to his game face—*all is well and easy to handle*—to try to calm her down. Her switch to panic mode would only make the job tougher. "We need to figure out who did and why."

"And then get to the bottom of Davis's attacker," Pax said.

Lara reached for the file but dropped her hand. "The attacker could have followed me. He came in Davis's house right after."

Davis had already thought about that possibility and discarded it. "Did you see him following you?"

"No..." She bit her lower lip. "I don't know."

Pax looked out over the boat slips and exhaled loud enough to start a tidal wave. "What a mess, but at least some things never change."

"Like?"

"Ken." Pax pointed at the man still struggling with his pile of equipment, this time a net he'd accidentally stepped into and got caught around his feet. "Thinks he's a boater."

More like a menace, as far as Davis could tell. "I'm afraid he'll hurt himself or, more likely, someone else."

"The chances are limited. He never leaves the dock. He gathers stuff, sits on the boat and then goes home. It's an expensive hobby." When Ken glanced up, putting his hand over his eyes to block the sun, Pax waved. "Weird but harmless. But back to the attacker issue."

Her body fell. "So, what are you guys saying?"

"Looks like we're going to be spending a lot of time together." And that idea didn't bother Davis at all.

She gnawed on her lip again. "Oh."

He winked at her. "Welcome back."

Chapter Five

NCIS special agent Ben Tanner straightened his tie as he waited in the carpeted outer office of the deputy director's suite. Ben had been the special agent afloat on the USS *Forrestal* and stationed in field offices as far away as Bahrain. After sixteen years of navy and investigative experience, plus a stint at the War College, he'd faced danger daily. That didn't mean he liked walking into his boss's office and delivering bad news. Not to this guy.

The deputy director of NCIS wasn't known as a patient man. Ronald Worth thought nothing of grinding special agents under his shoe. When he got bad news, the person delivering it often felt the wrath.

The deputy had earned his position. His appointment was not part of the good-old-boy network that sometimes came with prime assignment. But he insisted, irrationally so, that things run smoothly and let everyone feel his displeasure when that didn't happen.

Ben had heard stories. Standing there in the outer office of the suite, he remembered every single one of them.

The deputy's assistant, Wayne Kline, knocked on the door and only pushed it open after being ordered in. Even then he didn't venture fully inside. "Sir, we have a problem."

Deputy Worth waved them on without looking up from

the files spread out in front of him. "Not the words any boss wants to hear at the end of a long day."

Ben glanced around the office. These weren't the usual government digs, but NCIS Headquarters had moved to this space in Quantico, Virginia, only a few months ago. The suite was large and plush and, unlike the old offices at the Navy Yard in southeast D.C., had windows that opened and you could see out of.

Behind the huge desk loaded with two computers to match two wall-mounted screens sat Worth, the NCIS legend who had stopped an attack at Camp Pendleton years ago by taking a domestic terrorist down before anyone could get hurt. His career had gone stratospheric after that. People tolerated much because of his past.

The deputy continued to flip pages. "What is it?"

Wayne cleared his throat. Even looked a little green around the mouth as he talked. "It's about Martin Coughlin."

"Spit it out." Ronald looked up. For the first time his eyes focused on something other than paperwork. "Who are you?"

"Special Agent Ben Tanner."

"Right. I remember."

Ben had no idea if that was good or bad.

Worth looked Ben up and down with a scowl that suggested he'd sized up his opponent and found him wanting. A terrific way to start a meeting. "What is this about?"

Ben had heard the deputy appreciated facts, so he got right to them. "Steve Wasserman was murdered today."

Leaning back in his leather chair, the deputy's laserlike stare zeroed in on Ben. With an elbow on the armrest and a pen flipping between his fingers, he frowned. "Why does that name sound familiar?"

Ben stepped up and slid a file across the man's desk. When the deputy kept staring, Ben launched into an oral briefing. "You knew him at the Naval Academy in the mid-eighties."

"I'm aware of when I graduated. Get to the point."

"Wasserman was one of the witnesses on Coughlin's security-clearance interview list."

And that was the problem. Martin Coughlin was Worth's old friend and choice for appointment as the NCIS's senior intelligence officer. The deputy had pushed for Martin and insisted the security-clearance steps be fast-forwarded. Martin had been in the office as recently as two days ago to talk about the position.

The tap, tap, tapping of the pen continued. "Are you asking to investigate this matter?"

"Yes, sir." Ben shifted his weight from foot to foot because this guy's intense stare had the power to make you question everything. "There are some jurisdictional issues, but the matter is delicate. We should handle it internally."

The deputy stared for what felt like a full minute then nodded. "Do it. I'll pull the necessary strings. Is there anything else?"

"The case is unusual in that Wasserman volunteered to talk as part of Coughlin's security-clearance investigation. And, in general, there are suspicious circumstances surrounding the death."

The pen stopped waving. With careful precision, the deputy set it on top of his stack of files. "Isn't that always the case with murder? I mean, was the killer hovering over the body?"

"No, sir," Wayne said from his position just inside the office door.

The deputy never broke eye contact with Ben. "Then, while the death is sad, I'm still not seeing the problem. Investigate and report back."

Ben waited until the deputy reached for the papers in a

classic we're-done-here signal. Ben couldn't back down because he needed the guy's attention and was determined to get it. "There is a bigger issue."

"Unless Coughlin is too distraught to go forward with the appointment as a result of this, and I doubt that since I've known the man forever, you've lost me." The deputy's voice changed, now monotone and more than a little bored.

"A woman was there—"

The deputy swore under his breath. "You're saying this is a sex scandal?"

"The problem is the murder occurred while the female investigator was there to talk with Wasserman about Coughlin."

"Was she hurt?" the deputy asked.

"She's gone."

His frown returned. "Gone where?"

"Disappeared."

"Now I'm starting to see the problem. We have a dead lieutenant commander, a missing investigator and a potential NCIS appointment at the center of it all." The deputy exhaled long and hard. "Is there any evidence Coughlin is involved?"

Ben couldn't answer that, and that was the problem. "I don't know anything yet."

"Get to work. Talk to everyone associated with this woman and Wasserman. And find her. I want a preliminary briefing tomorrow."

Ben had no idea how to accomplish all of that in such a short time. He'd need manpower. "My team and I will—"

"Wrong."

"Sir?"

"Just you. You need to draw a circle around this. Keep the information contained until we know what we're dealing with. The death will be on the news, but right now it is an unfortunate death of a naval officer living in a very dangerous city. Nothing more, and Wayne will see that it stays that way." The deputy stared at Wayne until he nodded. "Everyone get to work. Time is of the essence."

After the deputy had rattled off his orders, he returned to the files on his desk. That fit with the reputation—rapid-fire action. You got his attention for a few minutes only, but when you had it, you had to use it.

Wayne motioned for Ben to leave.

In a daze, he walked across the floor. This was against protocol and common sense. He understood the political ramifications: the deputy and Martin were friends. Still, as a one-man job this task seemed doomed to fail.

Maybe that was the point.

Ben shook his head. No, this one had landed on his desk. Somehow he'd manage to get enough preliminary information to request more help, but until then, sleep would be elusive, if not impossible.

The door had barely closed when Ben heard mumbling on the other side. He thought he heard the words "watch him" but couldn't be sure. To be safe, Ben would cover his tracks. No way was he losing his career and all he'd worked for over Steve Wasserman.

Chapter Six

Lara stood at the railing on the back deck and watched the last of the sun's rays skim the water and dip into the horizon. The sky was on fire with a burst of orange and bright pink.

The sounds of the marina filled the quiet night. Boats swayed and bobbed, and metal clanked against metal on the sailboats. A few rows over people laughed as they sat out on their decks and enjoyed the summer night.

Despite the danger swirling around, being outside made her smile. It was inside that was the problem. The boat had a claustrophobic kitchenette and a bedroom that consisted of a mattress specially designed to fit under the front end of the boat. She didn't know much about sailing, but she knew about being sick, and staying down there, all closed in, almost guaranteed it.

To be safe she'd nibbled on the bread from her sandwich for dinner and skipped everything else. She wasn't hungry anyway. Her life had tilted and she was barely hanging on the side. Dead men at her feet and police buzzing around her life. It was all too much.

"You hiding from your former fiancé?" Pax came up beside her and assumed a stance that mirrored hers.

The comment was right, in part. After spending a short time with Davis, they'd morphed right back into old couple patterns. He'd stepped into the role of rescuer and didn't think twice about bossing her around using the "it's for her own good" excuse he liked so much. Oh, he didn't say it out loud this time around, which made her realize he had learned something during their time apart, but everything else felt strangely familiar.

He got near her and her heart tumbled. He kissed her and her brain spun with excitement. The attraction pulled between them as strong as ever. But loving him, wanting him, had never been the issue. Accepting everything else was.

"Thanks for bringing dinner," she said, verbally pulling Pax in another conversation direction with all her might.

He laughed. "Changing the subject?"

"Definitely."

"Well, getting here was no problem. I live nearby and was willing to use any excuse to see you."

"Aren't you the charmer?" She balanced her head against his shoulder and felt the firm muscles underneath.

Both brothers made her feel safe. With Pax the emotions never boiled and bubbled. If he ticked her off, she just rolled her eyes. And he'd never made her heart hammer, while Davis had that effect on her just by walking into a room.

She chalked all of that up to her buddy-type relationship with Pax. Amazing how taking the sexual attraction and romantic-love parts out of a relationship simplified everything.

Pax pulled back and looked her up and down. There was no heat, just a joking familiarity. "You look good. Always do."

"Why hasn't some woman snapped you up?" She knew the answer. Because he ran as fast as possible in the opposite direction whenever they tried to tell him their last names.

"I always said women were smarter than men."

"No arguments here." She watched the last of the orange streaks fade away into the dark sky.

The water stretched out in front of her in a vast nothingness. The waves she loved so much during the day took on a dangerous edge at night. That was a familiar theme in her life. Hours ago it looked a soothing, shiny blue. Now she only saw a deep, mysterious black.

They stood, soaking up the evening as dishes rattled below. A shadow moved around down there. She assumed Davis was cleaning up or maybe burning off some extra energy. He wasn't really the type to hang out on a boat and do nothing. That was Pax's thing.

Davis was constant motion, which was why she'd agreed to buy a fixer-upper with him. She'd figured he'd spend every extra hour making it shine. So when she had stepped inside earlier and seen boxes and blank walls, it surprised her.

She also knew from the way Pax tried hard not to say anything that something big rattled around in his head. The guy was like a little kid sometimes, nearly vibrating with excitement and the need to tell.

His determination only lasted a few more seconds. After a quick glance into the open doorway, he shifted to face her. His voice dropped to a whisper. "Anything you need to tell me?"

"About?" But she knew. Pax wanted her with Davis. He never pretended otherwise. He'd called for weeks after they broke up, asking her to come back before Davis turned more miserable than anyone could handle.

"My eyesight works just fine, and what I walked in on didn't look like two people happy not to be together."

The kiss. Yeah, she was still struggling to set that straight in her mind. She wanted to write it off as leftover attraction or a punch of adrenaline from the out-of-control day. To her soul, she feared it foreshadowed much more.

All these months she'd been trying to get over him and failing miserably. No other man even clicked on her radar.

"The problems haven't changed," she said. "Davis wants to be free to go all over the world, even if it scares me to death. On his list of priorities I'm near the bottom."

And that was the insurmountable problem. When she'd needed him, lying in that hospital bed crying for him, he'd been across the country saving someone else's fiancée.

"That's not true, Lara." All the amusement and laziness left Pax's voice. "I was there. I saw what losing you did to him."

"I lived it, Pax." Pain swirled around her until she thought it would suck her down. She tightened her hold on the deck railing to keep from going under.

The silence stretched longer this time. She noticed for the first time that the radio played in the kitchen area.

She was about to break the tension when Pax spoke again. "Did he tell you about his last job?"

The question surprised her. Her mind went to the discolored skin around Davis's middle and the way he grimaced when he lifted his arm too high. "You mean the rib injury?"

"I mean the reason for it."

This was new. Pax rarely did an end run around his big brother. They were two years apart and had lived through being abandoned and passed around to relatives who only cared when they received a check from the state for the boys' care. The dysfunctional upbringing and fighting to survive bound them together.

Their past also had forced Davis into a fatherly role before he'd hit his teens. Over time the relationship morphed to a more mutual one, likely because they'd worked together for most of their adult lives. It was a bond that grew out of respect and love, and neither brother tested it. But she sensed Pax was pushing the boundary by dropping hints about something he wanted her to know.

Picking her words carefully, she asked, "What are you trying to tell me by not telling me something?"

"That's quite a sentence."

Just like his brother. "Answer the question."

Pax's crooked smile didn't reach his eyes. "I thought I was being subtle."

"There is nothing subtle about the Weeks boys."

He winked at her. "On that note, I'm going to head out."

She grabbed his arm before he could move an inch. "Without giving me an explanation?"

"Don't give me that look. It says you are right on the edge of unloading on me, and I don't want any part of that."

"Then don't evade."

"We both know you're talking to the wrong brother." Pax called a goodbye to Davis then hit the ladder, but not before calling over his shoulder to her. "Good night."

DAVIS WAITED UNTIL Pax left...then waited another ten minutes. He wasn't a man accustomed to hanging around. Outside of work, patience wasn't any kind of virtue that he could see.

Despite the uncharacteristic pacing, Lara's head never peeked below to say hi. Even now he could look out the opening to the deck and see her sitting curled up on the back bench with her arms wrapped around her legs. Her cheek rested on her knees, and her head was turned to face the other boats in the row.

Enough with the hiding. He got the message. Hands off. If only his body would obey the order from his head.

He stepped out onto the deck, letting his sneakers thump against the floor so as not to scare her. "What are you doing out here?"

She didn't even move. "Getting some fresh air."

"It's sticky as hell." Though he doubted she felt it in that tiny shirt.

"I'm fine."

He exhaled, but the growing case of male indignation was lost on her when she continued to stare out over the water. He dropped down on the other side of the bench with his thigh touching hers. A rush of relief poured through him when she didn't pull away.

"I can control myself, you know." The words were barely true, but he wasn't an animal. He'd never forced a woman in his life, nor would he.

The idea she didn't want him as much as he wanted her was like a sucker punch to the gut, but living without her was something he had been doing for months now. He could manage that and still keep her safe.

She slowly turned to face him. "What did you say?"

"That's what this is, right? Stay away from the idiot male so he doesn't jump on top of you."

The marina light shone down next to the boat's deck, casting the water around the boat in deep shadows. It was tough to make out much, but he could see her face. The frown was hard to miss.

Her legs slipped and her feet fell to the floor. "You've got this all wrong."

"Look, I know I can be demanding in the bedroom, but I'm not a jerk." He believed in monogamy and a healthy sex life, whether the relationship lasted a few days or a few weeks. With her, it had lasted almost two years and he was all in. He thought only of her, always of her.

"Your bedroom preferences aren't relevant because we're not together."

The words sliced through him, but he refused to let the wound show. "I'm not sure that matters for us. Bed is the one place we've always communicated just fine."

"You're such a guy."

"That's what I'm saying. It's been a long, crappy day. You had two men die at your feet and are still standing. I'm really impressed. Everything about you makes me proud, but I won't pretend I don't want you."

Her eyes widened to the point of popping. "That's the first time you've ever said that."

"The wanting thing? Uh, I don't think so." He was pretty sure he'd said it several times tonight.

And there was no way she couldn't know. People who passed them on the street and had never met them knew. Hell, Mrs. Winston saw them together for two minutes, not touching, and got the point.

"Not that." Lara waved a hand in the air before putting it on his knee. "The impressed part."

He stared at her fingers. Looked at her hand where it flexed against his leg and felt his frustrations drain out of him. Without thinking about it, her inclination was to touch him. He didn't know what that meant, but it gave him hope again.

All those calls the first few weeks after the breakup had gone unanswered. The visits where she wouldn't open the door. He'd stopped because he refused to be a stalker and would not beg a woman who wanted him gone.

Now he wondered if he'd given in too soon.

"That's not true. I know I told you that before." When she shot him a nice-try look he searched for an example in his memory. Nothing came to him. "Then I am a jerk."

"Let's agree you have had a few jerklike moments."

Not good enough. He wasn't going to let her give him a way out with a joke. This was too important. She was too important.

He slipped his fingers through hers and willed her to believe. "Honey, I'm proud of you every single day. You're strong and independent, and don't get me started on how beautiful you are. Just looking at you makes me hard."

She leaned into him. "Sweet talker."

He brought their joined hands to his lips and kissed the back of hers. The soft skin drove him wild, but he needed to prove something to her. "I can sleep up here if that makes you more comfortable. You take the bed."

"Being out here really isn't about you."

"Lara—"

She squeezed his hand. "Davis, listen to me. It's not you."

He wanted to shrug but couldn't get his shoulders to move and fake the gesture. "Feels like it is."

"I'm sick."

"Wait, what?"

"Sick."

The lightbulb didn't just go on in his head, it exploded to life. He should have thought that through. She wasn't used to death. The usual bad guys in her life consisted of losers in the grocery store or those boring attorneys she used to work with, including the one partner who'd made a pass and almost had Davis's fist shoved down his throat in response. Contract killers were at a whole different level.

"It's probably a reaction," he explained.

"Yeah, to the boat."

"What?"

She tucked her face into the space between his shoulder and his neck. "I'm seasick. When you broke out the peanut butter, I thought I was going to hurl."

The information bounced around his mind. "Like that one time we went boating?"

"Exactly like that, complete with rolling stomach."

"But that was a weird circumstance. You don't usually get sick." He pulled back and cupped her chin in his hand.

"Not if I'm on dry land."

He laughed but stopped after he saw her grumbly frown. "Why didn't you say something?"

"You were in hottie-rescuer mode."

He could live with that. "As if that's ever stopped you before."

"Honestly, I was willing to do anything if it meant I was safe and strange men stopped jumping out to kill me."

"I can see that." He threw an arm around her shoulders and pulled her in as close as his bruised ribs would allow. He'd wrapped them earlier after Pax checked them out, but certain movements still had him hissing air through his teeth.

"So, I'll sit here until the world stops spinning, which I'm hoping is soon or we're going to see that bread I ate one more time."

The words vibrated against his bare skin. "I'll join you in sitting and just hope the rest calms down."

"You don't have to."

"Maybe I want to." His thumb slid into her hair. "Do you feel sick now?"

She looked up at him. "Are you about to make a pass?"

"Depends on the answer to my question."

"We need to be smart about this." The way she grabbed on to his shirt contrasted with her comments.

"Oh, definitely." Slowly, and giving her plenty of time to pull away, he lowered his head to kiss her.

She put a finger over his lips. "I am not sleeping with you."

"No. Of course not."

She lowered her hand to his chest. "That was too easy."

Oh, they would, and at some point they'd have to deal with the issues that drove them apart. It was clear to him this was more than the easy-to-ignore straggly ends of a broken relationship. These were threads that needed to be tied together again. He was never so sure as when he stared into those stunning eyes and saw nothing but welcome there.

Still... "The timing is wrong tonight," he said, only half meaning it.

"Gee, you think?"

But they could still kiss. He leaned in. Just before his eyes closed, a movement in the water grabbed his attention. At first he thought it was a buoy or dinghy that had broken loose.

Her smile faded as her head whipped around to follow his gaze. "What do you see?"

He was impressed she whispered despite the panicked tone to her voice. "Something."

Bending forward, he opened the storage cabinet under the bench. He felt around, moving over ropes and something that felt like a pulley. Then he felt it. Wrapping his fingers around the smooth plastic, he brought out a flashlight.

"Stay here." He motioned to her as he stood up and went to the railing.

The focused beam moved over the dark water. The rhythmic thunking didn't stop and he aimed for the sound. Following a line, the light landed on a small boat. The pieces fell together. It was the kind of boat you'd never take to the ocean but might spend hours loading down with unnecessary supplies.

She appeared at his side. "What is it?"

"Ken's boat." The light traveled over the craft but no one moved. The bigger concern was how close it sat to Pax's boat.

"I thought that Ken person never actually took his boat out."

Smart woman. "Exactly."

"What do—"

He put a hand over her mouth when he heard a thump at the front of the boat. "We've got company, and it's not Pax this time."

Chapter Seven

Not again.

Lara tried to stop her insides from shaking hard enough to rattle her back teeth. She grabbed on to Davis's hand with a death grip that would have broken the bones of a weaker man. Intuitively she knew she had to let go because he'd need two arms to fight off whatever new threat headed their way, but her brain refused to telegraph the message to her fingers.

After a reassuring squeeze, he did it for her. He turned his flashlight off with a snap and tucked the slim end into his back pocket. Next, he motioned for her to duck down. The textured floor was rough against her palms and bruised knee, but she didn't say a word. Couldn't.

Tucked against the seats behind the ship's wheel, she made her body as small as possible. Davis didn't have that luxury. With those shoulders, his body could only get so little.

Footsteps echoed against the bow lightly, but in the dead quiet of the night the still air carried the sound. Water lapped against the side of the boat, and all the associated clangs and dings continued, but the squeak of a step still stood out now that she was listening for it.

That put the attacker maybe ten feet away and slightly above them. The marina safety lighting hit the back of the boat and also highlighted their whereabouts. This guy had the clear advantage. And there could be more than one of him.

Davis pushed his palm against the small door under the seat in front of them and made a face when it clicked out loud. With quick and efficient movements, he drew something out. It didn't flash under the light, but she knew what it was. A gun, probably one of many hidden on the boat.

Back when they'd been together Davis had been adamant she know about weapons. Cleaning, firing, storing. He'd gone over the routines several times. He'd insisted the lessons were about more than simple self-protection. If he kept guns in the house, she needed to understand as much as possible about them or risk being a victim.

He touched a light hand to her lower back. "Get off the boat." The husky whisper blended into the sounds of the marina.

Her stomach ached as if she'd been kicked repeatedly. "You mean both of us."

"Eventually." He put a finger against his lips and raised his head enough to see something that had him ducking again.

She loved the big protective alpha-male thing. But she hated the idea of leaving him behind. Knowing he was in danger would freeze her to the dock. The rib injuries and long day of fighting might prove too much for him to overcome.

Thinking to call in reinforcements, she slipped her hand into her pocket to grab her cell, until she remembered she'd left it on the table below deck. The only thing she had with her was a springy pink hair tie. Nothing helpful about that.

Davis signaled for her to slip over the side. "Stay low. I'll stand to draw fire."

Her breathing actually shuddered. "Terrible plan."

"Go."

Her mind raced to find another solution. He was the expert, but she couldn't let him make this sacrifice or take on this danger. Her gaze bounced around the deck until she felt his hand against her elbow. He gave her a sharp shake of his head and pointed to his right.

Nothing subtle about his orders this time. His stern frown suggested he was ready to throw her over the side.

Because his attention should be on the bad guy, she gave in. She glanced over and tried to see the dock from her position. It fell out of her line of vision. She knew a six-foot drop should put her on a stable walkway, and she could run from there. But without the ladder or anything to break her fall, it was going to hurt. Not the best solution but maybe her only one.

Crouching on the balls of her feet, she didn't have much traction. She shifted to get her balance as a thud vibrated next to her ear. She looked up just as the attacker reached down and grabbed her. Her scream cut off when he wrapped his arms around her chest, stealing her air.

In the time it took for his face to register in her brain, he'd lifted her off her feet and had her pressed against him as a shield. Heat radiated off of him and a subtle vibration moved through him. She chalked it up to some sort of sick evil energy.

He was dressed all in black with his face partially covered by a hood, but she still recognized him. He'd made the trip from Capitol Hill to finish the job.

He pressed a knife against her throat as Davis got to his feet. The gun was missing but she knew he had it nearby. "It's him."

"Back for a second try? You'll fail this time, too." Davis's voice never wavered. He didn't look at her either.

The attacker rubbed his cheek against hers. "I've already won."

She jerked when the attacker's hot breath blew across her ear. She smelled musk and sweat. The mixture filled her senses and she had to fight to keep from gagging. The slight rock of the boat and salty fish smell of the water backed up on her and her stomach heaved.

The guy tightened his hold around her chest until she was afraid to move. In panic she clawed at the arm around her but the hold didn't ease.

"You and your girlfriend are going to get in the cabin," he said.

It didn't take an expert to know going inside meant death. Her heart raced so fast that she was surprised he didn't feel it. She vowed to go out kicking.

Davis glanced at the two steps and doorway to the area below deck. "So we can have an accident of some sort? No, thanks."

"I can cut her now and let you watch."

The blade nicked her skin. The shock of pain was a promise of things to come. "Davis."

The attacker's whole body shook with a harsh laugh. "Listen to the terror in her voice, Davis. Use your head."

For the first time since their unwelcome guest had arrived, Davis glanced at her. Those intense eyes blazed, and for the briefest of seconds his gaze slid to the floor then came back up again. It was a clue. Something about hitting the floor. Desperation ate away in her stomach as she tried to figure out exactly what he wanted her to do and when.

"Hands up." The attacker barked the words more than said them.

After a flash of hesitation, Davis raised one hand and took a step. He came even with the attacker's side. Davis's stare bored through her as he moved.

She couldn't come up with a scenario in which Davis going into the galley ended with them surviving. And if she knew that endgame, he definitely knew. His mind never stopped analyzing and assessing. That meant he had a plan and even now was unrolling it.

He touched the stair railing. Instead of going below, he flipped around and yelled, "Down!"

The sudden change of direction had the attacker flinching. Without thinking, she angled her head to the side and dropped before she could worry about the knife. Her legs collapsed under her, leaving her sitting in a heap at the attacker's feet. When Davis launched his body and slammed into the other guy, she was trapped between their legs. Right in the line of fire.

Her breath thundered in her ears as she looked for a space to slip through. She crawled a few inches but couldn't break free. With one hand, Davis lifted and pushed her out of the way. She ducked as he jumped over her to get to the attacker.

Her last thought was to run but her body went airborne. Her back smashed against the doorway to the front cabin before she landed hard on her butt. Bones rattled and a surge of dizziness had her head swimming and her vision blurring.

When her eyes focused again the urge to vomit hit her hard. She choked down the taste as she dragged her body, half falling and half stumbling, back to her feet as she looked to the other side of the deck.

The men rolled across the deck in an echoing series of grunts. Arms and legs flailed. A knife flashed in the light. Air refused to fill her lungs as she watched the attacker wrestle Davis to the deck. They landed with a thud as the fall knocked Davis's gun from his hand. The men scrambled, crawling over each other, using clothes and anything else they could grab for leverage.

Davis's hand wrapped around the weapon but the attacker pushed it away. Before Davis could make another attempt, the attacker slammed a knee into his back. Davis's body bent back. Tucking again, he rolled over and smacked the heel of his hand into the guy's face.

The attacker wailed as blood spurted from his nose. Instead of falling off Davis, the guy slammed his weight harder against Davis's stomach, doubling him over as he gasped.

With a final blood-freezing scream of rage the attacker brought the knife down in a swooping arc. Davis shifted his head to the side at the last second and the blade stabbed into the floor.

Fearing Davis couldn't win this one, not when he was already hurt, she struggled to her feet and looked across the bow for something, anything, to aim at this guy. She saw cans stacked up at the far end and blinked. Her mind didn't grasp the importance or even understand what she saw until she inhaled and the harsh scent of gasoline ran through her.

He was going to blow them up.

She spun around in time to see Davis whip out the flashlight and deliver a bone-crunching hit to the other guy's jaw. The attacker's head actually snapped back. For a second his eyes slipped shut and Davis used the opening to shove the guy off. Up on his knees, Davis stretched out for the gun.

"Davis!" Her scream bounced off the fiberglass and had him turning to face her. "Gasoline."

She barely got the word out over the terror shaking her body and kicking life into her muscles. She wasn't even sure he'd heard or understood until his eyes went wide. His gaze traveled over the boat as all emotion vanished from his face.

Swiping the gun, she stood up, stopping only to kick the attacker in the shoulder when he struggled up for another round. Running, his arms pumping and cheeks hollow, Davis smashed into her. With a hand on her arm, he lifted and propelled her to his right. Her thigh slammed into the side of a seat as they went but she kept going. She didn't have a choice. Davis had her locked to his side.

The attacker got to his feet but Davis didn't stop moving. With a hand on her butt, he hoisted her up on the side railing. His body wrapped around hers like a blanket as he dropped them over the side. The air rushed around them. She closed her eyes and waited for the hard crack of the dock against her skull a few feet below. When they hit, she bounced against his chest and heard him groan.

Her eyes popped open in time to see him aim his gun at the side of the boat, as if waiting to see a face peek over. They were lower and couldn't see inside, but he was ready.

She heard a splash and Davis swore. He shifted and jumped to a crouch. A rumbling whoosh stopped him from going farther. One minute she sat there, trying to get her bearings, and the next a wall of heat punched her face. The bang rang out right before Davis slipped his arms around her and rolled them to the far side of the dock.

The floor beneath them fell away and they flew through the air again. She gasped as they hit the water. The smell of fish smacked her in the face as she struggled to hold her breath. Her eyes opened as a ball of red and orange exploded above the water. Even under she could hear the booms and crackle.

Something slapped the water near her head. Davis kicked and they swam, bubbles giving away their path, as chunks of wood and things she couldn't recognize through the haze of water crashed around them.

Just as her air ran out and she thought her lungs would explode if they went one more foot, they broke the surface. She hung on to his shoulders and he grabbed on to the side of the small hill leading to the road and the firm land beyond.

Flames shot up from the center of what used to be Pax's boat. "We would have been in there."

The explosion numbed every part of her. Her mind barely functioned, yet somehow her hands held on to Davis.

"That was the idea." Even through all the noise his voice sounded harsh and raw.

The water bobbed around them and sirens squealed in the

distance. Men raced to the scene, screaming for help while the few people on the boats in the slips ran up the docks to safety. The fire consumed Pax's boat and the impressive sailboat next to it. Lara didn't see any sign of the attacker, but she had a trickle of a memory that made her think he got away.

She remembered Davis's promises about being safe and wondered if she'd ever feel okay again. "How did he find us?"

"I'll find out." His set jaw made his voice sound like a hard slap. "But your attacker miscalculated about one thing."

"You mean how he set the fire too soon?" Water splashed up and into her mouth, and she spit it back out. She tried hard not to think about what swam around in there with them or the garbage she had seen floating on the top earlier.

"I mean that he's made a new enemy. Pax is not going to take losing his boat well."

For some reason that made Lara feel better.

CLIVE PUT HIS palms against the floating dock on the row of slips at the far side of the marina and lifted his body out of the water. He rolled to his back and stared up into the orange-hazed sky. Shifting his jaw, he checked for any breaks. That idiot had swiped him with a flashlight. Oh, he'd pay for that.

Fire trucks blared into the parking lot. Clive lifted his head and watched their flashing lights illuminate the area. He lay far enough away, covered by his dark clothes and unexpected presence. For the next hour or so all attention would be on getting that fire out and roping off the area. Sneaking away would not be a problem. Recovering from this before his boss got word might be harder.

Firemen and policemen filed out of vehicles and surrounded the docks across from him. It was quite a scene. But the wrong kind of scene.

This was supposed to be a quiet ending. He hadn't counted on a late-night dunk in slimy water. Knock them out, stick them in the cabin and then light the fire. When the woman had struggled and the boyfriend stepped in, everything got screwed up. Too much time had passed, and the fuel exploded instead of sparking to a low burn.

His boss wasn't going to like this. He was a powerful man who preferred easy answers. This was too loud and called too much attention.

But Clive knew he could spin it, bring the arrow of guilt to point at Lara Bart. She wanted to hide her tracks and pretend to be dead. After all, she'd killed her lover Steve Wasserman and had to get out of town.

Yes, that story would work. Clive knew he could build it. First, he had to tie this off before the loose ends got any longer.

Clive admitted he'd underestimated his enemy this time. Investigative desk types rarely had this skill level. This Lara person only asked questions for a living, after all. Looked as though his intel on her was all wrong.

Clive hadn't counted on Davis Weeks either. That guy could fight—he'd avoided a fireball and a gunfight.

Clive admired Davis's will to live, but Clive couldn't allow it to go on. Lucky for him, he knew where to squeeze next. Davis had a weakness for the girl. The file mentioned a brother and a work team. That was where Clive would go.

He sat up and reached for the phone in his pocket. Waterlogged and useless. Guess that meant his boss couldn't track him down now. Breaking the phone in two, he whipped the pieces into different spots in the water. It felt good, freeing.

He glanced back to the spot where he'd seen the couple go over the side. They were out there and likely alive. He could feel it. They would not be easy to take out, but he would finish the job.

And he'd save that last bullet for his boss. No way could information on this botched hit get out. It would ruin his reputation, which meant they all had to go.

Chapter Eight

Davis stood with Lara chest-deep in the cool water and felt his muscles go numb. Hypothermia and fire were not his biggest concerns right now. No, the emergency vehicles racing into the marina parking lot held that title.

The huge light and sound show would draw attention from every direction—gawkers, news media, first responders, neighbors. They would all come running, and a helicopter was likely to show up any second. All things he didn't need right now. Or ever, really, but especially right now.

Being caught here would mean questions. Lots of them, and many he couldn't answer. Fingers would point and all that hard work in hiding his and Pax's ownership of properties and vehicles, including the boat, would crumble. Then none of them would be safe.

The police already wanted to talk with Lara. Davis was determined not to let that happen, not until he knew who'd killed Wasserman and why. Then he'd handle tonight's attacker. He'd taken two shots at Lara, and Davis would make sure there wasn't a third. Seeing that knife prick her throat had started a revving up in Davis's body that wouldn't stop until the attacker was on a slab or in prison.

Holding her now helped calm some of the fury thrumming through Davis. Another night like this and the explosion of the boat wouldn't be anything compared to the one in his head. He rubbed a hand over her arm and felt her tremble from the cold aftermath. He tried to silence the humming need for revenge, box it and control it, but the fire slammed in his gut.

While the heat inside him matched the one ripping through his brother's boat, her skin stayed cool as she continued staring at the flames. He needed her safe, dry and as far away from violence as possible. But first they had to get by the police roping off the scene.

Maybe they'd stayed a minute too late.

Climbing up the slippery rock hill would mean crossing the main path that separated the marina building and parking lot from the dock and slips. Talk about making them a target. They'd have to wind their way unseen through crowds and cars. It was hard to imagine how that would be possible because they were soaking wet and obviously not law enforcement.

They'd be right under the lights and in the open. And if people didn't see them, they sure would smell them. The mix of burned ash and dead fish would be tough to miss.

That left one really unpleasant option—swim under the main walkway coming down from the hill and keep moving until they could exit the marina on the far left side, away from the fire and crime-scene observers. It meant getting close to the flaming boat and passing in front of what was left of the hull. Wading, head nearly underwater through the muck that washed up on the rocks from the bay, might be the one step too much for Lara, who already looked ready to drop.

"We have to get out of here." When she nodded, he turned her face to look into her eyes. "Lara?"

"I'm okay."

With her hair stuck to her head and teeth chattering, she looked the exact opposite of okay, but their choices were limited here and the voices kept getting closer. "We're going to swim—"

"What?" Her gaze finally cleared and she frowned.

He took that as a good sign. Anger meant emotion and something still clicking inside her. He could work with that.

"We're going that way." He pointed to his left and did a double take.

Bright white lights skimmed across the water. A ship's horn sounded and an engine rumbled. As it got closer, he could make out fire hoses.

They were getting closed in from all directions now. With his arm still wrapped around her, he tried to maneuver over the rocks and drag her along with him. The ship's movements sent waves crashing harder against them. At the first smack of water, she slipped out of his grasp and went under.

She came up spitting. "This is impossible."

Wanting to shield her and limit the noise, he shifted until he stood on the outside, using his bigger body to block the floating debris and break the walls of water pushing into them. Flames shot up into the sky and floating debris brought fire closer to them until he batted them away.

Not giving her time to panic, he held her hand and brought her under the walkway. Each step felt like a Himalayan climb. The pressure of the water robbed their strength. He was bigger and just moving sucked the life out of him, so he couldn't imagine how difficult it was for her to lift her feet.

As they dipped lower, the walkway brushed against their heads. As they came out on the other side, voices rang out right above them. Diving on top of Lara, he dragged her out of the line of sight and pressed her body against his on the rocks. Sharp edges dug into his side and his aching ribs now thudded to the point where he had trouble catching his breath.

The water lapped around their still bodies as foam and charred debris brushed up against them. With her head tucked into his neck, he tried to blend their bodies into the hill separating the water from the land. When shoes hammered on the walkway down to the slips, he glanced up again.

People jogged down the floating docks. Hoses from the rescue boat in the harbor fired water into the flames. Male voices echoed around them.

They had to move.

Drawing her low in the water, he pulled her with him. Their mouths stayed closed and they moved quickly, cutting through muck and letting the dark water cover their bodies. The beeping sounds of trucks backing up and the thuds of boats knocking against the docks hid any stirring their moves might cause. Davis walked and kicked out, shoulders underwater as he ignored whatever wrapped around his legs and knocked into his ear.

All of his focus was on a less steep hill by the fishing-equipment rental shed. From there they could duck into the trees and follow the outside parking lot fence to freedom. By that time, everyone would be at the boat's side of the lot, overlooking the water. He and Lara would be at the back and on the run.

They finally reached the space he thought would work best for an escape onto land. Glancing back, he saw a line of men with their backs to them and the flames decreasing under the shooting water.

It would take hours to get the fire under control and hours after that to control the area and sweep for forensics. With most of the attention off the water and on other boats, now three of them burning from the explosion and being devoured by the lick of orange, they had a chance—as long as the other dangers lurking in the dark stayed away.

Narrowing his gaze, and wishing he had night goggles, he did a quick search for their attacker. Davis had his gun, but because it had been submerged in water he wasn't all that anxious to fire it. Sneaking away only to run into the attacker again would be Davis's luck at this point.

Lara's body collapsed against a smooth rock. Her chest heaved as she fought for breath. "Never thought that would be so hard."

"You did great." With his hands on her hips, he lifted her, sliding her body along the hill until her upper body reached the pathway.

Every time he let go to brace his hands and steady them both, her body deflated and whatever steam propelled her petered out. With her energy depleted, it was up to him to get them both up and on their feet.

Balancing his feet against the lowest set of rocks, he bolted up, careful not to cause a loud splash. The jump pressed his body against hers and she grunted in response. But he had leverage now. Pushing and pulling, he shimmied until he brought their bodies onto the path together.

Once his elbow hit pavement, he rolled off of her to give her some air. With eyes open, he stared up at the strangely pink sky. The fire had cut through the darkness, and smoke hung on the stale air. Without a breeze, all the smoke and fire stayed relatively contained, but much more and the haze would fall and they'd start choking on the foul, gas-tainted air.

He came up on his side and looked down at her. Her pale face stood out against the dark ground. "You okay?"

She peeked up at him. "I'm ready for a few boring hours."

"I think I can give you that."

She didn't say anything as she sat up and put her feet underneath her. She tried to stand but her knees buckled. She would have hit the ground again, but he caught her around the thighs. His arms trailed up to her waist as he stood. His legs didn't feel any stronger. The muscles had turned rubbery, so he held on. Maybe they could hold each other up.

After a few seconds, two trucks pulled up and stopped in front of the far parking-lot gate. News trucks. The new visitors tore some of the attention away from the fire. That meant it was more likely someone would spot them, so it was time to leave.

With his hand in hers and their bodies crouched down, they jogged the few steps to hide behind the fishing shed. He kept his back against the wall as he tried to judge the distance to the fence and the best way to go through it.

Going over it wasn't an option. Not in their current drained state. Not with water dripping off them and weighing them down.

He hoped the sirens got someone at Corcoran checking the marina cameras and seeing the devastation. That was his exit plan, but he had to get Lara to the fence first.

She fumbled with something in her fingers. He looked down at the bright pink band and watched her try to pull her wet hair out of her face. Her fingers were shaking and the band kept twisting.

He put his hand over hers. "Later."

Those huge eyes stared at him. Finally she nodded and looked down as she tucked the hair tie into her front pocket.

He pulled away, ready to head to the trees planted a few feet in front of them. He jerked to a stop when she didn't move.

He turned around, ready to give a quick and quiet pep talk. But she wasn't paying attention. She stood with the band on the tips of her fingers and stared at the ground. Her body seemed frozen in place.

Following her gaze, he saw the shoes. Shoes attached to legs. A man facedown on the ground. None of it made sense.

"How did...?" His voice trailed off because he wasn't sure what to ask.

She pressed both of her hands to her chest. "Is it him?"

He had no idea whom she meant until he saw the duffel bag and the cooler a foot away from that. He recognized both because he'd spent so much time watching them being dragged around. "Ken."

"Did he get caught in the explosion?"

Davis dropped into a crouch and slipped his fingers on the man's neck to check for a pulse. He didn't feel anything but cold flesh. When he pulled them back again, blood stained his fingertips and the pool under his head came into focus.

"Not an accident." This was body number three and Davis wasn't one inch closer to understanding what was happening.

Lara's head whipped around, looking from one end of the marina to the other. "The attacker did this?"

Had to be. The small boat next to Pax's had been the tip-off. That likely meant Ken was a sacrifice. Maybe he'd fought back. Davis didn't know but he secretly hoped Ken had inflicted some damage.

Thinking about the newest needless death started a spiraling tightness inside Davis. The attacker was willing to take out anyone to get to his target. Now Davis had to figure out who that was.

When he looked up again, he noticed the car idling on the other side of the fence. It sat fifty feet away, blanketed by the dark night. Between the smoky haze pressing down on them and all the commotion in the parking lot, the car blended in. A figure slipped around the front end and stood in front of the fence.

It was hard to make out the details from this distance, but Davis knew this wasn't an enemy. He'd been watching this figure his whole life, first as a pseudo babysitter then as a partner. Always as a brother.

Davis promised to refrain from saying, "I told you so," but running all those contingency plans for all those years had paid off. The DIA training and leadership at Corcoran made this all possible. Smart men who knew you had to be prepared for the worst case had taught him to be ready.

And now Pax had come to break them out.

BEN WALKED THE area around the fishing shed. Crime-scene lights bathed the entire area in brightness. After two hours of fighting the flames, the fire had died down to a smoke trail. Most of the police and fire vehicles still filled the parking lot as some of those in charge spoke with the press.

So much for keeping the investigation quiet.

He'd flashed his badge and explained the fire was related to an ongoing investigation. He walked onto the crime scene and tried to make sense of what he was seeing. Ben wouldn't even have come here if not for the emergency call from the deputy. Seemed Ronald Worth had got his hands on an unredacted file that led him from Lara Bart to a man named Davis Weeks. The confidential financial statement he'd filled out for his security clearance and work through a place called the Corcoran Team listed this boat as an asset.

It all struck Ben as too neat. Too convenient.

Lara Bart seemed to be at the top of everyone's threat list all of a sudden. Especially odd for a woman who'd sailed through her own security-clearance investigation to land a job preparing them for others.

Ben hadn't seen the forensics on Wasserman's house yet, but Wayne had called to let him know the deputy believed they would point to Lara and she should be the main target of the investigation. Without any real evidence or motive, people were very willing to believe she'd killed a naval officer.

Now Ben had arrived at another crime scene with a link to Lara Bart. Two dead men in one day. Either this woman had gone off the edge and was engaging in a wild crime spree, or something more sinister was at work here.

Funny how it all led back to Martin Coughlin and his NCIS appointment.

Even more interesting that he seemed to be the only one making that connection and wondering if Lara was being used.

Ben came around the side of the building, widening his circle as he scanned the area. His shoe pressed against something. He looked down, expecting to see a rock. Unless rocks turned pink from fire, this was something else.

He crouched down and grabbed an evidence bag from his pocket. Using a pen, he slid the hair tie into it. Examining the scrap of material, he wondered if it was related to Ken Dwyer's death or nothing more than a forgotten piece left behind days or even weeks ago.

His eyes narrowed as he studied it. Well, if it did belong to Lara they could know soon enough. The long blondish-brown hair wrapped in the band should give them DNA. She'd submitted samples to get her job, so a match, if there was one, would be easy to make.

Until the lab got back to him, he'd focus his attention elsewhere. First thing tomorrow—Martin Coughlin.

Chapter Nine

By the time Pax's car pulled into a driveway in the historic section of Annapolis, exhaustion had whipped through Lara, leaving her weary to her bones. None of them had spoken and the radio had stayed off on the short drive. Wrapped in a blanket and cuddled up against Davis's side, her muscles had released all of their tension. Despite being wet and smelling like a sewer, she could barely keep her eyes open long enough to take in her surroundings.

They pulled around a three-story redbrick house and to the garage that sat separate behind it. She didn't need to see the plaque by the front door to know it was a historic property. It was in the Federal style with a top floor only two thirds the size of the two below. Trees outlined the gravel drive. A bright light burned on the back porch and another attached to the garage clicked on from the motion of the car pulling in.

The place was so bright there was no way anyone could sneak up. She guessed that was the point.

Gravel crunched under the tires, and the car came to a stop. Pax and Davis jumped out a second later. The slamming doors revived her, but not enough that she wanted to race anywhere. She was too busy hoping her legs would hold her when she finally got up. The only way she'd even made it through the past half hour was to block the details of the day out of her mind.

Dead bodies. Explosions. Knives at her throat. She'd left the law firm on the hunt for something a *little* more interesting. But this was way over the top.

Davis opened the door and stared at her. That dark gaze swept over her body and an eyebrow lifted. Even soaking wet and half bent over, he was the toughest, sexiest man she'd ever met.

Somehow he had steered them through tonight's disaster. And to think one of her main complaints was the emotionless way he dealt with danger. Now she wondered if she'd been wrong. Maybe he needed the distance to survive.

She could accept that. Even apologize for being wrong. It was the rest, the secrets and messed-up priorities, she couldn't understand and had trouble forgiving.

But none of that mattered now. Not when he was looking at her as if he was two seconds away from dragging her to a hospital.

She knew exactly what he was contemplating in that whacked-out alpha-male brain of his. "Don't even think about picking me up. I'm not an invalid. I can walk."

A rare breeze rustled the leaves but disappeared as fast as it had come. Humidity thumped around them and her body grew sticky from the combination of wet clothes and hot air. None of that meant she wanted to be thrown over his shoulder and lifted off the ground.

His lips twitched. "You need rest."

"So do you. Rest and a doctor."

He winked at her. "Don't believe in either of those."

Pax peeked around his brother's shoulder. "Don't worry. I'll take care of the ribs and check him out. But we need to get you both inside and showered first."

"Where are we exactly?" She put out her hand and accepted Davis's assist out of the backseat.

"The Corcoran Team headquarters."

Clearly Davis thought that explained everything. "Your new office?"

"Offices are on the bottom." Pax pointed as he gave a verbal tour. "It's a residence on the top."

The last thing they needed was to destroy more of Pax's property. "Do you live here?"

He laughed. "No. Not really my style."

Davis scowled at his brother. "We can run through all of this tomorrow. Right now she needs sleep."

Davis ushered her toward the back door with Pax trailing behind. He whistled, acting as if his boat hadn't just exploded into a million fiery pieces. His loss put hers in perspective. At least she had a home to go to...eventually.

When they got to the door, Davis stopped and glared at his brother. "You done with the noise?"

"Didn't like the song?"

Davis shook his head as he pressed his right hand against an oddly out-of-place dark square next to the back door. Then he leaned down and stared into it.

So much for the not-a-spy thing. "What the—"

"Security." With a hand at her back and a no-nonsense tone to his voice, he pushed her through the doorway and inside.

The room whizzed by her, but she thought she saw a country kitchen with a farmhouse sink and blue cabinets. The six-burner stove had that made-to-look-old style about it. The place was homey and warm, complete with a bowl of fruit on the scarred wood table.

No way did the Weeks brothers live here. They went for straightforward and simple. This place had a woman's touch, a realization that had Lara's brain blinking back to life.

Pushing through the kitchen door, they stepped into a large open room filled with desks and computers; large cabinets lined the far wall and a conference-room table sat in the middle. No one needed to explain this part. It was work central.

"Rough night?" The voice came from the far corner.

Lara followed it and saw two men stationed in front of a huge screen watching the scene at the marina. She checked the corners for news-channel markings. Nothing. The picture was clear and aimed from slightly above. Lara was pretty sure she was seeing a private inside camera loop.

"Impressive," she said under her breath. All eyes turned to her.

She immediately regretted the whispered word. By the stunned expressions she guessed she looked like the wrong end of a zombie apocalypse. She ran a hand through her hair and gave up when she snagged knot after wet knot. Add in the blanket and what she feared was a pound of mud caked to her face and you got one scary-looking woman.

A terrific first impression.

The man who had spoken used a remote to turn down the volume. He stood like they all did, feet slightly apart and hands deceptively hanging by his sides but more likely just within inches of a weapon. It was as if all these guys had taken a class in appearing formidable and in charge.

Davis waved the concern off. "We're fine."

She thought he should speak for himself. She was not fine.

Pax scoffed. "I'm not."

"You have insurance," Davis said.

With all respect to the discussion about "things," she had something bigger in mind. "Then there's the part where we almost died. Again."

Pax smacked his lips together. "Sorry."

The man with the remote stepped up. All six foot three or so of him. The dark hair and blue eyes combination worked for this one. A smile opened his handsome face and the scruffy beard gave him a bit of an edge.

Something about the way he held his body, shoulders back and sure of his place in the room, made her think he filled the leadership role of the group. He was muscular but not as filled out as Davis. Still, it was as if these Corcoran men all came off the same shelf. They had the lethal look down.

"I'm Connor Bowen." He pointed to the fourth guy in the room. "The tired one with his head in the pot of coffee is Joel Kidd."

Yep, a matching set. The last one looked younger than the rest of them, probably in his twenties. And he took the scruff thing a little more seriously. The grungy look matched the black hair and near-black eyes.

Then he nodded to her, and she saw a touch of scoundrel in him. "Ma'am."

Because Davis didn't bother introducing her, she took over. "I'm Lara Bart and, honestly, I've had better days."

Connor nodded. "We know."

"What?"

"Your name. We know who you are." His smile grew even wider. "What can we do to help? Tell us what you need."

A bed and something to make me sleep for about a month. She was tired enough to drop but feared what she'd see when she closed her eyes.

She'd experienced horrifying trauma before. It had taken months for the memory of the pain and terror to dull. This time she wanted to race through it and put all the death behind her.

"In addition to the promise that I can get through the next twelve hours without being shot at?" Because, really, she'd pay good money for that promise at this point.

Joel shrugged. "That's asking a lot."

Connor talked right over him. "We'll certainly try."

She glanced at Davis but he just stood there. His shoulders were stiff and the strain showed across his cheekbones. He likely wanted to launch into work mode and she was messing up his schedule.

She was more than happy to duck out. "Then I'll settle for a shower and a change of clothes."

"I can run out and get you something." Pax's keys jangled as he grabbed them out of his pocket.

"Don't bother," Connor said. "Jana has something Lara can wear until we can get her something else."

That explained the look of the kitchen. Lara wondered if the upstairs had the high-tech industrial look of this space or if it more mirrored the kitchen's feminine style. She was hoping for the latter. "Jana is?"

Connor's smile turned a little sad. "My wife. She's out of town."

It didn't take years of training to know there was something else at work there, but Lara was too tired to ask. Besides that, she refused to judge relationships. Some of her friends had done that to her with Davis, questioning if his work trips were really about work, and she'd hated it. "You sure your wife won't mind?"

"If I didn't offer she'd kick my..." Connor cleared his throat. "Yeah, it's fine."

Davis nodded to her. "Go ahead and shower."

He'd suggested exactly what she had in mind but it was the way he'd said it. Like an order. With an edge of dismissal. Those days were over. "No."

"Excuse me?" The words carried a menacing thread. Davis was not a man accustomed to being questioned.

She was convinced that summed up what went wrong in their relationship. She never rolled over, but she'd let him get away with too much. Asked too few questions. Now that they weren't even dating, her tolerance for the tone was gone.

Ignoring their audience and her usual need to make a good first impression, because she'd blown that with the

hair-wrapped-in-seaweed thing, she launched into the tirade
that had been building since she'd hit that first guy with a
lamp this morning. "This is not going to be one of those
situations where the little lady leaves the room so the men
can talk. I'm in this. Don't want to be, but I am. If you talk
about the case, I'm here."

"I like her."

Davis practically growled at Joel over the comment before turning back to Lara with his full angry-man persona
in place. The tick in his cheek was new and drove home his
tenuous hold on his control. "You're going to get sick."

"Hardly," she said, even though she feared he was right.
To prove her nonexistent point she let the blanket fall to the
floor. "It's still over ninety degrees outside and it's two in
the morning."

Pax whistled as he slipped into one of the conference-
room chairs. "She got you there."

Davis's gaze dropped down her body. The heated stare
had her squirming in her skin. But she refused to check and
see what he was seeing. If her shirt was plastered to her or a
piece of garbage from the water hung off her shirt, she didn't
want to know. She didn't want anything to ruin her stand.

Davis held up a hand. "You'll get mad over this—"

"Then don't say it."

"—but the truth is there are things you can't hear."

The whirling in her head sped up then popped. "A man
got gutted in front of me. We can pretend this is about your
job, but I still think it's about mine."

Connor cleared his throat. "I tend to agree with her. She
was conducting an emergency interview for a pretty important NCIS position. A lot is at stake here for Martin Coughlin. We don't know what Wasserman planned to say but he
sure was hot to say it."

"Makes me wonder what this guy Coughlin is trying to

hide." Joel grabbed a file from the desk behind him and threw it on the conference table. It slid to a stop in front of Pax. "And I think we should find out."

"You all know about my interview?" She regretted the question as soon as she said it.

Never mind the confidential nature of her job—of course they knew. She'd filled Davis in out of necessity and he'd told Pax. It was like a covert-operative gossip circle. The news and theories likely spread among this group within minutes.

Pax winked at her. "We're on it."

There was a low rumble of laughter in the room. They shifted and filed into seats around the table. It was as if the tension had snapped and they felt safe to move again.

All but Davis. He stood stiff and still a few feet away from the conference table. "You're all forgetting the most important point."

Pax glanced up from the file. "Which is?"

"No one but the people in this room and a very few in the Department of Defense with the right clearance and a need-to-know have any idea about Pax's boat."

"May she rest in peace," Pax mumbled. Added a few profane words, too.

"Our financials are not available to just anyone." Davis folded his arms in front of him. The simple move, along with the monotone quality to his voice, had everyone snapping to attention and looking at him. "Our list of assets is confidential and buried deep. If the attacker found it, and it looks like he did because I know I wasn't tailed on the drive to the marina, someone handed it to him."

The theory made sense, but Lara wasn't convinced. When she closed her eyes she felt the storm brewing around her, not him. She truly believed whatever guilt he had about dragging her into this was misplaced. "You're still certain the attacks are about your work?"

"I think someone leaked the boat information and my house address to your attacker. The same someone who knew that you had ties to me and suspected you would come to me for help. My fear is someone came for me and decided the best way to get to me was through you."

The comment sat there for a second. Joel and Connor stared at her, probably realizing for the first time she was the ex. And wasn't that just great? She could only assume she didn't come out well in Davis's version of their breakup.

"We haven't been together for eleven months," she said because they were likely all thinking it.

Joel rolled his eyes. "Oh, please."

The air shifted again and she wasn't sure why. "What?"

"The last job..." Joel choked on the last word when Davis sent him the death glare. "What did I say?"

Oh, something was definitely going on. Something about her that they all knew. She hated that. "Someone explain."

Pax glanced at Davis and then back to her. "Joel's just talking out of his—"

"Davis." Yeah, that was where she would have to get the information. "Now."

Joel looked over at Connor. "Why did he break up with her again?"

"You think he left her?" Connor frowned. "Come on."

Davis turned the death ray of a look on them all, clearly not happy with whatever this was being played out in front of them. He should try being in her position.

He finally spoke up. "I was on an off-the-books job."

And that told her absolutely nothing. Well, except that whatever he was hiding was going to be bad.

She grabbed on to the back of the conference chair and dug her dirty fingernails into the soft leather. "Skip the covert-operative speak and tell me."

"Someone from an old job made a threat. It got back to me and I neutralized the guy."

Her stomach clenched. He made it all sound so mundane, but she knew better. "Neutralized?"

He shot her one of his famous you-can't-be-this-naive glares but stayed quiet.

Joel filled in the blank. "Killed."

Davis exhaled loud enough to drown out all the other noise in the room. "Yeah, Joel, I think she figured that out."

She blocked them all out except for Davis. She could see figures moving on the screen behind Connor and hear the buzz of the lights over her head. The only thing, only person, who mattered was the man trying so hard not to answer a straight question.

Davis's careful wording finally penetrated her brain. "What kind of threat?"

"Against you." Joel slid his chair back when Davis took a step in his direction.

"Wait, your rib injuries are because of me." She didn't phrase it as a question because suddenly she knew the right answer.

"Technically, they're because a guy hit him with a car," Pax said.

Davis never broke eye contact with her. "Don't help."

It all made sense. A sick kind of sense. "Someone was following me and you stopped them?"

Davis didn't even blink. "Yes."

She'd had more attackers following her and he'd never warned her. People she didn't know wanted her dead and he stepped in front of her and suffered in quiet on her behalf. "Who was it?"

"You don't know him."

"I can stand here all night, dripping on this floor, until you spill more facts."

Davis's gaze bounced down to her feet, then back up again. "We work with the Department of Defense and other agencies and private companies to conduct kidnap rescue missions."

He stopped there, acting as if that told her anything. "And?"

"We helped out recently when an off-duty service member got caught in the wrong place in the Philippines. A drug runner was killed and his brother didn't like it. He decided to make an example of me. Someone from my DIA days sold the information about your identity and our relationship, and the news got back to me. Simple."

Her life had turned into an action movie. "I think you're unclear on the definition of *simple*."

"The point is—anyone who investigates Davis's background will eventually find you." Connor shot her a sympathetic smile. "If they look deeper, they'll see he still watches over you and realize the bond isn't broken."

Davis closed his eyes and let out a small groan. "I meant to tell you to leave that last part out."

It was all too much. She'd given back the ring because he'd picked helping someone over being with her. She'd needed him as her stomach had cramped and she'd felt the blood rush out of her.

She'd lost their baby, miscarried, and he'd been so busy and gone so often that he hadn't even known what had happened. He thought they'd failed to get married and that was the biggest issue, but that was just the start.

The sudden rush of anger raced up and swamped everything. She was furious over his cluelessness and mad at herself for not confronting him all those months ago.

She'd accidentally left a door open and he'd found it and pushed his way through. Instead of moving on and forgetting about her, he still waged battles on her behalf. The last thing she wanted was for him to wade into even more danger because of her.

She pointed at him. "You stink at breaking up."

"I believe I warned you about that when you left," Davis shot back.

He'd actually warned her they weren't over but she hadn't listened. Now she didn't know what to think.

Inhaling as big a breath as she could gulp down, she turned and looked at Connor. "Where is this shower?"

He pressed his lips together as if he was trying to suppress a smile. "There's a crash pad on the top floor."

"I don't know what that means."

"An apartment," Connor said. "You and Davis can stay up there until we work this out."

The guy seemed nice and all, and definitely comfortable in his leader role, but no way was she following that suggestion. "What's on the second floor?"

His gaze shot around the room before settling on her again. "My home."

"Good. Davis can stay there." When Davis opened his mouth, likely to say something to make her temples pound, she held up her hand and sent him her best we're-done-here scowl. "I took out two attackers with a lamp. Don't tempt me to practice my furniture-throwing skills on your head."

This time Connor did laugh, but he tried to hide it with the worst fake cough ever. "I'll be right up."

Chapter Ten

Ronald Worth headed toward his front door. The usual headache-producing yelling that went along with having two teen daughters fighting over clothes had ended tonight with banging bedroom doors and his wife playing intermediary. Normally he didn't tolerate such nonsense for long, but he had other things on his mind.

He opened the front door to his assistant, Wayne, and motioned for him to follow into the study. The visit broke his usual rule of separating work and family. He wasn't a fan of after-hours meetings, but Wayne didn't exaggerate. If he took the risk of bothering his boss at home, an actual emergency did exist. Something that might be better handled outside of the office.

"What is it?" Ronald asked in a tone he hoped would signal a need to get to the point quickly.

Wayne stood with his hands behind his back, never leaving the safety of the door. Even though it was closed, Wayne looked as if he could bolt right through it.

As far as Ronald could tell, that was the norm for his assistant. Between the sweating and the heavy swallowing, the guy always looked ready to run.

After one of those throat-moving swallows, Wayne started talking. "Ben Tanner."

Ronald sat in his red leather chair. It was either that or give in to the frustration building inside him and whip something across the room at Wayne. Not that it was his fault. No, this was Steve Wasserman's fault. The man had stayed silent, observed the pact, for years. One day he grew a conscience and everything went to hell.

But Ben was supposed to contain this mess. He was the guy who understood that rules often didn't fit a situation and had to be...manipulated. Or that was what his record had said, the personality Ronald had counted on when he'd maneuvered the case to be dumped in Ben's lap. "What did he do?"

"It's more like where he is."

"I am not in the mood for cryptic word games."

"There was a fire at one of the marinas in Annapolis tonight." Wayne stepped forward and slipped a sheaf of folded papers out of the inside pocket of his blazer.

Ronald didn't see the logical leap from fire to Ben. "Did one of the academy midshipman do something?"

"Someone blew up Paxton Weeks's boat. He's—"

"I know who he is." Pulling every string and using every back channel to make sure the trail didn't lead back to him, Ronald had read the Weeks brothers' confidential files. He'd given Ben just enough information to connect the players and keep his focus on the Bart woman. Or he thought he had. "Why is Tanner there?"

"I don't know but he got onto the scene by flashing his NCIS badge. After a few calls, a detective got rerouted to me to confirm Tanner's legitimacy."

After only a day Ben Tanner was proving to be a liability. "Injuries?"

"One dead. A male, but it appears to be unrelated to the fire."

So, no Lara Bart, the woman at the very heart of everything. "This is getting too messy."

"Sir?"

Maybe this was a good thing. The more focus on the Lara-Bart-as-scorned-lover angle, the less attention on Steve Wasserman's accusations. "It looks like we have another link to Lara Bart. That woman does seem to turn up everywhere, doesn't she?"

"I'm not sure if anyone has made that connection."

This part Ronald could handle without using Ben. "Call your detective back and make sure they do."

SILENCE THUMPED THROUGH the room as Lara stormed up the steps. Davis had seen her hurt, seen her ticked off. Tonight was a whole new level of anger. She looked as though she could follow through with that lamp threat.

He just wished she'd saved that for a private conversation. He hadn't wanted to tell her about the car accident just yet. And having it unspool in front of these guys guaranteed he'd be hearing about it forever. The men had gone in together after their DIA team leader had got married and traded his job for a private-security company.

Pax and Davis had decided they preferred Annapolis over San Diego and came back home. Connor had convinced Pax and Davis to join Corcoran and then lured Joel from the government job that had him disillusioned.

Connor broke through the quiet. "That's an angry woman right there."

"I'm kind of in love." Joel took a long drink out of his coffee mug. "In fact, forget the 'kind of' part."

"She's had a rough day." Davis grumbled the words because that was all he could manage at this point. Lara wasn't the only one who'd had enough for one evening.

"Yeah, the *day* was the problem," Pax joked.

Davis was ready to declare this conversation over. He glanced around at the empty desks on the opposite side of the room, noticing clean tabletops and knowing that meant one thing. "Where's the rest of the crew?"

"Doing post-job cleanup in Mexico."

The idea of a new assignment and the chance to legitimately change the subject appealed to him. "What is it? Who's missing?"

"A diplomat's kid. It was an easy run and grab for us. The boy is still stunningly spoiled but he's home now." Connor shook his head. "But you don't get to spend even one minute thinking about that job. You have enough to worry about with your woman and figuring this mess out."

Davis liked the sound of Lara being his. Well, he usually did. Right now he wasn't sure.

The fighting wasn't his favorite. He could never understand why every minute couldn't run smoothly. You fell in love, lived together and—boom—things should straighten out.

Boy, had he been wrong on that score. "You might want to explain to her how she's mine."

"I'm not ticking her off by bringing your name up." Connor handed the remote to Joel, who immediately turned the volume up and flipped back around to rewind the tape. "But I will go get her some clothes."

As much as Davis wanted to ignore this, he couldn't. Letting things fester had helped to land them their messed-up relationship in this spot.

Still, he let out a long-suffering poor-males sigh. "Show me the way. I'll take care of getting her what she needs."

Pax whistled; this time it sounded like a warning. "Uh, are you sure that's a good idea?"

"Whether she likes it or not, we're in this together." Davis's only worry was that she really didn't like it.

Pax didn't back down. "Are you talking about this operation or the sleeping arrangements?"

"Both."

It actually took Davis longer than expected to get upstairs. Connor got the clothes and helped Lara settle in. Because every step hurt, Davis let Pax check his injuries and wrap his ribs. The pain pills Davis took had his eyelids drooping.

All he wanted was to climb into bed...with Lara. No sex because, really, he'd never stay awake long enough to enjoy it now that he had the painkillers in his system. But he could hold her.

When he opened the door to the crash pad, the room was dark. He didn't need a light. He'd stayed there for a few weeks at the beginning of his employment when he couldn't bring himself to actually move into the house he'd planned to share with her. For almost a month he'd debated selling it without ever putting so much as a shirt in the closet.

Now he saw the Lara-size lump in the bed and thought about lifting his T-shirt off. He gave up when he decided shifting around would only make his ribs ache more. The boxer briefs only stayed on as a concession to her. Sliding into the cool sheets, he lay back and nearly groaned in relief as his head hit the pillow.

She was up and twisting a second later. The light flipped on, highlighting the room in yellow.

"Hey." He threw his arm over his eyes to block the light.

She shoved it down and stared at him. "What are you doing?"

"Sleeping."

"Not here."

"I'm not going to touch you." Though he was tempted. Her oversize V-neck T-shirt hinted at the amazing body underneath. It had been a long time but he could still remember how soft her skin was and how perfectly her breasts fit his palm.

"Davis."

For a second he was worried he'd said that last part out loud. "Lara, look. I'm exhausted and in more pain than I want to admit." He added that last part in the hope the guilt might sway her. "Pax took care of the new injuries and gave me some pills. I could barely stand up in the shower."

"I'm happy you took one."

The smell of his shirt would have kept him awake. "I don't want to fight."

"I don't either."

Could have fooled him. "Are you sure? Because you're kind of good at it."

The flat line of her mouth went even straighter. "How much pain are you in?"

He guessed she was debating if she should add more. "Some. What about you and that knee?"

"It's no big deal. Not like your injuries." She nibbled on her bottom lip. "So, you're skipping the doctor?"

He was done talking about his ribs. That conversation could only lead to trouble. If she asked too many questions, they'd circle right back to what had ticked her off so much downstairs—the reason behind him getting run over by a car.

"Does this hurt?" He traced his finger over the small nick on her throat. The ends of her hair, damp from a shower, brushed against his hand. "I wanted to kill him for hurting you."

Her eyes did that thing where they got all soft. He had no idea how women did that. It was one of those secrets perfected over time and handed down through the generations. Women's eyes got big and sweet and men turned stupid. He was no exception.

She rubbed the back of her hand over his beard stubble. "You rescued me."

"Eventually." Almost too late, and that ate at him. He'd

see her face, the pleading as the terror threatened to swamp her, every time he closed his eyes.

She tilted her head and her hair slid over her shoulder. "Don't do that. You're not superhuman."

"But you are." Strong and sexy and so damn determined that his heart swelled just from watching her.

He still loved her. A piece of him had always known it, sensed the deep feelings had never gone away. He piled anger and regret on top of the love, but it thumped as strong as ever. Seeing her convinced him of that. Touching her, kissing her brought home the reality that he always would love her.

He had no idea what to do about his feelings or how to win her back. Then there was the very real part where he wanted her to explain and admit that leaving him had at least been a little difficult for her. She'd broken him and he didn't even know if she cared.

But now wasn't the time. His words were starting to slur and his brain skipped and stammered over making simple connections. Still, he needed her to know one thing. "You made me proud today."

Her smile was instantaneous. "Really?"

"Yeah, honey."

She dropped a kiss on his nose then scooted back to her side of the queen-size bed before he could respond. She glanced back at him over her shoulder. "Okay, you get to sleep here, but keep your hands to yourself."

"Oh, I can't promise that."

"You need your sleep."

He could hear the smile in her voice. "Then you're safe."

But for tonight only. As soon as the pain subsided he planned to remind her just how good they were together. If it took a battle to get her back he'd come armed for war.

Chapter Eleven

Ben rang the doorbell at Martin Coughlin's house the next morning. The one-story rancher in Virginia sat on a large lot with a leafy green front yard that defied the burning of the beating sun. Rows of perfectly trimmed bushes and bright red flowers highlighted the white bricks. The place was right out of a "work hard and you get this" public service announcement.

That fit Martin. He had graduated with honors from the U.S. Naval Academy, went on to serve with distinction and retired in time to get offered an impressive position with NCIS. He had plenty of experience, even worked in a joint command with NCIS, but another man had been the lead contender for the senior-intelligence-officer position. Then the deputy director had put his old friend's name at the top of the list.

Ben knew the details because there were no fewer than ten men in the special-agent field who had lined up to talk to him off the record. Martin was a favorite among the politically connected set, but men on the ground weren't impressed.

There was talk of an ego and outrageous sense of entitlement. More than one person commented on his heiress wife and the family's carefully crafted public persona, complete with two beautiful, blond private-school kids.

Although the gossip held a certain fascination, whatever

Wasserman knew that might have got him killed interested Ben more.

After the second ring of the bell, the door opened. Ronald Worth stood there. "Good to see you again, Ben."

Ben couldn't really agree. "Sir? Why are you here?"

"To supervise your interview with Martin." The deputy swept his arm across the foyer and in the direction of the mumble of voices to the right.

Because Ben hadn't told anyone except Martin about the meeting, that could only mean Martin had run to his old buddy Ronald. The inbred information of this case made Ben's head spin. There was nothing neutral about this case review.

When the case had landed on Ben's desk, he had wanted to dig in. Now he wished someone else had pulled the assignment. Of course, someone else might be willing to go along with the deputy's vision of the case, but Ben wasn't that guy.

He glanced around. Everything was in a shade of blue or yellow. Not a stick of furniture looked out of place. The no-dirt, no-clutter thing made Ben wonder where these people hid their kids.

He turned the corner and stepped into the doorway of the formal living room. The dark wood and small, shiny collection behind a glass-front cabinet didn't leave much room for question when it came to these folks' financial status. The place had an old-money feel to it.

So did Mrs. Coughlin. She sat perfectly straight in her chair with her legs crossed under her dress, and she sipped tea out of a tiny cup.

Ben shook his head. It was as if he'd walked into a Rockefeller family photo.

A man rushed forward. Fortysomething, fit and wearing dress pants and a tie while presumably relaxing on his day off at home. Yeah, that was normal.

"I'm Martin Coughlin. This is my wife, Nancy." She stood up with a smile seemingly frozen in place and came over to shake hands. "And this is John Gallagher."

Gallagher had a rich, useless look to him. Fancy watch and a smirk where a smile should have been. He, too, belonged to the business-suits-on-Sunday group. Made Ben grateful he lived in Georgetown because he preferred jeans on his days off.

No one bothered to define the man's role, so Ben guessed he should recognize the name. He didn't. He filed it away in case he didn't figure it out in the next few minutes.

He also made a mental note to polish his résumé because it was now clear the deputy had a telegraphed ending in mind to this so-called investigation, and finding out the truth didn't appear to be a priority.

"Am I interrupting something?" Which struck Ben as impossible because he had called the meeting.

"We're all here for your talk with Martin." Something in the deputy's tone suggested he expected to be made aware of all private meetings in the future.

Martin motioned toward the end of the couch. "Have a seat."

Ben obliged even though the seat put him right in the deputy's line of sight. Worth leaned against the wall right next to the baby grand piano. The bench had a cover that looked as if it had been brushed with a comb. Also, it didn't have an indentation that would suggest someone actually sat down and played the instrument now and then.

"You are in a difficult position." Martin sat perpendicular to Ben in a separate chair and assumed a serious man-to-man look. "We understand you need to go through the checklist, but the reality is the murderer's identity is known."

Ben tried to figure out if he agreed with any of that. "And that person is?"

"Lara Bart." John jumped to take this one. "Looks like a lover's spat gone wrong."

"It's terrible, but Steve always did struggle when it came to women," Nancy said, complete with a sympathetic head shake.

The entire conversation was too choreographed for Ben's liking. They each played a role, and none of them did so convincingly. He stared at the grandfather clock in the corner, watched it tick a steady beat and decided to play along. For now.

"Meaning?"

"He liked the type inclined to passion, and by that I mean fighting and screaming." Martin glanced at his wife and waited for her to give him a pursed-lip nod before continuing. "He'd twice had the police called when fights with a previous girlfriend escalated."

So the game was blame-the-victim. No surprise there. Ben decided to impart a little reality into the conversation. "Ms. Bart is a security-clearance investigator."

John waved him off. "And the last one was a stripper. The career choice doesn't matter. We're talking about the personality type."

Ben heard the dismissive tone and watched the fake smile slip. This guy, whoever he was, didn't like playing this game. "Refresh my memory. You are involved in this how?"

"John is a friend of the family and handles all of our personal legal matters plus those of my business." Nancy made the pronouncement as she took a seat in the only other chair in the room.

Ben didn't get her at all. In fact, many of the facts didn't fit. For all the fancy clothes and knickknacks, they lacked many of the trappings of obsessive wealth. The sprawling house, with its separate wings and three-car garage, was impressive by Washington, D.C., standards, where a square of property in a neighborhood with good schools cost a mint. But by all accounts this lady was so-much-money-no-one-bothered-to-count-it rich. Plenty of streets and parts of the metro area were filled with mansions. This wasn't one.

Ben made a mental note to take a closer look at the company she'd inherited. He remembered it starting as a financial-investment firm with its tentacles in everything from pharmaceuticals to government contracts training militia operations overseas. Before the financial markets collapsed, Nancy and her board had diversified, removing them from the commercial real-estate market that had built the firm originally. She'd earned praise for having foresight and gratitude for hiring while every other business fought not to go under.

Where John fit in, Ben had no clue.

He really hated having his time wasted. "While this show of support is impressive, and I think it says a lot about who Mr. Coughlin is—"

"Please call me Martin."

"I do have a few things we need to talk about. Maybe we could take a few minutes in private. We'll run through the preliminaries, answer some open questions and move on."

"Not necessary." Martin's wide smile faltered, taking on a more plastic cast. "You can ask me anything in front of them."

Because that would be productive. "That's not really the protocol for these types of things."

Ronald shifted at his place against the wall. "You can make an exception."

Which Ben took to mean he *would* make one or the deputy would end this pretend discussion prematurely. Ben balanced the pros and cons. No way would he get an honest answer. All he could hope for now was an honest reaction.

"It's a difficult question and I apologize in advance," he said.

"Just get to it." Martin's comment came out like an order. Adding the smile to the end didn't soften the impatience.

Ben steepled his fingertips together. Why bother taking notes? This was all about impressions anyway. "What information did Steve Wasserman have on you?"

Martin's eyes widened. "Excuse me?"

Nancy went with dropped-mouth indignation. "What are you saying?"

Before Ben could respond, the defensive shields snapped shut around the room. The air went from uncomfortable to choking with tension.

He told them what they clearly already knew as he watched for the smallest flinch or eye twitch. "Steve volunteered to be interviewed. He went to Hampton Enterprises' owner, Greg Parker, and because of the confidentiality issues Parker called NCIS. When Wasserman refused to speak with anyone in government, Parker sent Ms. Bart out there."

John reached into his pocket and came out empty-handed. It was the act of a former smoker, and the way he kept wiping his mouth suggested he needed a cigarette right now. "It sounds as if this Greg Parker got conned. Clearly Ms. Bart knew Steve. I'm thinking the entire interview was a front for something else, something going on between this couple."

Martin nodded. "Her personal items were found in the house. I told them." Martin leaned in. For the first time in this meeting he wasn't watching from the sidelines. "Figured they had a right to know."

Not under any investigative strategy Ben had ever heard of. He circled back to the question pounding his brain. "Do you have any idea what Steve intended to tell Ms. Bart or what he did tell her?"

"There's nothing to tell." Martin didn't offer more or try to convince them. He said his line then sat back in his chair. Other than a quick glance to his wife, he looked disinterested in what was happening around him and not one ounce threatened by the questions coming at him.

The clock chimed with a deep, heavy bong. Ben wondered if that was an omen. Maybe a signal of the impending death of his NCIS career.

"You can't think of anything that happened, maybe something you didn't think mattered but Steve could have let fester? It could be something minor that he spun into something bigger in his head." Ben tried to give them every out and shift the responsibility to the poor dead guy.

"Nothing," Martin said, ignoring the potential out sitting right in front of him. He looked to Ronald. "What about you? We were both there. If Steve was upset about something, it would likely affect both of us."

Ben stilled. The comment sounded suspiciously like a warning.

Ronald's intense glare never left Ben's face. "This line of questioning will not lead anywhere positive. Find another."

Ben was starting to get that. If he wanted answers, he'd have to go around his boss. "It's just for background. We ask these things to rule them out."

"Focus on Ms. Bart, Ben." The deputy's voice had a deadly ring to it.

"I plan to do just that."

The deputy glanced in the direction of the front door. "Then I will walk you out."

Ben took the hint. There was no information to be found here. Whatever they knew, and they clearly knew something, was buried under layers of loyalty and years of cover-up. That led Ben directly back to their days at the Naval Academy. The school bound them together.

He knew from only a few minutes of digging that Martin and Nancy had married at the academy's chapel right after graduation. The rich girl and the newly commissioned military officer. An odd match and a perfect place to start investigating.

Ben had almost made it to the front door when the deputy's furious voice smacked into the back of his head. "You are on a thin line."

Ben turned around. "I'm not doing anything any special agent wouldn't do."

Ronald's face was a deep flushing red. Anger radiated off of him and crashed into everything around him. "You're looking to ruin the reputation of a good man. You'll need to go through me to do it."

Because he'd already blown it, Ben took one more step in the direction of his firing. "Don't you think it's odd the wife and her partner insisted on being here?"

"No one insisted on anything." Ronald crowded them closer to the front porch and put his hand on the door as if to block anyone from getting inside.

"I just think it's interesting that the wife needed her assistant, but you didn't bother to bring yours."

The deputy's face fell. A thrumming tension pulled it down until the frown took over his entire face. "Are you trying to ask me something, Ben?"

"No." Ben grabbed his keys. "I think I have what I need here."

CLIVE SAT AT the window of the Thai restaurant across the street from the coffeehouse where he usually exchanged information with his boss. They passed everything in the middle of a newspaper left on the table for only a split second. One of them would get up and the other would swoop in.

Today he had put a buffer between them. He wore a baseball cap pulled low and sunglasses. In this neighborhood in the middle of summer, he fit in. No one outside of the usual trendy college, stare-at-their-laptops crowd was there.

Neither was his boss.

He waved the waitress away as he concentrated on the people passing on the sidewalk and all he had to accomplish. Time ticked by and the loose ends kept getting longer.

Because Clive had destroyed his main work cell in the marina, he was at a disadvantage. Sure, his boss had other numbers to reach him, but he hadn't tried any. The man followed the news closely, so by now he had to know about the marina explosion. Unless he'd totally fallen asleep, he should be able to move the pieces around and realize the marina fire had everything to do with this operation.

Clive turned his glass on the table, careful not to let it clank against the wooden top. His boss had wanted Wasserman out of the way. Clive had made that happen but hadn't been paid. The note inside Davis Weeks's file explained that the remainder of the transfer would occur when Lara Bart was neutralized. A task that turned out to be harder than expected.

In the meantime Clive had another problem. He knew many of the boss's deepest secrets, the kind that could not get out. Clive had done a lot of dirty jobs for him. His boss was a man dedicated to his own public image. Clive could destroy all that, but it also made him a target.

Lara Bart's boss had talked with Wasserman and set up her initial interview. She was supposed to have arrived later that afternoon and found Wasserman's body and the obvious burglary scene. She was to play the role of unwitting witness. One call to the police and all the work would have been done. Unfortunately for her, Wasserman had changed the meeting time, and the word had never got back to Clive to double-time his work. Everything had spun out of control from there.

She may not have had time to learn anything, but her boss at Hampton Enterprises did. That was Clive's in. The man,

Clive thought his name was something Parker, had talked with Wasserman. He had to provide Parker with a reason for wanting to be part of the clearance investigation. There had to be a kernel of something important in there. Knowing the reason Wasserman needed to die would provide Clive with much-needed leverage in case his boss decided termination was necessary.

All Clive had to do was convince Parker to talk. Every man had a breaking point. Most could only take a touch of pain before spilling their bladders and their supposedly top secret information.

Clive smiled at the idea of crushing the guy who made his living investigating the backgrounds of others. Yes, Parker would talk.

Then the real fun would come. After a bit of practice, Clive would wield his cutting skills on Lara Bart and her annoying boyfriend. There would be a blood trail all over town, and Clive would make sure it led back to his boss. Let's see how he liked to be set up for a murder rap. Being the decent guy he was, Clive decided to not even charge for taking out Weeks. That would be pure pleasure.

Clive raised his hand to get the waitress's attention. Because there were only four occupied tables, she scurried right over.

"Yes?"

"I need a menu." Suddenly he was very hungry.

Chapter Twelve

Davis leaned back in his chair and rubbed his eyes. Between the restless night sleeping next to Lara but not touching her and the morning of searching through files for an angle on the attack, Davis's vision blurred. The coffee helped, but after three cups the impact had worn off.

Connor had called in some favors and found out an NCIS special agent had been assigned to the Wasserman case. The police were crawling all over the marina trying to link the dead man near the parking lot to the exploding boat. Eventually someone would try to wrap a bow around it and package it all as Lara's fault.

The Corcoran Team had to beat them all to the evidence.

He glanced at the doorway to the main hall and listened for Lara's footsteps. She was up there showering, which had his lower body twitchy and the self-destructive part of his brain arguing that he should join her.

The chair across the conference table from him squeaked. Connor tapped a pen against the side of his head while he read the file in his hands. The chair rocked back and forth, probably without him even knowing he was doing all that bouncing.

It was a quintessential Connor pose. Deep in thought but his hand an inch away from a weapon if he had to use it.

"You okay over there?" Davis asked. "I'm the one some-one is trying to kill."

"You do have an interesting effect on people." Connor smiled as he glanced up.

"What has you so engrossed?"

"I'm double-checking the law-enforcement professionals assigned to investigate Lara to make sure we don't have an inside man. Someone is trying to implicate her. It would be easy for a person close to the case to do it."

"They all need to back off. We don't need help with this." The automatic reaction kicked up before Davis could stop it.

"You were never good at sharing."

Davis guessed Connor referred to their time together years ago serving on a Joint Terrorism Task Force. It predated Connor buying into and then taking over the Corcoran Team and reached back to his time in the FBI.

The work had solidified their friendship and made Davis's post-DIA return to nongovernment work an easy transition. He hadn't gone a single day without pay or a place to report to in the morning.

But Davis's thoughts ran even deeper. His patterns had been set long ago. Trust didn't come easily for him—and with good reason. For most of his life he could depend only on Pax. His mother had taken off after the car accident that had killed the father Davis had never known. It all had happened before a distinct memory could be formed of either of them.

Davis hadn't been saddled with a naive version of family. He lived the real thing. An endless parade of distant cousins with their hands out to the state for guardianship checks. Davis had broken away from his so-called relatives as soon as he could and grabbed Pax on the way out.

Pax, and now the team, held Davis's trust. But branching

out and bringing in police, instead of wrestling with the case on his own, started a spinning in his gut that wouldn't stop.

He'd let Lara in because he couldn't build a wall against her fast enough. He'd interviewed her on a DIA assignment that crept into her office building, and they'd started dating three days after the case ended.

From the beginning he'd believed in her. She had lost both her parents young, too, so they were matched lost souls when it came to family. And then she had packed her bags and left him to wallow all alone. Thinking about the past, turning the rock over and looking underneath, made him feel as if a weight had dropped straight down on his skull.

Time to get back to the work topic. "Where are Joel and Pax?"

"Lara's apartment."

"You thinking someone has already been there?"

"Pax reported back that the neighbor complained about all the people coming and going lately." Connor picked up the remote and turned on the largest screen. A shot of Lara's family room filled the screen. "They're inside now seeing what all those people were determined to find."

Davis focused on the furniture. "It's not tossed."

"No, the person or people erased their tracks. Joel thinks it looks too perfect. Not even an indent for a footprint on the carpet."

It was a common mistake. Davis had seen it a hundred times, and it usually fooled the police. "They erased signs of her along with signs of them."

"Exactly."

Davis watched the scene on the screen. He could see Pax's back, which meant Joel was either holding or wearing the camera. The lens focused on a basket of laundry and the underwear stacked on top. Davis preferred them on her.

He sure didn't like other men seeing them. "That should make Lara happy."

"Are her worries a concern for you these days?"

Davis dragged his gaze away from the monitor and to the man across from him with entirely too much amusement in his voice. "It's not like you to fish around in my personal life."

"I've known you for a long time and have been working with you exclusively for almost a year. It's not like you to fall all over a woman." Connor threw the folder on the table. "This one's special."

More than that. She was *the* one. The only one who would ever matter. "I thought so at one time."

"Whatever you have together looks alive and kicking to me." Connor reached across for the coffeepot and shook it. The inch of dark brown liquid sloshed in the glass.

"I'm not the problem."

"Are you sure?"

Davis gave up trying to read the words on the page. They'd mashed together into a long black smear. "Care to explain that?"

"You don't give away a lot. I can see where a woman might not like that."

"You talking from experience?"

"Yeah." Connor poured the last of the coffee into his mug then took off to the kitchen with the empty pot.

"Any chance you want to tell me where Jana really is?" Davis raised his voice just in case Connor tried to pretend he couldn't hear.

The guys had been talking about this issue for days. Without warning, Jana had packed up and left. Davis had missed it because he'd been too busy being hit by a car at the time, but according to Pax, they were more than two weeks into the sick-relative excuse and no sign of Jana.

Connor walked back in holding a replacement pot of coffee. They'd learned long ago one pot didn't work. "Visiting relatives."

"If you say so."

"I do." Connor slid back into his seat. "I've also heard your breakup story. I'm just saying you might want to go back over everything again and see what fact you missed."

To Davis it wasn't that complicated. He'd walked in the door and she'd left. He had called and she had ignored him.

"She was pretty clear when she gave the ring back." A fact that still killed him.

"That woman strikes me as a fighter. There has to be a reason she gave up on you."

The words bulldozed into him. "Yeah, you'd think."

A screen on the desk flickered to life. It focused on the front door to the Corcoran Team house and a guy standing there. He looked out at the street, then back to the door.

Connor leaned forward in his seat. "Who is that?"

"Someone who's not too comfortable about being out there and exposed."

"Smart man." Connor stood and pressed his thumb to the reader on the desk drawer. It popped open, displaying a choice of weapons. He picked a gun for his hand and a knife for his pocket. "You don't recognize the guy?"

Davis struggled to get a clear picture of the attacker in his mind. Between his details and Lara's they'd put together a sketch. He had to rely on her for most of the pieces.

He'd spotted the guy in flashes, and they landed punches. The attacker had worn dark clothes and kept his face out of the light. He had instinctively known where the cameras were and avoided them. The guy at the door was not him.

"No." Davis dug the cell out of his pocket and typed in the emergency code. Now he had to hope Lara had listened to the earlier instructions and kept her phone close.

Her job now consisted of staying tucked safely up there and heading for the safe room hidden by a door in Connor's closet. They'd practiced twice before she'd rolled her eyes and declared she needed a shower. He hoped two had been enough to get the point across.

He then sent the panic code to Pax and Joel. Davis knew they'd received it when the movements on the screen stopped and the picture switched to static.

Connor nodded. "Always good when a plan works."

Connor slipped into the main hallway and approached the door. Davis watched from his position just inside the conference-room doorway. His attention went from the live action in front of him to the screen showing him what was happening outside. No visible weapon.

He whispered the go. "You're clear."

Connor opened the inside door, leaving the outer reinforced one closed. His gun stayed just out of sight behind the door. "May I help you?"

"Ben Tanner, NCIS." The guy flashed a badge.

"I think you wandered into the wrong neighborhood. The Naval Academy is three streets over." Connor pointed as he spoke.

"We both know that's not why I'm here."

"I don't know what you're talking about."

"Really?"

"So, are we done here?"

The guy looked straight into the security camera. It would take an expert to recognize it in the strip above the door. He did. "I'd love to play this game, but we don't have time. I need Davis Weeks and Lara Bart."

That familiar churning of energy started in Davis's gut. He inhaled, letting the adrenaline flow through him. The oxygen fueled his blood and readied him for action. The meds from last night had long worn off, and the dull thump in his ribs gave way to the blood pumping through him at super speed.

He closed the double doors to the conference room and stepped forward, hovering just over Connor's shoulder. "You've got one of us. As for Lara, we broke up eleven months ago."

"Look, I get that you're protecting her, and you're right to do it, but she is in bigger trouble than you think." Ben glanced behind him, a move he'd been making since he'd hit the front steps. "Let me in."

Davis had read the NCIS file and recognized the name. Inviting the enemy to have coffee was not anywhere on his afternoon agenda. "We can't help you."

"How about this?" Ben opened his hand and a bag unrolled. "Look familiar?"

Lara's pink hairband, or one that looked just like it. Profanity filled Davis's brain, but he forced his expression not to change. "What is it?"

"In a pretty short period of time I'm going to get the lab results back and hear about the DNA. I'm betting the hair from that band matches your girlfriend. She gave samples to get her job, so I have a comparison sample."

"Aren't you enterprising?"

"The DNA will put her at the scene of two murders in less than forty-eight hours." Ben shoved the bag into his pocket. "I want to prevent that from happening."

The stare down continued for a full minute. None of them moved. To his credit, Ben didn't let two guys with guns scare him off. And he clearly knew they were armed because his gaze went more than once to the space behind the door where they aimed at him.

Davis ran through the options. He settled on collecting more information over sending the guy away. With the potential hairband evidence he didn't think he had much of a choice. "Fine."

Without saying a word, Connor unlocked the door and stepped back. Ben slipped inside and Davis slammed a hand against his chest while Connor conducted a pat down and scanned him. Once he got the nod the guy was clear, Davis stepped back again.

"Was that necessary?" Ben asked.

"Only if you want in."

They walked him into the sitting room across from the conference room. Connor lingered in the doorway until Ben sat down on one of the couches. Davis took the seat on the couch directly across from him. When he looked up again, Connor was gone.

That was fine. Davis knew the drill and kept the guy talking. "You've got the wrong woman. She's not the type."

Ben moved to the front of the cushion. "Can we not do this?"

"I'm answering your questions." Davis glanced out the front window. He saw the same scene that had been reflected in the monitor—one car and no one else. Connor was probably even now scanning the grounds. Because it would take Pax and Joel time to get back to Annapolis from Virginia, they had to buy time.

As if he sensed the walls closing in, Ben braced his feet against the floor and shifted so his back was covered by the couch. "You already know I left my weapon in the car."

Not a move Davis would ever make but good to know. "Sounds dangerous."

Ben exhaled. "She's being set up."

No kidding. "By whom?"

"I'm not sure yet."

"You're trying to tell me you're on her side?"

"I'm telling you exactly one special agent has been assigned to this case and he's being told to keep things quiet, and the hints about what the findings should be are anything but subtle."

When Ben stopped and stared, Davis decided he needed more information. "I'm listening."

"Those preferred findings center on an unfounded theory about Lara having a secret relationship with Steve Wasserman."

Davis was impressed Ben didn't try to proclaim he'd solved everything. He stuck to the facts no one could dispute and added just enough information to keep the interest alive.

It was the idea of Lara with another guy that had Davis slamming his back teeth together until he heard a distinctive crunch. "That's garbage."

"I agree. I think this is about Steve having some information about some very powerful people, information they don't want known. Your girlfriend was in the wrong place at the wrong time and now she is going to have all of this hung around her neck." All of a sudden, Connor appeared in the doorway and Ben glanced at him. "Can I have it back?"

"What?"

Ben held out his hand. "The badge. Did I check out?"

"Yes." Connor slapped the NCIS badge in Ben's palm. "I didn't think you knew I lifted it."

Connor didn't smile, but something about his expression showed he was impressed. Davis reluctantly agreed.

"It's what I would have done." Ben pointed to the lights hanging on the wall on either side of the fireplace. "Just like those aren't cameras. Right?"

Under different circumstance Davis decided he might like this guy. He was smart and pretty ballsy. He clearly had some information on Corcoran and the people who worked there. Knowing that, walking into this house showed more guts than Davis had found in most government agents. "How do you know about us?"

"I looked at the information on the laptop someone planted at Steve's murder scene. Lara's laptop. You figure prominently. After getting the name, I did a trace. If it's any consolation, you're not an easy man to find, but I happened to have a key."

"Explain."

"My boss at NCIS, the deputy director, handed me your file. The boat reference was in there."

"Interesting." Connor shot Davis a furious glance.

"Connecting you to the marina was a leap, but I guarantee you I won't be the only one who makes it." Ben tapped his pocket. "The hairband helps, but for now that's safe with me. If the police aren't inclined to share with me, then I'll return the favor."

"That thing could belong to anyone," Davis pointed out.

Ben smiled. "But it doesn't."

It was a lot of information to take in. The guy across from him scanning the room every time he shifted his head or body had some skills. He possessed an ego, which worked on this job, but not too much, which made him tolerable.

He said the right things, but that didn't mean he was clean. He had information he shouldn't have and Davis couldn't figure out if that made him a friend or an enemy.

His file on the agent didn't provide many clues. Ben appeared to play by the rules. But he could easily be the one who'd started this mess and wanted a piece of Lara.

Connor came around the couch to face Ben head-on. "What's in this for you?"

"If I'm leaving this job, and that seems pretty clear right now, either on my own or by being fired—" Ben blew out a breath as if the words were hard for him "—then I'm making sure an innocent woman isn't framed."

"Hypothetically, if we knew where she was, what would your plan be?"

Davis tried not to flinch at Connor's question. Letting Ben in was a mistake. The fewer people who knew, the safer Lara would be.

"I need to ask her what Wasserman said, if anything, and then talk to her about her boss."

Davis had expected that. Hell, he'd already been through all of that with her and there was nothing to find. "Why?"

"I think he could be the next target."

CLIVE HAD NOT moved in almost an hour. He'd perfected the art of perfect stillness over the years and had trained his muscles to endure the aches and stiffness.

He stood now, watching the security guard walk the same pattern around the top two floors of the Gimmel Office Building. Tapping into the closed-circuit feed had been easy. Just slip into the building and down the emergency stairs to the server room.

He clicked a button on the black box in his hands and the view switched to the glass-front double doors of Hampton Enterprises. He scoffed. Glass, as if the aesthetics should ever overwhelm an office's security needs. It was an amateur move by a man who'd spent his life in business rather than security.

No one moved in the area by the reception desk. Only the guard in the hall.

Five-nine with a stomach stretched and hanging low thanks to too few salads. Clive didn't fight off the smile. This would be too easy.

He leaned down and grabbed his backup gun from his ankle holster. No reason to waste his favorite weapon. This one would end up in the garbage. After, he'd blend into the

Georgetown tourist crowds filling the streets and walking along the water's edge, then slip away.

By his count, he had two minutes to get upstairs. He unclipped the listening equipment and smashed it under his heel. Nothing would trace back to him. It never did.

After a quick check in the hall to monitor for any surprises, he opened the door and slid out. A few feet more and he stood at the emergency stairs.

Minute-thirty.

Taking the steps two at a time, and careful to land his feet with as little noise as possible, he vaulted up the three flights to Hampton's floor. He reached his destination in record time, not even out of breath from the effort. With his hand on the lever, he pressed his shoulder against the door to the third floor.

A check of his watch told him he had thirty seconds.

He tightened his fingers and lifted his gun. The footsteps should sound at any minute. As soon as he thought it, he heard them. A sense of satisfaction pumped through his veins. It was about time something on this job went as planned.

He counted down. At ten seconds, he threw open the door and stepped into the hallway. The guard didn't even have time to blink before the bullet hit him.

Chapter Thirteen

"Greg is in danger?"

Lara had stayed upstairs as long as she could tolerate it. With a gun in her hand and a cell with 9-1-1 typed and ready to hit Send in the other, she headed down the stairs. She heard the low rumble of male voices, including one she didn't recognize. Rounding the corner she caught the comment about the threat to her boss.

Davis saw her and a mask of fury fell over his face. He pointed as he yelled, "Stay upstairs!"

"It's a bit late for that, don't you think?" Connor asked.

She saw the gun in Connor's hand and tried to make an educated guess about how many were in the room at that moment. She hoped at least one pointed at the guy she didn't know.

"I'm Ben Tanner." He stood up and held out a hand.

"I heard." She glanced at his outstretched hand but didn't shake it until Davis gave her a nod. "And, no, I didn't kill anyone."

"I'm looking into the Wasserman matter and any ties it may have to the Dwyer murder at the marina."

The guy didn't even know what he was dealing with. He was talking about two deaths and missing one that she couldn't forget. "For the record, the number of deaths is at three," she said.

Ben leaned forward. "Excuse me?"

"An attacker came for me in my home right after Lara's encounter at Wasserman's. He failed." Davis delivered the sequence with all the emotion of a guy being asked to clean the house.

"My people took care of the body," Connor said as he sat down on the arm of the couch. The gun rested on his lap, making exactly the kind of statement these guys did best.

Ben shot him a look. "I'd love to know how you did that."

Connor shrugged. "It's easy to make people disappear, especially when no one cares about them."

And that was just about enough of that conversation. Last thing she wanted to talk about were more bodies. She'd seen too many at her feet to last a lifetime.

"Had you seen the guy at your house before?" Ben sat back down as he asked.

"No." Davis blew out a long breath. "The one who killed Wasserman also killed Dwyer. Also blew up my brother's boat. He's the one still on the loose."

"Which is the only reason you're standing here," Connor said to Ben. "Someone tipped off the attacker about the boat. Someone with access to confidential information."

Ben's eyes narrowed. "Only a few people fit that description."

"Like the deputy director."

"Exactly."

Lara had lost the thread of the conversation. Somewhere along the line Davis and Connor had filled this guy in, which was a surprise. They kept the circle closed. Opening to a stranger struck her as a huge risk. If they were talking, things were more desperate than she'd thought. And that was hard to imagine because she'd painted a pretty horrible picture in her mind.

If it hadn't been for Davis crawling into bed with her last

night, she probably wouldn't have slept ten minutes. Not that she wanted to examine the comfort he gave her. That was confusion for another day. She had to live that long and stay out of jail first.

Best way to avoid the death and prison thing was to end all of this. She started talking before Davis could hustle her out of there. "Steve Wasserman didn't say anything. He offered me a glass of ice water and then got a call. He was in the kitchen so long that I went in and found him dead on the floor. That's when the fun started."

"How was he acting?"

She took the seat next to Davis and sighed inside with relief when his hand slid over her knee. The warmth of his palm gave her the energy she needed to keep going. "Nervous."

These were all questions Davis had already asked her. Whatever training this guy Ben had felt familiar. He kept the inquiries short and clear. He didn't let up or waver from giving her eye contact. Davis had used all those techniques on her one time or another, though she doubted he knew he did it.

One of the constant complaints of the relationship stemmed from his insistence on treating her like someone he needed to interrogate. He never noticed. She always did.

"Were there papers or anything in the apartment?" Ben asked, as if working through his mental list.

"Just my..." Her voice hiccuped in her throat.

Davis's fingers curled around her leg as he leaned in with eyes filled with concern. "What is it?"

The blood drained from her face. She felt it whoosh out and leave her head. The dizziness smacked her a second later. "I left my file. My work file. It had Wasserman's information and some of mine."

The breach was significant. With every other horrible thing happening it likely didn't matter, but it was so out of character for her that it hammered home how desperate she'd been to run from that house.

But the news did help a missing piece of the puzzle fall into place. For someone to attack her on Capitol Hill and launch a second attack about forty-five minutes later in Annapolis required significant planning. It shook her firm belief that the attackers traced back to her job and not Davis's. But this would explain it. If someone knew about her life, there could be another party somewhere overseeing and moving the people where he needed them.

Davis must have been thinking the same thing. "That explains how he tracked your name down and then got to me so fast."

Ben leaned forward with his elbows on his knees. His voice stayed calm but the air around him shimmered from the force of his will. "Wasserman didn't try to hand you anything or show you anything?"

"Really, we had just started when the call came."

Ben looked down, then his head shot up again. "You have the cell? There wasn't one in the house."

"There was when I left with the attacker on the floor." She tried to deliver it with a half chuckle but couldn't sell it.

Ben glanced at Davis before he continued. "Well, a lot of you is still at the house."

The way he put the words together tipped her off. She was not going to like this part. "What?"

"Personal things. Someone wants it to look like the two of you had a personal relationship."

"That's a lie." Shock punched into her. She didn't realize she'd jumped up until her feet hit the carpet. Her gaze bounced down to Davis. "It is!"

"We know, honey." He grabbed her hand and pulled her back to the couch. Once there he didn't let go. His fingers slipped through hers. "Why is her boss in danger?"

"Steve found out about the clearance investigation and contacted her boss, Greg Parker, directly. It's possible Steve said something." Ben made a hissing sound through his teeth. "Even if not, someone else might think Steve talked."

Connor got to his feet. He still held the weapon, but it seemed to have a different target now. "Let's head over."

Ben's mouth dropped open. "Me?"

"You came here asking for help," Davis said. "You're stuck with us now, especially since I'm not convinced you aren't at the bottom of all of it."

Ben swallowed hard enough that Davis could see his throat move. "That's comforting."

Davis's smile was almost feral. "So long as we all understand where we stand."

Lara had no idea what was going on. The room buzzed with energy. It was as if all the testosterone funneled into that small space and imploded. If anyone stormed the house right now, they'd run straight into a wall of male fury, including Ben. Somewhere along the line he'd been added to the Corcoran equation. His eyes hadn't stopped blinking since Davis had included him in the trip.

That left one person. Her. "I'm coming."

"No," Davis stated before she finished her comment.

He could yell all he wanted. This was happening. "This isn't a debate."

"Damn right." He dropped her hand and stood up. He'd probably have locked her in the closet if he got half a chance. "This could be dangerous."

She tried the one thing she thought would work—logic. To be safe she aimed it at Connor instead of Davis. "It's not during regular business hours. You won't get in without my key card."

Davis gave her a nice-try smile. "We're going to his house."

The man never learned. "Steve will be at work. He practically lives there. You should appreciate that since you're the same way. Work first always."

Davis frowned but didn't say anything to that.

But Connor was already moving. He stood in front of Ben. "So the deal is you stay quiet about Davis, and certainly about Lara, and in turn we look into this together."

"Yes, but if I find out I'm wrong and she did it, I'll deliver her to the police myself."

She wasn't worried about that because she hadn't done anything wrong. She had broken work protocol, but she doubted anyone would blame her seeing as she was being attacked by a trained killer at the time. A forgotten file couldn't matter that much.

Davis shook his head. "Connor, we should—"

"We need to drive to D.C. We should leave." She tried to telegraph a sense of urgency because the ball of anxiety bouncing around in her belly told her they didn't have time to waste.

Connor spared her a glance but kept his focus on Ben. It was clear Connor had downshifted into leader mode. "You could get into a lot of trouble for this."

"We'll all be in danger if I don't. You think whoever killed a navy lieutenant is going to just let this drop?" Ben shrugged. "Besides that, I don't think Lara should pay for something someone else did."

The man uttered the words that appeared to save his skin. Connor nodded. "Integrity. I like it."

"It's not exactly a novel concept."

"Right. That's why you plan to leave your government job after all of this is over." Connor looked as if he wanted to slap Ben on the shoulder but settled for a firm nod instead. Then he turned to Davis. "Lara goes. She'll be safer with us than here alone waiting for Pax and Joel to return."

Davis's eyes closed for an exaggerated second. "We could wait."

Both Ben and Connor shook their heads, but Connor got the words out. "Not smart."

She smiled at Connor. "Thank you."

He frowned back at her. "Don't make me regret it."

Davis scowled at all of them. "Let's get going. We have a drive ahead of us and I plan to break every law getting there fast."

CLIVE WALKED TO the window of Greg Parker's office. Towering glass panes provided an open view of the Potomac and Virginia on the other side. Off to the left sat the famous Kennedy Center. Boats sailed on this sunny day and people scattered in every direction on the streets and paths below.

Real estate in the waterfront section of Georgetown cost a small fortune each month. Renting an entire floor only increased the tab. Apparently, there was a good deal of money to be made digging into the personal lives of others.

Nosiness paid well—but not well enough to guarantee the supposedly "uncrackable" security would work as planned. Kill the guard, use his handprint and key card, and the door magically opened.

Clive tensed his hands against the windowsill. The view did nothing for him. He preferred the mountains to the water. Trees and as few people as possible. That was how he'd grown up, away from others, learning to shoot and live off the land. Lessons taught by a father who saw government as the enemy and an uprising of the people inevitable.

Put Clive in an enclosed space and the hypocrisy and general human waste choked him. Moving and living where he knew every leaf and stone appealed to him. He'd travel back to his cabin in West Virginia as soon as this job finished. No one knew him there. No one bothered him.

First, he had to dispose of Greg Parker.

He turned around and glanced at the type of man who disgusted him the most. He didn't produce anything or add to society. He made calls and held meetings. A well-trained animal could do those things.

But Greg's crimes surpassed laziness. He sat in an office and got paid to judge others.

Now it was Clive's turn to judge.

He stood on the opposite side of the oversize desk and watched Greg shift his hands, thinking he hid his movements as he tried to break free. That was not going to happen. Clive had bound the older man to the leather desk chair. Even now blood dripped from the slashing cut across his chest that slit his dress and had it gaping. The puncture wound on his upper arm didn't look any better.

Clive's only real concern was that Greg would have a heart attack before he coughed up any information. That was the problem with torturing men in their sixties. You tended to scare the life right out of them.

With his fists on the edge of the desk, Clive leaned in and saw Greg's eyes open on a bolt of fear. "It would be easier if you told me what I wanted to know."

Not that he could say anything with the gag pulled tightly across his mouth. The bloody knife sitting on the empty desk between them was there to make a point. One move and the blade would pin him to the chair.

Clive picked up the knife and touched the sharp end to his fingertip. Greg shook his head and mumbled into the gag.

"A quick admission would have meant a quick death. But you reached for that emergency button." Clive made a tsk-tsk sound. "I bet you're sorry you wasted my time now."

Greg strained his arms against the bindings. Sweat stained his armpits and dotted his forehead. His gaze shot around the room, and small thuds sounded as he shifted in his chair.

Clearly Greg thought there was a way out of this.

Clive found that notion amusing.

"Here's what's going to happen." Clive walked to Greg's side of the desk and grabbed him by the neck when he tried to shrink away. "I'm going to search this office inch by inch. For every drawer I go through and don't find something on Wasserman, you'll get cut."

Greg was whimpering now.

"After a few rounds I might give you a chance to talk again. Depends on how well you behave while I'm working."

The whimpering turned to actual sobs.

The pathetic sound only fueled Clive's need to keep going with the game. He crouched down so his face was even with the sniveling man. "For your sake, I hope there's something here worth finding or this is going to be a long and painful day."

Chapter Fourteen

A security guard lay in a sprawl in the middle of the third-floor hallway. Connor crouched to check his pulse. He shook his head but Davis didn't need the confirmation. A bullet hole through the forehead and blood pooled under the guard. Those clues said it all.

Davis heard Lara's soft cry and rough intake of breath, felt her body shake as she leaned into him. Once again he'd dropped her into danger. This was one more death and a desperate reminder of just how perilous it was for her to be at the Hampton offices.

He glanced around at the team and tried to think of a way to protect her, watch over Ben and shield Connor's back all at the same time. Dumping Ben on the sidewalk and leaving Lara in the car had been his vote. Connor had overruled him. For a man who trusted only after much hesitation, he seemed to want Ben's help.

Davis wasn't inclined to be that welcoming. If the special agent so much as twitched in a way Davis didn't like, he'd put a bullet in him and deal with the questions later.

Davis signaled for the rest of them to wait as he turned the corner and glanced down the hall. Seeing it empty, he motioned for the others to follow. He led and Ben shielded Lara. Connor brought up the back end, just as they'd discussed on the drive to D.C. Davis had verbally walked them through the plans several times and hadn't stopped until everyone could repeat them back without hesitating.

"This is bad," Lara whispered.

Davis stopped twenty feet from the main office door. "What?"

She touched her hands against his back and whispered into his ear. "Look at the bottom. The door is actually open and unlocked. It shouldn't be either after hours."

The situation was getting worse with every passing second. It was bad enough Pax and Joel had almost arrived in Annapolis when the rest of them had left for D.C., meaning they literally had passed on the highway at some point. This attacker had them running in circles. One more reason to want the guy dead.

Davis needed more data. He remembered the floor plan Lara had drawn in the car and mentally walked through it. "The only thing on the left is the conference room. Parker's office is on the right."

"At the end of the hall." Her killer grip on the back of Davis's shirt didn't unclench even though they stood next to each other now. "But there are many places in between here and there to hide. Rows of offices, the kitchen, closets—"

"I remember." She'd picked up his repetition issue but he didn't mind. More information always increased the odds of success.

Connor eased his surveillance behind them. Taking a break, he turned sideways and glanced at Davis. "Thoughts?"

He could see only one option, and he didn't even like that one because it separated him from Lara. "You take Ben and Lara out of here and I check it out. I'll signal for backup if I need it."

"No," Ben said, his voice not lifting above a scant whisper.

Lara tightened her grip until the edge of Davis's shirt dug into his neck. "Absolutely not."

Davis responded to her before Connor could jump in. "You've been attacked enough."

With all that had happened and the threats that still lingered, Davis couldn't believe he had to explain. The narrow-eyed looks he was getting suggested he did.

"Greg didn't do anything wrong," she said. "He needs our help."

Ben leaned in and glared at them all. "And we're wasting time."

The man had a point. Davis weighed the odds and couldn't come up with a way to make them work to his favor. He didn't trust Ben, but the man had done everything right so far. His file hinted at a bone-deep willingness to do what was necessary to finish a job. He could have turned on them, shot them or steered them into an ambush many times since he had shown up at Corcoran's door, but his resolve had never wavered.

Still... "If it turns out I shouldn't have trusted you—"

Ben nodded. "You'll put a bullet in me. You've made that clear."

Just in case, Davis drove the point home. "There won't be anywhere you can hide."

"Understood."

Davis pushed ahead before his doubts took over. If he hesitated, common sense might kick in, and then he'd have to get Lara out of there. If he tried, he'd likely have a mutiny on his hands.

"Connor and I go left. Ben stays in reception." Davis's gaze shot back to Ben again. "If anyone goes for her, you sacrifice yourself to keep her alive, got it?"

Lara tugged on his shirt. "Davis, that's enough."

"Got it," Ben answered at the same time, returning Davis's stare, head-on, man-to-man.

Davis took that as the vow it sounded as if it was. With a nod, he finished the orders. "Let's go."

With silent steps, they moved toward the door. Before Davis could open it, Connor held up a fist. They all stopped while he dropped down on one knee and investigated the bottom of the door.

He glanced up and delivered his opinion in a near-silent voice. "No wires or explosives."

Davis let out a long breath of relief. At least the attacker hadn't stopped to booby-trap the door. One thing fell their way.

Lara gently pushed on the door and it opened with a swish. The noise barely registered, but in the thudding quiet, it was as loud as a blaring radio.

Waiting to see if an unwanted visitor turned the corner, Davis held up his fist. When no one appeared, he motioned for Connor to move. He sent Ben a final warning glare and winked at Lara.

They would all live through this day. They would go back to the crash pad and he'd tell her he loved her. That he had always loved and forever would. Getting to that moment was his motivation to survive the next hour. Saving her was his only mandate.

Davis and Connor slipped by the reception desk, first checking the conference room. They swept in, ducking under the table and opening the closets lining the one wall while Ben covered them from his vantage point in the reception area.

Next came the office on the right. Their gazes scanned and guns shifted to cover each hidden corner where someone could hide as they walked down the long corridor. They passed open office doors and a supply closet. Nothing in those, but the door at the end of the hall with the big plaque on it was closed and a light shone through the strip underneath.

Davis glanced at Connor and he nodded. Faster now they jogged to the end of the hall. Their feet scratched against the carpet but they didn't stop. Davis tested the knob and found the door locked. Looked as if they were going in the hard way. Not a surprise.

As Davis angled his body for the best leverage, Connor lifted his leg and kicked the door in. It bounced off the inside wall with a crash as Davis stormed by, with his knees bent, ready to fire at anything that moved. They rotated going high and low, their guns moving the entire time.

Something crunched under his foot and Davis looked down to see papers…everywhere. The room was in shambles—drawers dumped, files ripped and documents lining every inch of the floor until the carpet underneath was almost invisible.

Connor checked the closet and private bathroom while Davis ripped back the curtains blocking out the natural light. The rings screeched along the rod as the two men stopped, shoulders touching, in front of the desk. Blood seeped out of what had to be twenty cuts on Greg Parker's body. But it was the deep slice across his throat that had killed him.

"We're too late," Connor said, the vibrating anger in his voice matching the fury thrumming through Davis's blood.

"Think the attacker found anything?"

"That is an angry death. I'm guessing Parker held out." Connor tore his gaze away from the macabre scene. "Good man."

"But still dead." Davis decided he'd seen enough death. This one and Dwyer hit the hardest. They weren't trained killers. They were men in the wrong place at the wrong time.

Davis lowered his gun and whispered an apology under

his breath for being too late. His fingers shook from the force of the adrenaline pounding him.

"Let's go get Lara," Connor said as he turned around.

Davis grabbed his friend's arm before he could exit. "No matter what, she doesn't come in here. I can take papers out to her, but she stays out. It's too much."

"Agreed."

They'd almost made it to the door when they heard her scream.

LARA STOOD IN the reception area with her back wedged in the corner and the NCIS special agent plastered to the front of her. She strained to see over his shoulder, even a peek to make sure Davis was safe, but she mostly got an eyeful of black jacket and formidable shoulders.

Her thigh hit the edge of the table and the lamp bobbled. Ben's free hand shot out to catch it before it slammed to the ground and potentially broke. After using lamps as a weapon in her past two rounds against attackers, she figured it would serve her right to have her location exposed by one.

The catch didn't solve her problem. Her legs cramped and she shifted to get into a more comfortable position, but being penned in stopped all movement. When that didn't work she tried a request. "Any chance you could move forward an inch?"

The only thing keeping her from running down the hall after Davis was the knowledge that she'd be in the way. If he worried about protecting he'd become an even bigger target. Bulletproof vest or no, even with all his training, he was human and she would not watch him bleed out in front of her. Just the thought of him being injured made her stomach ache from all the violent clenching.

"No." Ben continued scanning the area in an arc that

started in the general direction of the conference room and continued around reception and out through the glass doors.

He stayed still, didn't make any noise and kept his gun at the ready. Seemed he took Davis's threat pretty seriously.

She still wasn't taking any chances. She had the gun in her hand and hours of practice sessions from Davis just in case. It had been almost a year since she'd shot a gun. She hoped it was like that bike thing and you never forgot. She also hoped she could hit an attacker as well as she hit a paper target. Davis had warned her about the human factor and how it changed everything.

"The moving thing was more of a statement than a question," she said in a low whisper.

"I'd rather your boyfriend didn't kill me."

"He's not my boyfriend." The response was automatic. Someone mentioned Davis and the line floated through her head.

Ben shot her a quick frown over his shoulder. "Does Davis know that?"

Fair question. They'd been shooting mixed signals at each other ever since she had run into his arms at his house. The kiss had been a green light that suggested their breakup was more of a rest period than a true ending. But neither of them tried to push forward. Physically, yes, but not emotionally.

They had so much baggage piled between them. The baby he didn't know about, how his work was more important than her and the letter from his long-lost mother that he hid and to this day hadn't mentioned.

He was a man who thrived on secrets and kept his duffel packed by the door for escape. She craved stability, but right now she'd trade it all to know Davis was okay back there. Waiting for the horrible sound of gunfire to ring out or for Connor to report that Davis was in trouble was enough to buckle her knees in terror.

Because she needed all of her energy to stay focused and not let her mind wander to worst-case scenarios, she went with a response that said everything and nothing at the same time. "Our relationship is complicated."

Those shoulders in front of her shrugged, pushing her even deeper into the wall. "What relationship isn't?"

"No, really."

This time Ben's quick look suggested she was a little slow. "And I say again, no, really, they're all complicated."

She put her head back, rested it against the wall and fought back the urge to scream. There was just something about the way males like Ben and Davis and everyone she'd met at Corcoran downplayed important issues and lived in the moment that made her head feel as if it were being crushed until it might cave in.

But maybe that was good, because anger at their macho behavior gave her somewhere to channel all of the anxiety flipping around inside her. Between being squished from the front and suffocated from the fear clogging her throat, she needed all of this to be over. The attacker had escaped twice. He could not be so lucky a third time.

As Ben glanced to the left, Lara looked to the right. She blinked when a pair of boots dropped out of a ceiling tile. She screamed when a man slipped out, jumping to the hallway floor and straight into a shooting position. Ben's head whipped around but the crack of the weapon beat him.

Something whistled right near her hand. As she watched, one of the glass doors in front of them shattered into a giant spiderweb pattern but didn't break. A small hole formed but the glass didn't crumble into a million pieces as she'd feared.

Ben shot as she felt his body buck against hers. His shooting arm dropped to his side and just hung there. When he grabbed for his arm, his hand came back smeared with blood. She tried to reach around to help him but he shifted their bodies, shoving her behind him and facing the attacker head-on.

Not *an* attacker. *The* attacker.

Her gaze locked on the man now a few feet away and aiming again. She swore she saw a sick smile form on his lips the second before he aimed again.

They were open targets. Nothing hid their position from the hall. The only thing standing between her and a bullet was Ben. If anything, he stood up straighter, making his body even more of a shield.

She refused to be a victim. She turned to look for anything to duck behind and saw Davis come flying around the corner with Connor right behind.

The attacker's attention wavered at the streak of motion and Davis got off a shot. Ben fired, too. Through the thunder of booms the glass door broke apart, sending shards raining into the reception area.

"Lara, get down!" Davis commanded.

She was already ducking. With her hands over her face and body bent in half, she tried to avoid the glass shower. She almost fell over when Ben knocked into her. His footsteps wobbled and he started to slide.

Her only thought was to get him to the ground and out of the main shooting area. With her arms locked around his waist, she dragged him against her and dropped. His body fell hard against her, pinning her half against the wall.

Hard cubes dug into her skin through her jeans. She glanced down and saw the glass had broken into what looked like a million perfectly smooth squares. It must have been safety glass of some sort. Whatever it was, she loved it.

Everything else had her heart hammering. She looked around, catching the last glimpse of the attacker's shoes as he disappeared down the hall and around the corner with Connor a few steps behind. She struggled to find Davis, desperate to see him safe and hidden behind something.

He stood over her. "You okay?"

Her relief at seeing him turned all of her muscles to liquid. She had no idea how or when he'd got to her and she didn't care. "Fine, but Ben is—"

"Fine." Davis's glance dropped to the man in her arms. "Stay here. Shoot anything that isn't me."

UNABLE TO WASTE even a second holding Lara and checking to make sure she was fine or checking on Ben's injuries, Davis took off after Connor and the attacker. Glass crunched under Davis's feet and his shoe slipped on the desk chips and flurry of magazines and papers that had been kicked up during the shoot-out.

He blocked Lara's face and the blood all over her hands. *Not hers.* He repeated that five times as he pivoted to turn the corner and grab the door to the emergency stairs before it slammed shut. Momentum sent him shooting across the landing and right to the railing.

Leaning over, he looked down the spiraling steps.

He saw flashes of black one floor below him and another splotch the floor below that. Footsteps thudded on the metal stairs and harsh breathing thundered all around him.

Connor yelled twice for the attacker to stop. The guy answered by firing over his shoulder and into the air. The crack echoed through the confined space as the bullet pinged and ricocheted, chipping into the wall a few feet from Davis's head.

He took off. Ignoring the tug from his sore ribs, he jogged, taking two steps at a time and gaining space on Connor. They were still more than a floor behind each other and the attacker when the door clicked on the main floor. Picking up speed, Davis hit the main floor a few seconds after Connor. They both slammed into the door but Connor yanked it open.

The door led to a small hallway, then to an emergency exit. Davis pushed against the bar and winced when a shrill siren split the air. The sun nearly blinded Davis and the humidity smacked him in the face.

"Where did he go?"

Connor slid his gun into his vest. "Maybe another door. He didn't sound the alarm."

The noise in question wailed as a light next to the door flashed.

Davis's mind wouldn't accept that answer. Frantic, his heart racing with the need to finish this, he turned his head back and forth, looking for the retreating attacker. When Davis decided to try left, Connor grabbed his arm and held him back.

"Look around you." Connor panted as he said the words.

Davis noticed for the first time the groups of people walking the streets. Moms with kids in strollers. Couples with dogs. Many people using their cells and one guy frantically waving at a security guard a few doors down and yelling about the police.

Several people stared at them and a few pointed. Probably more than one had taken their photo and Davis had no idea how to fix that.

Yeah, the attacker had dumped them in a busy Georgetown area. People used this path to get from M Street, the main shopping area, to the water. And there they stood wearing their vests and holding guns.

Not good.

Connor's mouth turned to a grimace. "Let's get out of here before we have a PR disaster."

"The attacker is—"

"Gone." Connor finally looked at Davis. "Lara needs you."

Guilt smacked him as he remembered the blood. "She's trying to save Ben."

Chapter Fifteen

The men crowded around Ben as he sat on the Corcoran conference table, his shirt balled up beside him. Discarded bulletproof vests had been piled right behind him, and they all watched as Joel cleaned and dressed the injury.

He'd been hit just under his vest, almost in his armpit. A few more inches and the attacker could have caused unbelievable damage. Joel said something about hitting a lung.

Ben took the ad hoc medical attention and accompanying chorus of questions well. He jerked when Joel hit the wrong spot and swore through most of the treatment, but he never showed any other sign of weakness. Never demanded an ambulance or trip to the hospital.

Lara thought about rolling her eyes but barely had the energy to stand. Even now she held on to the back of a conference chair to keep from sliding to the floor in a less-than-graceful exhausted faint. Keeping her eyes open proved harder.

But just once she wanted one of these guys to suggest calling in the police, the fire department—heck, even the coast guard—when something went wrong. They functioned as an independent unit and ignored the rules the rest of society followed for this sort of thing. To her, dialing 9-1-1 was a no-brainer.

Maybe clunking their heads together would help. They'd

spent the first ten minutes, as Ben stripped down and Joel collected supplies, trading stories about their battle wounds. It was sick and deranged and so macho it had hair all over it.

Joel dropped the last bloody cloth in the small bowl Ben held. Joel eyed the bandage. "It's a through and through. You lost some blood but will be fine in a few days."

"Are you a doctor now?" Ben asked.

Joel's smile looked less than wholesome. "Nervous?"

She shook her head. Here she was ready to fall over and possibly sleep for six or seven solid years, and they were joking. Gunfire, chases—nothing slowed these guys down.

Davis was the worst. He stood to the side, by the doorway to the kitchen, and watched over the medical activities. With arms crossed over his chest, he'd shift now and then and bite down on a wince. His ribs hurt but heaven forbid he admit that or ask for treatment.

Stubborn idiot.

As if he read her mind, Davis pushed off from the wall and came over to stand in front of her. The other men continued their one-upmanship on scars as Davis stared at her with his gaze wandering over her face and down her neck.

This was the calmer version of Davis, not to be confused with the Davis that had nearly squeezed the life out of her when he'd got back upstairs after the office chase. He had asked her repeatedly if she had been hit. Even though she'd answered no, he'd brushed his hands all over. She'd half expected him to strip her down right there on the broken glass. He'd refrained, but she guessed the control cost him.

"How are you?" he asked.

His husky voice washed over her and she had to fight off the shiver at the back of her neck. "Still fine."

"What—never seen a guy get shot before?"

She didn't realize the male conversation had stopped and

all eyes had turned to the couple in the middle of the room until Pax shot his sarcastic question her way.

Fine, she'd shoot right back. "Not before the past few days."

Ben slid off the table, half bent over, and with a loud groan turned to face Davis. "You going to make good on your threat?"

Davis held out his hand. "Thank you."

Ben's eyes narrowed as he stared at the outstretched arm. "I let the guy get shots off."

Her head still was reeling from Davis's uncharacteristic gratitude when the reality of Ben's comment hit her. So, that was what this was about. A case of rescuer's guilt. They all seemed to be suffering from it.

Never mind that she was fine except for a few cuts from the safety glass. "The attacker was hiding in the ceiling. Who could prepare for that?"

Davis didn't drop his arm. "And you blocked Lara. You could have run or done anything, but you protected her. I saw it and appreciate it."

Ben blew out a long breath as he shook Davis's hand. "Anytime."

"I'd prefer if the attacks didn't become a habit," she mumbled.

Connor brought out the omnipresent coffeepot and a handful of mugs. The fact it was almost ten at night didn't appear to faze him. "Look at us all getting along."

"So, now what?" Pax sat down and looked at the stack of files in front of him. A second later he distributed them around the table to the other guys.

For some reason the move, so normal and out of touch with the danger pulsing around them, ticked her off. "Maybe we could take a second and feel bad for Greg."

"That goes without saying, honey," Davis said without looking up from the file in his hand.

He still didn't get it. She'd seen flashes, moments when his fear for her or anger of a situation would take over, but mostly he was a blank emotional slate. It was so unhealthy and so intimidating. She hated that side of him.

She also despised this thing where they compartmentalized human beings into body counts. "We should say it. He deserves that much while whomever Connor called goes over the murder scene and does whatever he does to separate it from Corcoran."

Davis dropped his arm and the file dangled from his fingers. "What's wrong with you?"

Even Ben winced over Davis's tone.

"Oh, I don't know, Davis. My boss was massacred, likely because of something I saw, Ben got shot—"

He waved her off. "I'm fine."

"—and I got trapped in the middle of a shoot-out that should have killed me. If you hadn't turned that corner when you did..." Her voice cracked and she wanted the floor to split open so she could sink right into it.

Something hard moved in Davis's eyes and he looked away for a second before turning back to her. The file crumpled in his hands. "I'm sorry I didn't get there sooner."

No one made a sound. It was as if they held their collective breaths, waiting for her response. "Are you even listening to me?"

His mouth flattened into a straight line. "I thought I was."

"I was worried for you." She stepped up and poked him in the chest before sweeping her gaze across the room. "For all of you, and in light of the ongoing attacks, I would like you to admit, just once, that a man being killed is a big deal."

Davis's head snapped back as if she'd slapped him. "What are you talking about?"

When Joel and Connor started shifting and looking at the
floor then the ceiling and Ben shot her a sympathetic smile,
she gave up. "Forget it."

She shifted to circle around Davis and leave. She needed
a few minutes to think. A few more to regain her game face
and figure out how to go along with the crowd on this, to
pretend she was as hard as they were. She didn't want them
dropping her out of this because she was too emotional. But
she needed some air before her head exploded.

Davis stopped her with a hand on her arm. "Of course it's
a big deal. People are dying."

"Then why act like you don't care?"

"To survive." The answer came from Connor but they
all nodded.

Davis's hold turned to caressing fingertips against her
elbow. "That's exactly it."

"Explain it to me."

Davis looked around the room with an icy glare. When
none of the other men even pretended to have something
better to do, Davis let out a long-suffering sigh. "Let's take
this somewhere private."

Pax folded his arms behind his head and leaned back in
his chair. "We're all good with hearing this conversation."

"I won't feel bad about punching you."

The room whirled until Lara wasn't sure what she should
say. Now that she remembered her audience, the idea of privacy sounded good. Problem was privacy likely meant a bedroom, and the bed could prove to be a distraction.

She'd promised herself she'd tell him the truth once she
got him alone, to explain everything that had happened
eleven months ago and everything that bothered her now.
She'd tried before and he wouldn't listen; then she was too
hurt and devastated to give it a second try.

But she wanted his comfort and his strong arms wrapped

around her. If the heat in his eyes and desire pulsing off of him were any indication, he wanted more than that. One step upstairs and they'd probably be all over each other. She couldn't figure out if that was a good thing or a bad one.

Connor took the decision away from her. He pointed toward the staircase. "Head up and we'll regroup tomorrow."

Ben reached for his shirt. "I'll head home."

That fast, Davis's attention snapped from her to Ben. "You're not going anywhere."

"Excuse me?"

"The second you walked into this office you made yourself a target. The safest place for you to be is with us," Davis said.

Connor nodded. "I agree."

The I-don't-think-I-do expression on Ben's face suggested he fell into a different camp on this issue. "Well, I don't need a babysitter."

Joel put his hand over the bandage. "And we don't need a dead NCIS agent, so listen to the boss or we will knock you out."

Ben's mouth dropped open as Joel's hand pressed harder.

Ben's eyes actually watered. "You'll have to do better than that. This isn't my first interrogation."

Connor nodded. "You heard the man."

"The guy's been in the field. Press harder. He can take it, though it would be smarter if he broke sooner rather than later," Davis said.

Before she could speak up and stop the testosterone-fueled nonsense, Joel obeyed, even holding Ben still when he started to squirm. "Do you agree now, Special Agent?"

"I can't..." Ben's voice died on a sharp intake of breath.

Connor shook his head. "Ben, don't be dumb. Think of it as an opportunity to study us."

Much more of this and they'd accidentally send him to the

hospital, so she tried to step in and offer a spark of common sense. "Pretend it's part of your assignment."

Joel shifted his weight. "This has to hurt."

"I'm fine," Ben said with a strained voice.

Men. It was all she could do not to roll her eyes. "You're about to pass out."

Ben tried to shove Joel away. When that failed, Ben treated them all to a small nod then slumped in a panting heap when Joel finally let go.

"See, it's always easiest if you just concede," Davis said to Ben, but looked at her.

She wondered if he realized that theory ran both ways.

RONALD PACED MARTIN's gourmet kitchen. Nancy had dragged their lifeless but impeccably dressed children off to the symphony or some nonsense that young kids would dread. Glancing out over the acre of backyard, Ronald wondered if those poor kids ever got to play out there. No swing set or toys. There hadn't even been a bike in the driveway when he'd pulled up.

But that was Nancy, always more concerned with appearances than anything else. Ronald knew from talking with Martin that she only agreed to live here, in a house she found inferior and a neighborhood she described as pedestrian, until Martin secured his NCIS position. He didn't want her wealth to be an issue and insisted they maintain the pretense he paid most of the bills.

Ronald didn't know if it was an ego thing or spite. It was hard to tell when dealing with a marriage based on lies and deceit.

Waiting until she left the house had tested Ronald's patience. He'd never liked her and that opinion hadn't changed one bit over time. If anything, he liked her even less now.

"This situation is exploding," he said, jumping right to the point.

Martin wandered around the kitchen, picking up stray cups and wiping off counters. "Meaning?"

"Lara Bart's employer is dead."

Martin stopped while brushing some crumbs only he could see off the marble island. "I don't know anything about that."

That was Martin's party line. He professed to never know about anything that could harm his reputation. "This all traces back to Steve. Who else could he have told?"

"I still don't believe he intended to tell anyone."

"He asked to be included in your security clearance. He contacted this Hampton company to add his name to the list. Who does that?"

"His loyalty never wavered."

Ronald looked at his friend of over twenty years and wondered what life he was living. "When was the last time you talked to him before he was killed?"

"It had been more than a year. He tried after, but we didn't connect."

"What does that mean?"

"A few weeks ago he called here to talk to me, but I was out. He may have called back." Martin waved the thought away. "Doesn't matter. The point is Nancy and I talked about it and decided I should ignore the call. We agreed nothing good could come from renewing that friendship."

Nancy—of course. Ronald figured she'd be at the center of any Martin screwup. Nothing had changed over the years on that score. "You didn't think to tell me that piece of information? It explains everything. Steve didn't just blurt something out. He tried to talk with you."

"No. Steve wasn't agitated or making threats. It was a routine check-in and nothing more."

No, Ronald thought. It was the beginning of the end and Martin had missed the signs.

Chapter Sixteen

"Are you okay?" Davis waited until they'd reached the third-floor landing and stood at her bedroom door before asking again. He'd been tempted to carry her up there but figured she'd put up a pretty big fuss. She seemed to be spoiling for a fight.

He was in the mood for other things.

Instead of giving him the usual strained answer, she threw open the door and walked inside, each step stiff and her head held high. She'd made it all the way to the chest of drawers before she whipped around to face him. "Do I look okay?"

Yeah, definitely wanting a fight.

That shade of angry red was not normal for her face. Neither was the way she stood there with her hands balled into fists, ready to punch if he said one wrong word, which he feared was inevitable.

Although he was starting to wonder if he knew anything about women, he did know this much. "This sounds like one of those questions women ask and men can't answer without wandering into jerk territory."

She leaned back against the chest hard enough to shake the sturdy wood. With arms folded across her stomach she assumed the we-need-to-talk stance.

He despised that pose.

Her eyes narrowed and her head tilted to the side. She'd

pulled out every furious-woman gesture. "Is it that you hide your feelings or that you do not have any?"

This was worse than he'd thought. Whatever fury had been brewing at her office after finding Greg had been murdered boiled over now. He'd try to find a neutral topic, but he had no idea what one would be.

"What exactly is going on here?" he asked like the lost guy he was.

"Don't act like you don't know. We've been over this a million times." She dismissed him by turning around and searching through the top drawer.

The woman had exactly three shirts and three pair of underwear in this house, but she acted as if she needed to search through her extensive wardrobe for just the right thing to wear. As if he cared about that. As far as he was concerned, they worked best without clothes.

He opened his mouth to point that out, but he stopped when he saw her expression reflected in the mirror in front of her. Lines of strain around her mouth, and eyes almost dead of emotion. Seeing her wrung out drained the coiling anger from his body.

He'd spent the past hour desperate to hold her. Watching her protective instincts kick in as she wrestled Ben out of the line of fire, all while maintaining her aim at the attacker, hit Davis with a dual punch of pride and terror. He thought having her threatened was the worst. But, no, repeatedly seeing her at the wrong end of a gun was the nightmare scenario. Even the memory had the power to grip his heart with a pressure so strong it could burst.

He stood there feeling oversize and uncomfortable. He wasn't one to suffer from bouts of insecurity. In his line of work that meant death, but she had him shifting his arms and shuffling his feet like an embarrassed schoolboy. The bed was right there, yet well out of his grasp at the moment.

One more glance at her face and her strange sudden fixation on whatever was in that drawer had him rethinking his usual strategy. He could play the angry male or he could try one more time to make her understand he was more than an automaton with a gun.

"You want to know that truth? I have feelings for you I can't control and can't shake no matter how hard I try."

She frowned up at him through the mirror then turned around to treat him to the direct version. "We're not talking about us."

"I am."

"I'm referring to how you act on the job and how you deal with death and danger."

He wasn't. Not now. Not after all this time. "I'm talking about being so driven under with my love for you, so desperate to have something real and lasting with you that I can't get my vision to clear. That's how I feel about you."

Her frown eased. "Davis—"

He gave in to the need to touch her as he slipped into the space between her open arms and wrapped his arms loosely around her trim waist. "You have to know how much I love you. I never hesitated to say it and I always meant it."

Those eyes so sad a second ago went soft and a little cloudy. "I do know."

"But you don't fully believe it." A wild mix of love and attraction zapped between them. This close he could feel her breaths grow short and the frantic beat of her heart. "You think I don't feel, like I'm immune or something, but with you it never stops. It flips me over and rips me apart."

She sighed as her hand brushed across his chin. "I love you. That's never been an issue. The question is whether it's enough."

It had to be. "For tonight, let it be. We can figure out the rest in the morning."

He watched as emotions raced across her face. Doubt, excitement, maybe a touch of hope. He read it in the way she nibbled on her lip to the way her fingers tightened against his skin. When she leaned in and placed a short, almost sweet, kiss on his lips, a heart-stopping need rushed through him.

"Lara?"

Her hand went into his hair and she tugged his face down closer to hers. "Yes."

The simple word set fire to something inside him that had been smoldering for months. His heart jumped and his hands moved all over her. Touching, kissing, mouths linked and pressing deep. He could not get close enough to her or break away even for a second.

His palms slipped under the hem of her T-shirt and fingertips hit bare skin. Warm and soft just like he remembered. As the kiss crescendoed to a fever, his blood scalded his veins. He couldn't get their clothes off fast enough.

With a sweep, he lifted her shirt up and off. Before he could lower his arms, she had tugged his shirt out of his waistband and stripped it up his chest. Her lips went to his exposed shoulders and her fingers fumbled at the snap to his jeans.

They were lost in a frenzy of hands and mouths. The heat that had always flamed between them exploded into a roaring wall of need. Turning as he kissed her, he pushed her toward the bed and followed her down when her knees buckled.

The bra came next. With a slip he had it off and on the floor. Nearly shaking with want, he looked down at her, at all that creamy skin that drove him wild. His mouth covered her breast and her back lurched off the bed as he rolled his tongue over the tip. He closed his eyes, enjoying the friction of their bare chests rubbing against each other.

He opened them again when her hand slipped inside his boxer briefs. She touched him as she trailed a line of kisses straight down his stomach. Her hand closed as it slid over him and his breath stuttered to a halt in his lungs.

Another minute of that and his body would explode. Shifting his weight, he reached for the condom he'd thrown on the nightstand earlier in a burst of optimism. The position put her head near his erection and she took advantage. She peeled his pants down and her mouth slid over him. The delicious mix of her hands and tongue put a wrecking ball to the last of his control.

Careful not to hurt her but with more force than he'd intended, he pushed her back against the mattress. He was about to apologize when she pressed the backs of her hands against the bed next to her head and smiled up at him.

On this they were always connected. She was as ready as he was.

A few tugs and he pulled her jeans and panties off. He wanted to spend time kissing her thighs and exploring every amazing inch of her. The screaming in his head wouldn't let him. It had been so long, so many lonely months, that he couldn't tolerate another second of not being inside her. He ripped the condom packet open and touched her to make sure she was ready for him.

She shifted, opening her legs wider. "Now."

That was all he needed and more than he ever thought he'd have again. He didn't wait another second. He slid inside her. One deep, long push before he could breathe again.

With a final burning kiss, he started to move. His body pressed and her mouth dropped open. The sounds and scents, the feel of her around him all came rushing back. It felt right and perfect and he cursed himself for ever letting her get away.

Her fingers trailed down the deep groove between his shoulders and she whispered his name. When her body tightened around him, he couldn't find the air to speak. When she told him to move, he did.

THE COFFEEHOUSE CLOSED in ten minutes. Clive stood on the sidewalk, just out of sight from the big front window, and watched his boss take his usual seat at one of the small tables. He glanced around, eyeing up the blonde at the cash register then returning his focus to the table.

No wonder the guy depended on other people to do his dirty work. His idea of blending in included an expensive business suit and wiping his hand through his hair to hide his face.

Amateur.

His stern frown was in place as always, but something was different. He played with the lid of his to-go cup and kept glancing at his watch. His usual controlled affect had given way to jerky moves and an air of desperate panic.

Clive found his first smile since killing Greg Parker. Looked as if his boss had got the message. Clive was no longer taking orders. He was more in the mood to give them.

He stepped inside. Instead of indulging the boss and playing their practiced newspaper-switching game, Clive sat down right across from the man who had yet to transfer the full payment for Steve Wasserman's extinction. That was a mistake the boss would pay dearly for.

His eyes widened and he glanced around at the few other occupied tables in the place. "What are you—"

"Right now I'm enjoying the look on your face." It almost made having to deal with the Lara-and-Davis duo tolerable. Almost.

The man's face flushed to a deep, angry red. "How dare—"

"Relax." Clive had had just about enough of the side-show. What had started out amusing was now wasting his time. "You're a smart man. You know jumping around like that calls attention. Sitting and talking is normal in a place like this."

The boss's hand slashed out and his coffee cup tipped. He grabbed it, causing the lid to pop off and sending the liquid spilling down the sides. "There is nothing normal about what's happening."

"You do look like you've had a hard day." Clive hoped the man hadn't slept. That would make some of this annoyance worth it. Not the race through the office building or the clip he'd taken in the shoulder and nick in the thigh, but he planned on exacting revenge for that later.

His boss flicked the coffee off his hand and made a show of wiping his suit blazer off with a napkin. He completed the move by crumpling the wet napkin in a ball and letting it drop to the floor. "This isn't how we do things."

"It is now." Clive leaned back, making sure his gun still pointed at the entitled idiot in front of him. It was almost a shame littering wasn't a capital crime. "You didn't give me all the information I needed to complete this."

"Such as?"

"How do I get into Davis Weeks's house? I've been there and seen the security. I figure your contacts know a trick or two."

"You don't need to do that."

"Oh, I do if I intend to lure Davis there for a chat."

"Why touch him?"

That should have seemed obvious, but Clive spelled it out anyway. "Where he is, Lara is."

"This job is over."

Maybe technically but not in Clive's mind. He liked the title *rogue agent*.

The idea of not answering to this guy appealed to him. The thought of him bleeding out all over the coffeehouse floor sounded even better. "I'm afraid not. See, I always finish the work before I move on. You should know that from our past dealings overseas."

"Keep your voice down."

The harsh whisper did more to draw attention than anything Clive had done. The man had no idea how close he was to getting shot. "Right now I have a few very annoying loose ends to tie up. Or maybe I should say *cut up*."

"You had your chance."

"You're not hearing me." Clive leaned in when a college-age student sat at the table two down from them, just in case her earphones proved an insufficient buffer. "I am going to continue my work and you are going to pay me."

"Why should I?"

That one was easy. "Because I *do* know where you live."

LARA TRIED TO roll over but her leg was trapped under Davis's heavier one. Instead of breaking free, she slid her arm across his chest and snuggled in closer. He mumbled something as she tucked her head against his neck.

Even though his love of danger made her skittish and confused, she'd welcomed it the past few days. He'd stepped in and taken charge. He'd protected but never slipped into self-destructive mode. He'd even listened when she'd begged to go along to Hampton and then praised her when she hadn't got herself killed.

Truth was she loved him more now than she ever had. Deep to her soul where it wiped out the echoing darkness that had settled in at losing him and the child they'd created. She wasn't even sure how she had lived a life with so few connections and now craved one with him to the point where she doubted she could ever be complete without him by her side.

He rubbed his hand over her arm. Even in his sleep, he had to touch her, comfort her. Maybe the thought should scare her a bit, but all she experienced was a bubbling of something deep in her belly that she suspected was hope.

So much of the man she knew hadn't changed. He had exchanged one terrifying job for another and chased after someone who he thought might hurt her, never bothering to warn her about the danger. Always the lone wolf.

But she'd seen glimpses of his other side. The sweet side, like in the way he handled Mrs. Winston, shielding her and giving her a touch of excitement and the attention she desperately craved. And his quick acceptance of Ben never would have happened a year ago.

She guessed Davis was angry and confused about the way they'd left things all those months before. He'd said as much and so had Pax. Sure, she'd explained her fears at the time and begged Davis to understand. She'd tried to communicate and even suggested they talk to someone to help them, which he immediately rejected, but she'd never told him the one thing he deserved to know.

In that way, she was as guilty as he was. But his tendency to hold back went so much deeper.

Still, she needed to tell him the awful truth. Keeping it from him hadn't been from spite or even anger. It just happened. When he returned she was home from the hospital and determined to make him understand how staying in San Diego had crushed her. He blew off her concerns and left her no choice but to reach for her packed bags and get out.

The time to tell him had never been right after that, and she'd been so lost in her mourning of the baby she'd already loved and the man whom she'd love forever, that she couldn't see a way out of the pain that blanketed her.

She'd switched jobs and tried to start over. By the time she'd emerged from the crushing despair she couldn't see what telling him would do other than shift part of her burden to him. If she did that and he shrugged it off as he did every other moment of emotional discomfort, she didn't know if she'd recover.

He stirred under her gentle caresses of his bare chest. "Why are you awake?"

"I love you." She said it because she wanted to and because she thought he needed to hear it.

His eyes popped open. "A man could get used to waking up to that sort of declaration."

"It matters?"

"It means everything." Those big eyes brightened. "I love you, too."

The words washed over her, smoothing out the rough parts. "I think we should—"

"Oh, wait. I have an idea." With his hand over hers, he slid her fingers lower. His erection pressed against her palm and his body thrummed with a sudden awareness.

They'd made love twice already that night and he was still ready to go. Now, that was the Davis she remembered.

He rolled over, pushing her to her back as his head dipped to that ticklish place right behind her ear. He made this appealing little moaning sound as his mouth moved over her and he whispered her name.

The explosive combination zipped through her senses, pushing out the exhaustion. Her hand slipped into his hair before she could stop, but she made one last grasp for common sense. "Davis, we—"

His lips hovered over her eyes, placing nibbling kisses on her nose and cheeks. "Can talk later."

And then his mouth covered hers and all she wanted was more.

Chapter Seventeen

The next morning Davis finally felt as if his life had adjusted and slipped back on track. He'd gone from being on edge about Lara's safety to feeling calm and relaxed. It was about more than good sex, which was spectacular. Though he hated the idea and they wouldn't mean anything or feel as good as being with Lara, he could find other women. This was about a deeper connection with that person who brought the right mix of comfort and shocking heat. With Lara he got it all—sexy, smart, giving and loving.

The only casualty to restarting their relationship might be sleep. He yawned for the fourth time and looked across the conference table to find Pax glaring at him.

"Now you're just showing off," he grumbled.

Davis refused to feel guilty. He'd spent some of the worst months of his life replaying every minute of his time with Lara, desperate to figure out where it all went wrong.

He couldn't wrap his head around her complaints about the danger. She knew about his life and work going into the relationship. He'd been honest and disclosed more than was safe earlier than he should have to prevent a claim of bait and switch.

He pushed the details out of his mind and just enjoyed the morning after. "I took your advice. Well, yours and Connor's."

Pax closed the file in front of him and put it on the checked stack. "I'm happy for you."

"I can tell by how ticked off you sound."

Joel spun his chair around and used his feet and the rollers to drag it from the bank of computers to the conference table. "If you two don't stop talking about sex I'll get my gun."

Davis picked up on the load of male grumpiness in the house this morning. For some reason the angrier they got, the more he wanted just to laugh. "No one said *sex*."

Footsteps creaked on the hardwood floors. They all looked up to find Lara, fresh from a shower and in white jeans and one of those slim-fitting tops women wore to torture the males of the species.

He sometimes feared a heart attack from just looking at her. She shot him that megawatt smile and his chest ached from the power of it. From across the room he could smell her, read every gesture and watch as her skin flushed remembering last night.

She put the tray with the new pot of coffee and pile of toast in the center of the table. Joel and Pax dived for the food. Davis grabbed the coffee before they knocked it over.

"It sounds like a locker room in here." She rolled her eyes. "Kind of looks like one, too."

Pax pulled out the seat next to him, the one that put her right across from Davis. "Technically, that's your fault."

"Pax, shut up before I let Joel shoot you." No woman wanted to be a punch line. Just because Joel and Pax were too stupid to know, that didn't mean Davis had to suffer.

"I can take it." She winked at him. "Where's Connor?"

Off breaking the law, but Davis decided not to phrase it that way because Ben was lurking around somewhere and the guy still had an oath to adhere to. "Taking one last run at some FBI files he's not supposed to have access to."

Joel held up a finger. "Hypothetically taking a run."

"Got it." She ran her hand over the side of the tall pile of files next to Pax. "Where are we in here? Looks like you've done a lot of gathering and reading while I was doing lazy things like sleeping and showering."

And other things, but Davis kept that quiet. The heated look he shared with Lara let him know she was thinking about those things, too.

"That's the bad news." Joel leaned back in his chair and talked while he munched on the toast. "I've been through the Naval Academy records and newspaper articles over a span of a few years. No school scandals and nothing in the background of Martin Coughlin, Steve Wasserman or the NCIS deputy director. They're linked by school, but not by anything that got the attention of the police, school board or media."

"And it gets worse. I used Connor's FBI contacts to dig deeper. Looked at juvenile-court records and academic files and transcripts, even went back to high school on those three, combing through all the stuff I shouldn't have access to. There's nothing." Pax tapped his hand against the top of his stack. "I even pulled the twenty years since college and, while I still have more to look at, so far I don't see anything."

Joel picked up the bad-news trail. "Their security-clearance records don't show issues either."

Lara's eyes narrowed. "How did you get ahold of those?"

Joel smiled. "I'm resourceful."

Like that, Davis's good mood slipped away. The light-hearted calm gave way to something dark and furious that was much harder to control. It took all of his concentration to stop his jaw from tightening, all his focus to keep his mind on track and not be derailed into what-if territory.

His future actually depended on it.

Giving in to some of that brewing frustration, he tossed

the notepad in his hands harder than he'd intended and watched it slide across the table. "We're missing something."

Pax shook his head. "I can't see where."

The men started throwing out ideas. Each possibility Davis put forward, Joel or Pax shot down and vice versa. They discussed other databases and the unlikely possibility that this tied to something that happened overseas during military service. That should be in the files they had, but Ronald had a lot of power. He could bury pieces, but it was hard to imagine him being able to make a big issue completely disappear.

Lara paged through the notepad, rarely glancing up or getting sucked into the adrenaline flow surging around the room. If the argument and raised voices bothered her, she sure didn't show it. She didn't even flinch when Pax slapped a hand against the tabletop to make a point.

After a few minutes she put the pad down and stared at them. Her lips curled in the start of a smile as she glanced around the table. Ben jogged down the stairs and into the room, and she shot him a conspiratorial look.

Many of the questions died before they got to an answer. One discussion trailed off entirely. One by one all eyes turned to her.

She waited until silence fell and only the low rumble of the police scanner on Joel's desk filled the room. "The non-school records."

Davis knew she had more than just the confusing phrase. The look of pure female satisfaction told him that.

Joel frowned at her. "I said—"

"You're searching school records and criminal records. What about the other stuff?"

Pax grabbed another piece of toast. "You lost me."

It was as close to an *aha* moment as Davis had ever experienced. The light clicked on and he heard the snap in his brain. He'd missed the hole and shouldn't have. They were running around searching but skipping crucial steps. He swore at his unusual lack of finesse on this one. They were all guilty and it took a nonexpert to see it.

Rushing right behind the temptation to kick his butt came a surge of pride. Most people would have been rocking in a corner after being attacked and seeing dead body after dead body. She didn't run or panic or even burst into tears, though she was entitled to do all of those. No, she dug in and didn't hold back even when it meant challenging them all.

No wonder he loved her. It was a miracle no other man had swooped in while he was stumbling around waiting to figure this all out. And he knew that was true because he'd watched over her from afar, dreading that day. He said a silent thank-you to the universe that that had never happened.

He winked at her. "The beautiful and equally brilliant Lara is right. We're going about this the wrong way by searching for an incident and trying to work from there. We need to look for a missing piece. Forget what's there. Find the hole."

That smile of hers turned up even brighter and she aimed it right at him.

He had to swallow twice before he could continue. The urge to drag her upstairs was that strong. Talk about bad timing. "Whatever this is won't be in an obvious record because it has never been found out. It's hidden. It looks innocent or at the very least not problematic."

"Interesting." Pax put down the toast and grabbed the files again. "We need to spread out over Annapolis and all of their hometowns in case whatever this is happened on vacation. Go through their families, expand to parents and siblings."

"Add Martin's wife." They were the first words Ben said since he'd walked in the room.

"Why?" Lara asked.

He leaned over and grabbed an empty mug and the full coffeepot. "She's a socialite from a wealthy family who plays the role like a pro, yet she married a blue-collar guy and agreed to travel around from base to base with him? I don't think so."

Lara shook her head. "Maybe it's true love."

Davis was inclined to go with Ben's gut feeling on this. Davis believed in love, but he also knew other emotions drove a lot of weddings these days.

Washington, D.C., being a purely political town made marriages-of-power-convenience all too common. If power could drive people together, maybe a scandal could, too.

"*Disdain* was more like it." Ben took the seat next to Davis, but not before he grabbed a few of the files from Pax's pile. "Something doesn't check out. She is a stereotypical all-for-show type but lives in a nice house but not a mansion, even though she could afford one and that life better fits her personality. I can't get a handle on her."

Lara's head fell to the side as she glanced at Davis. "Do you ever wonder what people say about us as a couple?"

"That he is one lucky bastard," Pax said.

Joel didn't even look up from his papers. "Pretty much."

Ben shrugged. "I didn't say it out loud because we just met, but I definitely thought it."

RONALD DISCONNECTED THE line on his regular Monday-morning videoconference with the field offices' heads. A knock sounded at the door before the images blinked from the screens. That could only mean his assistant had hovered at the door waiting for the two-hour meeting to end and decided a one-second break was sufficient. Because he wanted in and didn't use the intercom, the interruption could also mean bad news.

"Come in." Ronald got up from the couch and walked

over to his desk. He didn't bother to sit down because he had back-to-back meetings all morning. "What is it, Wayne?"

"There is an issue."

"There always is. Be more specific."

Wayne glanced at the paper in his hand. As usual, he hung by the door and raised his voice to talk across the room. "We've had a security alert."

"Sit." Ronald mentally watched as his schedule disintegrated. He pointed at the chair right in front of his desk and sat down in the big one behind it. "Be more specific."

"It would appear someone is looking into your background."

Not the news he expected. His mind still focused on the work discussion he had just had about Naples. He forced a topic switch.

"A security-clearance update?" Although that didn't make much sense because his update wasn't due for another year.

"This is off the books." Wayne tucked the note into his pocket as a trickle of sweat broke out on his forehead. "The flag you put on your academy files tripped the warning."

Ronald's stomach dropped, which was a good thing because he needed room for the fury boiling in his blood. "When?"

"Over the past twenty-four hours."

"Trace it back." Ronald knew where it would go, or he assumed he did. Somehow this would trace back to Martin and the killings and that damn Lara Bart and her boyfriend.

Ronald balanced his chin on his fingertips and blew out a shaky breath. He'd served his country with distinction. He'd made sacrifices and paid his dues. The idea that a twenty-year-old decision, one that wasn't even his, could rise up and slap him in the face refused to compute in his mind. He should be above this, his behavior unquestioned.

Martin had done this. Martin and Nancy. They'd left the girl that night and sent them all careening down this road.

Wayne cleared his throat. "That's the thing, sir. We can't."

It took an extra second for the words to settle in. "That is an unacceptable answer and you know it."

"I already talked with the tech experts—"

"You did what?"

Wayne was moving around and swallowing, his face blanching a scary white. Much more and the guy might pass out.

Not that Ronald cared. He wanted work done correctly and all signs pointed to a disaster from the beginning of this Steve Wasserman mess. Ronald never liked that guy and could not mourn his death, no matter how violent it had been.

"I didn't reference your situation specifically or give any clues that could lead back to you," Wayne said.

"You're my assistant. It's a logical leap."

"I took precautions to prevent anything like that from happening."

If he had, he was the first one associated with any part of this disaster to have done so. Even Davis's oldest friends failed on that score. "Continue to talk to whatever experts you need, keeping my name out of the picture, and find another avenue to track this down."

"We're going to get the same answer. The person breaking in is an expert. Like, can-beat-the-Pentagon's-security type of expert. This isn't just about a firewall."

"Wayne." For some reason his assistant was not understanding the import of this assignment. Ronald decided to make his position clearer. "Just do it. You have until the end of the day or be prepared for a new assignment in the worst detail you can imagine."

Chapter Eighteen

Lara worked around the Corcoran conference table with the
men for two more hours, meticulously dissecting every detail, going line by line. Previously she'd viewed them as
weapons experts and nothing more. They were the guys you
called in when you needed muscle and a way out of an impossible situation. Necessary but limited in their role.

She'd forgotten, or maybe she'd never realized, that for
their work to be successful, it required research, planning and
strategy. The job dealt with puzzles, human and otherwise.

They sifted and analyzed data and none of those skills had
to do with shooting a gun. Somewhere along the line she'd
sold them all short. She vowed not to do that again.

The process continued without deviation. Each of them
looked at a file. They checked, double-checked, then checked
again. When they passed it around and all took a look, they
passed the file to her for a final look from fresh eyes. Un-
trained eyes that might see something they'd skimmed over.

Being included, working side by side with Davis instead
of being left behind, thrilled her. She never lost sight of the
fact they were dealing in human lives, but she could move
that to the side and focus on the piece in front of her.

Her head shot up.

That was it. All Davis's talk about facts over bodies, all
his arguments about the job consisting of more than chasing

and shooting—she'd never got it until now. She wasn't sure it was possible to mentally sort it all out unless you lived through it. Now she had.

Davis slid his fingers over to hers. "Are you okay?" Concern lit his eyes and his concentration suddenly centered on her.

This wasn't the right time or place. The reality was that she needed more time to work reality out in her mind. But for the first time in a long while, something flickered in the distance. A tiny dancing flame of hope she thought had been snuffed out months ago.

Last night she'd felt love and passion. In this minute she saw a possible future. So many land mines lay buried in the path, but the breath of understanding gave them a place to start.

She smiled at him, caressing every inch of his face with her gaze. "I'm fine."

His eyes narrowed and he looked ready to say something when Ben thumped his fist against the table.

"I think I got it." He turned the document around for all of them to see. "A dead girl miles away from Annapolis on the last weekend of summer before junior year."

Lara read the headline. "College Girl Found at Beach." It actually hurt to say the words because the meaning was so horrible.

She didn't see the direct connection, but she noticed how Davis smiled as he scanned the lines. The black-and-white photo attached to the article on the front page showed a girl, pretty and young. The first paragraph pointed to her background—rich and privileged. Her father was the head of some company and she'd attended a private high school before going to the University of Virginia.

Lara didn't understand why any of that mattered. None of the people in the case went to that school. And why was the young woman's school even relevant? The article should focus on who she was as a final sign of respect. She'd had dreams and a future and it all had died with her.

She glanced up to see Ben's nod of satisfaction, but she still didn't get it. "Okay, so..."

Davis pointed to paragraphs farther down as he read an edited version out loud. "'She overdosed at the beach and was left to die. Evidence at the scene suggested multiple footprints and a parked car gone by the time the police arrived.'"

The poor girl made Lara take back all those complaints she'd had as a teen about not having many friends. She'd pick alive over popular any day. "That's terrible."

Davis kept going. "'The police believed other kids were there for the party but they left.'"

Joel flipped his chair around to face his computer. "That might be a stretch but it's worth looking into."

"Especially because there's a woman named Colleen Bradford referenced in the article." At Ben's words, spoken in a clear, booming voice, all eyes focused on him. "The reporter caught up with Colleen at the memorial service. She says she didn't know the young woman who died but talks about how she saw the story in the newspaper and had to come out of respect."

Since no one else asked, Lara jumped in. "Who is Colleen?"

Davis shuffled papers. "The name is vaguely familiar."

Ben smacked the back of his hand against the file. "Because for one semester, she was one of Nancy's roommates."

The light popped on in Lara's head and refused to blink out again. "They were all there."

"Nancy, Martin, Steve and Ronald, the deeply screwed deputy director. I'm betting we dig and we'll find some ties between them and the dead woman. Or, more likely, we'll see a profound absence of ties—even things that would be natural coincidence will be missing because someone scrubbed the records clean," Pax added.

Davis rubbed his thumb over the back of Lara's hand. "Well, that kind of secret certainly could be an interesting basis for the shaky Coughlin marriage."

The idea made Lara's stomach flip. Tying your life to someone out of guilt was bad enough. Having a pact revolving around some poor girl's death was the ultimate marriage made in hell. "If it's true, they deserve each other."

Davis must have sensed her anxiety or heard the anger in her voice. Without looking at her or saying a word, his hand tightened around hers. The touch, so basic and freely offered, was about comfort, not sex, and the fact he knew the difference confirmed she'd picked the right man for the right reasons.

"I wonder why Steve started talking after all these years." Ben tapped his pen against the table. "There were numerous times when it would have mattered. I'd think Ronald getting the NCIS deputy position would have rung a bigger bell in Steve's mind."

"Guilt, or maybe he got sick of everything working for Martin and not for him. Martin and Ronald remained friends. Steve could have resented their bond." Pax threw up his hands. "Really, it could be anything."

Lara glanced at Joel's monitors and the big screen with the names and photos of all the suspects. The screen showed normal people who had kids and the usual worries about traffic and other mundane things. The kind of people she passed in the grocery store all the time.

The evil lurking underneath was what scared Lara. "So, which one of these folks is the actual bad guy here?"

Davis barely spared the monitor a glance. His face screwed up in an expression that spoke to his disdain. "If they left that girl to die, all of them."

Lara didn't disagree but her concern was more immediate. "I mean, who's writing the checks to the hit man?"

Joel shook his head. "I don't see anything in their personal finances to reflect big payments."

The smile that spread across Davis's mouth was slow and satisfied. "Then check the business one." He looked over at Ben. "You did say Nancy ran a company, right?"

"Why, yes, she does."

BY LATE AFTERNOON, Davis had checked in with Connor, who was on his way back from D.C. They were on a half-hour break. When Lara disappeared up the stairs, shooting him a sexy wink over her shoulder, he'd planned to race up after her. Connor's call had stalled that.

Sitting now at the computer with all of Joel's fancy programs and password-detection software in front of him made Davis think about the things he didn't know. Not about Martin and those other clowns, but about Lara. There were months unaccounted for, that time while he was away and running for his life and the month or so after she'd left when he'd pretended he didn't care about her.

He'd been an idiot. It took only a minute of honesty for him to realize she'd never leave his head.

After a quick look around to make sure he was alone, he started typing. It took only a minute for data to fill the small screen on the left.

"What are you doing?" Pax's voice came from behind Davis's shoulder, but the disappointment lingered.

Davis hit a button and the screen went blank again. "When did you start sneaking around?"

"That indignation would be more convincing if you weren't stalling by answering a question with a question." Pax put his mug next to Davis's keyboard. "You use that trick a lot."

"I'm checking something."

Pax's mouth formed a thin, disapproving line. "I got that part already."

"Something Connor said." Davis wiped a hand through his hair and tried to explain something he didn't really understand. "He suggested I go back to the breakup and figure out what else was happening. It's been bugging me since he said it. I've watched over her since we've been apart but I don't know what happened in those three weeks."

"We were away and she got sick of it. That's what you told me."

Pax wasn't giving an inch and that didn't surprise Davis. Pax and Lara had always been close and Pax had a soft spot for women. When Davis was slow to trust, Pax jumped in.

"There's something else, Pax. Has to be." Davis was honest enough to admit that he didn't know what he was doing.

Guilt crashed over him and his mind raced with excuses, but the bottom line was this check felt more invasive than anything he had done before. The rest of the investigation had been about keeping her safe and making sure the danger of his life hadn't seeped into hers. This was about picking her privacy apart.

Pax balanced a hand against the desk and leaned in. "What happens when you find it?"

"Meaning?"

The muscles in Pax's face dropped. "I'm going to let the answer-with-a-question thing go this time, but know that tactic isn't helping your case. Think this through. You're back together with Lara."

Davis wanted that to be true. Even as the guilt ate away at his insides, he justified his behavior by saying he needed the information for them to finally, once and for all, put the sordid parts of their relationship behind them. "Maybe...I'm hoping. I don't know."

That wasn't quite true. He knew what he wanted. He knew they loved each other. He didn't know where all of that put them.

Pax shook his head. "Wow, she has you chasing your tail."

"Get to your point."

"If things are back on track and you have a shot of convincing her to give you guys a second try, whatever you find—hell, the fact you're even digging around in her life—might mess your chance up."

It was all so logical but carried such a huge risk. The real issue was the way Pax said the words. They seemed to be carefully chosen and placed.

"What do you know?" Davis asked, dreading the answer he might get.

"Nothing about what happened then, but I do know you love her and should be with her." Pax dropped to his haunches with his hand across the back of Davis's chair. "Look, we haven't exactly been lucky in the women department, but somewhere along the line she broke that cycle. She's the one. Don't lose her."

That qualified as the most impassioned speech Davis had ever heard his brother give. The words came alive under the force of his voice. It was as if he wanted to bend Davis to his will.

He wanted to shrug it off. More than that, he wanted to stand up and not research. But at that moment he couldn't choose. "I'll think about it."

Pax's chest fell. "You mean you'll ignore it."

"If you were in my place—"

He glanced down to the floor. "I'd be on my knees begging her to come back."

"That seems extreme."

Pax stood up again. "I'll remind you of that if she leaves when this case is over."

After Pax skulked from the room, Davis put his hands on the chair arms to get up. In midpush he glanced at the blank screen. Then to the keyboard.

He balanced there trying to decide what to do.

A second later he slid back into the chair and hit the space bar.

THE INFORMATION CLIVE received about the security codes and hidden cameras at Davis's house made him nervous. Not that Clive thought he would get caught or that he couldn't break the system. He was too good for that.

No, the worry was that his boss had put together a competent double cross. Hard to imagine, but the man sat in a position of power and that didn't happen without some skills, even if those skills amounted to nothing more than having an impressive address book.

It was entirely possible his boss fed wrong information in the hopes of landing a new person to blame for the Wasserman murder and all the fallout that came after. Clive had no intention of going to jail, regardless of whether he actually committed the crime.

To prevent that possibility, Clive took the direct approach. He'd staked out the neighbor, a Mrs. Winston. She was the older, nosy type. No real family and few visitors. She collected government benefits and somehow survived on that pittance. But the character trait that interested him the most was the nosy one.

Perfect.

Clive lingered near Davis's front door. Even ventured around the side, making a big show of trying to see if anyone was home. The goal was to look as if he belonged there. Last thing he needed was for her to call the police.

"May I help you?" Mrs. Winston's shaky voice came to him only a few minutes later.

Clive smiled. There was nothing better than when a plan fell together. He turned around and lowered his gaze. The lady stood all of five foot nothing, wearing what looked like a robe and a heavy dose of blush.

He shot her his most genuine smile. He practiced often enough. "I was looking for Davis."

Her eyes narrowed as the grip on her cell phone tightened. "He's out of town."

"I talked to him a few days ago."

The older woman waved the comment off. "He comes in and out."

She also looked around, hesitating when her gaze fell on the camera hooked to the wall on the side of the house facing hers. She could stare all she wanted because he already had taken over that video feed and was even now running an endless loop to make it look as if nothing was happening in the yard.

He took his hat off and twisted it in his hands, hoping for the concerned look. It was foreign to him but he'd seen it in others often enough. "Normally I would not ask you something like this, but is there any chance you have a number or address?"

The last of her friendliness came down with a crash. "We're not close."

He could almost hear the wheels turning in her head. He glanced at the cell again and decided that was the answer. If she didn't play along with the plan in his head and invite Davis here, Clive would kill her and come up with another way to make the meeting happen.

He took another shot at the role of worried friend. "I understand. Really, he's not the one I need. I have to get in touch with Lara."

"You know Lara?" The older woman's frown disappeared. "She's lovely."

Now Clive had his way in. He would have bet Davis was the woman's weakness. Turned out Lara was the answer. Again.

"A very interesting woman." Clive had to force his mind to even come up with that. He had a lot of words to describe Lara, and none of them worked in this scenario. "But I don't want to bother you."

Clive played the last card. He turned as if he was ready to move on.

Mrs. Winston bought it. "Why do you need her?"

Clive turned around with that same friendly expression plastered on his face. He was going to need a shower after this.

"I can't really say." He leaned in as if sharing a big secret. "See, it's a family matter. The kind you can't talk about over the phone."

The woman's hand went to her chest. "An illness?"

Worked for Clive. "I'm afraid so."

"Oh, no. The poor thing." Mrs. Winston lifted the phone, even gave it a look then let her hand drop again.

"I thought if she was with Davis, he could help her through it. He's very protective of her." Which was why Clive planned to kill him last. Imagining the guilt and shame on that moron's face while the knife sliced into his woman's perfect skin had kept Clive going all day. It would play like dinner theater. "Maybe I can check back. I just worry it could be too late."

He dropped the comment but didn't leave. The woman was near tears with worry over Lara. After a few seconds of hesitation, she said the words he'd been waiting for.

"You know, I could call him and see if he's nearby."

Clive tried to look confused, although he wasn't exactly sure what that one would look like. "I thought you didn't have a number."

"I can't guarantee it will work." She gestured toward her

house. "Have a seat on my porch while you wait. I can see if he's close enough to stop by and bring Lara with him. There's no need to upset Lara in the car."

Yes, Clive certainly wouldn't want to upset Lara. He smiled at the older woman as he debated the pros and cons of letting her live. "You've been very helpful. Thank you."

Chapter Nineteen

They didn't have time for a side trip but Lara insisted. When the call had come from Mrs. Winston fifteen minutes ago, Davis had picked up. She talked about making him a pie and leaving it on his table. It all sounded innocent, but the comment sent a fissure of panic through Lara. The last time anyone was in that house someone had died. She had no idea what state the place was in, but she knew Mrs. Winston was too old and too fragile healthwise to take that sort of shock.

Figuring out what had Pax and Davis sniping at each other before they'd left Corcoran was the bigger mystery. The argument had ended when Davis told Pax to wait at the house for Connor then ordered Joel to keep digging into the financial aspects of the killings. That left her and Ben riding along while Davis drove in silence.

The pulse of discomfort had her tugging on her seat belt. Because she didn't know what had happened or what had Davis staring at the road with a practiced blank expression, she tried for neutral conversation. "Do you usually see Mrs. Winston every day?"

"When I'm home."

So much for conversation. Clearly something had happened. As usual, she was the last to know. "Okay, then."

"This is an in and out, right?" Ben scanned the area as they pulled onto the far end of Davis's street. "I'm not comfortable with any of us hanging around town until we finish driving this thing to ground."

Lara had to chuckle at that one. "Not to scare you, but you already sound like one of them."

"Who?" Ben asked.

"The Corcoran Team."

"She's a nice old lady who is probably lonely." Davis's flat voice cut through the amusement and weighed the air back down again. "Really, I think she took a liking to Lara and wants to see her again. She was clear about bringing you along."

"That's sweet." Would have been sweeter if Davis bothered to look at her when he'd said it.

He tightened his grip on the steering wheel. "She told me to pull up in the back..."

Ben leaned forward between the seats. "What is it?"

Davis slowed the car and pulled it to a stop on the side of the street. Gone was the blank demeanor. Now he shifted around and looked over the area with the watchful eye she'd come to know. "How could I miss this?" he asked.

Lara knew the tone, too. Dreaded it, recoiled from it and hoped she'd never hear it again. It signaled something scary and dangerous, and just hearing it made the bile rush up the back of her throat.

She didn't want to know but she asked the question anyway. "What are we talking about?"

Davis thumped the heel of his hand against the steering wheel. "The back. Mrs. Winston is telling me someone is at the back of her house."

"Maybe it's just—"

He finally looked at her with dead eyes and a face drawn tight with worry. "She thinks I'm a spy and that this is some sort of helpful game."

Ben watched the street, his gaze hesitating on two men

standing near the stop sign up ahead. "You think our killer is there?"

"It was someone who didn't feel right to her." Davis was talking out loud but the words sounded as though the conversation was playing in his head. "Someone who made her want to warn us."

Ben gave a humph. "Way to go, Mrs. Winston."

Davis glanced into his rearview window and put the car back in gear. "I'm taking you back."

Lara slapped her hand over his and held the car in Park. He'd break the hold soon, so she rushed to get her point out. "No. She could be hurt...or worse. You're good at plans, so come up with one."

"You've been through enough." His voice wavered on a thin line between concern and frustration.

She'd heard it before but this time it wasn't going to work. They could call in reinforcements and shoot the place down so long as Mrs. Winston got out of there alive.

Lara could not live with one more death on her hands and certainly not that of an old woman with a cute crush on Davis. "We're going in."

They all sat there. Davis didn't drive away but he didn't turn the car off either.

"Wasting time." Ben's head popped up between them. When Davis let out a noise that sounded oddly like a growl, Ben shot back. "You know I'm right."

Davis swore. "We do what I say and how I say. Got it?"

Before they agreed he'd started the car moving again.

THIS WAS A death wish. Davis couldn't help but think that as he and Lara walked up to Mrs. Winston's front door. Lara wore the one protective vest he had in the trunk with his long-sleeve shirt over it. It was large enough to hide the bulk but it dwarfed her. In this heat, it would likely have her sweating any second.

She'd put up a token protest about being the only one with the added protection, but he wasn't in the mood for an argument. Ben ended any discussion when he told her to hurry up. Davis liked that guy's style.

In the tense second before he knocked on the door, he thought about asking her the question kicking around in his mind and messing him up. Hell, he'd been so messed up over Lara that he almost missed the clue from Mrs. Winston, the clue he gave to her never thinking this situation could happen.

He'd found Lara's hospital record and it had him reeling. Well, the bill and admittance information. He was still waiting for a copy of the medical records to show up on his cell. With all the privacy restrictions, that information was buried and hard to access. Being able to tell Joel and put him on the task would have cut through the trouble. But because Davis was going it alone, everything took longer.

"Are you okay?" she whispered without moving her head.

He decided to answer the one he expected her to ask. "We're going to be fine."

He reached out and rang the doorbell. He had a key but he didn't know where anyone stood inside and didn't want to put Mrs. Winston in additional danger.

The door opened and her worried face peeked out. "Davis?"

Clearly she thought he'd messed up the signal. She couldn't know Ben had circled around the house and would come through the back as their element of surprise. "You said you had cake for me. Coconut, I believe."

Some of the tension left her face when he mentioned the one thing in this world she was allergic to. A wobbly smile came next.

To make sure she understood he got it, he nodded to her and motioned with his head for her to step to the side. "May we come in?"

"Both of you?"

Davis had asked the same question a dozen times while walking up the porch steps. "Lara would like to say hello."

The smell of mothballs hit him like a pan to the face the second they stepped inside. He knew from experience Mrs. Winston was a fan. The harsh scent mixed with a hint of Earl Grey tea as she walked them through the family room.

Collections of glass figurines and other knickknacks filled cabinet after cabinet lining the dining room. The only thing Mrs. Winston had more of was detective novels. They were stacked around every room, making the place more of a maze than a livable space.

With each step Davis scanned the area, his gaze moving over every corner as he waited for their unwanted and very violent guest to appear. Clearly the guy had something special planned and was drawing out the moment.

The emergency call had gone out to the rest of the team right before they stepped inside, but Davis hoped they wouldn't be needed…and wouldn't find dead bodies when they got there.

Davis kept his hand on Lara's back and more than once had to propel her forward when her steps faltered. He didn't blame her. Walking into a guaranteed shoot-out was dumb. If the attacker was smart he'd lie in wait and hit them with a sniper shot.

But this didn't feel professional to Davis. This had turned personal and that might be their only chance. If the guy wanted a final moment, he'd have to show himself.

No sooner had Davis thought it than he heard the soft press of a shoe behind him. He would have missed the sound if he hadn't been waiting for it. He shifted just as the guy leaped forward. Instead of landing on Davis's back, his momentum carried him forward and into Mrs. Winston.

The small woman went flying. Lara reached out to keep the older woman from crashing into a cabinet in the corner between the dining room and kitchen. The catch gave the attacker the extra second he needed to smash into Lara's path.

Before Davis could get a clean shot off, the attacker had his hand wrapped around Lara's upper arm and Mrs. Winston at the other end of his gun. He stood behind their bodies like the weasel he was. "It looks like I have your women."

Davis kept his gun aimed while his second weapon burned through his shirt and into the skin at the small of his back. "Let them go."

"I don't think so." The attacker tugged Lara closer until her back pressed against his front. "It's not as if this was an easy plan to set up."

"You want me, then take me."

"If only it were that simple." He treated them all to a tsk-tsk sound. "No, see, your girlfriend here caused the problem."

"How?" she asked as she tried to shift and put a bit more space between her body and that of her attacker.

"You showed up at Wasserman's place early. The entire scene had been planned for you to arrive and find a break-in and dead body, but someone switched the meeting and I had to improvise."

Lara swallowed as her pleading gaze fell on Davis. "Steve."

"Ah, yes. He was very excited about turning in his friends."

Davis tried not to look at Lara. He needed to stay focused, and seeing her crumble or her eyes fill with fear could snap his control. With Ben nearby as backup, the goal was to collect as much information as possible.

This guy in front of him was a hired gun, which meant someone paid his bill. Davis wanted to know who.

"The people you work for wanted to remove Steve from the scene."

"I work for one person. One powerful person." The attacker shot Davis a smile so full of evil venom it was good the women couldn't see it. "But he is not your problem. I am."

This guy had gone full tilt. Davis would bet he was working on his own now. No way would his boss have wanted this kind of bloodbath, not on top of the dead bodies piling up all over town.

Even knowing it wouldn't work, Davis tried. From the way the women were listing and shifting around he knew he was running out of time. "Tell me the name and walk away. I'll go after your boss and you can leave with whatever he paid you."

"I'm still waiting for part of that, and Ms. Bart needs to die in order for me to collect."

That was a very bad piece of news. The attacker still had a reason other than revenge or anger to come after Lara.

Davis rushed to take away the incentive. "If she dies, you can't frame her for murder."

"You are a smart one."

Smart enough to have a contingency plan. Even now Ben slipped in the back door with his gun ready and slid into a small alcove, out of sight from this guy.

Davis switched the grip on his gun, holding his fingers up in a form of mock surrender. "We can think this through and come up with a solution."

"I've got it covered." The attacker began backing the women up, right into the kitchen doorway where Davis wanted him. "As I told you, I'm not working alone."

A bolt of panic shot through Davis. That suggested another player. Someone else on the property. With the gun odds evened, Davis no longer had the same confidence in his plan. He could throw his body over one woman and shield her, but not both. Not realistically.

"You first." The attacker motioned with the gun to Davis.

No way was he putting his back to this guy. Instead, Davis shuffled, keeping his gun steady and one slip from shooting. As he stepped into the kitchen, Ben came fully into view. He stood with narrowed eyes and a serious expression. As long as he could rapid fire, Davis didn't care what the other man looked like.

Just as the attacker turned into the kitchen, Ben stepped out with his gun raised.

The attacker just smiled. "It's about time you got here. I thought I would have to fight Mr. Weeks on my own."

"Ben?"

Davis felt as confused as Lara sounded. His head spun as he conducted a fast rewind on every conversation and action from the past day. The guy showed up and things fell together. He was too good to be true.

"Interesting." Davis shifted from confused to ticked off in a second. Whipping out his second gun, he aimed one at each of the other men in the room.

He thought he heard Mrs. Winston whimper, and the stunned looked on Lara's face, all wide-eyed and pale, made Davis hate Ben even more.

Ben didn't even flinch. He kept his gun on the attacker. "You're lying."

"You said you'd get him here, convince him his neighbor's call was legitimate then do the 'I'll be your backup' thing. It worked."

The attacker's words were convincing, delivered in a sure tone and without hesitation. Either he was a perfect liar or Ben was a plant. Davis went back and forth between the two possibilities. Until he decided, he planned on keeping a gun trained on each of them.

Ben shook his head. "He's playing you, Davis. Don't buy it."

"He sounds pretty clear to me." Davis waited for some sign. Any sign.

"What's his name?" Lara asked.

The attacker tightened his hold on her arm until she hissed out a breath and her knees gave way. He ended with a little shake. "I didn't tell you that you could talk."

Davis jumped in before the guy could really hurt her. Yelling, he brought the attention back to him. "If he's who you say he is—"

"I don't have to prove myself to you." The attacker glanced at Ben. "You want the young one or the old woman?"

"I'll take the loser between them."

Something about the way Ben had said it sounded genuine. If he was in on this, he should be moving. He had the element of surprise and could have ended this.

Davis wasn't good at trust, but he was desperate enough to believe in Ben.

"Fine. I'll decide." The attacker pulled both women in closer and let them go. He stepped back as a second gun appeared out of nowhere.

The room moved in slow motion as he raised both weapons, aiming for the dead center on the backs of each woman.

Ben's mouth dropped open and he started moving a second later. One arm wrapped around Mrs. Winston, tucking her head against his chest as he dived into a roll. The other arm came up to get off a shot.

The timing was wrong. Ben couldn't grab both women and that left Lara without protection.

But Davis was already moving. He motioned for her to

drop as the room exploded in a rash of yelling and booming gunfire.

Lara screamed as Davis crashed into her from the side and sent her spinning toward the cabinets. They slid across the linoleum floor and landed with a bang as they flew into the oven door.

Glass shattered and plates crashed. More than one book stack toppled over. It all happened as Ben slammed a bullet into the attacker's side and Davis hit him in the forehead. The attacker's eyes flew open as his body lifted up and back. He bounced against the wall then slid down, leaving a blood trail along the white paint.

Davis pulled Lara against him, trying to block her view of the gruesome scene. She let out a soft cry into his neck and held on to his waist. Not even a breath of air separated them and his hands were shaking so hard from the relief that she was okay that it took him an extra second to tour them over her, looking for wounds.

When the echo of the shots stopped and the smoke cleared, Davis watched Ben lift away from Mrs. Winston. The small woman lay in a ball under his chest. Ben touched his fingers to her neck and her eyes flew open.

She stared up at him. "Are you one of the good guys, then?"

Davis answered. "Yes, he is."

THEY'D BEEN BACK for less than an hour and had just washed up and settled down when Deputy Director Ronald Worth showed up at the front door of the Corcoran property and leaned on the doorbell. No guards and no other people. Just him standing outside as if that were the most normal thing in the world.

But the team had expected him. Connor had got word before he'd arrived home from D.C. that Ronald had traced the breach of his privacy records to them. He likely jumped in the car and was close on Connor's tail to get here, which was exactly what they'd wanted when they'd opened the virtual door just long enough to let him peek in.

"You sure you're okay with this?" Connor stopped looking at the monitor long enough to stare at Ben.

He shrugged because there was really nothing else he could say. His life had been whipped into a frenzy over the past few days. This was the only play they had left.

They knew who'd done the actual killings. Now they had to figure out which one, or if all three, had ordered the deaths. This was imperfect but the best way.

Joel wasn't finding a money trail, which meant it was likely buried deep in Nancy's company and would take more time to unravel. But that was a race where someone could cover the tracks before Joel could get in.

"I was just in a shoot-out. Talking to my boss will be easy," Ben said, not quite believing that to be true.

"Yeah, you'd think so." Davis leaned against the conference table with an arm wrapped around Lara. She hadn't moved since they had come back, and all of the men were starting to send her worried glances.

"You have one shot at this." Connor repeated the words he'd said twice already.

All this concern was starting to make Ben nervous. He'd been fine with the plan until the big push. He knew this was about the risk he was taking—not physical but with his career. He appreciated the thoughts but they had to get this done, uncover the conspiracy, before any other innocent people stepped into the middle.

"I get it." And he did.

Davis nodded. "Then go get him."

Before he stepped in there, Ben had to do one more thing.

He stopped at the double doors to the foyer and ignored the third ring of the bell. "Davis? Thanks for believing me."

"I was just happy I didn't shoot you before I figured it out."

Ben nodded and slipped out into the lonely hallway. He didn't realize Connor had followed until he reached around him to open the door.

The deputy's shoulders fell as his voice dipped low. "Ben. I should have known you'd be behind this."

"Come in." Ben motioned toward the room across from the conference room. "This is Connor—"

"I don't care who any of you are." Ronald stopped walking. He stood in the middle of the hall and made his stand. "I want an explanation before I call the authorities and have you all arrested."

"We're not guilty of anything," Connor said.

"You looked at confidential records."

"Did we?" Connor pretended to think about the allegation. "I think if you check again you'll find a decided lack of evidence."

Ben didn't care about any of this. The idea this man would stand in front of him complaining about records after what he'd done was enough to make Ben want to punch the smug look right off his face. "Your hit man is dead."

Ronald's eyebrows fell into a thin line. "What are you talking about?"

"The one who killed Steve Wasserman, Greg Parker and Ken Dwyer." Ben refused to buy into the act. He'd watched an absolute pro try to convince Davis and almost succeed. Davis denied it now, but Ben had seen the look that had washed over the other man's face and the pain in Lara's. Ben would remember that moment of panic forever. "The same guy hired to cover up a twenty-year-old terrible decision that resulted in the death of a young woman."

"Andrea McClintock," Connor said.

Ronald's face went slack. It was as if gravity had taken hold and wiped the emotions clear. "I don't—"

"Don't." Ben could take a lot but not that. "The only question we have is how deep you're into the current conspiracy."

"I'm not involved in any of it."

Ben felt his temper spiral. He glanced outside at the sunny day and thought about how lucky he was to have survived the morning, but even that couldn't bring his thudding heartbeat back under control. "The girl died."

"I drove a car." When no one said anything, Ronald continued. "I picked Martin, Steve and Nancy up from the beach."

"And started a lie that would go on for decades, but someone doesn't want it out now, and Steve threatened to expose you, so, again, who is making the payments?"

Ronald shook his head. "I don't know anything about a hit man."

"But you suspected." Ben held out a cell phone. "Call Martin and tell him you're coming to see him."

Ronald looked appalled by the idea. "Why would I do that?"

Connor stepped forward and grabbed the phone. Shoved it right into the dead center of Ronald's chest. "Because your career is over. What you're playing for now is a chance to stay out of prison."

A charged silence followed Connor's threat. Neither man moved. When Ronald finally shifted, he took the cell and started dialing.

Chapter Twenty

Lara turned her hands over, rubbing them together until they turned red. They wouldn't stop shaking. Yeah, she'd been cool and sure when she'd gone over to Mrs. Winston's house, but she had come out a tangled mass of nerves. She had no idea how Davis handled this stress on a daily basis.

And it wasn't over.

Mrs. Winston was safe in the conference room with Joel. When Lara sneaked away to come up to the bedroom, Joel had been showing the elderly woman the different monitors and the camera angles on Davis's house. Mrs. Winston was like a schoolgirl, flirting with Joel with an expertise that made Lara think the older woman should give lessons.

Fearing her knees would be the next to go, Lara sat down hard on the edge of the bed. She decided to rest for a second, bring her body back under control, before the crowd left for Virginia and the showdown with Martin. Davis would balk about her going, but she had to see it through.

This mess, accident or not, poor timing or not, started with her and she had to finish it. She owed that much to all the people who'd lost their lives during the charade, including poor Andrea McClintock. She'd have her revenge; it was just a shame it took twenty years for her to get it.

After a sharp knock, Davis stepped inside. Between the scruffy and disheveled hair, the dark circles under his eyes and the exhaustion tugging at his mouth, he had a rough look that said his adrenaline was running thin.

"You okay?" he asked as he shut the door.

"I'm ready for a bout of boredom."

He let out a harsh laugh as he sat down next to her. "I'm with you on that."

The sheepish look and way he avoided eye contact worried her. She'd known this was coming and steeled her body for the fight. "I'm going."

He finally looked at her. "What?"

"Aren't you coming up here to tell me I'm not going to Virginia?"

"You're not going, but that's not what I want to ask." He balanced his elbows against his knees and stared at the floor.

She thought she'd seen him in every state—sure, demanding, controlling. But this one, all bent over, struck her as... vulnerable. But that couldn't be right. That wasn't who he was or how he acted.

"Oh," she said because she didn't know what else to say.

He took a big inhalation and let it go. "Why were you in the hospital?"

The question came out of nowhere and slammed into her with the force of a body blow. It didn't follow what they'd been talking about before and it stopped her heart when he said it. "When?"

"When I was in San Diego."

Shock knocked her breathless. She gasped as she tried to find breath. When she finally pushed the words out they sounded breathy and jumbled. "How did you—"

He reached into his jeans pocket and pulled out a folded piece of paper. "Here."

She opened it a bit and looked at the top. That was enough. She'd been in the hospital exactly twice in her life and she knew to her toes he wasn't asking about her broken arm at age nine.

This time, the one on this page, almost killed her. Certainly turned her into a cracked shell for months.

But that didn't explain why he'd gone digging or how he'd found it after all these months. He could have asked her. They could have talked. She tried to do just that, but he skipped into investigator mode and made her one of his suspects.

She shook the paper at him. "Where did you get this?"

The mattress squeaked under his weight as he sat up. "Just answer the question."

She unfolded the paper then refolded it. She looked at it but only saw black streaks where the lines should be.

All the anger at his sneakiness drained out of her. This was so much bigger. So much more devastating, and she ached for him and what he was about to hear. Just saying it would rip away a part of her she'd never be able to get back.

Regret choked her until she gagged on it. "This isn't the way I wanted to tell you."

He shifted until he faced her. "It can't be worse than what I'm thinking."

Then she saw it. Not anger but guilt. A huge mass of it that crushed in on him from every direction, pushing down his shoulders and stomping on his heart. His face was painted with it. It radiated out of every pore.

"Tell me what you think." She whispered the words because it hurt to say them.

"That you were really sick. That's why you begged me to come home and I didn't get it." The grim line of his mouth barely gave him room to spit out the words. "I can't figure out how I missed the clue. Was it cancer or something?"

The words were pure torture. "I lost a baby. Our baby."

He blinked a few times. "What?"

"I was pregnant. I found out right before you left but was

waiting until you got back to tell you. Then you stayed all those extra weeks." The surprise in his eyes gave way to something else. A deep sadness that broke her heart, actually shredded it right in two. "I woke up one morning to these cramps and there was blood all over the bed.... I lost the baby."

"Why didn't you tell me?" Shock robbed his words of any punch.

She felt the thuds all the same. Blame and guilt—she'd wallowed in it for so long. "You made your choice."

He stood up and glared down at her. "That's not fair. You didn't give me the information."

He was right and she knew it, but she couldn't stop fighting. She needed him to understand how crushed she had been, how her mind had been foggy and that she'd stumbled around in a grief-stricken haze back then. "I pleaded with you."

Anger flushed through his face. Gone was the concern. This Davis she knew. Furious and hovering, determined to get his way.

"Do you really think if I knew about the baby I would have stayed away?"

She didn't know how to answer that, so she asked a question of her own. "Would you have gone if you knew I was pregnant?"

His mouth opened and closed a few times before answering. "I don't know."

She had to give him credit for honesty even as the words sliced through her. She looked down and expected to find blood on the floor. "You would have because your list of priorities had me at, maybe, number three."

"That's not true."

She stood up because she didn't like him looming over

her. "You picked helping someone else's fiancée over helping your own."

"I didn't know!" The whole house shook from the force of his scream.

Her fury exploded to match his. He threw around concepts about trust, but he failed to show her any. "And I didn't know your mother contacted you."

His face went blank. "What?"

He had the nerve to pretend he didn't know what she was talking about. "That's right. I found her letter to you right after you left. I wasn't snooping, just looking through the desk for something and I found it stuffed in the back."

"I didn't write back to her. It meant nothing."

"Which is why you kept it and never told me, right?" Even now he refused to understand. He saw his life as his own and didn't let her in. Yeah, he'd open the door for sex and a few other things, but he stayed closed up and alone no matter how many times she pounded and begged him to open up again. "This huge emotional thing and you cut me out."

His eyes widened. "So you got back at me by not telling me about the baby."

She was stunned by that conclusion. No, she couldn't let him think something so horrible. "It wasn't like that."

"Are you sure? Because it feels like it."

Pain shot through her. "I would never use our baby as a weapon."

"Lara, you—" He exhaled as he brought his hands to his face, and then he dropped them again. "Were you ever going to tell me?"

"I tried the other night."

He stared at her with a face ravaged by a mix of rage and pain. "You should have tried harder."

Then he walked out the door, slamming it behind him.

Her legs held her for another second then her knees buckled. She was sobbing, her chest heaving from the force of her tears, before she hit the floor.

PAX CAUGHT DAVIS'S arm as he got out of the car in Virginia. They were down the street from Martin's house, ready to spring Ronald on them and end this thing. Joel was back at the office with Ben and Mrs. Winston handling the tech and comm stuff. Connor was guarding outside the house.

Davis just wanted this over.

"You going to tell me what's going on?" Pax asked as he secured his vest.

"Nothing." That wasn't a lie. Davis couldn't even feel anything.

The world was this odd shade of brown and his body had gone numb. They rode the entire drive from Annapolis in silence. Lara stared out the window, her chest hiccuping from spent tears and her cheeks stained with the tracks of her pain.

He wanted to comfort her. Thought more than once about leaning over and reaching for her hand. But he couldn't. She'd shaken his world.

A baby. His baby and he never knew.

Guilt pummeled him, but so did the pain. He'd lost so much and hadn't even known. She hadn't trusted him enough to tell him.

He wanted to blame her but he knew part of this was his fault. He hadn't told her about the letter because he hated that it mattered. He'd wanted to hear from the woman who'd given birth to him and not care, but that was not what had happened. The letter had shaken every part of his world, and maybe he did close off and hide his emotions. But he didn't deserve this.

Connor left Lara sitting in the car and came over. "Last chance to switch places."

"It won't work." The plan was for Ronald to take Davis

and Lara in, presenting them to his friends. The goal was to figure out who was behind this before the friends figured out Ronald had turned.

Connor nodded then left again to drag Ronald out of the car.

Pax watched him go. "That was the most uncomfortable car ride in the history of man. And you two weren't exactly quiet upstairs."

Davis couldn't do this now. It was all too raw and his emotions shot in every direction. "She shouldn't be here."

"Neither of you should. Not like this."

"I'm fine."

"Get your head in the game." Pax handed Davis his vest. "We're confronting people who—"

"I know what we're doing, Pax." Davis forced his mind to focus. He had to get through these next few minutes, then he could go off somewhere and think this through.

"Look, I don't get it and I won't pretend to, but when this is over, get into a room and talk with her. You love her. She loves you. Whatever is screwed up, fix it."

The advice fit Pax's life philosophy. He was a black-and-white guy. Davis was starting to think the whole world was gray. "It's not that easy."

"Yeah, it is."

Lara walked over, leaning into Connor as she stepped. "I'm ready."

She looked ready to throw up. If her skin grew any paler she'd be transparent. Davis wanted not to care.

Ronald came around the car. "Let's get this over with."

It was the first time Davis had agreed with something Ronald had said. "You have a mic on."

"I am aware of that."

Even after everything, the sense of entitlement still hung on this guy. "Just wanted to be clear who was in charge."

"Fine." Ronald took off walking.

Lara followed without looking up. Davis fought off the urge to touch her. It didn't matter that she was upset. She *should* be upset, but still...

They walked fifty feet and he couldn't take one more step. He slipped his hand under her elbow and spun her around to face him again. Now that she was looking up at him with those red and puffy eyes, he couldn't think of anything to say.

Before she could turn away again, he leaned down and kissed her. Soft and sweet and with a touch of hope that they could somehow work their way through this. By the end she was holding on to his shirt.

"It will be okay." He didn't know if he believed it, but he wanted it to be true.

By the time they reached the door, adrenaline had started pumping through his body. His energy soared and his shoulders straightened.

He *could* do this. He walked into danger all the time and there was nothing more dangerous than being in love.

He would finish this job and the next day would come and he would figure out a way to make everything right. He believed it. This was not the end of his life or their relationship.

Martin opened the door and escorted them inside as Pax disappeared around the side of the house. They walked through the foyer and into the fussy living room filled with even fussier people.

From the photos in the conference room Davis identified Martin and Nancy. The hit man, whom they now knew to be Clive, had referred to the person who paid him as a he. That left Martin, likely funded by his wife's money.

"What's going on, Ronald?" Nancy asked, clearly upset that people she didn't know were traipsing through her house.

Davis answered for Ronald. "This is Lara Bart. I thought you might want to meet the woman you keep trying to kill."

Martin's nose wrinkled in a perfectly executed frown. "That's nonsense. What are you talking about?"

Davis knew he could toy with them and draw this out, but he wanted it over. Needed it over. "We know about Steve and about Andrea and about the lifetime attempt to hide it all."

Two sets of eyes went to Ronald but no one said anything, so Davis jumped in again. "The deputy, or should I say soon-to-be former deputy director, here confirmed the information surrounding Andrea's death."

Nancy put a hand to her chest as she gasped. "We don't know what you're talking about."

"Lady, you are playing with the wrong guy."

"No, Mr. Weeks, you are."

The guy Ben had identified as John turned the corner and stepped between Martin and Nancy. So much for the theory of him being a useless sideman to Nancy.

The problem wasn't in him showing up. The issue was the gun in his hand. Davis hadn't been ready for that, but he had people listening in and Pax loomed around here somewhere.

This time Lara stood by his side and Davis was going to make sure no one grabbed her. If someone wanted to shoot through him, fine. But Lara was walking out of here.

Martin looked at the gun and did a double take. "What are you doing with that?"

Davis didn't think that one was fake. Everyone looked surprised to see John's toy except John.

"Cleaning up."

Davis wasn't impressed. "Did they teach you to shoot that in law school?"

"Since my employee failed—several times, in fact—to finish this job, I see it's up to me. I believe your luck has finally run out, Ms. Bart."

That answered that question. Connor should have it on

tape so that whatever happened now, they would be able to prove his guilt.

"John, stop." Nancy put her hand over the gun and tried to lower it. "This isn't—"

He shoved her aside. "What—necessary? Of course it is. I've been cleaning up your mess for years. Marrying this one." He pointed at Martin. "Covering the trail for this McClintock woman."

"Why?" Ronald asked.

"You think this is the first time someone crawled out from under a rock to dig into that case? Dear Steve was just the latest to try to capitalize on the situation." John aimed the gun at Davis. "But you will be the last."

That explained part of the plan but not all of it. Davis wanted every last piece. "You weren't involved back then. Why step up now?"

"Because I own a percentage of the business and it's grown every year. I have a significant financial interest in this family and they owe me." John waved his hand in Nancy's general direction. "Oh, she'll claim she grew the fortune, but it was all me."

In her fancy dress and high heels, she launched at her business partner. "That's not true."

Her husband caught her before Davis could rush in.

"If they go under, so do I and, frankly, I can't allow that to happen." John shook his head. "Not after all this time and effort."

"Nancy wasn't involved in Steve's death?" Lara asked.

Davis understood the question. He'd thought this would trace back to Nancy, too. And it still might, but the true genius behind the plan to quiet everything down was pretty obvious. He had the gun in his hand.

"Me?" Nancy screeched, all signs of the regal woman gone now.

"The hit-man money came from your company." John laughed. "Brilliant, wasn't it?"

Davis watched Pax slip into the doorway behind John. Davis returned the smile with one just as sick and deadly. "Up until now."

John shrugged, clearly not seeing that there could be an end here that didn't wrap up in a positive way for him. "What happens now?"

Pax stepped up. "Me."

John was turning when Davis got off his shot. He clipped the man in his side and watched him fall against the chair as blood spread over his white dress shirt. He hit the floor with a thud as a second crack vibrated through the room.

Davis looked around, ready to take on a second attacker, but everyone was frozen in shock at the sight of John sprawled across the floor. Nancy dropped to the carpet, her expensive dress forgotten as she threw her body over John's still form and cried what looked like actual tears.

Not wasting any time or allowing for another surprise, Davis took a few long steps to bridge the gap and used his shoe to trap John's gun against the floor.

When Davis stared back down at Nancy, he saw her weeping over the man who was supposed to be nothing more than a business partner. Martin watched, too, as the force of his new reality crashed over his face.

Connor rushed in the front door and started issuing orders. Sirens wailed in the distance as reinforcements and medical help stormed up the quiet street.

It had all worked out. Just as Davis had promised and insisted to Lara. He looked over at her and smiled, grateful when she smiled back.

Davis glanced over to congratulate Pax on his excellent timing.

It took Davis a second to realize his brother had fallen to the floor. The blood didn't register until Lara screamed.

Chapter Twenty-One

Lara sat in the chair next to Pax's hospital bed. Machines beeped and the heart-rate monitor took off every few minutes for a new test. Pax slept through it all.

John had got off a shot as he fell and it had gone straight into Pax's thigh. The bullet had lodged there and the bleeding had taken some time to stop, but he was going to be okay. Davis hadn't left his brother's side for hours, and now would only venture as far as the cafeteria for a cup of terrible coffee.

"You can go home." Pax's eyes stayed closed and his words slurred together from the medicine.

She jumped at the sound of his voice, relief flooding through her as she squeezed his hand. "I'm fine here."

"I was hoping you'd go sleep with my brother." Pax fell right back to sleep after making the comment.

That was okay because she kind of hoped for the same thing.

When the tears had dried and the pain had stopped thumping in her head, she thought about that moment in the bedroom. Davis's devastation was understandable. She'd dropped a terrible piece of information on him. She'd fired back about the letter from his mother. Actually, she was just the woman who'd given birth to him. Lara didn't think she deserved to be called a mother.

After all the death, after watching Nancy weep over a man

who didn't seem to care if she lived or died, Lara viewed things differently.

Davis wasn't perfect. He was shaped by a tough upbringing but so desperate for her love that he didn't hesitate to tell her. He didn't hide behind a fear of commitment or some other nonsense. He loved her for her and she returned the favor by insisting he be someone else.

He still played a part in their rugged past that he needed to own, but seeing one more person hold a gun on him today had shifted her world into perspective. Somehow they would get through this. He would forgive her and she would forgive him. They'd work on trust and build a life together.

"He loves you." Pax's head fell to the side but his eyes stayed closed. "He's stupid with it."

She patted Pax's arm, trying to calm him back down. "I know. Save your strength."

"I don't know what happened..."

She watched the monitors to make sure his heart rate didn't kick up to danger levels. "It doesn't matter."

"But he—"

"This won't break us." For the first time in a year she believed the words as she said them. "We'll make it through."

"Will we?" Davis stood in the doorway with a cup of coffee in each hand.

Her heart hammered so hard she was surprised all these machines didn't pick up the beat. "Yes."

Waiting for him to say something, anything, ate away at her. She wanted a restart with him. But he had to want it, too.

She swallowed back her pride and dropped all of her instincts and every last breath of self-preservation. "Or am I going to fight alone?"

He took his time setting the cups down on the tray and walking around the room to stand in front of her. He didn't touch her but his presence reached out to her. "I never stopped fighting."

Her heart soared as she realized that was true. "I walked away. I had to because...well, I'm not even sure it matters."

The backs of his fingers trailed down her cheek. "It does."

She closed her eyes on a wave of unexpected pain. "Please, Davis. I don't want to fight."

When he lifted her chin and pressed his lips against hers, her eyes opened again.

"It matters because I need you to know there is no one more important in the world to me than you. Nothing ranks above you." With a gentle touch he slipped her arms around his neck and brought her in close. "I haven't done a good job of showing you that, but if you give me another chance I will."

Her breath hiccuped in her chest and tears clogged her throat. This deliciously strong, incredibly loving man stood in front of her offering everything she'd ever wanted. "Yes."

"The idea of you going through the hospital alone..." His voice cracked on the last word.

"I should have told you, let you in." She pressed a finger against his lips and closed her eyes when he lowered his forehead to hers. His body shook with a slight tremor.

He rubbed his head against hers. "You'll never be without me again."

"And we'll have more babies. Big, fat, healthy babies."

He pulled back and stared at her. "Are you sure?"

"I want to experience everything with you. The families we never had, the loving homes we always wanted."

"About my mom—" He swallowed. "I couldn't deal with it."

"I know." Lara kissed him. "We'll figure that out, too."

"I love you."

"And I love you."

Then his mouth closed over hers and all those months apart fell away. She felt love and commitment, promises and devotion.

His lips pressed against hers, deep and rich. It was a kiss that filled in those empty days and gave hope for the ones before them.

"Are you two done?"

They broke apart at the sound of Pax's voice and his words running together.

"How are you feeling?" Davis asked with laughter in his voice.

"Fine." Pax opened one eye. "Are you back together?"

She didn't know that she could feel so happy, be so free. She tried to nod but was pressed too close to Davis's chest to move her head. "Yes."

He kissed her forehead. "Definitely."

"Then get out of my room and let an injured man rest." Pax's eyes closed as he ended the sentence.

Lara started laughing at the outburst.

Davis looked at her with eyes filled with amusement. "You heard the man."

"He suggested I take you to bed."

"Excellent idea. But first we go get your engagement ring. I want to see it on your finger again." When a tear rolled down her cheek, he kissed it away. "And it will never come off again."

She nodded. "Never."

CONNOR WALKED INTO the conference room and set down two beers before slipping into the seat across from Ben. "Pax is going to be fine."

Ben had already heard the news from Joel but was happy to hear it again. "He knows how to get attention."

"You have no idea." Connor tapped his fingers against the

table in the same sort of frantic rhythm young boys used on new drum sets. "You did good work here."

Satisfaction flowed through him. Ben wondered if that was the last he'd have of that feeling for a while. "Maybe that will help in my administrative hearing at NCIS."

Connor shrugged as he took a long draw from one of the bottles. "I'm thinking you'll be fine."

"You going to pull strings for me?" Ben said it as a joke.

Connor took it very seriously. "I know some people."

Ben was humbled and grateful and a whole bunch of things he hadn't felt in a long time. This was a good team. An honest team. He thought he'd found that at NCIS, but those days were gone. Even if they did take him back, he might not want to return the favor. "That's not necessary."

"Yeah, it is." Connor stopped peeling the label and spinning the bottle and looked up. "You could have played this a bunch of ways and you picked one that showed integrity. I told you before that's not as popular a choice as you might think."

"And not a characteristic I find at NCIS right now." Ben grabbed the other bottle and leaned back in the soft leather chair. "I know that's not fair but it's hard to be excited about returning to a desk there."

"Then don't." The ripping tear of the label cut through the room.

"You going to pay my rent?"

For the second time Ben joked and Connor gave a serious response. "Actually, yes. I'm offering you a job."

The idea worked its way into Ben's brain and settled there. "Here?"

"It's the only business I own, so yes." Connor put his hands on the table and leaned in. "You know the work. You've met part of the team. I can't promise every case will end well, but I can promise you we'll try to make it happen."

"I don't—"

"And we have dental."

Ben lifted his hands in the air. "Oh, well, then."

"Think about it." With a knock against the table, Connor stood up.

Ben stopped him before he made it to the kitchen. "When can I start?"

* * * * *

A sneaky peek at next month...

INTRIGUE...

BREATHTAKING ROMANTIC SUSPENSE

My wish list for next month's titles...

In stores from 19th July 2013:

❑ Sharpshooter – Cynthia Eden

& Falcon's Run – Aimée Thurlo

❑ The Accused – Jana DeLeon

& Smoky Ridge Curse – Paula Graves

❑ Taking Aim – Elle James

& Ruthless – HelenKay Dimon

Romantic Suspense

❑ Colton by Blood – Melissa Cutler

Available at WHSmith, Tesco, Asda, Eason, Amazon and Apple

Just can't wait?

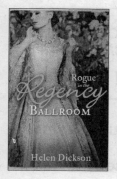

The World of Mills & Boon®

There's a Mills & Boon® series that's perfect for you. We publish ten series and, with new titles every month, you never have to wait long for your favourite to come along.

Blaze.
Scorching hot, sexy reads
4 new stories every month

By Request
Relive the romance with the best of the best
9 new stories every month

Cherish
Romance to melt the heart every time
12 new stories every month

Desire
Passionate and dramatic love stories
8 new stories every month